A Very Artistic Affair

E.M. Phillips

Cover illustration by Julie Hepenstal

TO THE MEMORY OF

NICKOLAS (NICK) BIRD

1943–2004

HAM ACTOR,

INSPIRED DIRECTOR,

PLAYWRIGHT & THEATRE BUFF,

AN EXHAUSTING, MADDENING GENIUS

AND MUCH MISSED FRIEND

A Very Artistic Affair

E.M. Phillips

A Very Artistic Affair

Published 2010 by Sagittarius Publications
62 Jacklyns Lane, Alresford, Hampshire SO24 9LH
Tel: 01962 734322

Typeset by John Owen Smith

ISBN 978-0-9555778-6-4

Printed by CreateSpace

Prologue

'I don't sleep with old married men,' she told him bluntly; but eventually she did, on the night of Buchannan's party, in a single bed in her room above a bar. For a man of fifty-three she had been a revelation, her directness and total lack of inhibition almost shocking.

'How old are you?' he'd asked from the bed afterwards, watching as she prowled, half naked and unselfconscious, around the room, dressing again with the off-hand negligence of one to whom doing so in crowded dressing rooms had made second nature.

'Twenty-three; how old are *you*?'

'Forty-three,' he tried.

She gave a gurgle of laughter. 'And some – but it was OK, wasn't it; d'you want to do it again sometime?'

He was nonplussed, stumbling like a callow youth over his 'Yes… Yes, I do,' realising even then that he was entering dangerous waters. Caution told him to finish with that first night, but the sheer excitement of her, the feel of her young girl's skin, had brought the irresistible intoxication of once again tasting the forbidden fruit – and such forbidden fruit…

PART 1

Sigh no more, ladies, sigh no more,
Men were deceivers ever,
One foot in sea and one on shore,
To one thing constant never.
Then sigh not so, but let them go,
And be you blithe and bonny;
Converting all your sounds of woe
Into Hey nonny nonny.

W.S.

1

Olivia asked doubtfully, 'Are you *sure* you want another egg? I only ask because you're always so fond of telling Carol they'll clog her system.'

With precision Giles Ryder cut the egg on his plate into two perfect halves, allowing the yolk to flow evenly across the surface towards the twin triangles of crisply fried bread. He said, 'That's because Carol is fair, fat, over forty and heading for gallstones. I may be fair and over forty but there the resemblance ends, so I'd like another egg, if that's not too much trouble.'

OK, so to hell with your gallbladder, arteries and anything else that may get blocked. Olivia broke a second egg into the frying pan, when what she really wanted was to smack it on top of the head now bent over the British Medical Journal. He turned a page and she averted her eyes from a full colour splash of a ruptured spleen. 'Giles, do you *have* to read that at breakfast?'

'Why? What's the matter with it?'

'Nothing from your point of view, but it puts *me* off my food.'

'Then don't look.' Forgetting he was still holding his fork he pushed a hand through his hair, dropping a globule of egg on the close cut blonde curls.

He didn't notice and she decided on impulse not to tell him. Serve him damn well right. She hadn't, as he'd assumed, been asleep the previous night when he returned from the party; watching through half closed eyes she had seen his clothes were rumpled as though they'd been pulled on in a hurry. It was a very long time since he'd played away from home, she was sure, but it didn't do to be too complacent about Giles; one look at some girl with her PVC Mary Quant skirt up to where her knickers should be but probably weren't, and he'd be unable to resist a good try.

Olivia sighed, overcoming her immediate desire to beat him about the head with the frying pan. 'No need to be quite so obviously an egghead,' she said, and wiped his curls with a clean tea towel.

*   *   *

'I should have left it there.' Carol bit into her cream slice. 'I don't know how you've put up with him all these years. He really is the

9

most impossible old letch…what makes you so sure it doesn't still actually lead anywhere?'

'I'm *not* sure,' Olivia pushed her own cake to the side of her plate and stared out of the window of the Cadena Cafe onto a wind-swept, rain-soaked Winchester High Street, 'but I can't rock the boat. I have Adam to consider: fifteen's a funny age.'

'When all that trouble blew up with Sister What's-it's and you had the great "This is the last time or else" showdown, you said ten was a funny age.'

It's all right for *you*, Olivia though resentfully, your old man's a pathologist and works with a woman who looks like Mick Jagger on a bad day, whereas Giles…Olivia sighed. She expected it would have been some perky little nurse he'd been groping; it usually was until the perky little thing realised that the handsome sexy Mr Ryder had absolutely no intention of giving up his comfortable married state to take things any further. A spot of bottom pinching in the consulting room between patients was all she was likely to get, however perky and accommodating she may be.

'What beats me,' Carol was on a roll now, 'is how he keeps getting away with it…I mean, people must *notice*: his colleagues, that old bat of a Matron…You can't hide much in a hospital, can you?'

Olivia made an impatient gesture. 'Oh, God, *I* don't know. I suppose it's the same as it was in the forces during the war…all that groping and knee-trembling behind quarters; almost everybody was at it, and those who weren't wished they were. Anyway, hospitals have always generated that kind of adolescent hanky-panky; Giles was offering me a full medical within a few days of our first meeting and I couldn't wait to take him up on it!'

'That was in the middle of a war when all anyone seemed to think about was jumping into bed with the nearest thing in a uniform, but you wouldn't do it now, would you? Giles is fifty three for heaven's sake, and you've been married over *twenty years.*' Carol was well into her stride

Olivia shrugged. 'Mostly they do the chasing and he just waits until they catch him. Anyway,' she added provocatively, 'I've not had all that much reason to complain; he's terribly good in bed and we've had one hell of lot of fun along the way.'

She grinned at Carol's quick intake of breath. Already plump and matronly, mother only to a Persian cat and with sweet, quiet Chris for a husband, Carol couldn't even begin to understand what life with Giles was like; or had been with the odd exception up until about a month ago. Olivia began to gather her bag and gloves. 'I must get back. Adam is ringing at lunchtime. Don't forget dinner tomorrow evening.'

'Fat chance – Chris can't wait to exchange my cooking for yours.'

Carol watched her friend as she threaded her way through the busy café, musing that the day might come when Giles would push his ideal wife too far, then all hell would break loose. With a bit of luck, she thought cattily, she might be around to see it happen and cheer from the sidelines.

*   *   *

On the hill down into Ranleigh, Olivia came to with a start and the sudden realisation that she hadn't been concentrating properly on the road. Sod Giles. One day she'd drive right up a tree worrying about what he was up to. She left the dual carriageway, driving more carefully on the narrow lanes towards Larksbridge and home. The rain had changed from downpour to drizzle and she looked hopefully for some sign of blue behind the clouds. If the rain let up she could spend the rest of the day in the garden.

By now Sandra would have gone, the bed would be made, the house tidied and polished. Sometimes Olivia felt guilty about employing someone to do the dirty work around the house, but she wasn't a natural-born getter-into-corners and Giles was so blasted *picky*, everything around him had to be just so. Bloody control freak, she thought mutinously. Sandra was a good cleaner but he still managed to find something to whinge about. Only that morning he'd complained, 'She moves my papers about on my desk and I'm damned sure she has a good swig at my booze every time she comes. I don't see why you need her here at all. It isn't as if you've anything else to do but keep house.'

'Of course not,' Olivia had been mildly sarcastic. 'Not a thing: only shopping, cooking, washing, ironing and gardening; taking and fetching your suits from the cleaners, getting the cars serviced, entertaining your colleagues and our friends… nothing at all really, compared to hacking into a couple of chest cavities a day and drinking coffee in the consultant's rest room.'

She swung in through the gates of Riversmead and felt her rear wheel arch scrape the low brick wall.

'Bugger!' She slammed the car door and climbed out to inspect the damage: a scrape of paint off the nearside arch of the Vauxhall and a raw spot on the wall. Poking a finger into the moist soil she rubbed it over both marks before returning to the car and driving into

11

the carport. With a bit of luck Giles would never spot either, and she could get the paint scrape seen to at the garage in the next day or two, thus saving a load of chauvinistic digs about women drivers.

Pausing only to pour a generous gin and tonic she went up to the bedroom, sniffing appreciatively at the mingled smell of spring flowers and fresh polish. Kicking off her shoes she lay down on the bed and leafed idly through last week's Gardeners' World while she waited for Adam to ring. What did he want this time she wondered…most probably more pocket money.

When the phone rang she picked it up saying crisply, 'No, you can't have a pound for chocolate and strong drink!'

He laughed. 'Hi, Mum how did you know?'

'Call it intuition…'

'How about a five bob P.O then – just for the chocolate?'

'That's more like it; anything else?'

'Er, yes.' His voice became coaxing; she heard an echo of Giles in it and was immediately suspicious. 'Would you and dad mind if I spent a few days with gran and pops over Easter?'

'Alone?'

'No – actually with Flynn … he's in the sixth, but I know him quite well, his dad moved down into the same village last Christmas and he wants me to stay and go sailing.'

'Who is Flynn and how experienced is he,' she asked cautiously, 'and do his parents know about this visit?'

She heard his quick impatient intake of breath. 'I told you, mum, he's in the *Sixth* … he's seventeen, almost eighteen and he's been sailing for years … I'll be absolutely safe. His dad's an artist of some kind and hates kids, which is why I need to stay with gran.'

Olivia was dryly amused. 'I pity the man's poor wife and children.'

'Oh, *mum,* he hasn't *got* a wife. Flynn says she did a bunk years ago. He likes to sail in the vacations 'cause it keeps him out of his old man's way.'

'Well it all sounds very odd … I'll speak to your father tonight. Now is there anything else?'

'Only the P.O – I'm a bit short … you will swing it with dad about Easter won't you?'

'We'll see.'

'Thanks, Mum – and don't forget the five bob.'

'Five shillings,' she corrected. 'Yes.'

She replaced the receiver and finished her drink. On the table by her side of the bed were two photographs in a double silver frame. She picked this up now and studied the two faces. A school photograph of Adam at fourteen, almost a carbon copy of his father: the same crisp fair curls, the straight half-frowning gaze, the gentian blue eyes. The other of Giles, taken just before their wartime wedding, Surgeon Lieutenant Giles Nikolas Ryder, RNVR, a young Adonis, the blonde hair curling engagingly from under the cap, the blue eyes that always appeared shot with silver, the air of confident charm. She sighed. *You haven't changed, have you? When am I going to find out what you were up to last night- and with whom?*

She looked across to the table on Giles' side of their bed. Only one photograph there: herself at twenty-three, in Wren uniform, posing glamorously on the bonnet of his old Sprite.

They had been so in love ... she corrected herself, *she* had been so in love, rushing blindly into marriage, living for the delirious, tempestuous reunions after each time apart, making plans for the future. But even in those first passion-fuelled months he hadn't been able to resist chasing every attractive piece of skirt that came his way.

*   *   *

She told Giles about Adam's plans over dinner that evening. He was cautious as she had been.

'He knows nothing about sailing... how do we know this Flynn boy is safe in a boat?'

'We don't, but Adam says he's been sailing for years.'

'Hmm, what about this artist chap? Now *he* sounds definitely weird. Why have kids if he hates them?'

'Darling, *I* don't know; why does any man do anything? You tell me ... the male psyche where sex and responsibility are concerned is still a complete mystery to this woman.'

'Oh, don't start, Livia. I've had a hard day.'

She said half under her breath, 'Perhaps not as hard a time of it as last night.'

He pounced. 'And what's that supposed to mean?'

'I wasn't asleep – I watched you. You came in looking rumpled and disgustingly smug...'

'Look,' immediately he was the picture of hurt innocence. 'I can't help it if some silly little idiot got the wrong idea at Buchannan's leaving party and grabbed me in the cloakroom, can I? If I come in with the odd niff of perfume, that's no reason for your suspicious mind to start working overtime.'

'Save it, Giles,' she said tiredly. 'I didn't notice the perfume, only

13

the fact that you looked as though you'd dressed in a hurry.'

For a moment he looked sulky, before the familiar, penitent little-boy charm began to operate. 'Well I hadn't.' He pushed his plate aside. 'She was just a silly kid who'd had too much to drink and came on a bit strong when I went to get my coat, that's all.'

'Well that's par for the course.'

'Oh, cut it out Olivia,' he was irritable and dismissive. 'You know it doesn't mean anything.'

'I'm sure *you* believe that.'

I feel like his mother, she thought and how many times have we been through this? Perhaps it had been no more than he said. A meeting at a party and a quick roll certainly wasn't his style, he was much too fastidious – and cautious, but recently he'd seemed vague and preoccupied, staying late at the hospital, then too ready to forego lovemaking for sleep...

She felt the anger of frustration begin to build. 'Giles, I'm tired of this, tired of being endlessly understanding, endlessly forgiving … it hurts, it matters. I'm forty-five, for God's sake, and I can't keep bouncing back.'

'Livy!' Immediately he was at her side; kneeling down he put his arms about her waist. 'Let's not quarrel. Please.'

She snapped, 'I'm not going to quarrel. I can't be bothered. Get up Giles; you're too old to be kneeling on cold flagstones.' She made to push him away but his hands were already on her, stroking, caressing and coaxing. She took his head, twisting her fingers in the tight curls as the warmth and urgency of desire began to flood through her body. 'Oh, *damn* you, Giles, you practically ignore me for weeks then as soon as I hit out you think you can make it up with a quick wham, bam, thank you, ma'am.'

'I know. I know.' With one experienced flick he unhooked her brassiere, 'but I *do* want to make it up to you, and right now I can't think of a better way!'

*   *   *

'Mother … not ringing too late, am I?' Olivia held the back of Giles' neck as he lay nibbling her shoulder. 'It's just that we've been tied up with other things all evening.'

'Since when was I ever in bed by ten thirty,' Margot Heyward's voice was dry. 'What can I do for you?'

'Adam called. He wants to go sailing with a school friend over Easter and wondered if he could stay with you. He says the family are

14

new neighbours of yours.'

'Must be Flynn the sculptor; he's the only newcomer in Lodscombe. I don't know about the boy but we see the girl about the village most weekends. I think she's a weekly boarder somewhere in Salcombe.'

'Oh, *that's* who he is; Adam just said he was an artist … Ah!' She put one hand over the receiver and caught at Giles' seeking hand, biting his fingers, whispering, 'wait!'

'Olivia, are you alone?'

'Of course not, mother, Giles is here,' she grinned and held out the receiver. 'Say 'hello' to mother, Giles!'

'*Hel-lo*, ma-in-law,' he breathed obediently. Olivia retrieved the phone and heard her mother chuckle.

'Why don't you ring tomorrow, then you can talk without any distractions and I can tell you what I know about our local celebrity.'

'All right, I'll call around ten.'

Olivia put the 'phone down as he reached for her again. 'Giles, we've spent the last two hours in bed,' she protested, 'we ought to go down and at least clear the supper table.'

'Tomorrow … tomorrow…'

'Is all this to make up for the infrequent, absent-minded apology for lovemaking that's been on offer for the past few weeks?'

He chose to ignore the sarcasm, only pulled her closer into his arms and felt her familiar response, which was both invitation and surrender and like nothing else he had ever known with another woman, even Zoë…Zoë, with the sleek, slyly innocente looks of a depraved choirboy, the voice of a bass viol…

His thoughts filled with an equal measure of guilt and lust he looked down on Olivia's face; on the softly waving dark hair, the calm, cat-green eyes. He whispered, 'I love you, 'Livia'.

'Swine…' she murmured and he laughed and again gave himself up to the pleasure of her warm and yielding body. He did love her. He really did.

2

'You *were* at Buchannan's leaving party last night, weren't you?' Carol, putting the finishing touches to her lipstick hogged the bathroom mirror, leaving her husband hovering at her shoulder trying to shave and making a pig's ear of it.

He said plaintively, 'You know I was. I drank too much cheap wine as usual, and you complained like hell when I had to keep getting up for a pee.' He fingered a painful nick on his chin. 'Er, could you move over a touch?'

She made a *moue* and shifted fractionally. 'Was Giles there?'

'Uh huh,' Chris nicked his chin again and swore, 'bound to have been. He never misses a staff party.'

'I suppose he was flirting as usual?'

'Didn't notice.' He was evasive, wondering the safest path to take. 'There were a lot of people and most of the evening I was busy talking to Charlie Makepeace.'

She shrugged and vacated the mirror.

'You all stick together … you wouldn't say if Giles'd had Matron on the floor behind the bar.'

'You'd have heard the cheering from here if he had; nothing worse than a professional virgin going through the menopause. Someone should do something about it before she explodes.'

'God, but you men are disgusting.'

Carol left the bathroom in a huff, and Chris gave a sigh of relief. Hope he'd sounded convincing about Giles; the old devil hadn't shown his face all evening.

*   *   *

'*Ambrose Flynn!*' Carol's eyes were alight with interest. 'Oh, but he has those huge exhibitions at the Constantine Galleries … you must remember, Olivia, we went to one last autumn.'

'Of course I remember … did as soon as mother said his name.' Olivia smiled at Chris, who was eyeing the last roast potato; she pushed the dish towards him. 'Take it, Chris, and do your gut a spot more damage.' She turned back to Carol, 'Giles and I have talked it over, and as my parents are happy to have him, he might as well go.'

'What did Margo say about their local celebrity?'

16

'Only that he was attractive in an ugly sort of way; with a beard and sandals and a young village girl who cleans the cottage – and according to dad also probably caters for his night time needs as well. But then my father's always thought that all male artists are immoral and beyond the pale.' She grinned across at Giles who had kicked off one shoe and was busy running his foot up her leg. 'Oh, yes … and he doesn't appear to be a very demonstrative and loving father, particularly to the boy. Mother says he doesn't hide the fact that he didn't want children in the first place, and that the damned woman – that's his wife, presumably – should either have taken them with her or at least had the boy put down.'

Carol patted her mouth with her napkin. 'Well he *is* a genius and they probably upset his creative flow. Children can be such a nuisance – particularly adolescent boys. I know I should never have been able to make such a success of the boutique if I'd been tied with one child, let alone two.'

Carol's horror that she might one day accidentally produce even one offspring was legendary, and it was common knowledge that poor old Chris had practically to claw his way through barbed wire to get his occasional well-protected oats.

Giles mouth twitched ominously and he gave Olivia's thigh a particularly hard dig with his big toe. She shot him a warning look and said firmly, 'Come and help me with the sweets, Giles,' so that he had hastily to push his foot back into his shoe and follow her from the room.

'Just stop it, will you,' frowning Olivia shut the kitchen door. 'I don't want you stirring it with Carol, she'll only start on Chris and the poor old chap has a hard enough time as it is.'

'Oh, all right, but she gets up my nose and I can't help wanting to take her down a peg. We all know her poor bloody staff run that shop, she's hardly ever there…and she's a thoughtless bitch, too, yakking on about kids being a nuisance.' He put his arms around her, suddenly gentle. 'She knows you wanted more children.'

'That's just thoughtlessness; she doesn't mean it maliciously.'

He gave a wry smile. 'I married a saint.'

'No you didn't, but please don't spoil the evening by squabbling with her.'

'OK, darling, I'll behave.' He let her go and picked up the bowl of whipped cream, dabbing in a finger he looked at her out of the corner of his eye. 'Hey, I can think of something absolutely marvellous to do with *this*!'

She eyed him severely. 'Just put it on the trifle, will you, and clean your mind, because they won't be going home for hours yet.'

*   *   *

'I've a series of weekly lectures to attend in Salisbury over the next few weeks.' Giles stretched lazily, hooking an arm about her waist as she closed her book and leaned to switch off the lamp. 'So don't expect me back until late-ish on Fridays from this week.'

'How late-ish?'

'I'm not sure … you know how it is at these things … one always gets talking afterwards.' He began to stroke his fingers down her back, lingering over the smooth curve of her hip.

'I suppose I should be grateful it's only once a week. It's just that I'm feeling a bit restless. You've been at that damned hospital so often in the evenings over these past weeks … I suppose I just don't have enough to do.' She began to move slowly against him, nuzzling his neck. He chuckled and tightened his hold. 'I thought I might start dusting off my paints,' she ventured, 'perhaps enrol again for an Art course … just to brush up after all this time.'

Even as she said the words she felt his withdrawal. He twitched away from her, pettish as a spoilt child.

'Oh, not *that* again … mess everywhere and no time to cook a decent meal.'

'It doesn't have to be like that, I've plenty of time to do both now.' she protested.

'I'd hate to take a chance on it – and if you've all that much spare time you might try getting rid of Sandra – she's been at my booze again.' He loosed his arms and turned away, pulling the bedclothes up over his shoulder. 'Anyway, it's too late to talk now. I've a busy list tomorrow. I need to be up by seven-thirty.'

She closed her lips on an angry retort. He was playing the old game: *Keep my life running smoothly, don't rock the boat and I'll keep you happy … in and out of bed.*

Suddenly she wanted to scream and pound her fists on that turned back, but only lay raging silently; furious, when after a few minutes he began to breathe quietly and evenly, in apparently untroubled sleep.

The darkness stifled her until she had to get up and open the heavy curtains. For a while she sat on the window seat, unconscious of the chill night air, thinking that tomorrow she *would* sort out her art materials and to hell with Giles. With the warmer days she could work down in the summerhouse, and then he couldn't complain about the

18

house being cluttered with all her paraphernalia.

Olivia thought bitterly of how he'd always blocked every attempt she'd made to resume her painting. She had been an artist of promise and just starting to get noticed when war called a halt to her career. Afterward, when she'd again taken up her brush, they'd been married and living in a small flat in Islington, all they could afford on his salary as a Surgical Registrar. There had been rows when he came home to find her still before her easel, the flat untidy and meals unprepared. Then, after they had moved to Riversmead and Adam was born, she'd finally given into his demand that she should stop painting altogether. Reluctantly she'd suppressed her own needs and put away her materials, to become instead an efficient housewife, a good hostess, a loving mother – and a faithful wife, who over the years had watched her husband stray, not once, but several times.

And just what was he up to now? She was suspicious of the sudden burst of lovemaking after weeks of very occasional, almost absent-minded coupling. That he had necked with his little nurse the night of Buchannan's party she knew would mean nothing to him, so why did she have this feeling that he was beginning to slip away from her again?

She fretted and worried until it became too cold to stay at the window any longer and she slid back shivering into the bed, nestling against his warm back. If only she wasn't driven by the simple physical need for him and for the reassurance that he still needed her…

He stirred, rolling onto his back, smiling in his sleep.

'Sweetie!' he murmured and Olivia froze. In all their years together she had never heard *that* sickly endearment from his lips. In sudden fury she leaned to deliver a sharp pinch on his buttock, feigning deep sleep when he yelped and shot up onto the pillows.

*   *   *

At breakfast the next morning he was morose. 'Something bit me in bed last night!' he complained. 'God knows what it was, but I've a damned great red mark on my behind.'

She took a bite of toast and munched thoughtfully.

'Try TCP,' she suggested, '…and don't look at me like that, because I'm most certainly not going to kiss it better while I'm eating my breakfast.'

*   *   *

Adam Ryder didn't really enjoy smoking, but he wasn't going to risk looking a twit in front of Flynn. He sat back, inhaling slowly and trying not to cough. 'You sure we're safe here?'

'Yeah, no sweat man,' negligently, Liam flipped ash. Adam looked at him admiringly. Flynn didn't care about anyone and he could do everything when it came to sport ... and what about all those girls he said he'd had? He asked tentatively, 'Doesn't it spoil your wind? you know ... smoking and girls and all that?'

'Not yet; by the time it does I'll be too old to care,' Liam laid back, hands behind his head and cigarette canted expertly between his lips. 'I quite like the idea of dying young ... after all, you've pretty well had it by the time you're twenty-five, haven't you?'

'I dunno.' Adam was doubtful. 'I'd rather like to hang on a bit longer than *that*; besides, my old man u'd never forgive me if I popped my clogs too soon; he expects me to do medicine.'

'Ugh!' Flynn recoiled in exaggerated horror, 'think of all those smelly bodies and disgusting floppy bits!'

Adam tapped a fraction of ash from his cigarette. ''S'matter of fact, I'm not all that keen myself.'

'Then why do it just to please your old man? Anyway, the Bomb will have got us all long before then, so make the most of what you've got: smoke yourself stiff, get drunk and have yourself a good time with the girls, pal.'

Adam felt a pleasurable but embarrassing stirring of excitement at the thought of having that sort of good time and changed the subject. 'Tell me more about your boat and where we'll be going.'

'Well, now.' Liam blew a smoke ring into the still air. 'She's named the Morning Star ... a Volksboat.' He sat up, and scrubbing at an area of grass with his heel, leaned forward and drew with his finger in the dirt.

'See, she's wooden hulled and has one mast ... *here*, and she's sloop rigged with a mains'l and fors'l jib. Below there's enough cabin room to sleep three and a galley. My sister Kate crews; she likes cooking so we can take food and have decent grub when we're out for the whole day – oh, yeah, and the bucket an' chuck is here.'

'What's a bucket and chuck?'

His companion gave a snort of laughter. 'A bog, you don't think we crap over the side, do you? You're a bit bloody green, but you'll soon learn...'

*　　　*　　　*

Tom Doyle watched from his study window as the boy with the head of a Botticelli cherub walked across the courtyard with an innocent nonchalance that simply oozed guilt. When barely a minute later, another familiar but less pleasing figure strolled from the same direction, hands in trouser pockets, his dark good looks marred by the obligatory Elvis sneer, Doyle shook his head and sighed. They'd probably been smoking behind the pavilion, he thought, hardly an original sin, illicitly indulged in as it was by half the school, and he personally was prepared to turn a blind eye within reason, but young Adam Ryder was a nice, uncomplicated kid, and Doyle was suspicious about this sudden friendship with the older, would-be sophisticated Flynn; drugs might well be on *that* young man's list of Things To Do Before You Die.

For a few moments he considered dropping the devious and untrustworthy Flynn in it with his own housemaster, but dismissed that as a waste of time. The boy was almost eighteen, in his last year and unlikely to take the slightest notice of any reprimand, from his own housemaster or anyone else.

Virtually all boys were artful and as much trouble as the proverbial wagon load of monkeys, he thought wryly, but some, like Adam Ryder were worth any amount of trouble, because one could be certain that, eventually, they would turn out to be quite reasonable human beings.

But the Liam Flynn's of this world? Doyle shook his head; now with them you never could tell which way the cat would jump.

He turned back into the room. No point in making a mountain out of a mole hill, but in future he'd keep a closer eye on the pair of them. Tobacco was one thing; drugs another.

*   *   *

Giles came to the long straight stretch of the old Roman road and let the Jag have its head. Ella Fitzgerald was singing 'Let's fall in Love' and he leaned to turn up the radio, lifting his voice and harmonising along with Ella.

It had been a long busy week with no free time in which to make this journey, but now he was on his way again. There would just be time to book in to the Crown, have a quick shave, then get to the theatre before curtain-up. He must remember to order a late supper, with champagne to celebrate the first whole night they would spend together.

Against his will his thoughts turned to Olivia, seeing her as he had that morning as he drove away from the house; standing at the gate and clutching her shoulders against the chill of morning, then smiling and waving as the car turned the corner ... *Oh, Livvy, Livvy ... I can't help it this time. Really I can't.*

He despised himself for spending the week just passed making love to her as he had. Deprived of Zoë's company he'd been randy as an old goat. 'I'm a swine,' he muttered to himself. 'I should have got over this itch. I swore to Olivia I wouldn't let her down again after that last time.'

And he had stuck to that for almost five years; just the odd flirtation that he thought she didn't really mind, might even have been amused by, only occasionally lashing out as she had the other evening. But oh, dear Lord ... *Zoë.* He must be crazy.

Let's be rational about this. He gripped the wheel firmly. *I have a lovely, loving wife, still exciting and desirable, so why am I chasing after a certainly less than loving girl young enough to be my daughter?*

Because, he answered himself savagely, she lights a fire in me that is beyond all reason, and keeps me on the edge of arousal each time I see her, or even hear her voice...

*   *   *

The curtain went up on The Taming of the Shrew and from the moment Zoë entered and spoke her opening lines in that extraordinary voice, Giles sat enthralled and motionless in his seat, impatient as a boy each time she left the stage, desperate for her return when he could resume his worship.

He was no devoted playgoer and it had been Olivia who had dragged him all those weeks ago to see Twelfth Night, then rhapsodised afterwards over the talent of the young actress playing Viola. He'd been deliberately lukewarm in his response, although already stirred by the sight and sound of her, knowing even then that he would have to see her again, and at closer quarters than from a seat in the stalls.

And so it had started. Almost at the very end of the run at the Playhouse, when he'd sat through her performance several times, he had stifled his conscience and sent a note asking her to join him for a drink after the play.

She had come, absurdly young, walking like an impudent boy on her long shapely legs. 'Could I have a simply enormous gin with a great deal of ice and tonic?' she asked, grinning like one of Murrillo's street urchins. 'I sweat like a pig in those cloth tights but the thinner ones always make me want to slap my thigh and burst into song!'

He had laughed and ordered the drinks, knowing then that if he was not yet in love, he was most certainly in lust. When the company moved on for a short tour through the Southern Counties he had telephoned every day, and was there to meet her off the train when she returned.

And within a week of that return they had become lovers for the first time.

Now he leaned forward as the curtain rose on Act Five; thirty minutes, forty at the most and he would see her walking towards him again…

*   *   *

Olivia wandered down to the end of the long garden where a narrowed tributary of the Test ran clear over a gravel bed, the sound of its ripples and eddies clearly audible in the still peace of the warm evening. Kneeling on the cold grass of the bank she trailed her fingers in the water, thinking of her son's coming trip to Devon, envying him the endless sea and high, wide sky of the coast where she had spent her childhood.

'I must have water,' she had told Giles when they moved from London to Hampshire and she was pregnant with Adam, 'even the river. I can't bear to be without water that moves and changes. I've missed it so much since I left Lodscombe.' Then one morning in early spring, they had found Riversmead, and she had fallen in love with the old brick and flint cottage and the wild, tree-filled garden with the river winding through it.

A wooden summerhouse stood by a willow, at a spot where the stream shelved into a deep pool and there, all through that first long summer she had spent a part of each day. Floating on her back under the green canopy of trees and watching her belly become high and round as their baby grew within her.

She pushed open the door of the summerhouse and surveyed the clutter: deck chairs stacked haphazardly against a wall, Adam's holiday sports paraphernalia and the camping gear he'd had for Scouts all dumped in a corner, a pair of steps which should be in the shed, leaning drunkenly against a grubby window. She half closed her eyes, seeing it all stripped clear, the floor scrubbed, a table for her paints by the large window, her easel by the door for the best of the light.

She would begin on Monday as soon as Giles had left for the hospital. It was time she did something she wanted for a change, she thought rebelliously. In comparison with what he had been up to over the years, a few late meals would hardly constitute grounds for divorce.

The telephone began to ring as she stepped through the cottage door and she crossed the hall to the sitting room to answer it, hoping it wasn't Carol wanting to come for a chat. She needed this evening to herself, to plan how she would organise her work. As well as clearing the summerhouse she wanted to get into the attic and sort out her canvases and paints.

It was Giles. 'Liva, I'm going on to dine with a couple of the chaps here. We shall probably sink a bottle or two so I'll stay overnight … don't want to risk driving back afterwards. You don't mind, do you?'

'No, but what about tomorrow?' she asked, trying not to sound too delighted at the thought that now she could spend as long as she pleased rooting in the attic. 'You'll need a change of clothes.'

'Oh, I'll nip in home first. It's a short list in the morning. I'll ring and let them know I'll be a tad late.'

'How's the evening going?'

'Very well – we've only stopped briefly for coffee, so I'd better get back. See you tomorrow … love you.'

'Goodnight, darling – '

She broke off as a sudden burst of Tannoy sounded from his end. He cut the line quickly, but not quickly enough.

'Ladies and gentlemen will you please take your seats for…'

Olivia put the receiver down on the half moon table and for a few moments stood gazing into space. There was a vase of tulips and daffodils by the telephone and she fingered the squeaky stalks of the tulips, a frown puckering her forehead. That was an odd way to call delegates back to a lecture hall, she thought, it sounded more like a theatre announcement.

Suddenly the nasty cold finger of suspicion poked at her back. Surely he wouldn't be stupid enough to use the excuse of a professional commitment to cover for something else? No, of course not; she dismissed the thought. He'd know she could easily check – and why on earth should he be in a theatre when it simply wasn't his scene? He only ever went with her occasionally and under duress, and even then would invariably sleep through most of the performance.

At the kiosk in the theatre foyer Giles put the receiver down carefully and sagged back against the wall. Hell, but that had been close; thank God he'd shown himself at the hall before his dash here.

He knew his Olivia; she wouldn't be able to resist checking up on him.

*   *   *

Olivia reached for the 'phone again and dialled the hospital. 'Sister Marsden?' She kept her voice light and unhurried. 'Would you be a dear and let me have the telephone number for the Salisbury lectures?'

'Of course, just a moment, Mrs Ryder – yes, I have it here. They are at the Kingdom Rooms in Catnal Street,' she rattled off the number, Olivia thanked her and rang off. Well, the lectures were real all right. She dialled the new number, then waited dry-mouthed while the receptionist checked the list of delegates.

'Yes, Mr Ryder has signed in. Would you like me to have someone fetch him?'

'Thank you, no,' Olivia eased the receiver that she had been gripping tightly in both hands. 'I don't want to disturb him. It isn't that important.' Feeling foolish and ashamed she replaced it on the telephone rest. She really *was* getting paranoid. She simply must stop imagining women under every bush!

3

Zoë Ormonde leaned closer to the mirror, working the cold cream vigorously into her face. She reached for her roll of cotton wool, thinking what bliss it was to have a dressing room of her own for this run, even if it was the size of a rabbit hutch and cold as a crypt.

Last night Jimmy Yelland had taken her to dinner; watching her with his lazy, considering eyes as she ate, then when she had finished announced in his clipped camp voice: 'You are doing splendidly, darling. I am very, very pleased with you. Some day you shall be at the Old Vic, but not yet. There is still a great deal to learn before *that* becomes a possibility.'

Then he'd dropped his bombshell, informing her in his disconcertingly casual fashion, that she was to play Desdemona in the summer. Her knees had threatened to clatter like castanets and she'd felt sick with excitement.

She paused for a moment, staring at her reflection, reliving that moment. 'Do you really think I'm ready for that?' she had asked, suddenly unsure.

'No, not yet, but you will be,' he smiled. 'I shall be very strict and work you very hard. We shall open here, then Reading and Oxford and five other venues before finishing the tour in Scarborough. Eight weeks in all and then back for a last week in the Great Metropolis!' He arched his brows significantly. 'The Kings Theatre, my sweet, and I shall be very, very cross indeed if you are not in bed, on your own, by midnight each night!'

She giggled suddenly at her reflection and began to clean the make-up from her face. A good job he wasn't interested in girls. She didn't think she could cope with him *and* Giles at the same time.

But two *months;* Giles wouldn't care for that. It would mean fewer candlelit dinners and fewer enjoyable hours in bed. But then how much did those things matter? How important to *her* were Giles and dinners and bed?

She paused again. She'd thought he would not return after that first time. She knew that, if not exactly shocked, he had at least been shaken by what he called her masculine attitude towards sex. She had laughed at him then for being old-fashioned. 'You are just not with it, are you?' she'd teased, wondering even then why she found him so attractive. Older men really weren't her thing, but there was just something about Giles that was different; he was not only still very good-looking, he was also nice, he was fun, and he was kind.

And she was excited by just the way he held her, as though she were something precious and unique. He made her feel warm and special and he made love beautifully, his practised hands and strong, wiry body stirring in her a new intensity of sensual pleasure.

Was it because he *was* so much older that she felt as she did about him − perhaps seeing in him a carnal replacement for the hard-drinking, hard-living, end-of-the-pier, third-rate-comic father she had once loved but now could scarcely remember?

She sighed and spoke aloud to her mirrored image. 'Keep it cool; don't get too involved. He's not the sort to leave his wife, and you can't afford to let any man take over your life, especially a married one. Your foot is now well and truly on the ladder, kiddo, and you are going right to the top!'

Quickly she cleaned off the last of the cream, then made-up carefully. Giles could arrive at any minute now and she hated him to come to her in the dressing room; finding her shiny-faced and pale and surrounded by the tawdry trappings of the theatre, the spilled powder, scattered sticks of make up and grubby towels.

She threw a panicky glance at the clock. He was late. Perhaps he'd grown tired of waiting.... Shrugging into the thigh-high plaid skirt and skinny yellow sweater she scooped up her shoulder bag and left the dressing room like a whirlwind. Running down the stairs, calling 'Good-night' to Wardrobe, still hanging costumes, then blowing a kiss to William at the stage door, she clattered down the iron steps just as Giles turned into the narrow alleyway behind the theatre.

She ran to him. 'I heard you laugh. I know your laugh from everyone else's...' She put her arms about his neck and hungry for praise asked, 'Was it good? Was *I* good?'

'Don't you know?'

'I thought I was, but you can't always tell when you are up there.'

'You were wonderful.' He wrapped his arms around her. 'I wanted to shout 'Hurrah! Encore!' and rush straight around, but thought I'd give you time to take your wig off first.'

She kissed his mouth, then pulled away breathless. 'I've missed you ... it's been a bloody awful week.'

'Don't swear,' he reproved, 'with that voice it is a sin.'

'OK,' she was flippant; tucking her arm in his she demanded, 'so what do we do first ... dinner, or bed?'

He shook his head, but his eyes were sparking with laughter.

'Hussy, what would your mother say if she heard you talk like that?'

'Have a blue fit, I should think, she pretty well disowned me years ago; I was bad for her image, you see … all hell and damnation and polishing the chapel pews, that's my mother.' She was mock solemn. 'How she ever came to marry Jerry, let alone allow him close enough to impregnate her with me is one of life's greater mysteries!'

'You really are a brat.' He stopped suddenly and pulled her hard against him, putting his lips close to her ear. 'I've missed you, and I want to take you straight to bed…'

'Oh, yes, lovely…'

He let her go, tucking her arm again in his and walking on. 'I might want to, but we shall both enjoy it more if we have a nice civilised dinner first, with a great deal of champagne. After all, we do have the whole night before us…'

*   *   *

'How was your evening?' Olivia poured their drinks then sat down beside Giles, where he sprawled on the couch. 'You were in, changed and out again so fast this morning I didn't get a chance to ask. I thought you might ring me when you got to the hotel last night. I waited until eleven thirty then gave up and went to bed.'

'We were pretty late and I didn't want to disturb you.' He leaned back, closing his eyes. 'Lord, but I'm tired tonight … think I'll turn in early.'

Olivia said, 'I'm going around to Carol for an hour. She needs some ideas for decorating their guestroom. Ma and Pa-in-law are coming to stay over Easter and she wants to spruce the place up.'

'Left it a bit late, hasn't she?'

'Oh, she has her usual little man all lined up and ready to go.' Olivia leaned to kiss his forehead. 'Do you want to come with me and keep Chris company?'

'Not tonight … you go off when you want. I'll probably fall asleep in front of the TV.' He opened his eyes, looking deeply into hers for moment before putting his arms about her and pulling her head down onto his shoulder.

She rubbed her head against his chin. 'Nice … what brought that on?'

He grunted. 'Nothing in particular … what did *you* do with yourself last night, then?'

'I was making a few plans for the summer house; I thought I'd

28

clear out the junk and use it to start painting again.'

'What … pictures?'

'Of course,' she spoke decisively, keeping any hint of coaxing out of her voice, determined not to sound conciliatory as she had before and risk another rebuff. 'I need to have something positive to do apart from keeping house. You're so busy now and I'm not a social animal … well I am, but I've never been the sort who can join things and get excited about Beetle Drives or Local History or whether or not someone's seen a sedge warbler…'

He interrupted. 'There are other things.'

'Unlike you I do not have, nor do I want, a load of buddies with whom to play tennis and golf.' She lightened her words with a smile. 'Also Adam is growing up fast and won't need his mother to plan his vacations for much longer. He'll have his own ideas about what to do with those, and quite rightly so.'

Giles was silent for a moment or two before answering, and she steeled herself for an argument. 'Well, I suppose it's all right if the painting helps fill a gap and you don't start getting too serious about it,' he said eventually. For a fleeting moment she wondered what he would do if she was to hit him, right here and now, very hard. 'But try not to let it take over completely' he continued, unaware that he was being anything but graciously understanding, 'you forget … I've lived through it all before.'

She said gravely, 'I shall do my best to maintain your high standards.'

Filled with a sudden possibility for snatching more time with Zoë, he missed the underlying sarcasm. 'Tell you what,' he tried to cover his excitement, 'why don't you spend the Easter holiday down in Lodscombe with your parents? Not the whole time Adam's there of course, he might think you were checking up on him. Go the second week. You could take your paints and canvases and have a really decent break – stay until it's time for him to go back to school if you like.'

'Really, are you sure you wouldn't mind?' Olivia turned her head to look at him. She said dryly, 'You're not just getting rid of me so that you can hold an orgy or two are you?'

'Of course, how did you guess?' He hoped his answering laugh was sufficiently light and carefree. 'I'm going to have Carol and Chris's assistant from Pathology *and* matron here every evening, so that we can roger the night away four in a bed!' He slid his hand up the inside of her thigh, taking the soft skin between his fingers and pinching it gently. 'Now, go on next door and let me nod off and snore without being prodded awake every five minutes by you.'

He left his hand on her thigh for a moment; she said straight-faced, 'Move that and your snoozing days are over.'

'Get out!'

She leaned to kiss his mouth. 'You know, in a funny sort of way, I still love you, although I can't think why.'

After she'd left him Giles lay with his eyes closed for several minutes, then sighed and picking up a cushion held it to his chest.

The hell of it is my love, that in a funny sort of way I also love you and everything about you. So why am I being such a stupid bastard and sending you away so I might spend more time with Zoë, when all I really love of her is what her body does to mine?

*   *   *

'So when are you off to your folks?' Carol busied herself with making coffee while Olivia sat at the kitchen table, dipping her hand into the biscuit barrel.

'Oh, I'll give Adam a few days on his own before I show up.' Olivia munched on a Ginger Thin. 'Keep an eye on Giles for me whilst I'm away, will you? Feed him the odd meal. You know what a lazy sod he is over doing anything for himself; the place will be littered with empty packets and pie cases by the time I get back – and I warn you, he's promising himself a four in a bed orgy with you as *primo uno*, so better start polishing your hormones, ducky!'

'He should be so lucky.' Carol put the mugs on the table. 'No more problems with lover-boy, then?'

'No, that was just me being paranoid.' Olivia sipped at her coffee for a few moments in silence. 'Actually, he's being rather sweet lately.'

Carol gave a snort. 'Watch it, he's probably snogging that new half-baked receptionist in Physio.'

'Possibly, but I'm trying not to get my knickers in a twist about him. So long as he continues to save the real thing for me I'll not complain.'

'After twenty years you still actually enjoy all that don't you?' Carol regarded her with curiosity tinged faintly with envy.

'Enjoy all what?'

'Sex you ninny.'

'Ra-*ther*; I hope to still be enjoying it in my dotage.'

Carol gave a short laugh. 'Any woman of your age who goes about still looking like a vestal virgin ought not to think so dirty.'

'Jealousy,' said Olivia primly, 'will get you nowhere.' She stood. 'I'd better have a look at this room of yours. If I leave Giles snoozing for too long he'll be grumpy as hell when he wakes.'

*   *   *

Returning to Riversmead she walked slowly around the garden, enjoying the effect of moonlight on the slow moving stream and the pale, closing faces of the primroses lining the banks. She loved the mornings and nights of early spring: the sudden brightening of the garden and the sharp chill at evening and first light.

She let herself in at the back door and went quietly into the sitting room. The television showed only a snow flecked screen and Giles was slumbering peacefully, his mouth opened a little to emit the occasional fluttering snore. Switching off the television she stood looking down on him, feeling particularly tender and quite a bit sexy. But she wouldn't disturb him, she thought; there were lines of tiredness and strain around his mouth and he was frowning slightly.

She knelt down and carefully eased off his shoes then loosened his tie, murmuring, 'You can have another ten minutes, I suppose, although you'll be all snarly and grumpy when you wake-up and blame me for letting you sleep so long, you tiresome old man.'

As she leaned to switch off the lamp he opened one eye. 'I heard that, woman – less of the old!'

'You were snoring like a pig. Get up and go to bed.'

He smiled sleepily and wedged his head more firmly into the cushions. 'Wake me again when *you* go to bed, then I can be grumpy and snarl at you properly…'

His voice faded away. She waited until she heard the faint snore again then went into the kitchen. Pulling the dusty wooden case full of paints and brushes from its hiding place under the dresser she became lost in nostalgia, her fingers darting through the contents, releasing into the room the mingled smells of oils and varnish and old musty turpentine rags.

*   *   *

Next morning, when she laid her chequebook on the counter of the Art shop, Olivia blinked hard at the final bill for the oils and canvases. What the hell, she thought, and recklessly added another half-dozen brushes to the pile. Most of those she had neglected for so long would be of little use now and she might as well do the thing properly. She

31

wrote the cheque in the certain knowledge she'd be in Lodescombe when the bank statement arrived, and thus be spared Giles' howls of anguish. Not that he was mean, far from it, but he did enjoy the occasional ritual of pretending that poverty was staring them in the face, especially if he could lay any extravagance at her door.

Clearing the summerhouse, and trying to keep the worst of the resultant chaos and upheaval from disturbing him, kept her busy until it was time to collect Adam from school. Usually Giles undertook the journey to and from Somerset, but had suddenly pleaded a heavy workload. So like him, she thought resentfully, to push one more task onto her, when just for once she was busy with her own affairs. She would also have to stay overnight when she drove Adam down to her parents, so that she might check up on this Flynn character a little more before entrusting her precious son to him. The father could obviously be given a miss as it seemed unlikely Adam would find himself in *his* company, but hadn't there been some mention of a sister? She must check if Giles had done his stuff efficiently and seen Adam was all clued up to the dangers, as well as the pleasures of sex, and *au fait* with the havoc that could be wrecked by uncontrolled teenage passions.

Not, she mused wryly that Giles was the obvious example for avoiding trouble, although he could undoubtedly give a few good tips on how to wriggle out of tight corners…but please God, she crossed her fingers, that wouldn't be necessary yet. It would be altogether too much if she had to spend the next few years watching Adam following in his father's footsteps.

* * *

Giles stood in the doorway surveying the transformation of the summerhouse.

He had come up quietly, unobserved by Olivia, absorbed as she was in sorting through her canvasses, her usually neat hair tied back carelessly in a scarf, her hands and face smudged with dirt. Picking up a small square painting of a child's head he studied it carefully. 'I don't remember seeing this; it's lovely,' he said, and as she turned at his voice added lightly, 'Such a pity he had to grow up!'

Olivia gave a slight shrug 'I painted that when he was about two … almost the last thing I did. If you remember that was about the time we had the big blow-up…when I finally gave in and stopped painting.'

'You talk as though it were all my doing.' He laid the picture

32

down and moved behind her, putting his hands on her waist. 'You agreed that you couldn't do everything…something had to give. Now things are changing and you can start again.'

'Perhaps,' she smiled faintly. 'Although I wonder how you'd feel if, for my sake, you'd had to give up surgery for years, then have me tell *you* that it was OK to start again.'

'I don't see that's the same thing at all.'

'No, darling, you wouldn't … and of course you're right as usual; I'm sure everyone would agree that the scalpel is mightier than the brush.'

'On the other hand…' he kissed the back of her neck. 'Which would one rather look upon, the Mona Lisa, or part of a lung resection posing daintily in a kidney dish?'

She laughed outright. 'Idiot, I was getting ready to be quarrelsome tonight and now you've spoiled it.'

'Why should you want to quarrel?'

She gestured around at the canvasses. 'Looking at these, realising how much I've missed it all, I was getting angry because you pressured me into giving it up. You were, still are, a totally selfish pig, you know.'

'Blame my dear departed mama. She spoiled me.'

'So she did, and I continued where she left off: my big mistake.' She rubbed her dusty hands with a clean rag. 'Come along, I don't *want* to feel cross tonight. Let me lock up here and then I'll have a quick bath and you can take me out to dinner.'

'Why?' He shot her a suspicious glance. 'I thought I saw a naked chicken looking hopeful in the 'fridge this morning.'

She looked guilty. 'Yes, well … I'll cook that tomorrow.

'You'd forgotten all about getting dinner, hadn't you?' he accused. 'My God, Livia, but it didn't take you long, did it?' For a moment he struggled between annoyance and laughter before giving a strangled snort and taking her arm. He said menacingly, 'Men have committed murder for less than this, however, tonight, your wish is my command … but only if you let me scrub your back.'

*　　　*　　　*

'We should do it more often.' Olivia looked around the quiet restaurant and raised her glass. 'To us and may you continue to mellow with age.'

He lifted his brows. 'I've always thought myself the perfect husband, apart of course from being selfish and unreasonable, and

33

wanting everything my own way. Small faults, I know, about which some wives might be picky.'

She put her hand over his. 'I don't know why you're suddenly being quite so exceptionally nice and understanding, but I do want you to know that it's noted and appreciated.'

Abruptly he picked up the menu, ostensibly to choose a dessert, but in reality to avoid meeting those direct green eyes. The still small voice of conscience that had seldom troubled him before was now shouting loud in his ear.

He would have to put a stop to the meetings with Zoë soon, he really would. He couldn't go on like this. If he were half a man he would come right out with it … tell Olivia, beg her forgiveness, give up wanting it all ways…

He groaned inwardly then, thinking of Zoë with her gamin grin, her appalling language and that terrible Zizzi Jeanmaire haircut … and the beautiful, wanton, young girl's body…

All at once he felt he was quite literally being torn apart down the centre…. Making a tremendous effort to compose himself he put down the menu and returning her pressure on his hand forced a smile. 'I'll have the treacle sponge,' he joked, 'then you can sit and listen to my arteries hardening!'

*   *   *

She was a little early, no sign yet of Adam amongst the thirty or so boys milling about the school steps. Parking alongside an opulent red Mercedes, Olivia swung herself out of the car. Nodding and smiling at one or two familiar parental faces, she strolled across to the small rose garden to stretch her legs, before facing the long drive back to Ranleigh, but she had barely made one circuit of the beds before she heard her name spoken.

'Mrs Ryder.'

Adam's Housemaster stood before her, smiling his apologies. 'I didn't wish to disturb you, but I saw you come in here and thought I'd let you know Adam is on his way.' He fell into step beside her. 'Are you holidaying anywhere special this Easter?'

'Not really. Adam is sailing with Liam Flynn, another of your boys who now lives close to my parents. I shall join him later for a week or two.'

She paused, taking a deep red rose between her fingers, bending to inhale the perfume a moment before continuing, 'I thought I should check out his sailing companion before I leave him with his grand-

34

parents tomorrow, although I daresay they'll already have made a few discreet inquiries.' She hesitated and gave Doyle a sideways glance. 'Adam is clearly in the throes of hero-worship, but I can't help wondering what the attraction is for Liam. Most young men of his age would run a mile rather than be saddled with a younger boy for the vacation.'

Doyle grinned, making no attempt to side-step her implied question. 'If you are thinking what I think you are, you've no need to worry about ulterior motives where the Great Flynn is concerned. His bad habits stop short of the seduction of younger boys. He probably just needs someone to crew for him.'

Olivia halted, her cheeks pinking. 'You don't mince words, do you?'

'No, that's never wise when one deals almost exclusively with the young.'

He stood looking down on her, his brown eyes crinkling in amusement and for the first time in almost three years of their brief, very occasional meetings, she took the opportunity to have a really good look at Papa Doyle, as the boys called him.

He really was rather an attractive man. The mouth within the close-cropped beard and moustache had an air of dry humour that went well with the wry, lived-in, rather sardonic face. She knew the boys had nicknamed him Papa because of that beard, and wondered briefly if he was aware of it. She thought, I've never kissed a beard and felt the beginning of another blush. Lowering her gaze she said hastily: 'Thank you for being frank.'

'It's Tom, actually.'

He winced exaggeratedly as Olivia laughed. 'That is a terrible joke,' she said and his mouth twisted again into that engaging smile.

'It goes with the job –' he broke off as Adam came into sight, to ask mildly, 'where have you been for the past ten minutes … smoking around the back of the sports pavilion with the other bad boys?'

Adam first paled then blushed. He stood awkwardly, twisting his cap in his hands and Olivia felt suddenly protective. She put an arm about his shoulders. 'Are you ready to go?'

'Yes. I put my case in the car.'

'Come along then.'

He mumbled, 'Goodbye, sir, see you next term.'

'I imagine you will … for one thing or another.' The master gave one of his faintly mocking smiles. He took Olivia's hand, the smile warming, his eyes lingering on her face. 'If you have any more problems, you know where I am. Goodbye, Mrs Ryder.'

He stood watching them walk away, musing for a moment or two on the pleasure of a beautiful woman's smile and how, despite its conventional length, Olivia Ryder's dress failed to conceal the attractiveness of her tight *derrière* and long, shapely legs.

*   *   *

Adam threw his cap onto the back seat then sat in silence for a few minutes 'What were you talking to old Doyle about?' he asked eventually.

She gave a sidelong glance at his face before turning out onto the road.

'You, of course, darling.'

He looked alarmed. 'Crumbs … what was he saying?'

'Nothing much; should he have been?'

'No.'

Olivia remembered Doyle's look and the reference to smoking. 'All right,' she said resignedly, 'what have you been up to?'

'Nothing, absolutely nothing, mum.'

'Adam,' she sighed, 'you are such a rotten liar.'

He bit his lip. 'I think he might have seen me smoking … but you won't tell dad will you?'

'No, but you will.' She was cross with him; silly little fool. 'You know how he feels about that. You're to own up, and it will serve you right if he sends you down to gran and pops without any pocket money.'

He muttered rebelliously, 'Dad smokes, and so do you, sometimes.'

'I know I do, but only occasionally. I'm not like your father who simply must have them in the house. He doesn't want *you* to begin because he knows only too well that once you start, it's not so easy to stop.'

'I wish I hadn't told you,' he was sulky. 'This is a rotten start to the holiday.'

She relented, taking one hand off the wheel to ruffle his curls. 'All right, then, *I'll* tell him, once you're safely in Devon.'

Irritated he twitched away. 'Don't *do* that, mum. I'm not a kid anymore … and I'm sick of chaps calling me Shirley Temple. I want my hair cut short this vac; really short, like Burt Lancaster.'

She laughed. 'Don't be ridiculous. You'd look like a convict and your ears would stick out like jug-handles. You can have it cut shor*ter*, but don't go mad, because apart from shaving your head

36

completely, you've no chance of getting rid of those curls.'

Really, she thought as he settled into an offended silence, always some new bit of angst these days … how on earth could a man like Tom Doyle choose to spend his days surrounded by dozens of such stroppy adolescents? She smiled remembering those dark eyes looking down on her, wondering fleetingly if he was anything like Giles; seizing the opportunity to flirt with any woman who wasn't actually hideous.

'It's not funny,' Adam said crossly, misinterpreting the smile.

'I wasn't thinking about *you*!' she snapped.

Puzzled and aggrieved, he gave her a stony stare before observing, 'You've missed the turning!'

Childishly, she stuck out her tongue at him. 'Just shut up, will you Adam.' She did a forbidden U-turn across the central grass of the dual carriageway, adding *sotto voce* through gritted teeth, 'Sometimes you sound just like your father.'

*　　　*　　　*

Giles was waiting by the gate when they arrived back at Riversmead, and as Olivia slowed the car, Adam was out and running to meet his father, stopping a few paces away as though suddenly remembering the loftiness of his years. But Giles was unembarrassed, pulling Adam to him with a welcoming hug, which was warm and affectionate, but brief enough not to damage his son's dignity.

'How dare you keep growing up behind my back?' He squeezed Adam's shoulder. 'Come along in. We'll see to your things later.'

*　　　*　　　*

'You are good with him.' Olivia prodded the potatoes and turned to smile at Giles, where he sat on the kitchen table, putting cherries on the trifle. 'I don't get it right with him now; he's dodging my mothering and I no longer have the right touch.'

'Don't worry. He'll come around later. You're just feeling now how I did when he was younger.'

'I'm sorry, was I a doting mother?'

'Yes, but it was nothing to do with that,' he popped a cherry in his mouth, 'just ages and stages.'

She made a face. 'I tried hard to be the perfect wife – always putting you first; even before Adam.'

'You made a very good job of it.' He grinned, 'incidentally, we had a *very* informative walk around the garden. It's all right – he let you off the hook. I know about the smoking.'

'Oh, you do? What did you say?'

'Told him not to be an ass, of course, and promised him a quid for each term he could come home and tell me he hadn't had a cigarette – and a damned good bollocking and clip around the ear if he had!'

'You see, I even got that wrong, I came the stuffy mother bit and threatened him with you.' She spread her hands helplessly and he laughed, getting off the table to hug her much as he had hugged Adam.

'Cheer-up, I shall never be your rival in the matter of cooking his favourite steak and kidney pud!'

She took a back seat that evening, leaving them to play chess and chat about sport in general and cricket in particular. Giles led his son on to talk about his holiday plans, shooting Olivia the odd wry smile as Adam waxed enthusiastic about Liam Flynn, Devonshire and sailing … and Liam Flynn again.

'Got a bad case of the hero worships,' Giles commented, after his son had taken himself off to bed. He cocked an inquiring eye. 'I suppose this chap Flynn is, er, *safe*?'

'If you're thinking along the same lines as I was earlier, it's all right. I had a word with the legendary Papa Doyle, who incidentally is quite a flirt in a quiet way.' She settled next to him on the couch. 'He obviously doesn't like him overmuch, but assured me he's quite definitely harmless in the younger boy department.'

'Thank the Lord for small mercies.'

He put his arm around her and she settled back against him. 'I wish you could come with us tomorrow.'

'I can't. I have to be in Salisbury, remember?'

'How many more of those damned lectures are left?'

He said vaguely, 'Only a few.'

'You'll be sorry when they've finished,' she twisted her head around to look at him.

'Not really.'

'Liar, you enjoy staying in posh hotels and boozing with the boys.'

'There is that of course.'

She said teasingly, 'I met Johnny Porter's wife last week, apparently *he* manages to get home every Friday night. I'm surprised he doesn't stay and join the party, you two being such pals.'

'That's because he's a miserable, stingy bugger who doesn't want to stand his round.'

He wondered that she hadn't felt his heart lurch. God damn it all to hell, wouldn't you just know something like that would come up out of the blue? Johnny wouldn't have given him away, but all the same he'd have a word with him in the morning before he did his rounds, just to be on the safe side.

*   *   *

It was when Zoë and Giles were dining the following evening that Giles received the second nasty jolt in twenty-four hours, when a half-remembered voice fluted in his ear and a hand touched his shoulder.

'Mr Ryder, what brings you here? I was only saying to Harry a few weeks ago that we must ask you and your lovely wife to dinner one evening … a small mark of gratitude for saving his life!'

Giles stood up, his scalp crawling, horribly conscious that the woman's eyes were now coolly assessing his companion. For a split second he panicked, then, with the merest warning flick of his eyes towards Zoë, gave a professional smile and took the proffered hand. 'Mrs Wynn-Davies, Harry,' he said smoothly, 'how nice to meet you both again,' adding, with only the barest hesitation, 'I don't think you know my daughter, Zoë.'

'What a charming name … I didn't realise you had such a grown-up family, Mr Ryder … your son must still be at school. We met him at the hospital fete last year – such a delightful boy, and so like *you*.'

She looked questioningly at Zoë's straight, ragged, dark hair and pointed features.

Without faltering, Zoë smiled innocently. '*I* take after mummy's side of the family,' she replied. Scooping up a spoonful of ice cream, she treated Harry Wynn-Davies to a wide-eyed, schoolgirl smile while closing her lips over her spoon with the virginal air of a postulant nun receiving communion

He stroked a finger across his moustache. 'Lucky mother,' he said. 'Such a pity she isn't here, but I'm sure you more than make up for her absence.'

Demurely, she cast down her eyes. 'You'll have to ask daddy about that.'

Oh, my God! Giles felt his palms begin to sweat. *Don't let her overdo it. Just let the buggers go, or the ground open … please…* He said weakly, 'We were just about to have coffee. Won't you join us?'

*   *   *

'Christ!' Giles sat down, very slowly and carefully, as Mrs Wynn-Davis and her beaming spouse finally departed. 'I'm getting too bloody old for shocks like that ... and did you *have* to flirt with him? God knows what you've done to his blood pressure. You may have ruined a very expensive bit of surgery there.'

'Language daddy...' Zoë propped her chin on one hand, looking at him solemnly with the same wide-eyed innocence she had maintained for the past half-hour, then she collapsed into muted hysterical giggles. 'You should have seen your face, you lying toad!'

'I'm sorry ... dropping you in it like that. It was all that came into my mind on the spur of the moment. Do you think they were suspicious?' Giles picked up his napkin and dabbed at his forehead.

'Not a chance; I'm an actress, remember?'

'Yes, but I'm no actor.'

He was rather more shaken than he cared to show by the encounter. Now where the hell did those two live, he wondered feverishly; it was somewhere in the back of bloody beyond, but just where exactly? Why hadn't he asked them? He teased his brain. Was it the Channel Islands? No. The Isle of Wight? Ah, yes. That was it! He relaxed.

They must just be visiting. Not much chance of running into them again, though why the hell they should be thinking of asking them to dinner on the Isle of Wight, God only knew ... but supposing she asked his whole damned family for a weekend? "I can always find you at your hospital when Harry comes for his check-ups," she'd said coyly. A small moan escaped Giles' lips.

Zoë was still watching him. 'You worry too much,' her voice softened. 'It might have been better to say I was just a friend. Nobody takes that much notice these days...' and she touched his hand. 'It really was terribly funny!'

It was an unusual gesture for her to make and he felt a little flutter under his ribs. Oh hell, he thought, I mustn't let you get too close; this is a relationship that can lead nowhere; that one or other or both will eventually tire of, and that is the way it must end.

'Don't look at me like that.' Her brows were drawn in a frown and he was reminded that beneath the flippancy of youth, and the occasional, deliberate 'don't care' of an out-at-elbows urchin, lay a considerable intelligence and an exceedingly sharp mind.

He rubbed a hand across his face. 'You don't know a thing about the Mrs Wynn-Davies of this world, nor the havoc they can wreak when they get gossiping with others of their kind.'

'Well, don't start trying to hide me away, because I won't do that;

not for a dozen Wynn-Davies and all their friends and relations…'

He smiled. 'Don't get uppity with your father or I shall make you go to bed early!'

She looked up at him from under her lashes.

'Yes, please,' she said.

*   *   *

'It's very odd. I seem to know the daughter's face, but I can't think from where.' Sylvia Wynn-Davies settled into the Saab, her forehead creasing in a frown of concentration.

'You need new glasses, my dear!' Harry gave a bark of laughter. 'You *should* recognise her because you've watched her all evening, although perhaps not as closely as I have. And she did have a great deal more hair on stage. She played Bianca … the fetching little baggage!'

'Well, how extraordinary … but surely not; you must be mistaken. She only looks about eighteen, and I didn't notice the name Ryder in the programme.'

'Hardly surprising my dear. She's billed as Zoë Ormonde.'

'Well, theatre people, they do that sort of thing: use another name, don't they?'

'Uh-huh,' he was non-committal. She looked hard at his sceptical smile. 'Harry, you don't think…?'

'I most certainly do. I've never seen such an amazingly smooth cover-up in my life. The girl is brilliant … but his eyes gave the game away.'

'Well … *really*!' she was lost for words.

'Just forget it.' Harry patted his wife's arm. 'The man saved me from an early grave; I have the scar to prove it. For my money, he can run a full harem and I'd wish him nothing but well.'

'But we're living not more than five miles away from his hospital now … how awkward if we ever meet him with his wife.'

'Quite, so I guess that just about knocks your idea of a cosy little dinner party right out of the window, doesn't it?'

Harry Wynne-Davies drove home, still shaken by intermittent chuckles. God, but that little kitten reminded him of when he was a subaltern in Basra in 'forty-four. He'd shown the adjutant's very willing daughter a thing or two then…

His wife was a great deal less amused. It just didn't seem right. A man in that position shouldn't be parading around with a young girl half his age. It was just the sort of thing one might read in the News of

41

the World. Not that she took such a paper, of course, but one heard about its content from the less intellectual; Mrs Harris, her daily, was always a positive mine of salacious Monday morning information about the similar goings-on of professional men who should know better.

*   *   *

'Do you actually care for me at all?'

Giles was seated on the bed holding Zoë between his knees. He began to undress her, letting each garment slip to the ground.

'Perhaps,' she teased, beginning to unbutton his shirt. 'Why? Does it matter?'

'I don't know.' He was watching her eyes. 'I can't imagine what it would be like now, not to be able to do this with you, but I don't expect it to last.'

'That makes two of us.'

'Is there anyone else?' He knew it was the one question he shouldn't ask.

She frowned. 'I don't sleep around, as a matter of course, if that's what you mean, and one at a time is my motto.'

He said, 'How does anyone get as amoral as you at twenty three?'

'By being born a generation later than you, sweetie,' the tawny eyes were mocking him. 'These days it's a big bad world out there, you know. A girl can no longer afford to be a shrinking violet ... especially in my business. If she wants anything, including sex, she goes and gets it. If not, she just says "bollocks" and gets on with her life. Where sex is concerned I'm very choosy, so generally I just say bollocks. But I'm in a minority there.'

'What an appalling philosophy; thank God that I don't have a daughter.'

He was grinning. She turned on him, anger sparking in her eyes.

'To me that's an even more appalling philosophy; in fact it's bloody obscene. You're quite happy to screw someone else's daughter, aren't you?'

He winced. 'Zoë ... don't.'

'Why not, it's true, isn't it? That's how you think about it?' She mimed looking at her watch then giving an affected little shriek clasped a hand to her forehead. 'Heavens, it's six o'clock; time I got home to the wife.'

He stood, putting his arms about her. 'No, it isn't. It isn't *like* that. Zoë, darling Zoë, don't be angry ... please.'

42

'Shut *up*. Just shut up, will you.' Furiously she turned on him again. 'I'll get as bloody mad as I like!'

'What have I done? You knew how it would be…'

She dug her fingers into his shoulders. 'Of course I knew, stupid.'

The feel of her almost naked in his arms was making his pulse race, the heat crawl through him. With something like terror he realised that he'd been a fool to think this was just another short affair that would run its course and finish amicably, with only the usual small sense of regret. From the very beginning this had been different. He rocked her against him; smoothing her hair, kissing her forehead. 'Hush. Don't be angry with me, because I don't want it to finish. More than anything in my life I want you … need you. I swear it.'

'Don't be so damned nice to me, or I might start wanting it too and *then* where would we be…'

I love you. He tried it out experimentally to himself. It sounded right. It felt right. But it couldn't be. There was Olivia and Oh, God – there was Adam.

'I love you,' it burst from him; he repeated it louder: 'I love you. I *love* you.'

She raised her head. 'You don't have to shout.' She sounded like a cross child.

'Dear, dearest Zoë,' he kissed her with great tenderness. 'I'm very much afraid it's beginning to be true.'

'Well don't be. You're just an old married man with a twenty-year-itch … that's what's true, isn't it?'

'Is that how you see it?' he sighed. 'Perhaps you're right … and you?' he stood her back, holding her shoulders, 'what are you?'

'Me? I'm an actress remember? And I'm going right to the top.' She threw back her head as he'd watched her do, night after night on stage. 'I like you, Mr Giles Ryder; I like you a lot. I don't know if I love you … I'm not even sure if I know what love is; so let's stop all this talk of needing and love and just go on having *fun*…'

4

Margot Heyward stood above the harbour, watching the yacht take the breeze and head out across open water; Liam at the wheel, the girl handling the sheets with easy competence, Adam at her side, eagerly taking in all the instructions.

'They obviously know what they're doing.' She turned to Olivia. 'Are you still not sure about Liam?'

'He's very sure of *himself;* a bit of a smart-arse in fact. I think Adam's Papa Doyle has him sussed.' Olivia shrugged. 'But what can I do – Adam's getting too old to be tied to my apron strings.'

'Oh, he'll be fine.' Margot said comfortingly, as they began to walk back towards the cottage. 'All the same, I'm glad you laid down some ground rules and insisted he tells us where they're proposing to go each day, and a rough estimate of when to expect them back.'

'It seems a lot of responsibility to put on you and dad, but I think they'll play fair.' Olivia chuckled. 'Adam will, anyway. I told him straight this morning … if he messes you about he comes back home on the next train. Anyway, dad won't let him get away with much, will he? Not unless he's mellowed considerably since *my* teenage years.'

Margot took her arm as they began the climb up the steep lane from the harbour. 'Your father can't wait for you to come and stay next week, and he's so pleased you've started painting again. He could never understand what made you give it up like that, just when you were doing so well.'

'Artists are not meant to be wives and mothers.' Olivia replied dryly. Always loyal to Giles, she had never given the slightest hint to anyone that his wishes had been paramount in the gradual death of what she, and everyone else, had expected would be a successful career. Now she narrowed her eyes against the sunlight, already planning where she would set her easel above the harbour, wishing she could stay now and begin work right away.

She said, 'I've done a fair amount of sketching during the past few weeks but I feel a bit rusty on the painting after all this time.'

'I remember you saying when you joined up, that as a born artist it was like riding a bicycle, you'd never forget the skill.' Margot reminded her, and Olivia laughed.

'Let's hope I was right … arrogant little toad that I was!'

44

When they reached the cottage a pot of coffee bubbled on the range, and Clive Heyward was putting mugs and a jug of yellow cream on the scrubbed kitchen table. Margot sank down thankfully on the nearest chair, while Olivia leaned to peer into the jug, exclaiming, 'Oh Lord, this really is heart-attack country! Have you some of this I can take back for Giles? You know he simply loves it.'

'Of course, and bring that man of yours down with you next week.' Her father looked up from pouring the coffee. 'Do you good to have a break together.'

'So that you and Giles can both go off fishing and leave mother and me to slave away here? No thank you!' Olivia wrinkled her nose. 'Anyway, he's too busy these days, and a fat lot of peace I'd get to paint if he *was* here.' Olivia sipped her coffee, looking at him over the rim of her cup. 'You can take me fishing one day instead.'

'With pleasure, darling,' he raised his own cup. 'Cheers … roll on Friday week!'

She was loath to leave, making them promise to 'phone when Adam returned that afternoon, turning back from the car to hug them both again before she finally got in and started the engine.

'She looks well.' Margot waved until the car was out of sight.

'Umm,' Clive took out his pouch and began to stuff tobacco into his pipe. 'But I get a feeling something isn't quite right. She's less chatty than usual and she dodged me when I suggested she brought Giles down. A few months ago he would have been here with her like a shot.'

'Darling, she said he's busy…'

'Doing what? Don't surgeons get time off any more for good behaviour?'

'Well, we'll see … perhaps he'll change his mind,' she soothed, 'after all, who could resist the offer to join you in murdering a few innocent fish?'

*   *   *

Kate looked at her watch and put down her book. 'It's coming up to four-fifteen: time to head back.'

'Give it another ten minutes.' Liam was laid full length on the cabin roof, one arm flung across his face to shield his eyes from the sun.

'No. That big round thing up in the sky is already beginning to sink.' Kate stirred him with her foot and winked at Adam. 'But stay there, you lazy slob; *we* can take her back … just fetch up the anchor will you, Adam, and then take the helm.'

Adam tried not to look too openly as she moved smoothly and unhurriedly about the boat. He thought she was just gorgeous ... quite the prettiest girl he'd ever seen, with her long straight brown hair caught up in a pony-tail, and eyes startlingly blue in her tanned skin. His heart beat fast and he shifted uncomfortably when her slender body in the brief shorts and thin shirt brushed his back as she passed behind him. He'd never been this close to a girl before ... God, wait until he got back and told Marshall about this holiday.

He was suddenly aware that Liam was sitting up watching him watching Kate.

'Did you say you were going into Torcross tomorrow, sis? I hope so then Adam will be able to concentrate on the sailing!' Liam smiled his knowing, adult smile and Adam blushed scarlet. 'We'll drop you off to do whatever it is you want to do and pick you up on the way back.'

'Please yourself.' She was pulling a sweater over her head; she paused to smooth back her hair. 'I can take the bus.'

'Get some cash out of the old man, did you?'

'No, I have enough; I've not spent much this term.'

'More fool you ... I'll get you some. I'm not afraid of him.'

She flushed, but didn't answer. Adam looked at the horizon and made a show of ignoring these exchanges. Brothers and sisters, he supposed, always argued with each other, and it was decent of Liam to say he'd get some money for her. He slid his hand into the back pocket of his shorts, fingering the five-pound note his father had given him, wondering if he dared offer it to Kate ... but no, she might be embarrassed, or even worse, annoyed.

They were back in good time and after making the boat secure in her berth the three sat on the harbour wall, chatting and making arrangements for the next morning. When the clock on the tower of the little church struck six, Adam left them and scorning the roadway, climbed the cliff up to Captains Cottage.

Tea was on the table and gran and pops waiting to hear his news. He settled down to talk, well pleased with his first day's sailing, and the added bonus of being able to watch Kate Flynn moving around all day in those shorts...

'I took the helm on the way back. Flynn said I did all right. Tomorrow we're dropping Kate off in Torcross and going around Start Point to fish. Flynn says it's OK for me to crew because the forecast is so good.'

'That's quite a way to go,' Clive put in mildly as Adam paused for breath, 'and I'm glad the forecast is good, because I shouldn't care to think you were sailing around the Point in anything but fair weather.'

'Have you ever done any sailing then, pops?'

'Quite a fair amount when I was your age, and I've seen more than one lot of wreckage washed ashore after a gale ... and from bigger boats than the Morning Star.'

'You don't have to worry, Flynn knows what he's doing.'

'So does his sister, to judge by the way she was handling the sails when you went off this morning.' Margot smiled, 'Such a pretty girl!'

'Yes, well...' Adam coloured. 'She's OK, but they squabble a bit ... Flynn says she can put a bit of a damper on things some times.'

'I daresay that means she doesn't like taking any risks.' Clive buttered a roll, looking at his grandson over his spectacles. 'I might feel a touch easier if your friend wasn't *quite* so sure of himself.'

'That's only because he's so good at everything!' Adam was hot to defend his idol. 'You've no idea, pops ... he's just the most terrific sportsman.'

'I'll take your word for it.' Clive winked at Margot. 'Perhaps we might have the honour of entertaining him to supper sometime.'

'I dunno...' Adam was frankly horrified at the thought of Flynn being quizzed by his grandfather, who could be pretty direct when he started and for some reason didn't seem to like Flynn, which wasn't fair. 'I think he goes off somewhere in the evenings, he doesn't get on with his dad.'

Margot shot her husband a warning glance and moved to Adam's rescue. 'What about his sister? Perhaps she'd like to have somewhere to go in the evenings? She would be very welcome to come for supper anytime.'

'Thanks, gran ... I'll ask her. We're not sailing on Monday because Flynn's taking the bus into Dartmouth on his own. He's getting some stuff for the boat. She might like to come then.'

'Fine, just let me know in time.'

*   *   *

Adam and Kate lay on the grass at the edge of the cliffs, watching the waves break on the rocks below, waiting for Margot to call them to supper.

'I wonder what Liam's doing in Dartmouth all this time?' Adam sent a stone bouncing down the cliff, leaning forward to watch it land on the beach below. 'I always get bored in the towns ... we live out in the sticks a bit, which is great in the holidays; plenty of fishing and swimming in the river all summer.'

'That'd send Liam batty.' Kate sat back, pulling her legs up and resting her chin on her knees. 'He'd loathe it here if it wasn't for the sailing. His idea of heaven would be to moor the Star permanently somewhere like Plymouth, then he could get all the – '

She broke off and Adam eyed her curiously.

'Get all the what?'

'Oh … ciggies and things,' she was suddenly vague, gazing out over the water.

'Your dad must have given him some money, I suppose,' he said naively, and she gave a small smile.

'Yes. I daresay big brother wore him down eventually. Dad's working on a commissioned piece at the moment and can't afford the time to row with Liam, who can keep going all night if necessary.'

'Look,' he was suddenly shy. 'If *you* need any cash I could let you have some; my dad gave me five pounds and I've only spent a pound of it, so if you want – '

'No. It's all right, really, but thanks all the same. I can always have money from dada when I need it.'

'But Flynn said, and you said, the other day…'

Vehemently, she broke in on his stammered confusion. 'Don't you ever tell him I told you or I'll never speak to you again! Dad hates giving Liam money because of what he might spend it on, that's all. He may be a bit of a dead loss as a father, but he's not mean and I could spit right in Liam's eye when he talks about him like that!'

'All right … don't get mad at me.' Adam was alarmed. 'I only know what he told me. I won't say anything. Honestly.'

'OK. Sorry.'

They sat in silence for a few minutes, Adam not sure what to say next, so that it was a relief when he heard pops calling them in to supper.

Kate slipped her arm in his as they walked up the path, rather as he'd seen girls walking arm in arm together, and gave his elbow a little squeeze. 'Don't spend *too* much time kissing Liam's boots, will you?'

He didn't answer because he didn't know what to say, and besides, the feel of her small breast moving against his arm was causing him a bit of a problem. This holiday was turning out to be rather different than he'd imagined. Suddenly, there were undercurrents and eddies that he could feel but not understand. But the rapidly growing heat in his groin he could both feel and understand only too well.

*   *   *

Giles helped Olivia to pack her holdall and painting kit into the car, laying the easel on top he shut the boot carefully. 'Take it steady, and stop if you feel tired. Everyone seems to be heading southwest this Easter … my regards to Clive and Margot.'

'Can't you possibly manage at least a couple of days? Dad's dying to go fishing with you again,' she put her arms about him. 'You've never before been as busy as you are now. We've scarcely had an evening together this past week. It's quite absurd. Besides, I shall miss you.'

'Think of it as a necessary sacrifice,' he kissed her. 'I'll come down with you in the summer. Adam can sail with his friend, if they're still on speaking terms, I shall fish with your father and you can paint.' He laid his cheek against hers.

'Just see you do.' She held him a little longer then turned to the car. 'I'll ring you tomorrow.'

'No,' he answered swiftly, 'let me ring you … in case I'm kept late.'

'All right,' she put the car into gear; blew him a kiss. 'Be good!'

He watched her out of sight, standing for several minutes leaning against the gate and staring down the lane.

He'd been longing for this moment; counting the days until he could have more than just a few snatched evening hours with Zoë. Now he felt wretched and completely at war with himself. I don't know what to do, he thought. I can't go on forever pleading overwork.

He turned to look at the home he and Olivia had made together. It seemed such a short time ago that he had carried his son through the doorway of this cottage for the first time. He thought of all the laughter and the loving, the fights and the making-up. The terrible never-to-be-forgotten day she had almost died giving birth to their tiny premature stillborn daughter. Her unbearable grief when he'd held her in his arms and told her there could be no more children…

He felt moisture start to his eyes and put up a hand to wipe it away.

What am I going to do? What can *I do now which won't destroy or cause pain to one or other or all of us?*

*   *   *

With Adam only too clearly not needing her company, but happy to sail with Liam or swim and walk with Kate, Olivia began to spend every day out in the village, or along the cliffs and down in one or other of the small coves which dotted the coast. She was glad of this time to be alone, the pleasure in working again dispersing in part the cloud that seemed recently to have been hanging over herself and Giles.

He'd always had mood swings, but lately they'd been more noticeable and very trying on her patience. Surely by the time a man was past fifty he should be secure enough and mature enough to keep his emotions on an even keel? He'd spent the last weeks alternately making love to her half the night, or lying hunched and uncommunicative under more than his share of the bedclothes.

Sketching and painting from early mornings through to the late afternoons, working with passionate concentration, she found her peace of mind return. All the old skills resurfaced and she filled her canvasses with the remembered beauty of buildings and landscapes, so utterly absorbed and happy that it was a shock to rise one morning and realise the holiday was almost at an end.

'I don't know where all the time has gone,' she complained ruefully over the breakfast table, a couple of days before they were due to leave. 'Now I shall be counting the weeks until Adam's summer vacation when we can come down again, with Giles, I hope; so long as dad keeps him out of my hair when I'm painting!'

'Liam and Kate want to take the Star over to France in the summer,' put in Adam tentatively. 'May I go with them? He says it's better with three because of having to keep watch at night. It'll take hours and hours; twenty or more to reach Brittany from here, you know, and then we'd be sailing right along the French coast almost as far as Spain.'

'We'll see.' Olivia smiled. 'Still not fed-up with being Liam's cabin boy then?'

'Oh, *mum*! You're as bad as pops; he's always getting in digs like that!'

'Umm, well, I still think he's too sure of himself, but you certainly haven't come to any harm so far. If his sister is going along as well, and if your father agrees, I should think a trip across the channel might be on the cards. Kate has a sensible head on her shoulders and I'd take a bet she'll keep you both in line.'

'Yeah … she's all right,' he muttered and began to shovel cereal into his mouth at speed. 'Got to hurry … we're going out a bit further today after mackerel.'

Clive snorted. 'Call that fishing? They practically give themselves up around these waters!'

'Yes, but pops, you've still got to use the right spinners and know where to find them…'

Olivia winked at her mother and left them still arguing. Collecting her bag, stool and easel on her way out, she decided that this morning she'd try the view of the harbour from nearer the top of the hill.

*   *   *

'Very good, but the light is going and you'll end up with one hell of a stiff back if you sit crouched like that any longer!'

Reluctantly Olivia brought herself back into the real world. Annoyed by the sudden interruption she screwed up her eyes at the burly figure by her side; outlined against a brilliantly setting sun, he was just a looming dark mass.

'Oh God,' continued the deep, rumbling voice, 'd'you *have* to squint like that?'

The man moved to the other side of her, so that he no longer had his back to the sun. Olivia gave him a cool look.

'You broke my concentration. You should know better, Mr Flynn.'

Very white teeth showed briefly in a luxuriant, grey-flecked brown beard.

'Do I know you? Should I know you?' Beneath the deep, cultured speech, his voice had an upward lilt and a rhythm that betrayed his origins. Again the teeth showed. 'I'd damned-well *like* to know you!'

'No, to your first two questions and I will, as our American friends say, take a rain check on the last one. Now will you please go away and leave me to finish.'

He gestured at the rapidly setting sun and gave a growl of laughter. 'Too late; in any case…' he squatted beside her, so that his great head was on a level with hers, 'you've been sat in this same spot, painting that same damned picture since this morning, only stopping for precisely ten minutes at noon to eat your sandwiches!'

She began to screw the caps back on her oils. 'How do you know that?'

Her fingers moved neatly, gathering up her materials and slipping them into her bag, and he watched her for a few moments in silence, until she glanced up at him with a frown. 'Must you stare?'

'Sorry. I could see you while I worked. My studio is up there….' he gestured to a long low cottage on the hillside behind them. 'That's

51

my house. The ghastly pink one.'

'I know.' She looked out over the harbour to where the Morning Star was creeping towards its moorings. 'Here comes my son, and yours … only just making it back in time.'

'Good God!' He stared at her. 'So you're the intrepid woman who's entrusted that baby to the devious and untrustworthy fruit of my loins.'

'Well you said it, I didn't, although I'm inclined to agree with the character reference you give your son.' Carefully, she lifted her canvas and placed it in his hands. 'Hold this a moment, will you?' She began to fold the easel. 'Although I think you're being rather harsh. Cocky and too sure of himself would be my description, but then he's probably inherited that.'

He gave another rumbling laugh and, holding the canvas at arm's length, said, 'This is really very good, you know, very powerful. I abhor pretty pictures.' He waved an expansive arm, 'although I think you should make the buildings your main subject. They are splendid; you have an architect's eye.'

'Thank you.' Olivia smiled and he stared intently down at her in silence for a full half minute, during which time she could feel herself becoming distinctly warm about the face. 'Beards,' she thought inconsequentially, 'there are altogether too many beards around lately!'

'Ye-es…' he said eventually. 'I'd like to sculpt that head … how about next week?'

'Next week,' she answered dryly, 'I shall be back in Hampshire with my husband.'

'Pity,' he grinned. 'Kate will be sorry. I gather you've fed her from time to time.'

'My mother has,' Olivia swung her bag onto her shoulder and picked up her easel, 'it's been a pleasure. She is a lovely girl.'

'Is she?' He looked surprised. 'Yes, I suppose she is.'

'And Liam is a good looking young man.'

His face closed. 'Unfortunately he knows it,' he turned as though to leave, and she raised enquiring brows.

'I thought perhaps you had come down to welcome your offspring home.'

'No. I came to see if what you were doing was any good. But I don't mind hanging around a little longer, if you think I should.'

'I have no views whatsoever about what you should, or should not do, Mr Flynn,' Olivia started towards the harbour and giving vent to another growl, which might have been either of amusement or exasperation, Ambrose Flynn fell into step beside her and they walked in silence down the hill.

*　　　　*　　　　*

'Hi, mum!'

Adam was unusually pleased to see her. She remembered in time not to hug him, but to her surprise he came close, leaning against her, greeting Liam's father with a politely reserved: ''Evening, sir,' which made the recipient pull down his brows and give his pirate grin, before shifting less friendly eyes to Liam, who stood stony-faced and silent, a half dozen mackerel dangling on a wire from his hand.

'Better give your friend his share and chuck the others at Kate … she's getting the tea tonight; Miriam's off dancing.' Flynn's tone was sarcastic. Expressionlessly, Liam unhooked half of the fish and handed them to Adam, then, with a muttered 'See you in the morning,' he walked on up the hill.

His father shrugged. 'Must be one of his strong silent days.' he turned to follow his son, 'Good night, Mrs and Adam Ryder. Enjoy your fish.'

Adam took the easel from her and she put her arm about his shoulders as they began the climb up to Captains Cottage, aware of how lanky and loose-limbed he was, and that his head now was on a level with her own.

'Had a good day, darling?'

'It was OK.' He was uncommunicative, keeping his eyes lowered. She squeezed his shoulder comfortingly.

'Not quite so good, then?'

'They can't all be, can they?'

'No. Want to talk about it?'

He shook his head. 'It's nothing, really.'

OK, she thought philosophically, so they've fallen out over something at last. I daresay tomorrow everything will be wonderful again, and Liam Flynn the greatest thing since time began.

Adam trudged on, his head down. He wanted to tell her, but that would be sneaking, and anyway it hadn't happened before. Tomorrow Kate would be there again, so everything should be all right.

But he wished it hadn't happened. Liam had said it didn't matter, that everyone did it; that it made you feel good. But he wouldn't try it and Liam had first laughed, then got annoyed and called him a wanker. Just to make up for refusing the reefer, and to prove he wasn't a wimp, he'd drunk some of Liam's whisky and now he felt queasy…

He walked on in the shelter of his mother's arm. No, there was no need to tell. It probably wouldn't happen again.

*   *   *

Kate took the fish from her brother and gave him a hard look. 'You idiot – you'd better get on upstairs before Dada gets a good squint at you and twigs.'

'Shut up; he never notices anything.'

'Then you're lucky, aren't you? He'd put a rock right through the bottom of the Star if he knew you'd sailed in that state … and if you've been getting Adam to join your nasty goings-on – '

Liam interrupted her. 'Don't fuse your knickers. The kid's all right.'

'He'd better be, or I'll bloody well shop you to dad myself, you bastard.'

'Amazing the language young ladies learn in a Convent school, isn't it?'

They glared at each other in silence. Then Liam began to grin. For a moment Kate struggled, then her mouth twitched and they both exploded into laughter.

She said, 'You're such a twerp; wasting your money on that stuff … and the booze. You don't really need it. Nobody does. It's just a stupid fad.'

'It makes living with that old sod more bearable.'

'You do talk a load of rubbish about dad … and don't you dare involve Adam. I mean it. I'll drop you right in it.'

'OK,' he smirked infuriatingly, 'he fancies you like nobody's business – can't wait to get into your knickers!'

She grabbed a tea towel and snapped at his retreating back. 'Go and sleep it off before supper.' She watched him up the stairs then turned to deal with the fish.

'Men,' vigorously she chopped at heads and tails, 'who needs them!'

'Women do,' her father's powerful frame filled the doorway. He jerked his head towards the stairs. 'What's up with him?'

Kate shrugged.

He scowled. 'I thought things might be easier here; I should have known better. How much freedom does he want?'

'I don't think freedom is all he needs, dada.'

'Then what – I keep off his back; leave him alone…'

She lifted her shoulders then let them drop again. 'Perhaps he's lonely.'

His face darkened. 'Well, he's never wanted *my* company for the past five years, has he?'

'No, dada … and quite a lot of the time he doesn't want mine, either.'

He looked at her bent head; hesitating slightly, he put out his hand to briefly touch her shoulder. 'You're a good girl, Kate.'

She forced a smile. 'So how about peeling some potatoes? I don't see why I should be the only one slaving over a hot stove this evening.'

Just give me a hug, she thought, just cross the barrier … tell Liam he's OK and not to blame for what happened. Just do *anything* rather than bottle it all up and go on keeping us both at arm's length.

But he only grinned and picking up the knife began to peel a potato and, as always, keeping a distance between them.

5

Olivia walked through the house, unable to credit the evidence of her eyes. No pie packets. No empty cans or bottles... No *life*.

She walked from the hall to the bedrooms, voicing her thoughts out loud. 'He hates Sandra coming when he's alone. He'd rather pay her to keep away, but he must have had her here at least to clear up – Good Lord!' She stared at their bed, the coverlet turned half-back, almost as she had left it; the same sheets and pillow-cases, all scarcely creased and looking remarkably clean...

Disturbed, she returned to the kitchen, and lifting the lid of the pedal bin found it empty of everything but the clean, unmarked paper she'd used to line it with before leaving for Devon.

It was creepy and she wished she'd brought Adam back with her, instead of dropping him off in Salisbury to do a rush job on the holiday task he'd neglected in favour of sailing.

'I can do it in an afternoon, mum,' he'd assured her. 'It's only about English Cathedrals and I can get most of what I want in Salisbury and find out the rest from books.'

'Lazy little devil!' she'd said, laughing, 'but I suppose I did much the same thing at your age. All right, you can ring me before you get the train and I'll meet it at Romsey; but you *must* get back before seven. I don't want dinner late tonight. I'm tired.'

Now she stood irresolute, checking her watch. Almost one-fifteen, Giles must be at the blasted hospital again. Thanks to Adam and his project, she was back much earlier than she'd expected ... she should have rung Giles before they left Lodscombe. She went back to the hall and picked up the 'phone, dialling the hospital she asked his extension number.

It rang for a long time before anyone answered, then it wasn't Giles but some breathless female.

'I'd like to speak to Mr Ryder, please.'

'I'm sorry he's not in today. He never comes on a Saturday unless he's called.'

'Oh, of course not.'

Feeling foolish she returned the receiver to its cradle, although she really wasn't to know. He'd been called to the department on several Saturdays running before she'd gone away ... at least, that's what he'd told *her*, and if he wasn't there, then where was he?

56

She picked up her shoulder bag and went out again, locking up behind her.

Carol answered her door, opening it almost before Olivia let the knocker fall. 'Saw you coming through the garden … come in, the kettle's on. I'm glad you're back. Its been like a tomb around here, with Chris at the Crown Court giving evidence on that New Forest murder and Giles staying most of the time; in fact *all* the time, with his old pal, only showing up for the odd coffee and lunch.' Carol prattled on with Olivia only half-listening, her mind busy still with the empty house she had just left. '…and bloody Fuffkins has had three ginger kittens … I'll castrate that blasted yellow-eyed tom with the grapefruit knife if I catch him around here again – '

Olivia interrupted belatedly, 'What old pal?'

She felt a stab of guilt. Although her mother had taken several calls from Giles on her behalf, she'd been so wrapped up in her painting that she'd forgotten to ring him back. Her heart sank. He must have got fed-up and cleared off in protest, which would be a typical Giles' reaction. Now she supposed she'd have to coax him out of a hurt, how-could-you-go-and-forget-all-about-me, mood…

'Some old student friend … lives near Whiteparish.' Carol filled the teapot. 'Hogg, Hogget … something like that.'

'Hodges?' Olivia queried and she nodded.

'That's right. Pete Hodges.'

'But I thought Pete took a Sabbatical and went to Canada weeks ago, to do research for a paper.' Olivia shrugged 'I suppose he must have been delayed. How was Giles when you did see him?'

'Blooming and looking like a little pig in clover. I expect they've been chaps together in the pub every night. How was *your* holiday?'

'Wonderful. I've got a mass of painting done … loads of sketches and three completed canvasses.' She grinned mischievously. 'Actually, Ambrose Flynn thinks I'm very good.'

'Lucky cow; I must visit your mother in the summer! What's he like?'

'Huge, bearded, sexy dark brown voice, over the hill a bit age-wise … what else can I tell you?'

'That sounds like quite enough.' Carol offered the biscuit barrel. 'You look positively blooming, too. Not been doing anything you shouldn't down there, have you?'

'If I had, would I tell *you*?'

The kitchen 'phone rang, making Olivia jump. Carol took it.

'Hello. Yes, it's me.' She rolled her eyes. 'Of course she's here, where else d'you think she might be – in bed with the milkman? Hang on…' She handed it over, 'Giles, for you.'

'He must have his spies everywhere.' Olivia took it. 'Hello, darling, what made you ring here?'

'I bumped into Adam in Salisbury High Street; I tried to ring you at home but there was no answer. I guessed Carol was your most likely port of call.'

'What on earth were you doing in Salisbury on a Saturday afternoon?'

'Well, I stayed overnight as usual after the lecture and decided to wait a bit and have lunch … shop for some bits and pieces; shirts, socks, you know, but I didn't find anything worth having. I'd have been back if I'd known you were returning early.'

Immediately she knew he was lying: knew it instinctively, absolutely. God knows, she thought, with a sudden spurt of anger, she'd had enough practice…

'How's Pete?'

His hesitation was only momentary, but it was enough.

'Fine, he sends his love. Look. I'm running out of change. See you for supper. I've told Adam I'll wait and pick him up from the Cathedral Close at five-thirty and save you a journey. 'Bye…'

The line went dead.

You liar; you lousy, two-faced, liar…

She smiled at Carol.

'I think I'll forego the tea … looks as though I can get supper early and I have to shop first.'

Back at Riversmead she paced backward and forward along the bank of the stream.

You must be rattled to make that sort of mistake you rat. Even the smartest, newest phone boxes don't have the Home Service on radio, nor the sound of someone moving around in the background! I reckon that's the second time in the past weeks you've pulled that one on me…

She kicked off her sandals and sat on the bank, putting her feet in the water and letting the small brown trout parr fuss around her toes, wondering desolately if Giles now cared a solitary damn about all they had put into building their lives in this place she loved so much.

*   *   *

As they left the city, Adam sat back in the Jaguar, enjoying the sort of speed Olivia never reached, thinking how safe and strong his father's gloved hands were on the wheel, and how good it felt to have him all to himself for a while.

It had been a real stroke of luck, seeing dad on the crowded High Street. Funny, he'd thought at first there was another boy with him; or it might have been a girl in shirt and trousers, but after he'd called out and battled through the crowds, his father was standing alone. He'd smiled and looked around saying: 'What a surprise! Is mummy with you?' Adam hoped he might suggest they went for tea and cakes, but no such luck…

'Sure you have all you need for your project?' He looked up as Giles glanced at him with a conspiratorial grin. 'I bet your mother roasted you over leaving it until the last minute!'

'Not really, and I don't go back until Wednesday so I've plenty of time to finish it.' His brow creased in a puzzled frown. 'Dad, did I interrupt anything important today? I thought you had someone with you.'

'What sort of someone?'

'A boy … or I suppose it might have been a girl; someone not very tall, anyway.'

'No. We must get your eyes tested.' His voice was teasing. 'Can't have you seeing things that aren't there, can we? Now, tell me about the sailing. Mummy won't want to be bored listening to it all over again tonight, will she?'

Pleasantly diverted, Adam settled down to sing a paean of praise for all things to do with sailing and the sea.

*   *   *

Giles kissed her cheek then raised his head to sniff the air appreciatively. 'Umm, smells delicious … you've been a busy girl.'

'Haven't I just.' She took his overcoat, throwing it with unaccustomed negligence over a hall chair then turned to Adam, 'Dinner in fifteen minutes. You can go over to Carol's first if you like; Fluffybums or whatever it's called has had kittens. Carol says they've just got their eyes open.'

'Fab; can we have one?'

'No.'

'Shame!' Adam shot off. Giles raised his brows.

'Was that necessary? We've only just got here.'

'So you have. But I though you might want a few minutes alone with me – might even want to ravish me on the spot. It must have been hell for you with only another man for company all this time. How's Pete?'

'I told you. He's fine.'

She heard the note of caution in his voice, and smiled mockingly.

'Oh, good, I must ring him and say thanks for taking in a lonely lodger … you did tell Carol you were staying with him, didn't you?'

He turned his back, walking into the sitting room. 'I need a drink, what about you? Or have you already had more than enough? You sound damned odd, I must say.'

'Not a drop has passed my lips and I don't need one now. What's Pete's number? The least I can do is ring and offer him dinner sometime.'

He poured a large whisky and sat in his armchair, frowning and fiddling with the glass. 'Too late, he left for Montreal this morning. You've just missed him.'

Olivia sat down, crossed her legs, then carefully arranged her skirt an inch above the knee. He watched her warily, nursing his drink.

She smiled pleasantly.

'Do you have to work very hard at being a lying, hypocritical bastard, or does it just come naturally?'

'Now, Olivia…' he started forward.

'Don't you dare try to flannel your way out of this. I'm not prepared to discuss it yet, I just thought I'd let you stew until Adam has gone to bed.' She stood again and walked towards the door. 'I should drink that one up and then have another. You're going to need it.'

He stayed where he was, his agile brain already re-writing the scenario for the past fortnight. Throwing the whisky down in one he shuddered as it hit the spot then poured another.

She might suspect but she couldn't prove anything. He would have to convince her he'd just been enjoying a little flirtation… How about a female colleague from the lectures? No, that would only stir a different hornet's nest; it would have to be something connected with Pete; that was too good a cover to waste.

Damn. How could she have known? He thought he'd covered it nicely with the story to Carol. He chewed a fingernail. There was no way he was going to bring Zoë into this, he thought, feeling slightly sick at the remembrance of the close shave with Adam; he'd only just kissed her as they'd met before the matinee. Afterwards he had been so shaken that when he'd got rid of Adam he'd had to sit in her dressing room for half an hour before he could summon the nerve to call Olivia… God, there just *had* to be some way out of this … Of course; he almost snapped his fingers: Flossy, Olivia would believe anything about Pete's batty old sister. Why hadn't he thought of her before?

It would put him on the spot for all that guff to Carol and he'd be for the dog house without a doubt, but it might just wash…

*   *   *

Olivia watched him over the supper table, knowing with a sick, controlled fury that he'd almost certainly found a way out. She knew him so well … every expression, every nuance of his voice. But this time he wouldn't get away unscathed. She had already taken the first hesitant steps for getting out of the rut of being nothing but a dutiful wife and mother; perhaps the time had also come to really dig in her heels over his adolescent wanderings. The humiliation was more painful to bear now than in the past; then she had had the resilience of youth on her side.

There would be a row. He'd fall back on his usual getting out of trouble tactics: either belittling her with biting sarcasm, or contrite and pleading. Whatever the ploy, he'd eventually end by getting her into bed. Perhaps it was also time she took a stand there, even if she would be depriving herself as much as him.

Skilfully Giles avoided her eyes, pretending an interest in his son's conversation and eating his meal with evident enjoyment.

'Look at me,' Olivia wanted to shout at him, 'what have I done wrong? Why aren't I enough? Does whoever she is make better love? Come quicker? Scream like an alley cat with ecstasy when you fuck? … Just tell me and I'll see what I can do…'

She wondered why, after all this time, she now had this determination to face him out. In the early days she had wept and raged, throwing herself helplessly against his assured, unshakeable confidence of her need of him; later, turned a blind eye and waited for him to end the most recent affair. Only that last time, when he'd been stupid enough to actually take a married member of his own staff to bed and come close to creating an almighty scandal, had she stood firm and said: "No more, or else…"

Since then it had only been supposedly harmless flirtation, and in self-defence she'd returned to the blind eye routine.

But now she *knew* that something out of the ordinary was brewing. She had no absolute proof, just the familiar voice of a radio announcer, and the certainty that there had been another person in the room…

But to catch Giles out one needed it foolproof, gilt-edged and tied up with red ribbon.

*   *   *

''Night dad, 'night mum,' Adam pecked Olivia's cheek and started up the stairs.

'Light out in half an hour, darling … it's been a long day.'

She turned away with a sigh of relief. She had found the evening a ghastly strain. Fortunately Adam had seemed enveloped still in the rosy afterglow of his holiday, his sporadic chatter covering any awkward pauses that threatened.

Giles had retreated smartly to the sitting room. She poured herself another coffee and followed him.

He turned immediately. 'Just don't start!'

He stood with his back to the empty grate, a drink already in his hand. Good old Giles, she thought with unwilling admiration, back right on form with attack the best method of defence. Now I *know* you've been up to something.

She said brightly, 'I can see you are bursting to tell me about your couple of weeks. I'm all ears.' She settled herself comfortably on the couch. Putting her feet up she regarded him over the rim of her cup with enquiringly raised brows. 'Do tell all.'

'There's nothing *to* tell.' Giles rocked a little on his heels then leaned a casual elbow against the mantle. 'Pete was delayed and only buzzed off to Canada the day after you left. His sister … you remember Flossy, the mad, scraggy, one whose husband, surprise, surprise, left her? She was supposed to stay at the Lodge until the people who've leased the place turned up at the end of the month. She thought she heard a prowler on her first night, panicked, and phoned me. I went over and she was so jittery I said I'd stay until you returned, after that she'd have to manage on her own. You know she's a complete neurotic, you've said so yourself. That's it. That's all. Nothing to get het up about, is it?'

'No, it all sounds terribly reasonable, and who could object to you spending a fortnight in an isolated cottage with a scraggy neurotic like Flossy, but why lie to Carol?'

'Because I knew she'd rush to tell you I was shacked up with some woman, probably embroider it and that you'd react just the way you have.'

'What about the 'phone call today, you weren't in any 'phone box, were you?'

'No.' Now he was completely confident and at ease. 'I was in a café; they let me use their phone, but you see how you are …

62

suspicious and nasty-minded. I told Flossy you would be. It was easier not to have to start explaining then.'

'Poor misunderstood Giles … and poor Flossy! Whatever will she do without you now?' she purred silkily. 'Perhaps she'd like to stay with us for a while?'

'No need.' He smiled; the Giles triumphant smile. 'The new tenants turned up on time – she'll be on her way back to Leicester by now.'

She was silenced. Putting down her coffee cup she lay back watching him through half-closed eyes, feeling suddenly drained and exhausted. How did he *do* it? He'd be a gift to MI5. She let the silence build until it rang in her ears.

He came towards her slowly, seating himself by her side, stroking the inside of her forearm with a gentle finger. 'I'm sorry, Livia. I should have told Carol the truth; I don't know why I didn't.'

'Don't you? Well I do. You can't help yourself … you'd lie your way out of hell,' she turned her head to hide the sudden moisture that welled in her eyes. 'Go away, Giles. Just go away.'

'Li-*vy*…'

His lips were on her throat. Carefully, controlling herself with an effort she pushed him away and sat up.

'Not now … I'm not in the mood.' She took a new, malicious pleasure in his expression of sheer disbelief. 'Perhaps you'd clear up in the kitchen. I'm tired. I think I'll go to bed and read myself to sleep. Don't wake me when you come up.'

She didn't look at him as she crossed the room to the hallway and walked swiftly up the staircase, but heard him follow her into the hall and knew he was stood at the foot of the stairs watching her. A light still showed under Adam's door and she called out 'Go to sleep!' as she went past. Gaining the sanctuary of the bedroom, she unfastened skirt and blouse and dropping them on the floor slid between the clean, bland smelling sheets in her cami-knickers, too weary and sad to even wash her face or brush her hair. Taking her book from the bedside table, she began listlessly turning the pages.

*   *   *

Left alone, Giles thought about another drink then decided against it. He went into the kitchen and surveyed with distaste the piled plates and pans. Bundling them anyhow into the dishwasher he poured powder messily into the container, slammed the door, turned the switch then walked out into the garden.

63

If I were religious, he thought, pacing up and down the lawn, I could go and confess all this and get it forgiven. It wouldn't solve the problem, but it might make me feel better. He wondered at his ability still to lie so outrageously and easily. A legacy, he thought, from his childhood. He had always lied: to his teachers, his friends, his doting and indulgent mother, who believed every word, and to a cynical father who didn't, but looked on in powerless despair as his wilful, disingenuous son was spoilt beyond redemption.

Giles stopped by the conservatory and rested his forehead against the chill, damp panes. *What sort of bloody stupid, unprincipled fool am I? I've been a complete cad to my wife; I've lied and cheated ... it's more than dishonest, more than immoral, it's disgusting ... but I'm a weak-kneed, pathetic swine, and I know I'll keep on doing it, again and again and again.*

He turned and retraced his steps towards the house.

*   *   *

Olivia slept, one arm pushed under the pillow the other flung across her forehead, half covering her eyes. Her book had slipped to the floor and Giles could see the trace of dried tears smudging her make-up. His throat tightened with pity.

Picking up her discarded clothes and hanging them over a chair, he went into the bathroom and showered, scrubbing his body hard until the skin hurt. For once he left the bedroom curtains drawn back, and, careful not to touch or disturb her, eased himself into the bed to lie with his back to her, staring for a long time at her photograph before falling into an uneasy sleep.

He woke slowly, feeling her arm across him, her fingers fluttering over his chest and belly. He lay silent for a few seconds before whispering: 'Livia?'

'Umm...' her voice was heavy and blurred with sleep, ''s'lovely dream...'

'If it is, we're both having it!'

He was cautious; unsure after the confusion of their quarrel, then aroused by her moving hands, turned to take her in his arms. Feeling the slip of satin under his fingers and meeting no resistance, he slid his hands up to pull the straps from her shoulders. She said something under her breath and he stopped.

'Is this all right? Say if it isn't.'

'Depends...' She was awake now. 'How was the mad woman Flossy in bed?'

64

'Terrible!' His heart ached. He slid down, closing his mouth on her breast, feeling her nipple harden against his tongue. She stroked his head and he whispered, 'I'm sorry I lied. It was stupid of me.'

'Just tell me about her, whoever she is.'

He shook his head. 'There is no her, and nothing to tell.' The lie was bitter on his tongue.

'Whatever am I going to do about you?' She sighed, rubbed her hands over the curly head. 'All right then, make love to me, you liar…'

*   *   *

He telephoned Zoë the following morning, while Adam was in the study, working on his neglected project and Olivia down in her studio. The 'phone rang for an age before he heard Zoë's breathless voice.

'Perfect! I was just coming back from the loo…'

Giles said, 'I rang the Feathers and they said you were at the theatre … what are you doing *there*?'

'Jimmy called a rehearsal. We're running behind time. Gosh, I wish we were going back to the hotel again tonight.'

'That makes two of us. I'll try and see on Wednesday, darling. I don't think I can get out of taking Adam back to school then, but I'll do my best to see you on my way back.'

'OK … not to worry; Yell is being an absolute bastard.' She gave a gurgle of laughter. 'We had a terrific row yesterday after you'd gone. He called me a moronic child because I hadn't touched the new text.'

'He doesn't approve of me taking your time, does he?' Giles felt a stab of jealousy. Even if Yelland *was* homo, he didn't like to think of him making demands on her; of being so close.

'No, he thinks you're bad for me and so you are,' she dropped her voice to a purr. 'Would you like to hear what I dreamed about last night?'

'Not while I'm fifteen miles away, I wouldn't. Save it for Wednesday.' He glanced up and saw Olivia walking towards the house. 'Look, I have to go now. I'll ring from the hospital tomorrow…'Bye.'

He met his wife in the hall. 'Forgotten something?'

'No. I fancied a coffee. Do you want one?' Olivia's tone was cool and impersonal.

He nodded and she led the way to the kitchen. He stood watching as she moved about the room. This morning she was composed, her every movement fluid and calm. He thought about the night just passed, her body first soft and yielding, then arched and passionate beneath his, and desire began to stir in him again.

She turned at that moment and catching the expression in his eyes turned away, hiding the pain and humiliation that had returned again with the morning light, her cheeks flushing at the remembrance of her own weakness and need.

He sat silent at the table as she measured coffee into the percolator. He thought I am becoming a complete schizophrenic. One day I'll get my wires crossed and blow the whole fucking thing sky high! Right now I'm totally shagged-out, yet still both the sound of Zoë's laugh, and the sight of Olivia's skirt moving over her hips as she does something as mundane as making a cup of coffee, is sufficient to get me going again…'

6

'If I find you with that instrument in your hand once more I really shall slap you.' Yelland took the telephone from Zoë and glared as she grinned guiltily back at him. 'In case it has slipped your moronic little mind, darling, rehearsals re-started five minutes ago and I am *waiting…*'

She pulled her mouth down at the corners, acting the penitent. 'Sorry.'

'So you should be.' He flung out an arm. '*Go!*'

Exasperated, he looked after her as she fled. She was a vulgar, irritating, lively, massively-talented pain in the neck. One moment she could bring him to the verge of wanting to throttle her, the next walk on stage; the sheer enchantment of her prickling the hair on his neck.

As he neared the rehearsal he could hear her. She would have rushed in he knew, apologised profusely, irritating the women, charming the socks off the men, known exactly where in the script they were, hit her mark, and gone straight into the scene…

''Make the doors upon a woman's wit and it will out at the casement; shut that and t'will out at the key-hole; stop that, t'will fly with the smoke out at the chimney…''

The husky voice spoke the words naturally and unaffectedly, with the same ingenuously naïve inflection that she would use to say, 'Oh, shit! … Just look, I've a ladder in my tights…'

Without needing to see her he knew how she would stand, hands lifting, palms upward, the smile starting, the negligent shrug. She had the fire and the tenderness and the magic that could still an audience in seconds and have them hang on every word. God knows how, or from where, she got it. Certainly not from the over-controlled holy-roller mother, nor from the blessedly deceased drunken old ham of a father; but somehow, from somewhere, someone, she had it.

Yelland walked in, clapped his hands for silence and scowled.

'Zoë, that was bloody atrocious. Now that *everyone* is here we shall go back to the beginning and do it all again…'

*   *   *

'I want you to start learning the Othello script in earnest now … you've already wasted enough time.'

Zoë finished her coffee and made a face. She asked, 'How do you suppose that machine manages to make anything taste so disgusting? Dishwater it may be; coffee it ain't.'

'Did you hear me?'

'Yes.' She was vague, at her most irritating, fidgeting and squashing the waxed cup in her hands. Her pointed face was drawn and white, with tiny vertical lines between her brows. 'I'm tired, Yell … give me a break, will you? You've been on my back all afternoon. It's not fair on a Sunday. You sent everyone else off simply *hours* ago. Someone should report you to Equity.'

'I released them one hour ago, to be precise, and we shall leave Equity out of this.' He leaned back in his chair and she glanced sideways at the thin hawk-like profile.

'You should have been an actor … all that hair and Gielgud looks, but you're not as pretty as him!'

'I *was* an actor, and don't you dare attempt to divert me by comparing me with the incomparable Johnny G.' Yelland cast a critical eye over her face. 'Try spending a night or two in your own bed, will you? I might then get some decent work out of you.'

Her shoulders drooped. 'Was I awful?'

'No.' His face softened. 'You were very, *very* good.'

'Then why give me such a hard time?'

'Because you can be more than good; you can be brilliant. You used to be so single-minded; now half the time you are wafting around on some nauseating pink cloud and I won't have it. Either get rid of that ageing Romeo, or forget all about the career you could have and settle for the life of a provincial actress.'

He leaned forward, looking down at her, where she sat cross-legged on the floor, his dark eyes sharpening. 'Spend the rest of your life with this Company, go home every night and cook dinner for your Giles while he still has his own teeth to eat it, if that's what you really want. But while that, my sweet, may be good enough for you, it's just not fucking good enough for me. *I* want to see you at Chichester and the Old Vic … and at the National if it's ever built, which I doubt.'

'Really, what should I play by then – Juliet's old nurse?'

'No. And don't be pert.' Yelland narrowed his eyes. 'Cleopatra, I think. Ten years of *very* hard work should see you ready.' She gave a splutter of laughter and he smiled. 'Well, perhaps not quite that long.'

She hugged her knees.

'Why are you so terribly cross about me and Giles? He's very nice you know, and he makes no demands on me.'

Yelland grimaced his distaste. 'Sooner or later he will face you with making a choice: the theatre with its lousy pay, hard times and uncertainties, or the soft option of marriage to him, with the assurance that there will always be food on the table and money in the bank.'

She protested vehemently, 'It isn't like that.'

'Is it not?' he was relentless, 'You are playing at love; Giles Ryder is not, and it is a dangerous game, Zoë; dangerous for your career, and for you as a person. However much of an act you may put on for him, you are still a long way from being properly grown up,' his mouth quirked in a sudden, sardonic smile, 'and remember, jealous wives have been known to shoot their husbands' mistresses!'

She sat silently with bent head, still twisting the cup in her hands. Yelland lit a cigarette; drawing deeply he sent a thin stream of smoke drifting up into the flies before continuing in a milder tone, 'However, we will leave the subject of Mister Ryder for the present. In one month from now I want to start rehearsals for The Moor and by then I want you living and breathing Desdemona. God knows, you make *me* want to strangle you at least once a day with your how-could-you-be-so-cruel act when you cock up a rehearsal and get your just desserts. Convince everyone in your audience that it's reasonable for Othello to feel the same and I may be quite pleased with you.'

She was fidgeting and looking vague again. He peered at her, demanding irritably, 'What is the matter now? Have you listened to a word I've said?'

'Yes, honestly; Giles and Othello and all that but please, Yell, can I go now? I've absolutely *got* to have a pee.'

He closed his eyes. 'Just bugger off right now, will you, darling, otherwise I may have to use your understudy on Tuesday night, because by then you may be *seriously* dead...'

*   *   *

Giles was annoyed at Olivia's insistence that he took Adam back to school, forcing him to revise his plans to spend the day with Zoë, but at the same time he had felt a stab of guilt. He knew he'd neglected Adam during the past term; even using his visit to Devon to persuade Olivia away from the house. Now the honeymoon was almost over. He dare not pretend the lectures were continuing after this week. There would be little free time between Zoë's new play and rehearsals for the next, and he'd come damned close to disaster with the cock-up over Hodges, let alone his near miss with Adam in Salisbury.

He drove automatically, listening with only half an ear to his son's chatter, his brain busy concocting alternative plans.

'*Dad*!'

Adam's exasperated shout brought him out of his reverie with a jerk that sent the car swerving onto the verge. A tree loomed and he wrenched frantically at the wheel, hearing the branches of the hawthorn hedge splinter as they raked along the coachwork.

Swearing fluently he righted the car and pulled back onto the road before exploding. 'Bloody hell, Adam, I'll clip your ear if you do that again!'

'But Dad…' Adam was shocked and truculent. 'I asked you three times and you didn't answer. I was only trying to make you hear. You nearly hit that tree…'

Giles slowed the car, pulling to the side of the road he stopped the engine. His hands were shaking and he sat for a moment holding the wheel tightly before turning to look at Adam's white face. 'I'm sorry. It wasn't your fault I was just thinking about something else.'

Normally placid, Adam's emotions were channelled by fright into a sudden eruption of anger. 'Hell, I've hardly seen anything of you this Easter. You even cleared off when I met you in Salisbury; I thought you might have at least taken me for a coffee or something.' His voice cracked. 'I thought we'd have a chance to talk now, but you can't even be bothered to listen, so I had to shout to get through to you. I'd rather have come back with mum – at least she knows I'm here, which is more than you have lately!'

'Adam, you are being insolent.' Giles felt his own temper beginning to rise.

'I don't care, it's true. You don't think of anyone but yourself and what you want – I'll be bloody glad to get away from you and back to school – '

Giles slapped his son's face hard, and was immediately appalled. Never in fifteen years had he done such a thing. Spanked him briefly a few times when he'd been a naughty small boy, once even taken a stick to his backside when he'd smashed a third window in succession with his football, but never lashed out like that. He swallowed hard. 'I'm sorry; I shouldn't have done that.'

Adam turned his face away. 'You don't have to take it out on me because you nearly killed us.' For a few moments he sat rigid, then his whole body began to shake

'It's all right,' Giles took his shoulders, pulling him into his arms, holding his head against his chest, repeating, 'It's all right. Look, we're almost there. We'll sit quietly for a few minutes then I'll take it very easy the rest of the way. That OK with you?'

Adam nodded. After a moment or two he sat up, brushing his

sleeve across his eyes. 'What a wimp,' he was suddenly gruff and embarrassed.

Giles looked at the mark of his hand across Adam's pale face and felt physically sick. He put out his fingers to touch it but Adam flinched and he moved his fingers instead to the thin wrist, feeling the thudding pulse. 'Are you all right? You didn't hit your head or anything when we swerved?'

'I don't think so. I'm OK … really.' Adam gave a shaky grin. 'I don't need a doctor.'

No, Giles thought, you don't need a doctor, just a father, and a damned lousy, useless one of those I've become.

*   *   *

He watched uneasily as Adam bounded up the school steps, swinging his case and hallo-ing at his friends, unusually loud behaviour for his normally well-mannered son. While Giles stood hesitating, thinking that he must report the incident to someone, just in case the boy developed any odd aches and pains, he saw Doyle's tall figure appear at the top of the steps and stop Adam's capering with a hand to the boy's shoulder. There was a brief exchange of words, Giles saw Adam shake his head vigorously then, after another short exchange, Adam turned quickly and walked through the door.

Without haste the master strolled down to where Giles still stood by the car.

'Good afternoon, Mr Ryder, I understand you've had something of a close shave,' he eyed with mild interest the scratched and scored paint along the side of the Jaguar.

'Adam told you?' Giles didn't hide his surprise. He wouldn't have had that kind of chitchat with any master when *he* was fifteen. Doyle smiled fleetingly.

'He didn't exactly volunteer the information, but as he doesn't normally behave like one of the lower primates there had to be a reason, so I asked.'

Giles gave a deprecatory shrug. 'It was nothing really. I was preoccupied, he shouted and we almost hit a tree. I was about to let someone know in case of any reaction later, but I'm pretty sure he's all right.' He hesitated. 'I'm afraid I … ah, lost my temper with him. We rather lost it with each other. You probably saw…'

'Yes. It would have been difficult to miss.' Doyle was blandly non-committal. 'I'll warn matron and keep an eye on him myself. He is, fortunately, one of the more stable members of this zoo,' he smiled

71

again. 'I must go now; please give my regards to your wife.'

Giles watched him walk away, feeling a stir of animosity at the air of easy authority and self-assurance, and Doyle's obvious influence over his son, which at present was probably stronger than his own. Remembering also Olivia's comment that the housemaster was quite a flirt, he knew a quick stab of jealousy.

The cheeky bugger!

He got back into the car and fired the engine, giving a short, humourless laugh. Just like me, really, he mused. Acting God Almighty to the minions and never missing an opportunity to give a pretty woman the eye.

As he turned out of the school gates he began to whistle, deliberately pushing Adam and the disastrous journey they'd just made out of his mind. Time for a quick visit to catch Zoë and talk over their arrangements for the next few weeks…

*   *   *

Adam dumped his case in a corner of the study then crossed to peer into the small mirror by the window.

Shit! You could see the finger marks and it was already beginning to bruise; he didn't need to have hit him *that* hard. He slumped down into a chair. He felt awful. His face hurt and his head ached and he wanted to yell and throw things. He *was* bloody glad to be back. Devon, apart from that horrible trip with Liam smoking that stinking stuff, had been great but home had been well, different; strange … and he was bloody angry about that humiliating slap. Dad shouldn't have done that.

He sat still, trying to think what had changed and why. He frowned in concentration. Mum and dad had both seemed odd these holidays, he realised. Of course mum had started painting again and was a bit away with the fairies, but when they'd been with gran and pops she'd been really happy and they'd talked for hours every evening. Once they'd returned home though, she'd been different and there was an uncomfortable feel about the house.

It was dad. The odd feeling started when *he* was around…

'Crikey! What happened to your fizzog?' Bill Marshall stood in the doorway feigning amazement, clapping a hand to his forehead, allowing tennis racket, books and a partially eaten ham sandwich to spill from his arms onto the floor. 'That must have been some fight … what did the other bloke look like?'

'Frigging awful … I hammered him.' Adam jumped up and

72

grabbed the sandwich. 'Bags I half.'

'You can have the lot,' his study mate wasn't to be deflected 'Come on,' he encouraged, 'who punched you up?'

'No one; I cheeked my dad and he slapped me, that's all.'

Marshall whistled. 'Some slap … some cheek.'

'Yeah, well, he was ignoring me and I yelled at him.'

'Oh, *that.* You should have been in my house when my parents were splitting up.' Marshall waved an airily dismissive hand. 'Neither of 'em ever heard a bloody thing I said, or if they did they ignored it. I might just as well not have been there.'

Adam said through a mouth full of sandwich, 'Oh, my mother's all right, it's only dad. Half the time he isn't on the same planet.'

'Ah-*ha,*' Marshall looked knowing. 'Then it's either something wrong at the office or he's got a bit of crumpet.'

'Don't be stupid.' Adam felt anger flush through him again and his heart began to race.

Marshall goaded, 'I'll bet its crumpet! Lots of old blokes fancy a bit on the side, you know. He's probably screwing his secretary – that's what he's doing.' His imagination took flight, 'he's having it off with her against the filing cabinet – or having a poke at some juicy nurse…'

'You *bastard,*' furious, Adam flung the sandwich aside and launched himself across the room. 'You bloody lying bastard!'

They crashed to the floor and Marshall rolled under him, giggling and trying to hold up crossed fingers. 'Pax, Pax!' He yelped in sudden pain. 'Ouch, you silly bugger, that hurt; let me up!'

'Take it back then or I'll punch your fucking head in.' Adam drew back a threatening fist just as his companion went unnaturally still; rolling his eyes backward his lips shaped one word.

Adam looked up to see Doyle at the open door, gazing down at them, his face like granite.

Marshall recovered first. Scrambling to his feet he straightened his tie and smoothed his hair, 'Sorry, sir, just a bit of larking about.'

'Really, it appeared to me that Ryder was about to do something *very* nasty to your head.'

'We were having a disagreement that's all.' Adam stood up slowly, still flushed and reckless with anger. 'I don't see it's anything for anyone to get excited about.'

'Do you not?' Doyle's mouth tightened ominously. 'I should have said you'd completely lost your temper, which I understand would be for the second time today. Then there is the small matter of your language …offensive at any time and even more so when yelled at the top of your voice.' He paused, his eyes flinty. 'Also you have just come dangerously close to being impertinent to *me*.'

Adam muttered a surly and unconvincing, 'Sorry, sir.'

'You will be!' Doyle stood. 'Both of you, my study, five-thirty ... and don't keep me waiting.'

They stared glumly after his retreating back.

'What a swine, making us stew for five hours.' Bill pulled his mouth down. 'Not very happy, is he?'

Adam's anger faded as he realised the sort of trouble that he'd landed them both in. 'Shit,' he blanched. 'My dad'll kill me if I get suspended.'

Bill grimaced horribly. 'Better that than have Doyle dust off that bloody cane he keeps in his cupboard.'

They gazed apprehensively at each other. Adam's stomach somersaulted at the thought of Doyle in a temper, and with three feet of bamboo in his hand. 'He won't,' he said, 'he hardly ever beats.'

The irrepressible Marshall began to giggle. 'My study, five thirty!' he mimicked Doyle's precise tones.

'And don't keep me waiting!' Adam intoned lugubriously.

Marshall threw a book, 'Stupid bugger, Ryder!'

Adam deadheaded his arm, 'Lying bastard, Marshall!'

'Come on.' Still giggling, Bill kicked the tennis racquet into a corner and began to pick up his books from the floor and dump them on the table. 'I need to copy some of your project. I haven't half finished mine. What did you do?'

'Salisbury.'

'OK ... I'll just take off the spire and pretend that it's Winchester. Old Jenner'll never notice the difference. He never reads our essays anyway.'

Adam stopped in the act of pulling a chair up to the table, seeing quite clearly in his mind's eye, like the instant a camera shutter clicks, a picture of his father across that crowded Salisbury street.

He *had* been with someone. Not a boy, but a girl. A girl with ragged brown hair, dressed in a green shirt and dark slacks ... and he'd had his arm around her shoulders.

Very carefully Adam took the books from Marshall and began to arrange them on the table, methodically squaring them into a neat pile. *Had* his father got a bit of crumpet? Could that really be it? She must be some tart he'd picked up; but why should he do that and, if he had, who was she and what would happen if mum ever found out?

Adam's stomach began to churn again and he felt sick.

                    *   *   *

Olivia finished the last brush stroke and stood back to cast a critical eye over her canvas.

'Not bad,' she murmured. 'Not bad at all.'

She had started the painting in Devon and gazing now at the wide sweep of Morgans Bay, the cottages tumbling down the hillsides, the towering cliffs, she was overcome with nostalgia. For twenty years she had lived in other villages, other towns, but nowhere, however beautiful, had ever taken the place of the Devon coast where she had spent her childhood. True, she and Giles had been regular visitors, but it was only now, when she had begun to paint again, that leaving it really tugged at the heart.

She began to clean her brushes. It would be dull now. No rolling hills and wide blue sea, and Adam back at school again until the half-term break.

She took a last stroll around the garden. As Giles had said he'd break his journey home to have a meal, she would just make herself a sandwich then perhaps go over to see Carol. The in-laws must have gone by now and Carol would have time for coffee and a good gossip.

                    *   *   *

'I'm glad you've come. Chris is out tonight.' Carol settled herself opposite Olivia at the kitchen table. 'If I didn't know better I'd think he was seeing another woman, but it's only something sordid and apparently human the river police have dredged up at Hamble.' She returned Olivia's grin. 'You don't mind having coffee in here do you? I've had a bellyful of draping myself elegantly around the drawing room every evening with Lucrecia Borgia and Boris Karloff … thank God they pushed off early this afternoon. One more day and I'd have run amuck!'

'They are pretty gruesome.' Olivia helped herself from the remains of chocolate cake and marzipan eggs; Carol's Easter delicacies slaved over to impress Chris's monumentally unimpressable parents. 'I'm more than grateful that Giles' father has the decency to live in Paris and only show up at Christmas. Although I enjoy visiting Nikolas by myself from time to time, he and Giles really do get on each other's nerves; it's one hell of a strain keeping the peace when he stays with us.'

'How is Giles, by the way? We haven't seen much of him lately.'

Olivia said vaguely, 'He's fine.'

In the past she would have had a gossip and perhaps a laugh with Carol, but now she couldn't bring herself to be light hearted about the suspicions that were festering in her mind.

Whatever he was doing, it was going on far too long. That she still wanted him to make love to her sometimes appalled her. Surely there was something incredibly weak about still wanting someone so badly when one was apparently surplus to requirements? It was pathetic and she cringed to think that others might see her as some feeble dependent creature, clinging to her husband at all costs. Half the trouble was of course, that Giles was just too damned good in bed, and the other half that she simply couldn't imagine being without him – and he knew it, the bastard. She sighed, thinking that she was doing a lot of sighing lately. Aloud she said, 'You know our generation was brought up all wrong,'

Carol twiddled her kiss-curls over her ears and gave her a puzzled look. 'What brought forth that pearl of wisdom?'

Olivia shrugged and gave a wry smile. 'Think about it; weren't we brainwashed from the cradle to think that a career was all very nice in theory, but all we needed to live happily ever after was a husband, babies, and enough money to buy our suits from Peter Jones. What have we done with our lives that's any better than our mothers and grandmothers did with theirs?'

Carol sniffed. 'I don't know about you, but I had a broader and better education than either of them … *and* I've not had to produce a baby a year!'

'Neither did our mothers, thanks to Marie Stopes – but I'll grant you the education.' Olivia nibbled on a marzipan egg, 'and I shouldn't complain, because mother and dad did encourage me to go to art school. All the same, my mother was in seventh heaven when I married Giles, and I'll bet yours was the same when Chris happened along.'

Carol retorted huffily, 'I didn't marry just for security, I married for love.'

Olivia looked around her friend's bright modern kitchen, loaded with every labour-saving device known to man and suppressed a grin. 'Didn't we all? Now we are nice little stay-at-home wives, cooking and cleaning and waiting for hubby to come back every evening and tell us what a hard day he's had. For God's sake,' she exclaimed, suddenly exasperated, 'the war taught us there was more to life than that and we chucked it all away.'

'I've got my own business…'

'Oh, come off it, Carol. You know you only go there once in a blue moon and Chris's accountant takes care of the business side; you spend almost as much time as me as an unpaid housekeeper.' Olivia hovered over another marzipan egg, then plumped for a chocolate rabbit and bit its head off. 'Just compare what we've settled for with what some of the young girls are up to now. They aren't in any hurry to become unpaid servants, they're too busy giving their parents two fingers, getting themselves decent, well-paid jobs, and being independent. They wear what they like, and damned well do as they like – and good luck to them, I say. If I were twenty years younger *I'd* let my tits hang free, wear my skirt up around my ovaries and give the chaps a run for their money!'

Carol propped her chin on her hands and made her habitual disapproving *moue*. 'You're being very bolshie, all of a sudden.'

'Yes, well. I've just had a week away from it all'...*and come back to that lying sod,* she added silently. She gazed pensively into space. 'Perhaps I should get a dog. It would be something to talk to while Giles is out fanning around his p.p's until all hours, or whooping it up with his buddies after work.'

Carol wondered for the umpteenth time if she should repeat Irene Porter's gossip; that when Johnny had been ill a few weeks back, she'd heard him on the telephone, arranging for Giles to pick up his notes from the Salisbury lectures. But when Giles had arrived at their house it was ostensibly to collect a hospital file that Johnny had supposedly taken in error...

Chris had been non-committal when she'd told him.

'Just leave it alone,' he'd advised, 'you don't *know* anything and Irene Porter is the biggest gossip in Ranleigh.'

For once Carol decided to take his advice, but thought privately that if there *was* anything going on, that blighter Giles would trip up sooner or later, and when he did she had a feeling that this time Olivia wouldn't let him walk away unscathed.

7

Adam staggered out of Doyle's study with glazed eyes.

'What happened?' whispered an apprehensive Marshall.

Adam groaned 'He'll rip you into little pieces and at the end of it you'll get gated for a fu...' he threw a nervous glance over his shoulder, 'for a blooming month!'

'A *month?*' Marshall gaped. 'Fucky-*fuck*!'

'Oh, don't,' Adam gave a pitiful whimper and banged his head against the wall. 'Just get in there and get it over with then we can both cut our throats and finish the job for him!'

As the door closed behind Bill he leaned his burning forehead against the cold corridor window. He could hear Doyle's hard measured tones, the words muffled by the heavy door and felt a pang of sympathy for poor old Bill.

It had been awful. He hadn't even been let to apologise. Doyle had just blasted his ears off then kicked him out. Adam felt the hot tears beginning to gather behind his eyes, and there was a lump in his throat that he couldn't swallow. It was all dad's fault, he raged, messing around with that rotten tart – and there wasn't anyone he could tell about it. He drew a long shuddering breath. He couldn't, he just couldn't go on as though today had never happened. He could have stood anything but the cold anger, the hard brutal message that he'd put himself beyond the pale.

He wiped his sweating palms on his trousers. He'd run away – tonight; to London; they wouldn't find him there. He was old enough now to get a job, then they could all stew and worry about *him*. Feverishly he totted up in his mind how much money he could lay his hands on: enough for the train fare anyway. He'd wait until evening chapel then slip out. With luck, he wouldn't be missed for at least a couple of hours, by then he'd be well on his way. He'd let mum know, but that was all. He hated his father, hated this place, but most of all he hated Doyle.

He'd never felt so lonely in his whole life.

Suddenly the door was wrenched open and Bill streaked past him and down the corridor like a frightened rabbit. The next moment the master stood in the doorway, looking after him, before turning to stare at the figure by the window.

'I thought I told you to get out of my sight.'

Adam stammered, 'I w-was w-waiting for M-Marshall.'

'Then wait somewhere else. I don't want you here contaminating my corridor.'

Adam opened his mouth but no words came. To his horror he felt the dammed-up tears threatening to overflow.

Doyle demanded mercilessly, 'What are you snivelling about?'

Adam flung his head back and glared, his anger returning with a rush. 'I'm *not* snivelling. I'm just pissed off with this place and everyone in it … I'm getting out of it now – tonight – and no one's going to stop me: not you or anyone else!'

Chest heaving he waited for the heavens to fall. There was a long silence, then Doyle sighed and crooked a beckoning forefinger. 'Back in here if you please, Mister Ryder.'

Adam hesitated, measuring the distance between the master and the end of the corridor.

'*Now.*' Doyle's voice cracked like a whip. Shaking, and with a horrible cold emptiness replacing the spurt of anger, Adam edged warily past him into the room. Doyle pointed to an easy chair by the fireplace. 'If you can spare the time before you go,' he said with mild sarcasm, 'I think you should sit down quietly, think hard, and tell me truthfully what this is *really* all about.'

Obediently Adam sat and gazed miserably at the floor. 'I can't. I really can't.'

'Yes you can. Come on … whatever it is, it's better faced. Fighting and running away, from here or anywhere else, won't solve anything. Your problems will still be there the next morning.'

'But they're not *my* problems and I don't know *how* to solve them!' The tears came in a sudden torrent and Adam buried his face in his hands, wailing, 'It's awful and disgusting and I don't even want to *think* about it.'

Doyle dropped a large clean handkerchief onto the boy's knees. 'Well, *I* rather think you should, so blow your disgusting nose and mop up, while I go and make us each a strong coffee – that is if I can trust you not to do a runner as soon as my back is turned – you won't will you?'

Adam snuffled into the handkerchief and shook his head.

'Good. So that's one problem out of the way!'

Adam gulped: 'Sorry about, you know, saying I was pissed off and all that…'

Doyle paused to look back over his shoulder, observing with mordant humour, 'So you damned well should be … and just in case you thought you were getting away with it, I've every intention of dealing later with that piece of quite breathtaking impertinence.'

*   *   *

Giles waited until the late news was finished before broaching the subject of the accident he had so nearly had. He stood to turn off the television, asking casually, 'Would you mind if I take your car tomorrow? Mine will need to go in for a paint job...I made a bit of a mess of it today. I thought that if you were shopping you wouldn't mind taking it into Carters and taking a taxi back.'

Olivia grinned. 'What did you do? Scrape the wall turning in at the gate?'

'No, I ran off the road for a moment ... nothing serious.'

She eyed him thoughtfully. 'Then why are you looking so shifty?'

'Adam was with me,' he admitted. 'He shouted. I went up on the verge and only just missed a tree, then scraped the ruddy thing along a blackthorn hedge ... made one hell of a mess of the paintwork.' He bent to take a cigarette out of the box, snapping his lighter irritably. 'You might as well know that Adam was extremely rude and insolent and I smacked his face for him.'

'Why?'

'I've just told you.'

'I mean why was he shouting?'

'Oh ... he was nattering away and apparently asked me something; I didn't hear him, so the confounded little idiot yelled right in my ear. I damned near pranged that tree.'

Olivia controlled her anger with an effort. 'You had no right to lash out like that – and he was right; you don't listen to anyone, because your mind is always elsewhere these days.'

'That's a polite version of *his* complaint.' Giles tried for a lighter tone, 'he actually had the nerve to swear at me and tell me in so many words that he'd be bloody glad to see the back of me.'

Olivia sat looking at him with those considering eyes as though she could make a pretty good guess at what had been going through his mind, and why his thoughts had occupied him to the exclusion of all else. Giles began to feel as though he were on some remorseless treadmill and unable to get off. He felt drained. After all the hours of driving, athletic sex with a twenty-three-year old in the middle of the afternoon, should have been postponed. Now everything felt slightly out of kilter: even this conversation...

'Giles, why don't we really talk any more?'

He shied like a nervous horse from her sudden question. 'We do

80

… we are.'

'No. We just exchange a few words. I generally tell you about my day. You tell me nothing. Or we snipe at each other or have a row. That's not talking.'

Her tone was reasonable but she was sitting very still, watching him closely as he stood slumped against the mantle shelf.

'I don't know. My fault I expect; the advance of middle-age perhaps.'

'I wish you could tell me what's making you so … so damned *difficult* lately.'

He gave a half smile. 'I thought I'd always been that.'

She didn't answer and he stood smoking in silence. What he really wanted to do was cross those few feet of carpet between them, kneel down, put his head in her lap, and lay down his burden of guilt. Let all the calm and the quiet and the healing he had always found in her flow over him. But Zoë now was in his blood and in his heart and he just couldn't walk away from her. Not for Olivia's sake, not for Adam's, not even for his own…but he would have to say something soon…

If I go to him now thought Olivia, and put my arms around him, perhaps the miracle will happen and everything will be again as it has been for these last few years. I won't mind him flirting when he thinks I'm not looking; I just want him to be mine again. But he is slowly going away from me and I don't know what to do…

He looked up; their eyes met and she froze in an agony of indecision. *No, don't tell; not now, not yet.* Giles saw the sudden panic in her face, the almost uttered words of confession died in his throat and he bent to stub out his cigarette. 'I think I'll take a turn in the garden before bed.'

'Fine.' she stood. 'I'm off now. Don't forget to lock the kitchen door.'

Giles let himself into the garden, and felt silence fall behind him like a dark, stifling blanket.

*   *   *

'*Christ on a bicycle*!' Zoë threw the script down on the bed and reached for another cigarette. Blast Jimmy, why couldn't he keep his bloody opinions to himself? She couldn't concentrate today. She lay back against the pillows and closed her eyes, trying to see the shape of the speech on the printed page. That usually did the trick, but today, nothing came.

81

Right from the beginning she'd deliberately kept herself from thinking about Giles' other life, telling herself that as she had no intention of having more than a temporary affair with him, what his wife didn't know wouldn't hurt. Now Yell kept shoving it right under her nose with his nagging about ageing Romeos and making choices and jealous wives, so that now she could think of little else.

He was giving good advice and she knew that she should take it.

She owed James Yelland a lot. She hadn't distinguished herself at Drama School and had at times been a rebellious student. Although she didn't have any noticeable regional accent, those who did had a pretty hard time of it, and she had been impatient with what she viewed as the ludicrous insistence on the ironing out of speech to fit an accepted pattern.

But Yelland had been in the audience for the end of course production and singled her out from the rest, although she had hardly shone in a small and insignificant part. Appearing in the crowded dressing room afterwards he had whisked her off to the dingy bar around the corner, and sitting opposite her at the sticky drink-stained table, offered her a place in his company. She had listened spellbound to the clipped, camp voice that she could later mimic to perfection, as he ticked off on his fingers the steps he was planning for her life.

'If you work hard for me and don't grumble when you have to make the tea for weeks before you open that lovely mouth to say just one line on stage; if you willingly and uncomplainingly shift scenery and collect props, go easy on the booze and the pot and do as you are told, we shall get along splendidly, and I will teach you all that you will ever need to know in order to climb the ladder of theatrical success.'

Then he had smiled and taken her hand in his and said: 'You are a scruffy, undisciplined little brat but I can make something very, very special of you if you just keep that wonderful voice and are a good, obedient girl. One day, people will say: "Have you seen Zoë Ormonde at the Shaftsbury this week?" as they now say: "Have you seen Coral Brown?"'

'You might be wrong.' She had grinned shakily.

'I am never wrong. Just trust me and you will see…'

She had trusted him. Done everything he asked without complaint. Now almost three years on from that night, here she was, on line for Desdemona.

She mustn't mess it up. She had to get it right. Picking up the script again, scanning it briefly, she closed her eyes chanting aloud: 'My noble father / I do perceive here a divided duty; / To you I am bound for life and education; / My life and education both do learn me / How to respect you…'

There was a tap on the door. She opened her eyes and scowled. 'Go away. I'm out.'

'No you're not. I'm coming in and if you haven't any clothes on, shut your eyes!'

'Oh, it's *you*.'

'Yes, light of my life.' Martin tripped across the room and she made space for him on the bed. 'Mine host has just opened the bar … are you coming down?' Taking out a tin and papers from his pocket he began to roll a joint.

'OK, she said, laying aside her scrip, 'although I doubt it's a good idea – nor is smoking spliffs. I'm having a problem learning lines today, even when I'm clear-headed and sober.'

He licked the paper, smoothed it with his fingers and struck a match. 'Bollocks, ducky, pot relaxes the mind and there's no point in having rooms over a pub if we can't sample the wares.' He drew on the joint twice, then handed it to her and picked up the script. 'Hmm… Desdemona it is then … lucky girl, but then, you *are* Jimmy's pet.'

'Bitch, just because he doesn't fancy you.' She giggled suddenly, 'Come to that, he doesn't fancy me, either.'

'Oh, my sweet, how true, but he never mixes business with pleasure.' Martin jumped up to peer into the mirror. 'I'm going to grow my own beard for Cassio. All that spirit gum plays hell with my complexion. I thought I found a spot this morning…'

'For God's sake stop prinking and come and help me with my lines.' She drew deeply on the joint before handing it back and scowled down at her script. 'I don't think I like her much … I don't wonder Othello throttled her if he heard her banging on about that bloody willow.'

'What's the matter, sweetie?' Martin came back and climbed onto the bed again; propping himself up on the pillows he put an arm around her waist. 'Have a few more puffs, lay your head on your Uncle Martin's shoulder and tell all, though I can't think what you are so bothered about. As Miss Jean Brodie would say, you are, even by Jimmy's exacting standards, the *crème de la crème…*'

She relaxed into his warm, sexless embrace, curling up against him like a child. 'He says I'm going nowhere if I don't give Giles the push.'

'He's right.' Martin's handsome young face creased with concern. He dug his chin into the top of her head. 'You can't have it all ways in this business. Have your flings, by all means ... don't we all, but avoid like the plague letting suave old gentlemen who are trying to recapture their youth, monopolise your time and energy,' he grinned, 'at least until you've climbed far enough up the ladder to be hoity-toity with producers and directors!'

She sighed and wriggled closer into his embrace.

'It's a lousy life ... why do you have to be such a fag? Here we are, cuddled up all warm and cosy ... we could have such a lovely fu–'

He put his hand over her mouth. 'Don't say it!'

'Why not?'

'Because it is rude and crude and my mummy warned me about girls who wanted my body.'

She pushed him away. 'I don't want it; I prefer real mature, experienced men ... like Giles.'

He wrinkled his nose. '*Eeeuw*; over-ripe, you mean, like old Camembert!'

They began to laugh and he pulled her off the bed. 'Come on, darling – drinkies.' He pinched the spliff and dropped it on the bedside table. 'That's for you later, sweetie. Now, we are going to get really sloshed, then we'll both have a go at the dark gentleman – trust me; after a few beers, it'll all come together.'

'All right,' she let him pull her unresisting towards the stairs, 'but I must stay sober until seven at least. Giles said he'd ring me then.'

'A pox on Giles,' he slapped her bottom and she yelped. 'Leave the old bugger to his own devices. Tonight, you and I are going to behave disgracefully in the bar of this sordid hostelry, and have ourselves a *very* good time.'

She hugged his arm. 'Let's shack up together ... you and me, Marty. I could go out when your blokes came, and you could do the same for me.'

'I should only consider that proposition if you were thinking of sharing yours, in which case they must be under thirty and very clean. I insist.'

She gave him a sly, sideways glance. 'Are you sure about that? I thought by the way you sometimes looked at him you might fancy Giles. He's old but clean.'

Martin grinned and pushed open the door to the bar. 'So I might, darling, but before we could get it together, *he* would need to fancy *me* and that would be a different matter entirely.'

8

'Adam 'phoned.' Olivia glanced up from peppering the steaks. 'He wasn't very happy … you didn't tell me you'd written him that you were too busy to see him next week end.'

Giles wished he'd gone straight into the living room and poured a drink, instead of putting his head around the kitchen door and straight into her line of fire. 'You *know* I can't make it to your parents' with you next week; I'll go another time. Adam understands I'm busy, and he'll enjoy fishing with Clive.' He made an effort not to let the irritation he felt sound in his voice.

'I suppose you'd forgotten it was his half term, even though I've reminded you at least four times over the last month.' She knew she was being deliberately perverse and provoking, but a headache had been threatening all day and she was feeling irritable and out of sorts and in no mood to be reasonable.

'No, I had not forgotten, and you know I have to spend the time catching up on paperwork. I told you so on Friday and you heard me making my excuses to your father last night, so just stop being so damned awkward.'

She went on preparing the evening meal her back pointedly turned. 'I thought you were supposed to be reforming and trying to spend a little more time with your son.' She chopped cabbage with unwonted viciousness.

'Amazing isn't it? When something's wrong, he's my son, when everything is going swimmingly, he's yours.' Giles sat on the kitchen table swinging his legs, looking, she thought spitefully, like some damned old pixie on a toadstool.

'Don't be childish. He's neither one nor the other, just ours, although you seem able to forget that when he becomes an inconvenience.'

Giles set his mouth, feeling particularly hard-done by as for once his excuse was valid. He *was* behind with his correspondence and had to bribe his secretary to work at Riversmead over the next weekend to help clear the backlog. Too many afternoons spent with Zoë before the Company went on tour had left him snowed under with a mass of reports and letters; these past few weeks he'd found it almost impossible to concentrate on the mounting paperwork. God only knew what he'd do when the long tour of Othello began. Try to get back to normal, he supposed – or as normal as life without Zoë could ever be.

Aggravated by his silence, Olivia reached for a saucepan and banged it down on the table next to him, making him jump. 'As the last time Adam saw you he got a smack in the face, perhaps it's just as well you'll be staying here with Joan Tucker … though God knows why she's agreed to come without me here to keep you out of her knickers.'

'If I'm ever reduced to the stage where I'll tackle a pair of celanese, elastic-below-the-knee passion killers, I'll let you know and you can chaperone her!'

'How do *you* know what kind of knickers she wears?'

Once we would have laughed about that, she thought, and wondered miserably what on earth was happening to them. Since Adam returned to school almost five weeks ago, they'd been squabbling intermittently, like a pair of bad tempered children.

What had started as a thinly veiled needling match, fuelled by her suspicions and his lies over the time she'd been in Devon, had gradually become an even more wounding sparring match until they had reached a state of barely controlled hostility. She had retreated into her painting and he'd spent more and more time away from the house. With increasing rarity they had the kind of occasional polite sex that barely satisfied her physical needs and her emotional needs not at all. It had all been quite dreadful.

She rested her hands on the rail of the Aga, trying to control the tide of misery that was beginning to engulf her. Her head ached and throbbed abominably. It was hot and she didn't want to cook this meal that neither would enjoy. She felt as though she was sinking into some dark pit with the walls closing over her head. If only she could go to sleep, then wake and find it had all been a part of some ghastly dream…

'I'm sorry.' She heard her own voice from a long way off. 'I don't think I can finish this…'

Giles leaped from the table and caught her arm as she swayed. 'Are you ill?'

She pushed his hand away. 'No … the stove … it's too hot in here.'

She didn't want him sounding concerned, treating her like a patient, but was by now too sick and exhausted to argue as he picked her up bodily and carried her into the sitting room. Settling her onto the couch he put a cushion under her head. 'Stay there,' he ordered, 'I'll get my bag.'

'Don't *fuss*.' She made to sit up and irritably he pushed her back down.

'Olivia, just for once, will you goddam do as you're told!'

'I do nothing else,' she answered pettishly, turning her head into the cushion, 'and stop bullying me.'

He stood looking down at her for a moment then she heard him leave the room and return almost immediately. 'Put this in your mouth … and don't grind your teeth.' Forestalling further complaints, he sat beside her and slid the thermometer beneath her tongue, then felt gently around her neck before taking her hot wrist in cool fingers.

He was in control now, calmly detached and professional, and she could have hit him. It was humiliating to lie like a jigsaw puzzle and watch him trying to fit the pieces together. Olivia glared balefully at him over the thermometer, but his head was bent, his eyes on his wristwatch. She shut her own eyes and pretended none of it was happening.

He reclaimed the thermometer and frowned over the reading. 'Your temperature is up and your pulse going like a mill-race; why didn't you say you were ill?'

She opened her eyes and struggled to sit. 'Because I'm not,' she peered belligerently at the thermometer he held for her inspection. 'I'm never ill … the damned thing's wrong.'

'What's this?' He caught at her left hand, looking at it closely, demanding, 'How long has this thumb been swollen? What did you do?'

'It's nothing. I punctured it on a nail when I was stripping an old canvas. I needed the frame.'

He exploded. 'For fuck's sake, woman, you're married to a doctor; you know better than to neglect things like jabs from rusty nails!' He pushed up her sleeve shouting, 'Look at it … it's already spreading past your wrist,' he pointed angrily at the thin red line running from the base of her thumb. 'Do you *want* to die of blood poisoning?'

She yelled, 'Don't you dare shout at me!' then crumpled suddenly and began to weep. Her hand did hurt; had been sore for days, but apart from dabbing the thumb with antiseptic she'd ignored the dull throb of increasing inflammation. At any other time, she thought miserably, she would have told him, but she'd been so depressed and distracted and he'd ceased to even notice she was there … it was all his fault, the rotten cad.

'You need to be shouted at. How *could* you be so stupid?'

She turned her head away again, aware that she was wallowing in self-pity but unable to stop. She said, 'I didn't care. It didn't seem to matter. Nothing matters any more.'

'Oh, Livvy,' he stroked her hair back from her face with a gentle hand. 'Sometimes you can be *such* an ass.'

For a few moments he continued to stroke her hair in silence and she could feel herself weakening under his touch; when he spoke again his voice was shaking slightly. 'Talking of asses … if you'll just hold still while I find a syringe – and promise not to sock me one when I put my hand up your skirt…'

'Hell, *no* Giles!' She was stung into a sudden response. 'You're a lousy needle man … I'll wait until tomorrow and have someone else do it!'

'You will not.' He was business-like again, rummaging in his bag, 'just ask yourself which is preferable – a quick shot of penicillin from me or galloping septicaemia?'

'Oh *God,* what a girl has to do to get a bit of attention these days!' She suffered in mutinous silence the painful jab in her thigh and continued to grumble as he half carried her up to the bedroom and began helping her undress. She gave a sudden giggle. 'This must be the first time you've ever taken off my clothes and left me unravished!'

'Behave yourself.' He slid her nightdress over her head, then lifted her onto the bed and pulled the covers over her.

'It's a long time since you've had me as a patient, isn't it?' Reaction was beginning to kick in and she giggled again. 'Sorry, I think that was one of those remarks that might have been phrased better…'

He smiled. 'You said something along those lines soon after we first met; when you came into Haslar with a fractured toe.'

She turned her head away. 'What a memory…'

'You are to come with me to the hospital first thing tomorrow and have McCarthy take a look at that thumb, but for now go to sleep.' Briskly he shook two tablets from a bottle, handing them to her with a glass of water. 'Now don't argue; take these.' He waited until she'd swallowed them before bending to lay his lips briefly against her forehead. 'I'll be downstairs. Throw something at the wall if you need me.'

In the kitchen he made a coffee and sat for a long time at the table, staring into space. At any other time I would have noticed that swollen hand, he thought, and was suddenly sick with disgust at how uncaring of her he had become.

They couldn't go on as they were. He would have to clear the air and take the consequences, whatever they might be. Olivia was not vindictive and she had always forgiven him before. Only this time it would be different. This time he couldn't tell her it was all over; it wasn't and it wouldn't be. He tried to visualise a future without Olivia and failed. But then neither could he imagine his life now without Zoë.

As soon as she returned from this tour he would see her. Rehearsals or no rehearsals, they must find time to talk. If Zoë needed him as he needed her, he knew he would be unable to turn his back and walk away. On the other hand, if he wasn't that important to her he still wouldn't be able to finish it. It was Catch 22 with a vengeance.

Propping his elbows on the table, Giles put his head in his hands.

Either way, they couldn't all win. Somebody had to end up the loser. There was also the undoubted fact that, if he were to become a permanent presence in Zoë's life, Yelland would be after his blood. He groaned aloud.

What a mess he'd made of everything. What a bloody *awful* mess!

*　　　*　　　*

'You didn't have to go to such lengths to see me; I would always have met you for a clandestine G and T!' Pat McCarthy grinned up at Olivia after examining her thumb. He held her hand gently in his. 'I think we have to let out whatever is lurking in there then give you large dollops of antibiotic. I'll do it myself now, then Giles can take you home straight away.'

'Will it be all right by next Friday? I'm supposed to be driving down to take Adam to my parents for his half-term.'

'Not a problem, penicillin will clear it up in a few days.'

She made a face. 'I don't want Giles near me again with a syringe; he should still be practising on oranges.'

'Some of us never acquire the knack; women are much better at it. But don't worry, you can take the cure in tablet form,' he stood up. 'Come along now. Just a quick jab of local, a spot of incredibly brilliant scalpel work from me and you'll be well on the way to recovery.'

*　　　*　　　*

'Not too bad, was it?' he asked fifteen minutes later.

Olivia smiled her gratitude, 'Brutal to watch Pat, but painless.'

He stood back as his nurse make a neat job of her bandage. 'Just pop in each morning for the next few days will you … to have the

89

dressings changed and check everything's OK? I'll get a message to Giles now that you're ready to leave.'

Olivia slung her shoulder bag and stood up. 'I'll go down and wait for him in the coffee lounge.'

After collecting her cup from the counter, she retreated to a small table behind a plastic potted palm. The last thing she wanted was to be seen by any other member of staff and have to explain her heavily bandaged hand. She was embarrassed now to think she had been so stupid and hoped Giles wasn't going to deliver another lecture on their way home. At least her accident had broken the ice a little between them and they'd actually conversed together, like normal human beings, over the breakfast table.

'I said one sugar for you, Sylvia, that's right, isn't it?' asked a woman's voice. Olivia heard the sounds of two people settling into a seat behind her and moved further under cover. 'Although why one must take it from the counter and not have the bowl on the table, I can't imagine...'

'More hygienic, I suppose.' The cut-glass vowels of the second speaker put Olivia's teeth on edge. Now where had she heard that voice before, she wondered? Irritated, she tried to close her ears to their conversation, but without success.

'I'm so glad I bumped into you this morning,' twittered number one. 'I always have a coffee before my stint with the Red Cross ... I'm in the shop today, and it gets so busy that there's no time for refreshments once I'm there.'

'Harry wanted me with him this morning.' Her companion gave a tinkling laugh. 'He's still a little nervous over his check-ups, although it's a year since the last one and he's had no trouble at all.'

'He was so lucky in his surgeon.' The first voice became arch. 'What a charmer that man Ryder is, all his women patients are crazy about him, you know.'

There was a short laugh from cut-glass vowels. 'So I imagine, and they are not the only ones. Giles Ryder spreads his charms well beyond this hospital, I can assure you.'

Olivia's coffee slopped onto the table and she mopped it hastily with a tissue, her face flooding crimson. Paralysed with embarrassment she sat listening as the voice continued: 'Harry and I met him in a Salisbury restaurant ages ago, with a mere slip of a girl, an actress...' There was a faint gurgle of well-bred laughter. 'I suppose it *was* funny ... Harry thought so. The man actually introduced her as his daughter.'

'No *really*?' her companion was avid for more. 'Who was she?'

'Zoë Ormonde – she's with that Salisbury Company … I can't remember the name of it; Harry would know. She's quite brilliant, but must be half his age – and it was no casual meeting. Although they haven't seen us, we've seen them several times since then, the last only a few weeks ago. They were hand in hand going into the Queen's Head, and as it was well after the restaurant had closed we presumed they had a room there.'

'How *awful,* I wonder if his wife knows.'

'I doubt it, poor woman. One can't help but feel sorry for her. Harry and I met her with him at last year's fete and they seemed such a devoted couple, but a man doesn't stray unless there is something wrong at home does he?'

Olivia wondered if she was going to faint. Her hands were clammy and she could feel a trickle of perspiration between her breasts. As the two women prattled on she hunted around for some means of escape, although even if she could summon the courage to walk out, she doubted her legs would support her. Trapped, she sat on, her coffee growing cold, listening to further graphic details of Zoë Ormonde, so that by the time the pair eventually left she felt she knew every fascinating inch of the blasted little slut's face and figure as well as did the loquacious Sylvia.

And she had actually been the catalyst that stared it all! *She* had dragged Giles to Salisbury to that fatal Twelfth Night. *She* had drawn his attention again and again to that girl with the lovely voice. Bile rose in her throat.

Feverishly she counted back. Four months; he had been seeing her all this time. No previous affair had ever lasted longer than a few weeks. What a stupid fool he must think her not to have found him out.

Now even in her misery she could feel satisfaction that her suspicions had been vindicated. Summoning all her strength she rose and left the coffee lounge, making quickly for the main hall, vowing that this time he had gone too far. He wouldn't get the opportunity to make a fool of her ever again.

'Archie,' she buttonholed the head porter, 'would you please ring for a taxi then get a message to my husband to say I've gone home and not to bother about driving me.'

'If you're sure you're all right, Mrs Ryder.' He eyed her, his face full of kindly concern. 'You do look pale.'

'I'm fine, really.' She forced a smile. 'I'll just wait outside for the taxi. Please don't tell my husband until after I've gone.'

Summat up there, Archie mused, turning to the telephone. *Such a*

*nice lady Mrs Ryder – I wonder if she knows what her old man gets up
to when he thinks nobody's looking?*

92

9

She had been home less than twenty minutes when she heard his car draw up, the bang as he slammed the door, then hasty footsteps crossing the hall.

'Olivia, what the *hell* are you playing at?' Bewildered, he stood on the threshold of the sitting room. 'You left me looking an absolute prat...'

'Join the club.' She invited. 'I was beginning to think I was the only member.'

'No riddles please; just tell me why you went off like that ... are you feeling ill again?'

'Sick, maybe; ill, no.' She spoke with cold bitterness. 'You stupid fool; how much longer did you think you could go on with your sordid little affair before someone dropped you in it?'

He walked to the window to stand with his back to her before asking: 'Who?'

'Some bloody woman called Sylvia. You were seeing her husband this morning ... Harry someone-or-other...'

'Wynn-Davies,' he supplied dully, 'but I don't understand. She hardly knows you; has only met you once.'

'Oh, I got it second-hand. She was in the coffee lounge, regaling her friend with the details. And very interesting they were.'

With an effort he turned to face her.

'I doubt that you'll believe me, but last night, after I left you, I made up my mind to tell you. I'm sorry I left it too late.'

'I bet you are, and I believe you all right ... you'd have the gall for anything.' She ran distracted fingers through her hair. 'I suppose *she* was the real reason you spent all those Friday nights in Salisbury; you didn't actually go to any of those lectures, did you?'

He shook his head. 'No, I just signed in.'

'And when I was in Devon?'

'I ... we, stayed at a hotel. I came back here a couple of times and had a meal next door.'

'I can't believe it, even of you I can't: that you could be crass and stupid enough to parade around with her in a public place.' She spread her hands in mute appeal. 'Why, Giles? When you were getting all the oats you needed right here, please, just explain to me ... *why*?'

'I don't know. I don't bloody *know*.' Almost, she felt sorry for him, then was swept with a painful jealous fury when he added: 'Yes I do … she makes me feel young again.'

'Well, bully for her!' She fought to keep calm. She rose and took a cigarette from the box on the mantelpiece, giving a grimace of pain as he automatically stepped forward with his lighter. She held his shaking hand steady for a second as she bent to the flame then straightened to face him. 'Are you in love with her?'

'Yes.' He couldn't meet her eyes. 'She got under my skin the first time I saw her and I've had no peace since. Don't ask me why … or how. She's not a patch on you. She isn't beautiful, she can be brash and vulgar and she swears like a drunken sailor. And she didn't chase me, I chased her.' he hesitated. 'I think she cares for me.'

'You think? After four months, don't you know?'

He said, 'It really doesn't matter whether or not she cares. I do, and right now that's *all* that matters.'

She stared past his shoulder, silently acknowledging that she had come to the end. 'When life has been so good to us that you've had no need to look elsewhere for anything, least of all sex, I'm damned if I'll fight to keep you any longer. This is the end, Giles. You can screw around and take the consequences. She can have you, if that's what she wants, and God help her…'

'What do you want me to do? Clear out of the house?'

'You may do as you wish. I don't give a damn.' She turned her back, 'You started it; you finish it in whatever way suits you. I wash my hands of the whole business.'

'Please Olivia, look at me!'

Unwillingly, she turned again to face him.

His eyes were brilliant in his white face, his lips tightly compressed. In the face of that look she found her resolve slipping and dug her fingers into her palms, fighting for control. How, she wondered wearily, could any man possibly be such a mixture of professional strength and moral weakness … She drew a deep breath. She couldn't, wouldn't go through it all again, not now, not ever. Under the unwavering deepening hostility of her gaze, his own fell. Defeated he said, 'I'll move my things into the guest room for now, if that's what you want.'

'What I want appears to be purely academic, but under the circumstances it would seem to be a good idea.'

His eyes pleaded. 'We have to talk.'

'Not now.'

Despite the warmth of the day she felt cold and walked past him into the hall. Taking a coat from a hook by the door, not noticing that it was an old jacket of his, she stepped into the garden, until she pulled up the collar and was immediately assailed by the scents of tobacco and after-shave; antiseptic and that own special, Giles' smell. The tears began to slide down her cheeks.

What was so wrong in their marriage that he'd *always* needed to go after other women? Was it her fault; something about her, something she had never got completely right? True she was past the first flush of youth, but her body was still slim and supple; until this recent trouble their lovemaking had never become stale and automatic. She was intelligent, enjoyed entertaining their mutual friends, always welcomed his colleagues. And much as she adored their son, she had always put Giles first.

She loved him, in spite of all he'd been and was. She needed him; the thought of living life on her own was terrifying. She stood at the river's edge hunched into his jacket, swept with a terrible longing to put the clock back; never to have stabbed her thumb on that nail, never gone for that coffee, never sat at that particular table, never faced him with what she had heard.

But no, she pulled the collar tighter about her throat. This was not like the other times when she might wait for the infatuation to pass. She shivered. This was like facing a dark and uncharted sea without lights or compass. This time she really couldn't see any way ahead that might lead to a peaceful conclusion.

* * *

'Tell me it's going to stop.' An hour later, still hunched into his jacket Olivia faced him, across what to her exhausted mind appeared to be about an acre and a half of carpet.

'I can't. Not this time. Not unless she wants it to finish.'

Giles was grey-faced and dull-eyed. He'd spent her absence in frantically seeking an answer to the unanswerable. He made a tremendous effort to gather his wits, to try and explain. 'I'm sorry ... I thought she didn't matter so much, but she does.'

'And she is more important than your wife, your son and your home, is she? After more than twenty years you can chuck it all away with barely a second thought.'

'Must it come to that ... can't we work something out...'

'Like *what*?' She cut across him savagely. 'Have her move in with us: a *ménage à trois*? Or am I supposed to sit around for some unspecified time, waiting for you to get tired of her, or her of you?'

'I don't know.' He shook his head wretchedly. 'I love you, Olivia:

95

I need you. I can't imagine my life without you. But she's so vulnerable; in many ways such a lost child...'

'And what about Adam – isn't he vulnerable? Won't he be a lost child?'

'Oh, don't!'

'Now there'll be one more career for you to cut short.' She couldn't keep the contempt from her voice and he raised startled eyes to hers.

'What do you mean by that?'

'Grow up, Giles. Take a good long look at yourself.' She viewed him with a mixture of pity and irony. 'This girl is an actress, who probably has a brilliant career ahead of her. You make her need you as much as you need her and you'll kill all that. It won't be enough for you to live on her terms, any more than you could live on mine ... it will have to be on yours. Can you *really* see her settling down as a good little housewife?'

'I hadn't even thought about it,' he flushed angrily and she gave a short, derisive laugh.

'Then you'd better start. You are selfish Giles, and frequently childish. You expect and take so much ... a woman's undivided attention, good sex, when *you* want it, your home comforts and a wife who will double as your mother to provide them ... and you need them in that order.' Now she was reckless, twisting the knife and not caring how much it hurt. 'In ten years time when you retire, *if* she is still around, she'll still be a young woman, wondering what she gave it all up for ... as have I, more than once.'

Stung into retaliation he sneered, 'Well, you'll be able to please yourself now, won't you? You can let the Artist in you out of its straight-jacket of marriage to me.'

She flinched and for a moment let slip her mask of icy contempt, looking at him with tragic eyes, so that he was washed with sudden bitter shame.

'Livia, I'm sorry, so sorry; please, just don't do anything in a hurry. Give me some time. I'll get out of your way...'

'Don't bother,' she recovered herself quickly. 'I'll leave. You may have forgotten that we have a son, I haven't, and at the moment he is my first concern. I won't have him back here in a few weeks time with you dodging in and out of her bed as you please. I'll pack and go next weekend as planned, but I'll be staying in Lodscombe after I've returned Adam to school.'

He was angry and flustered. 'What's all the flaming hurry?'

Because, she wanted to scream at him, *I can't bear to be in the same house with you now; because I cannot possibly play out this charade before our friends; because I still love you, and always will.*

Fighting down her rising panic she turned away with a dismissive shrug. 'Why not; what is there left to stay for?'

*   *   *

Olivia began to feel the journey would never end as, driving slowly, never letting the needle go above fifty, she forced herself to concentrate on the road.

She had just passed the worst week of her life: attending the hospital each morning, being bright and cheerful with Pat, pretending everything was normal. Arranging with a knowing-looking Sandra to clean once a week, no matter what Mr Ryder may say to the contrary; concocting a story for a clearly disbelieving Carol, that she was feeling run down and needing a break … the list of deceit and lies endless, most of it done to save face for Giles.

She passed the turn-off to Adam's school and thought, *Time enough to take that hurdle tomorrow,* and felt her muscles tighten and her stomach lurch, but once over the border into Devon and heading for Lodscombe, she could relax a little, knowing she was almost there, although what to say to her parents when she arrived she still had no idea. She'd funked telephoning her parents to warn of her early arrival, but knew she'd have to put them fully in the picture before she fetched Adam in the morning.

She drove on, oblivious of the gathering rain clouds until, arriving on the brow of the hill before the village she stopped the car to look down on Captains Cottage. Thin blue smoke spiralled from the chimney into the still sullen air and she gave a short, bitter laugh as her mind at last registered the coming storm. How appropriate she thought, and putting the car into gear, drove slowly down the hill.

Stormy weather; it would be stormy weather all the way from now on.

*   *   *

Her father opened the door in response to her knock; smiling warmly he held the door wide.

'Hello, darling … you're a day early. Nice surprise.' Nothing much ever fazed Clive Heyward. 'To what do we owe the honour?'

'Hi, dad,' she put her arms around him, laying her cheek against his, feeling the tears gathering behind her eyes. 'You are not going to

97

want to hear this, but I rather think I've run away from home...'

*   *   *

She sat on the old squashy sofa, snuffling into a handkerchief, gulping on the brandy he'd poured and handed her without a word, before seating himself by her side. He waited until her tears dried and she'd finished plying the handkerchief, then suggested, 'How about starting at the beginning? I suppose we should really wait for your mother, but she's shopping in Dartmouth and will be another hour or more: we can't sit here in silence until she returns.'

'If I start at the beginning I'll have to go back twenty years, because that's how long Giles has been chasing other women...' She broke off to glare resentfully at him as he put a hand over his mouth. 'Dad, this is no laughing matter.'

'Aren't you going just a little over the top, darling? I know he's a flirt, the man can't help himself; he even does it with your mother, but it seems harmless enough.'

She ripped a few stitches from the hem of the handkerchief and counted slowly to ten.

'Do you call several separate hops into other beds *and* a string of neckings and gropings harmless flirtation? Because I don't, I call it gross unfaithfulness, and I've had enough.'

Clive sat forward, taking her hand in both of his. 'Are you sure of your facts?' he asked. 'It's easy with a man like Giles to read more into his actions than is really there.'

'If I wasn't sure, I wouldn't be sitting here now.' Angrily Olivia pulled her hand away. 'Don't treat me like an unreasonable child, dad. He's admitted being unfaithful at least four times and I'd take a bet there were more,' her voice rose. 'I've coped with the skirt chasing ever since we were married, even managed to forgive him in the past for those he actually caught and took to bed, but now he's in the throes of a full-blown affair with someone half his age and I've had to listen to a load of hogwash, about how he apparently loves and can't do without, both of us. It's plain bloody insulting and I refuse to be reasonable and forgiving any longer.'

'OK.' He put up placating hands. 'I'm sorry, but when you've kept any hint of this quiet for all these years, it isn't easy to suddenly revise all my previous notions of your apparently happy and contented marriage.' Gently, he took her hand again. 'Come along now, take your time and put me properly in the picture.'

When Margot returned over an hour later, she found her husband

98

sitting alone at the kitchen table, his head bowed, and turning a glass of whisky in his hands.

Margot put her shopping bags on the floor and began to take off her coat, shaking it vigorously and sending rainwater spattering across the tiled floor. 'I see Olivia's arrived a day early. Why didn't she let us know?' She stared in surprise as he looked up, his face grim and dark with anger. 'Where is she, and what on earth is wrong with you?'

'She's upstairs; asleep, I hope. God knows she's exhausted enough.' He stood to fetch another glass then pushed the bottle towards her. 'Better sit down and have one of these, while I tell you the saga of our daughter's happy marriage.'

*   *   *

The storm built as they sat talking while daylight faded under the threatening clouds. Eventually Margot rose to switch on the lights and Clive got heavily to his feet; crossing the kitchen he took his oilskins from their hook by the door.

'I'd better empty her car now. She'll wake if there's much thunder and I'd like her to feel all her things are ready for her when she comes down.' He paused at the doorway to give a wry grin. 'What a mess; they are the very last couple I would have expected this to happen to. It just shows, doesn't it, how someone you love so much, and think you know so well, can cover up such pain for years and never say a word.'

She helped him to stack the cases in the hallway, noting all the painting equipment and canvasses, a clear intention she thought of their daughter's determination to stay.

'Was it wise, d'you think, to leave the field clear for Giles?' she asked, as later they sat in the living room, watching the first lightning sheet across the water. 'He'll be able to do just as he likes now won't he?'

Clive shrugged, 'Perhaps, but she's desperately worried about Adam and doesn't want him drawn into it...' he broke off as the door opened and Olivia stood on the threshold. She had washed her face and renewed her make-up, but nothing could disguise her ravaged face and the blue shadows beneath her eyes. Margot jumped up and put her arms about her.

'Olivia, we are so sorry. Are you all right? We were just talking about Adam.' She drew her to the sofa and sat down beside her. 'It's going to be so difficult for you both.'

'Thanks mother, I don't know quite what to do about him. I've

99

been thinking about him ever since I left the house.'

She was composed now, her weeping over. She felt she would never cry again, that all the tears had been spent over the past week. 'I don't want to tell him too much too soon, but I can't try to hide what's happened. He will have to know.'

'Think carefully, Olivia. Adam adores his father; is there no way you can return and try again?'

'No. I can't go back to Riversmead. If we were there for Adam's summer vacation he'd soon find out what's going on, and I won't have that. Don't worry,' she shook her head, 'I shan't say anything to make him think any less of Giles; just tell him that like many other married couples we're having difficulties, and are going to live apart until we can sort things out.'

'That won't wash with him for long,' her father put in abruptly, 'he's not a fool.'

She flushed. 'What else do you suggest I do?'

'Tell him everything and answer the questions he's bound to ask. He'll be sixteen in August, Olivia. These days that's almost a man. Treat him like one.'

'You're right.' She winced as thunder crashed overhead, observing mordantly. 'I could do without the sound effects!'

'We had a storm like this the night you were born,' put in her mother inconsequentially.

'Well, I didn't notice at the time,' Olivia returned drily, 'but perhaps someone was trying to tell me something even then!'

*　　　*　　　*

Despite the storm that raged for most of the night, she slept tolerably well and woke early, feeling refreshed, with only a slight, lingering headache, her first immediate thoughts of her son, and the difficult weekend ahead of them all. She shouldn't really have run home like this, she supposed, but with Giles and herself in separate rooms, and Adam looking forward to his half-term break and a few days out with Liam and Kate on the Morning Star, she'd had no alternative.

Rather than stay in bed with her thoughts, she got up to bathe and wash her hair, then stood at the window watching the sunrise and towelling her hair dry. It looked set to be a beautiful day and she planned to leave early for Chiltens, making a leisurely journey of it and giving herself plenty of time to rehearse what she would say to Adam.

Going quietly downstairs she made tea and toast and carrying them into the garden, stood by the low drystone wall to breakfast and watch the village come slowly to life. From here she could see Ambrose Flynn's pink-washed house, a long straight plume of woodsmoke rising from the chimney into the still air, the sun striking fire on the glass conservatory that was his studio. Remembering the lively eyes, and that dark brown voice with just a hint of Ireland in its depths, she smiled. She might have to watch that one if she was thinking of spending any protracted period of time in Lodscombe.

Despite the constant numbing pain of her separation from Giles she felt a sudden lifting of spirit and began to map out in her head how the days would go. Of course she would pull her weight with the shopping and cleaning and the getting of meals whilst at Captains Cottage, but the rest of the time would be her own.

For the first time in over twenty years she would be free to immerse herself again in the work she loved: to paint as much and for as long as she pleased. Then, if the unthinkable happened and Giles and Riversmead were lost to her forever, she would find a cottage somewhere along this beloved coast and become what she had set out to be: an artist; one who might perhaps, in the fullness of time, achieve some small measure of success.

She was putting her plate and cup into the sink when her father appeared, tying the cord of his plaid dressing gown, sleepy-eyed and with his sparse white hair ruffled like the down of a baby bird.

'Thought I heard someone moving about, and as your mother is still sleeping, it had to be you!' He smiled and put his hands on her shoulders. 'How does the world look this morning?'

'A little better than yesterday,' Olivia kissed his cheek. 'I'll make you some fresh tea.'

'What's in the pot will do.' He sat, yawning briefly. 'Did you sleep?'

'Yes, reasonably well.' She began to pour his tea. 'I've been thinking how much I should say to the school about all this. I don't want Adam getting himself into any trouble because he's upset and worried. He's not quite the amiable chap he used to be, you know; he can be damned difficult these days if something really gets his goat.'

'Takes after you, then, doesn't he? But I think you're right. Better ring the Head before you leave and arrange to see him before you speak to Adam.'

She handed him his cup then took her own and sat down at the table opposite him. 'I'm not washing my dirty linen in front of *him*!' She pulled a long face. 'He's a dear old thing but not really in this century. No, I'll give Adam's Papa Doyle a ring; he's reasonably easy to talk to, although I'm not telling even him anything more than the bald facts.'

'No time like the present.' Her father pushed the telephone towards her. 'Better see if he's free.'

'Dad – It's only eight thirty. I can't ring yet.'

He gave a sarcastic snort. 'Rubbish, he'll have been up for hours giving them all hell. Trust me. I remember my own schooldays only too well.'

*　　　*　　　*

Doyle certainly sounded wide-awake, and if he felt any surprise at her call he didn't allow it to show in his voice.

'Do you want Adam present?' he asked. 'No? Then I suggest we meet away from the school.'

'If that won't be too difficult,' Olivia was embarrassed, thinking she must be sounding like the proverbial tiresome parent. 'I'm sorry, I know you must be busy.'

'I'm very good at delegating.' She could hear his smile. 'Have you noticed a turning about a half-mile before the school, sign-posted Pendene? You have? Good. About a mile along that road you'll see a cottage on the right. You can't miss it, there's a very large sycamore tree overhangs the gate. I shall be there about eleven, but should I be held up my father-in-law will entertain you. His name is Bartholomew Kenny, but you can call him Barty and I promise you he won't bite!'

Olivia thanked him; putting the 'phone down she regarded her father with a barely concealed grin.

'Now there's a thing…' she propped her chin on one hand, 'he's got a father-in-law called Bartholomew. I didn't know he was married. What *do* you suppose he's done with his wife?'

'Whatever it is it's none of your business,' Clive looked at her warily, 'and certainly no reason for you to be getting that sort of a light in your eye.'

'Why not?' she answered him reasonably, 'it's about time that I did, and when last we met, he quite definitely had that sort of light in his.'

*　　　*　　　*

She found the cottage without difficulty and backed the car up onto the rough grass track running alongside a tall beech hedge. Stepping out she stood looking for some sign of life. All the curtains were drawn back from the latticed windows, but there was no sign of any human occupants, only a small tabby cat sat on the gatepost, pointedly ignoring her and industriously washing a paw. As she stood hesitating there was a crunch of footsteps on the gravel path and a tall, stoop-shouldered man with a shock of white hair appeared around the far side of the house.

'Ah – my expected visitor,' his arms were full of flowers and he beamed at her over a riot of lupins and delphiniums, 'come in, come in, the coffee should be brewed by now. Tom just 'phoned. He'll be here right away.'

Pushing the front door open with his foot he led the way into a sitting room that ran the length of the cottage, dominated at the far end by a big kneehole desk, covered with untidy piles of books and papers.

'I'll put these in the sink.' He waved the sheaf of flowers. 'Just sit you down, or have a browse while I get our coffee…' he appeared to be struck by a sudden thought, and turned back, giving her a sunburst of a smile, 'sorry … forgetful of me. I'm Barty Kenny.'

She returned the smile. 'I thought you might be. I'm Olivia Ryder.'

'Oh, I know that all right.' He gave a sly wink. 'I've had you described in detail.'

Oh have you, she thought, wondering what that meant. She gazed around the long low-ceilinged room, feeling immediately that this was a place in which one was instantly at home. There were several old comfortable-looking armchairs, a round rosewood table, a long, crowded bookcase, and more books piled on almost every surface. A cluster of fishing rods stood in one corner; a bag of golf clubs, cricket bat and pads jumbled together in another. The pleasant clutter of a leisured, but far from idle household, was evident wherever one looked.

A framed photograph on the low oak mantle shelf caught her eye and she moved to pick it up for a closer scrutiny, recognising the younger Doyle immediately; in Army uniform, still sporting the moustache but minus the beard, he was smiling and leaning back against the trunk of the sycamore, his arms around a fair-haired young woman whose hands rested on the shoulders of a small boy with wide, solemn eyes.

'My daughter and grandson,' the old man had come in silently and stood holding a tray with three mugs and a jug of coffee. He placed it carefully on a low table then straightened and came to stand beside her. 'Both they and my wife were killed by a flying bomb while visiting my sister in London. I was in North Africa then, and Tom in Burma. Ironic, isn't it? We were the ones who went to war, but they were the ones who died.'

'How dreadful ... I'm so sorry. It makes you wonder where God got to for five years, doesn't it?' She looked again at the picture. 'You must have lived here a long time; it was taken under the tree in the garden, wasn't it?'

'Yes, I brought Kathleen here when we were first married. Ross ... Rosalind was born here.' He smiled and replaced the picture. 'Kathleen took it on Tom's last leave before it happened. It all seems a long time ago.'

'And who's that, or am I being too inquisitive?' She gestured towards a much more recent and casually posed photograph of a youngish woman with short curly hair. She wore what appeared to be some kind of tropical kit and was carrying a camera. There were palm trees in the background and the face was vaguely familiar.

'Oh...' He gave a sideways glance at the photograph before bending to pour the coffee. 'That's Jayne Foreman, the war correspondent; you might have seen her photograph in the Sunday News; she's Tom's occasional lover.' He dropped his small bombshell in a carefully neutral voice. 'Her picture spends half the time chucked in the drawer and half up there, depending on his mood, and how long she's been away. He's always hoping she'll give up all the excitement and settle down here. I hope so too, but we're both probably living in a fool's paradise.'

Oh, ho, thought Olivia, you're quite a dark horse, aren't you, Mr Tom Doyle?

*   *   *

The object of her thoughts arrived within minutes, coming quietly into the room, the small cat cradled in his arms. Dropping the animal onto the couch he shook Olivia's hand and apologised for keeping her waiting, then greeted his father-in-law with a grin and an affectionate, 'Hello, guv'nor.' Helping himself to coffee he sat down. 'To business,' he said, 'and would you like Barty to leave?'

Olivia smiled. 'No, I rather think I'd like to have him stay.'

She gave them a broad outline of her problem, stressing that she would be telling Adam much the same unless he wanted to know more about the reasons for their parting, in which case she would be honest and tell him.

Doyle sat drinking his coffee in silence, watching her attentively

104

and thinking that he was in a particularly ticklish situation. This woman's restrained and cautious skirting around her marital problems meant he would have to tread very warily indeed. He had a growing suspicion that, following Adam's outpourings to him after his disastrous return to school at Easter, her son might know rather more than his mother did about what the two-timing Giles was about.

When she finished he put his cup down and scratched thoughtfully at his beard. Did she or didn't she know about the girl friend? And how on earth was he to handle this without breaking Adam's confidence and perhaps stirring even more of a hornet's nest between the parents?

At length he ventured, 'I rather think Adam may know, or at least suspect, more than you realise…'

She asked sharply. 'How, and in what way do *you* know?'

'There was a bit of a fracas with his study mate the day they came back after Easter.' Doyle took his pipe from his pocket and began to push tobacco into the bowl. 'I'd gone to their room to check that he was all right after the near miss your husband had with a tree, and interrupted quite a set-to. Adam was in a blazing temper and in a mood to take on all comers … he even chanced his arm with me.'

Olivia stared at him hard and saw his mouth twitch slightly. Now what on earth had been going on, she wondered, and what kind of state had Adam really been in to 'chance his arm' with this man?

Aware of her regard, Doyle concentrated on his pipe, continuing his narrative in a neutral, matter of fact tone. 'Frankly the pair of them were so totally out of order, that my first instinctive reaction was to just about skin them both, but on reflection, I ended up giving Adam in particular a severe verbal roasting, and gated them both for a month.'

'Oh.' She pulled her mouth down. 'I didn't know. He's not very forthcoming these days.'

'I don't think he would have wanted you, or your husband, to know either the cause or the ending of this particular episode.' Doyle hesitated momentarily and gave her a faint, embarrassed smile. 'I can't break his confidence. I'll just say that because he'd not only started the fight but gone verbally way beyond anything I could allow, I'd given him a very hard time; his friend got away much more lightly. However, I realised there must be more to it than just a schoolboy brawl when I found Adam lurking outside my door, looking rather damp around the eyes. It didn't take much digging on my part to find the cause. When he'd got it all off his chest he apologised very nicely for his lapse of manners and trotted off to supper, not too much the worse for wear.'

Olivia gave him a long, thoughtful look; sure there was more in all this than he was admitting. 'Poor Adam,' she said, eventually, 'I'm glad he had someone at hand to confide in. Usually he'd rather die than come straight out with anything the least bit personal.'

'That's the trouble with most adolescents; they think everything is beyond the understanding of anyone over twenty-one. They sit on their emotions for so long that when the geyser does blow all hell is let loose.' He struck a match, applied it to his pipe then glanced up at her over the flame. 'Will you tell him you've spoken to me?'

'Yes. As my father reminded me he can no longer be treated as a child.' She sighed, feeling a return of the hollow ache of loss. 'Giles was always so good with him, and Adam has swung very much towards him and away from me over the past year ... all a necessary part of growing up, I know, but it's going to be difficult for *me* to deal with him right now.'

'He will still need his father.' Barty spoke quietly from where he stood behind her.

'Yes, he will.' She was silent for a moment, then stood up and turned to Doyle. 'I've kept you long enough. I'll go and collect him now. Thank you, and I hope he won't give you too many headaches in the future.' She turned to smile at Barty. 'And thank you for your welcome and the coffee.'

'Come again whenever you wish,' he held her hand in his, patting it with the other. 'I'm always here, and if things start getting too difficult just hop in that car of yours and come for another coffee and a chat.' He jerked his head at his son in law. 'No need to let *him* know.'

Doyle gave him a dry look. 'Get back to your garden and behave yourself, Barty.' He took Olivia's arm and steered her towards the door. 'At your age you should be past issuing that kind of invitation.'

When they reached her car he opened the door asking: 'I wonder if you'd mind giving *this* old man a lift back? I cut across the fields coming here, but I ought to get back as quickly as possible.'

'Of course,' she stared straight ahead, holding the steering wheel tightly, unable to leave the subject of their talk just hanging in the air. Feeling foolish and uncertain she steeled herself to speak. 'I guess that whatever Adam had to say has given you a pretty clear idea of *why* Giles and I have separated. He may tell me in his own time what he has discovered, and how, but I shall not ask him. Thank you for taking so much trouble.'

'I'm happy to help in any way that I can. Adam is a nice chap and

I've always had high expectations of him. I shouldn't like to see him a casualty in all this.'

'But he will be, won't he?' She caught her lower lip between her teeth. 'When parents split, the children come off worst.'

He said, 'Not necessarily. Not if they feel safe and loved.'

She turned the key in the ignition, summoning a smile. 'I do like your Barty. He doesn't say much, but what he does is kind and wise, and straight to the point.'

'So it should be,' he gave her one of his amused sidelong glances. 'He used to be the Rector of this parish until he retired a couple of years ago.'

She blushed. 'I wish you'd warned me.'

'Why? Did you commit some frightful gaffe?'

'I was rather derogatory about God at one point,' she admitted.

He laughed. 'I shouldn't worry overmuch. I imagine he's heard worse, and he can be pretty forthright himself on some subjects.'

Olivia's blush deepened as she remembered Barty's comments about his son-in-law's "occasional lover". Doyle noted her heightened colour and wondered what the old devil had been saying to make that lovely face even more enchantingly beautiful. I don't know what you can be chasing that's so much better than this, Mr Giles Ryder, he thought with grim amusement, but I have a suspicion that you're going to cause more than one man something of a problem in leaving your woman lonely and unattended....

Later that evening he sat in the big leather armchair with long legs outstretched, feet propped on the old-fashioned brass fender; a deep pile of marked exercise books on the floor beside his chair and a diminishing pile on his knees.

'Oh, Lord,' he muttered and slashed a diagonal line of red pencil across a page. 'Why do I bother? I should have taken up grave digging or something equally useful...'

He paused to push the hair back from his forehead and his eye fell on the framed photograph on the mantelpiece. 'Go on, Ross – laugh your head off – this is the last thing you expected me to end up doing, isn't it? And as for *you*...' He stood up suddenly to take the photo of Jayne Foreman from its place; opening the table drawer he pushed it inside, 'you can go in there for a while, my love, and let me think in peace.' And he shut the drawer with a bang.

'Are you still at it?'

Barty had arrived with his habitual silent tread, bearing in either hand a large mug, 'Coffee for you to keep you going, cocoa for me to put me to sleep!'

Tom took the mug with a word of thanks, before casting an eye over the ancient grey plaid dressing gown and leather slippers. 'Those damned things will walk by themselves one day,' he said, 'why don't you buy some new gear?'

'No need. These will see me out.' Barty sank into his wide wing chair. 'How's life?'

'Bloody awful, guv'nor, the present Lower Fifth appears to be comprised entirely of single cell amoebae, and I'd rather do any number of things on half-term than sort through all this drivel. I can't make up my mind whether to return to the schooldays of Shakespeare himself and beat some learning into them, or just give up and go into a decline.'

'Is that really all that's wrong?'

'No.'

His father-in-law looked meaningfully at the mantelpiece and gave a cackle of laughter. 'I see you've given up on Lady Jayne again.'

'Are you trying to stir me up, Barty?'

'Time somebody did.'

'Anyway…' Tom reached to take his pipe and tobacco tin from his jacket pocket, 'she'll be home eventually, or I shall have to go chasing after her – again.'

'So long as she's all you chase.' Barty stared intently at the ceiling. 'I have noticed there are other women around.'

Doyle grinned. 'You should be ashamed of yourself.'

'I'm talking about you … I didn't see you looking away.' The old eyes were keen and searching.

'About all I can do, look.' Doyle gave his sardonic smile. 'That would be a bit like doctor/patient, wouldn't it? Mother and son's schoolmaster might be equally frowned upon – not least by the son.'

'And she is married.'

'As you say,' Tom continued filling his pipe, 'she is married, and my future, I trust, lies elsewhere. So the question doesn't really arise, does it?'

'I hope not, because at this stage Olivia Ryder may still be in love with her husband, and certainly rather lost and vulnerable … to all kinds of influences.'

'You don't miss much, do you Barty?'

'I thought I should give the matter an airing. I think she may come again … to talk.'

'If she does, then I shall try to keep out of the way as you so obviously want me to. But don't run away with the idea that's she's some fragile little thing and in need of protection, from me or anyone else. There's a fair bit of steel there, you know,' Tom clenched his pipe between his teeth and bent to pick up the discarded book, adding tersely, 'and I have to say, guv'nor, that having a vicar, even a retired one, in my life, has more than once threatened to cramp my style. But don't make it too hard for me now, will you? It might be rather nice to spend an occasional hour or two with a woman who stays put long enough for me to appreciate her company.'

10

Adam was glad Liam was spending time in Dartmouth again; it gave him the chance to be alone with Kate. Ever since mum had fetched him from school yesterday, and over dinner in the town told him about her and dad separating for a bit, he'd wanted to talk to someone. Gran and pops had behaved normally and not been at all embarrassing but he couldn't really talk to them … or his mother. Not yet anyway. He knew it had happened to Kate and Liam, and although he couldn't discuss a thing like that with another bloke, he thought if he told Kate she'd understand.

'My parents split up this week.' He tried to sound casual, although his voice wobbled a bit. 'I think my mother's going to stay here now.'

They were seated side by side on the cabin roof and Kate shifted round towards him, drawing up her legs to hug her knees. 'Gosh, hard luck; did she say why?'

'Sort of; that they hadn't been getting along … needed time apart to work things out … you know, the usual guff, but it's more than that.' He flushed. 'He's got some floozie. I saw him with her. I think that's disgusting.'

'Does she know about the floozie, d'you think?'

'I dunno; probably. They weren't talking much at Easter, and she's been kind of quiet. I think she would have told me more if I'd asked, but I didn't want to then.' Embarrassed, he stared at his feet.

'You should tell what you saw. If *she* knows she'll be keeping it to herself, like you, but I bet she'd feel better if she knows *you* know.'

He said, 'I don't think I'd want to know if it was me.'

Kate was silent for a long time and Adam watched her covertly, as she sat rubbing a finger along the brass trim around the cabin roof, her face flushed and her lips pressed close together. He felt a fluttering begin deep down in his belly. *You're beautiful, really beautiful. I'd like to touch you and kiss you...* He thought about Liam – shag a few girls, he'd said. Adam wondered how it would feel and how you knew when they'd let you. His palms began to sweat and he was so wrapped in the struggle with his turbulent thoughts and feelings that he jumped when Kate spoke.

'Liam blew it for us … I think dad never forgave him,' her face was red, the words jerky. 'He walked in on my mother and some

110

farmer from our village. They were – you know, in bed – on it rather; starkers.'

She stopped suddenly, her mouth snapping shut again. Adam knew his own face was hot. Her mother and some bloke doing it; *shagging,* and Liam had seen them. He passed his tongue over dry lips. 'What happened?'

'Liam went absolutely mad and rushed straight to dad. Stupid really, we knew she *had* a boy friend. Dad knew but pretended he didn't, and while nobody said anything we got along all right. Of course, with Liam swearing and yelling blue murder all over the show he had to take notice.' She cupped her chin in one hand, staring out over the harbour. 'There was an almighty row. I think dad threw her out. Anyway, next day she went off with the boy friend; six months later they cleared off to Canada, and that was that. I think Dad probably blames Liam for making him do it, and Liam blames *him* for doing it; neither of them ever talk about it and sometimes it's hell…'

'Do you miss her?'

'I did at first; but not now, not so much.'

Adam inched his fingers across to take her hand and they sat together in silence. After a few minutes the warm feelings began again, spreading and sending hot fiery waves surging through him. Kate's fingers were clenched in his, and when he dared to steal a look at her, she looked back at him questioningly, then, without speaking, and still holding hands, they stepped down below.

Kate sat on her bunk and Adam stretched to lie beside her, putting his head in her lap and his arms around her waist. For a few minutes they were still and quiet, then he pulled her down until her body was pressed tightly against his. His lips touched hers and they were cool and soft against his own; tentatively he began to explore her mouth, then, driven by his mounting excitement, dared to put his hand under her shirt and feeling a dizzying shock of delight when his hand found her small bare breast.

At his touch Kate gasped, then her hands were around his back, holding him tightly to her, her heart thumping, her body trembling violently as a heady mixture of excitement and fear surged through her. But when Adam began to push his hand down the band of her shorts she was shocked into protest and sat suddenly, bracing her hands against his chest, whispering, 'No, not there … I'm sorry; I wasn't teasing, honestly. I've never done anything like that before. I didn't realise I'd make you … that you'd…' confused she stopped, her face flaming.

Breathing heavily he released her, then following her downward glance gave a breathless embarrassed laugh. 'It's all right for you, you can't tell by looking!'

Her ponytail had come undone and the long silky hair hid her face. 'I liked what you did at first. But it stops at that – all right?'

Adam swallowed hard. 'OK, but it … you know, it's difficult not to go on.'

She kept her head bent. 'I wasn't expecting – I didn't know I'd feel like that.'

'Like what?'

'Wonderful,' she whispered huskily, 'all warm and sort of lit up inside; I didn't want to stop.'

'Nor me.' He was hoarse and cleared his throat, 'but you don't have to worry. I wouldn't try to – you know – go all the way.' They looked at each other uncertainly for a moment, then both began to giggle. Adam cleared his throat again and said boldly, 'Yes I would, if you'd let me!'

'Well I won't.'

'Not ever?'

'Ah, well,' Kate rolled over him and stood up, 'ever is a long time.' She pulled her shirt down and tucked it into her shorts. 'Sit up and I'll fetch that smashing cake your gran made us. I'm starving.'

Adam put his hands on her hips and held her loosely. 'So am I … but not for cake,' he ventured.

She blushed again, glancing at him from under her lashes for a moment before bending to swifty kiss his mouth.

Adam watched her go into the galley, then stood and stretched to his full height, pushing his hands against the underside of the deck. Suddenly he felt strong, in control, and older than he had been before these past few magical minutes. It was a heady feeling.

Something wonderful had happened to him; not just getting an erection, that could happen anytime, sometimes even when he wasn't even thinking about sex, but knowing Kate was special to him; so special that he hadn't minded, had even been glad in a funny, mixed up sort of way, when she wouldn't let him do more. The tumult in his mind and body began to subside, replaced by an almost overwhelming tenderness.

But he still wanted her and his groin ached when he thought how her skin had felt beneath his hand; it wasn't fair, he thought disconsolately, to have feelings like this and not be supposed to do anything for simply ages….

When they'd demolished half the cake and washed it down with Coke he lay down again on the bunk, curled on his side again with his head in her lap, breathing in the secret scent of her. Letting the new delicious warmth stir his senses and flood his heart with what he was quite sure must be love.

With his head heavy and warm against her thighs, Kate moved her hand slowly over the blonde curls, wondering in turn how it would feel to lie naked in Adam's arms and go "all the way". For five years no one had put their arms around her nor kissed her, not even on the cheek. Now she felt no shame at what she'd allowed him to do. Dreamily, she let the new stirring of desire for him build and flow gently through her body; bending she kissed the top of his head, knowing that in those few minutes when they'd lain together, they had both stepped over an invisible line. That nothing in their friendship would ever again be quite so easy and uncomplicated.

And if she should ever let him touch her *there* she wasn't at all confident she would be able to stop him, or herself, from "going all the way…"

*   *   *

By the time Liam returned they were seated at the cabin table deep in a game of cards. He looked from one to the other, adroitly interpreting the atmosphere between them.

Well I'm damned! Grinning widely he stepped down into the cabin and seated himself between them. *Fancy our Adam chancing his arm with sis – and getting away with it, the cheeky little sod.* Liam chuckled inwardly. *I'd thump him one if I thought he'd actually done it, but he wouldn't – at least, I don't think he would, even if she'd let him!*

'Now then, children,' he patted both heads with a paternal hand. 'Time to go home, or it may be tears before bedtime.'

Adam glanced up and grinned amiably, no longer the unquestion-ingly admiring younger boy. 'Bog off, Liam.'

Kate selected and played her ace with care, then gave her brother a gently satirical stare. 'Why don't you go and find yourself a bit of crumpet and leave us in peace to finish our game.'

Gracefully conceding the usurping of his authority, Liam dropped his long lashes over one bright blue eye in a conspiratorial wink.

'I won't tell on *you*,' he said, 'if you don't tell on *me*!'

*   *   *

On the way to her bedroom Olivia saw Adam's light was still on and

113

looked in to say goodnight.

He lay on his back, hands behind his head, staring at the ceiling, but sat up quickly as she entered. 'I've been waiting for you,' he said.

'Have you?'

He drew his knees up, making room for her to sit. 'Is it too late to talk?'

'No. I'm not really tired, but gran and pops were up later than usual last night, and the only way to get them to go to bed was to come up first. They do rather feel it's their duty to see me safely tucked up before they move!'

'Are you all right, mum?'

'I'm not sure yet. It takes a bit of getting used to. What about you?'

'The same,' he leaned his arms on his knees. 'Mum, did you leave because dad's got someone else?'

'Yes.' She was ready and didn't hesitate. 'It's something he has to work out for himself. I can't do much about it.'

'I've seen her.' Adam looked at her with straight, clear eyes. 'At Easter, when you dropped me off in Salisbury ... Mum, she's a *girl*. She can't be much older than I am – and he lied when I asked if he was with someone. He made a joke about it and told me I was seeing things and I *believed* him. I don't think I'll ever trust him again.'

'Oh, Adam,' he was so hurt and angry that Olivia could have wept for him. 'I think it really is something he can't help and it's made him very unhappy as well. I wish you'd told him you knew; he might then have felt able to be honest and explain.'

'I couldn't, because I wasn't sure at the time; I thought I might have made a mistake.' He was suddenly sheepish, ducking his head and picking at the blanket. 'I had a dust-up with Marshall after I got back to school. Dad had clouted me and I was angry and Marshall started talking about his parents splitting up, and that lots of old men went looking for crumpet. I went for him and we had a hell of a scrap...I was going to punch his head in because I thought he might be right and that made me furious. Afterwards when I really thought about it I knew I *had* seen someone with Dad. I remembered her perfectly ... what she looked like, even what she was wearing.'

'I know about the fight. Mr Doyle told me. I went to see him before I fetched you.' Olivia leaned to put her hand over his. 'Do you mind? I thought he should know, just in case you were to do something silly.'

'I'd already done that! But I don't mind that you talked to him.' Adam lowered his eyes again, rubbing his thumb along her hand.

'What did he tell you happened?'

'Only that you'd been very upset and angry, but had talked things over later. He was very understanding.'

'Yeah, he's all right … for a child-beater!'

She ruffled his hair and he didn't pull away.

'Liar Adam, you were gated.'

'So? He still clipped my ear for cheeking him.' He sounded so indignant that she was hard pressed not to smile. 'And he's a sadist; he made Bill and me stew for hours thinking he might cane us… I was scared witless all afternoon thinking about it. Besides,' he scowled suddenly, 'he's always somewhere you don't expect, or want him to be.'

'He needs to be on the alert with characters like you around.'

Adam gave an embarrassed, lop-sided grin. 'Not any more he doesn't, I'm not a kid, you know.'

'Well, he didn't treat you like one, did he?'

'No. He's a good egg, although when he really rips into you, then you just about want to die…' He looked away for a moment, hugging his knees tighter. 'How much did you tell him about dad?'

'Not much.'

He hesitated then took the plunge. 'I told him about him and that girl,' he eyed her anxiously. 'You aren't cross, are you?'

'No. You did the right thing.'

'I didn't mean to, but I was feeling awful because he'd really given me hell. When he started on me again a bit later, I told him I was clearing out of school because I was pissed off with the place and every one in it. I was going to run away, mum, I really was.'

She gave a grunt of laughter, 'Oh dear!'

He flushed. 'If he'd gone for you like he did me, *you* wouldn't have wanted to hang around either.'

She was suddenly sobered and filled with guilt. How could she and Giles have imagined that their son had noticed nothing, when all the time his world was turning upside down?

She said, 'Oh, Adam, I am so sorry.'

'It's all right.' he sighed, and rumpled his hair. 'Did you and dad have a big row before you left?'

'Pretty big, like you, I was angry. We both were. We said the wrong things and didn't listen to what the other had to say, or care how much we hurt each other. We didn't part very well, but I hope that the next time we meet it will be better.'

'I think it was like that with Kate's parents. We talked about it today.'

She smiled sadly. 'That's the trouble with rows between people who know each other too well.'

'I suppose so. I'll try not to be angry with him.' He made an effort to sound off-hand. 'Doyle thought I should 'phone and ask if he'll come down to see me one Saturday and I said I would.'

He looked at her with Giles' eyes; but such steady, grown-up eyes, and she thought: how did he get like that all of a sudden? He was watching her now; assessing her reaction to this suggestion. Faintly she heard an echo of Giles' voice: *"How dare you grow up behind my back!"*

She smiled and leaned to kiss his cheek.

'I think that's a brilliant idea. Come for a walk with me tomorrow and we'll have a really good talk. I don't want you to think anything is being done behind your back. From now on, I promise we'll keep it all up front and honest.'

'Sure. And don't worry, mum; you still have me.'

'Yes, I still have you.'

'Mum.' He stopped her at the door. 'Mum, is dad – you know – doing it with that girl...' he floundered. She looked into his beseeching eyes and resisted the temptation to lie.

'Yes, he is.' She gave a wry smile. 'That's what it's all about, you see: Sex. It's both the best, and the most destructive, thing, in the world.'

She closed his door and went to her own room and the bed that was much too big and empty for one. She leaned on the dressing chest and raised her brows at her reflection in the big oval mirror.

Well, let's hope he'll thank you one day for being honest and telling it like it is. You've been lucky enough to have him for almost sixteen years, so when it's time for him to find out for himself if the pleasure is worth the pain, just see you let him go gracefully – and don't you dare to be a clinging vine!

It had been a long day, but weary as she was, her brain refused to quiet and allow her to sleep. She sat on feeling tired and drained, listening to the dying gurgle of the bathroom pipes and the sounds of her parents preparing for bed; waiting for the house to fall silent.

When the last murmur of conversation had died away she took up a soft wool shawl and left the room, moving confidently and quietly in the dark down the familiar staircase and through the sitting room. Unlocking the French windows she stepped out; pausing for a moment to throw the shawl around her shoulders, she began to walk across the headland towards the village and the cliff path beyond.

She hadn't realised it would go on like this, the emptiness and sense of loss an actual pain deep inside her body. Only three days ago she had turned her back on Giles' stony face, wiped of all but a terrible blank hurt in his dull eyes, and driven away from their home without daring to risk even one backward glance, knowing that if she did, she would be lost; would stop the car and run back to fling her arms around his neck and say it didn't matter, and that she would never ever leave him.

But it did matter, and she had left him and now it seemed, was the beginning of the end of their marriage.

Because even if he should leave his Zoë, who made him feel young again, and wish to take up the threads of their life together, nothing could ever be the same. When trust had finally died for her in his ultimate betrayal of needing younger arms in place of hers, there was little chance of ever healing wounds so deeply inflicted.

But still she missed him and needed him and could only see the future stretching before her as a barren stony wasteland, offering little of comfort and nothing of joy.

She must have walked at least a half-mile along the narrow path bordering the cliff top before turning to retrace her steps. As she rounded the headland and the harbour again came into sight she heard the church clock strike one. Simultaneous with that a dark form loomed out of the shadow of an overhanging rock and the unmistakable rumbling tones of Ambrose Flynn observed: '"She walks in beauty like the night"… I thought I was the only one abroad at this God-forsaken hour!'

Half annoyed, half relieved at being jolted out of her melancholic thoughts, she laughed nervously, clasping the shawl about her. 'I don't usually prowl in the dark but tonight I couldn't sleep. I'm sorry if I disturbed you.'

'I'm not complaining. Sit down.' Ambrose patted the area of flat stone beside him. 'See, the moon on the water brings a pathway straight to this place. It's my favourite spot for sitting and thinking.'

'I think *I've* thought myself out, right now.' She sat beside him and leaned back against the rock face, aware suddenly of her aching legs and feet. He turned his head to give her a long look.

'Anyone on holiday should look happier than you, Mrs Ryder.'

'I'm not on holiday. I've come to stay and as it seems likely we shall meet from time to time, the name is Olivia.'

He offered a large, warm paw. 'Ambrose. But my friends call me Flynn. I hope you mean to stay for a good long time. What I saw at Easter was impressive – and I don't just mean your paintings.'

She took her hand from his and held on tightly to her shawl, thankful that the darkness hid her sudden blush. Idiot, she admonished herself, you shouldn't be sitting out here in the dead of night with this man and giving the impression that you're up for grabs.

Although relieved that he wasn't quite the same bluff, caustic-tongued person of their first meeting, still she found him unnerving. Studying him covertly by the light of the moon she decided that the combination of his broad brow, large, straight nose, vivid blue eyes and an undeniably sensual mouth, added up to rather more than her mother's pronouncement that he was attractive in an ugly sort of way.

Suddenly aware of how ridiculously vulnerable she felt without Giles in the background, she thought: *I should have kept my mouth shut; bloody men – one whiff of a married woman out on her own and they're right there.'*

'No need to coil up like that!' The laughter was back in his voice. 'I'm only out here to watch the moon. Even though you are an un-expected bonus I'm not a pouncer by nature.'

'The thought never crossed my mind.' She caught at the shreds of composure. 'I'm only coiling, as you put it, in preparation for getting to my feet and walking home.'

He settled back comfortably, folding his arms across his broad chest.

'Then good night, Olivia … and do please keep painting. I meant it when I said your work was impressive. It is. Very.'

'Such praise from a genius is overwhelming!' Now that she was on her feet again she felt in command of herself and could relax. 'I saw your last London exhibition and was rather more than impressed. But don't be alarmed, I shall not be pestering you for your autograph.'

His laugh followed her as she swung down towards the harbour, aching feet temporarily forgotten. She'd watch her step and keep a good distance between them, she thought virtuously, but for all his satirical mockery he might be rather fun, and she could do with the odd laugh now and again.

'You'll end up like Giles,' she admonished as she stepped back into the cottage and locked the door behind her. 'First you start getting ideas about Tom Doyle, now you're thinking about the possibility of getting pally with such a clearly unsuitable character as Ambrose Flynn.'

All the same, after so many years, it felt very liberating to find the shoe had shifted onto the other foot.

*   *   *

118

At Riversmead, Giles lay stretched full length on the long couch in the sitting room, an empty glass balanced on his chest; smoking without pleasure while viewing with clinical detachment the pollution of his lungs and liver. His mouth tasted sour from too much whisky, his throat thick with the acrid fumes of tobacco; he was completely exhausted in mind and body, his energy at its lowest ebb. Ten nights alone in the unfamiliar spare-room bed had been hell. Even after Olivia had gone he couldn't bring himself to return to their bedroom to sleep.

Right up until the last minute, when she'd stepped into her car, he hadn't believed that she would leave him. The slamming of the door and the way she had gone without even a turn of her head had been devastating.

She would ring, he'd told himself, as soon as she arrived at Lodscombe. She would ring and he would tell her again how sorry he was; beg her to return and help him find a way out of the waking nightmare that his life had become.

And she would come. She must.

But the telephone had stayed silent all that weekend as he fought his way through the neglected reports and correspondence; the clicking of his secretary's typewriter like minute hammers picking at his brain. Since then the hours and days had crawled by. Time after time he reached out to dial the cottage, always at the last minute drawing back. He might get Margot or Clive, or even worse, Adam. Then what would he say? What *could* he say?

In an orgy of misery and self-loathing he imagined them discussing him, despising him. What had she told her parents? And Adam, what had she said to him? He stared at the smoke spiralling towards the ceiling. "I shall tell him what he needs to know and nothing else," she had said. "I shall not blacken your name, or make you in his eyes any less than you have already made yourself."

He shuddered at the remembered bitterness in her voice, the hurt in her eyes. Tears of self-pity welled. He sat up with a convulsive movement, crushing out the half-smoked cigarette and sat, holding his head in his hands, feeling that his brain was in two halves, each pitted against the other. On the one side Olivia as she used to be: calm and warm, patient and forgiving, now alas, hurt beyond healing. On the other Zoë: laughing, living carelessly for the moment, swift and abrasive, passionate and needy.

I'm going mad, he thought, I really am going crazy.

Suddenly, shrill and shocking, making his heart race, the 'phone rang and he snatched at it, fumbling in his haste and almost dropping the receiver.

'Giles ... I'm sorry. I know it's late and I shouldn't ring you there, but I was worried ... you didn't call on Friday.'

'Zoë, ah, Zoë...' He closed his eyes.

'Don't be cross, Giles.' She gabbled on, he could hear her quick, nervous breathing. 'We got in last night and there was no message and I had to call you ... I couldn't let another night go by. I thought if anyone asked you could say it was the hospital calling you.'

'Zoë, don't rush. It's all right, I'm quite alone.' He sat back, cradling the 'phone and smiling stupidly, aware that he had drunk too much and was really in no condition to deal with midnight calls from anyone, especially Zoë, but flooded with gratitude and a tipsy joy that she cared enough to be worried about him. 'It's all right. I'm all right. I had to wait until I was sure...'

'Sure about what? Giles...' Her voice was uneasy now. 'Are you drunk?'

'Yes, very drunk...and alone.'

'Alone?'

'Yes.' He was suddenly apprehensive. 'Olivia has left. She went on Thursday.'

There was a silence; when she spoke her voice was unsteady. 'You've always said that she wouldn't leave you.'

'I was wrong.'

'Giles, I don't like this...' He pictured her quick frown, brows pulled down, her mouth set. 'I never wanted...'

He interrupted her. 'Look, it's happened; I can't explain now because I'm tired, and I'm pissed. Darling, I'll be with you tomorrow about five. We'll talk then.'

'We're rehearsing all afternoon.'

'Afterwards then, say six o'clock at the Crown.'

'OK, goodnight, then. Go and sleep it off!'

Unwilling to let her go he asked quickly, 'What are you going to do now?'

She chuckled, 'Learn my lines!'

'At past midnight?'

'That's my best time.'

'Not when I'm with you...' he waited a moment, 'I love you.' He waited another moment. 'What about you?'

'Probably, if I could figure out what is love.'

'That's good enough for me ... sleep well.'

He sat looking at the telephone, all tiredness vanished. Clearly and precisely he knew that he was in love: deeply and passionately in love. For the first time in his life he wanted to protect and cherish, care for and honour.

What have I been doing all these years, that I could have taken Olivia's love without being able to give the same in return? He was appalled and disgusted. *I loved her, still do; I adored her compliance, her surrender after quarrels – and I moulded her into what I needed to make my life easy and comfortable. Knowing that whatever I did, or however badly I behaved, no matter how bitter the words between us, I had only to say I was sorry and take her to bed. I took everything she gave me and did so little in return...*

He went into the kitchen, drinking copiously glass after glass of water before going up to the bathroom. There, sickened by his dry, nicotine-smelling skin and foul-tasting mouth he threw more water over his face and head and brushed his teeth.

He stood, rubbing a towel over his hair, watching himself in the mirror. 'Well.' He spoke aloud to his reflection. 'After twenty years of lying to and cheating on one woman, what makes you think you can do better the second time around ... even if she'll have you?'

Because she is all I'll ever want, all I could ever need. Because she is my love and lights up my life as no one else ever has, or ever will...

*   *   *

Zoë put down the phone and turned to Martin, who leaned against the wall and stared back with sombre eyes.

'His wife has gone. He'll be here tomorrow.' She put her hands up to her face. 'Oh, Marty ... I can't believe it. What am I going to do?'

'You just wait until Jimmy finds out.' He wetted a finger and drew it slowly across his neck. 'He'll fucking slit your throat, ducky. He really and truly will.'

She gave him a dark and menacing look.

'You tell him, *ducky*, and so help me, I'll really truly manage to slit yours first!'

11

When she came into the hotel lounge Giles stood, catching both her hands in his and drawing her down onto the couch beside him. For a moment he let his eyes rove hungrily over her. It was almost a month since they'd met. With the tour going as far as Coventry, there had been no way that he could find the time in a busy schedule of work to drive such distances.

'You look different.' He stared intently at her face. 'What is it? Not your hair … no, that's just as raggedy as ever!' He smiled and touched her sleek jagged crop. 'It's your eyes. They are bigger … how's that? What have you been doing?'

'Going to bed on my own and getting all my beauty sleep.' Zoë was teasing him, folding her hands demurely in her lap whilst sending the familiar invitation from the tawny eyes.

He caught his breath. 'Not yet!'

She raised her brows and chuckled. 'What else then after almost four weeks?'

'A walk; somewhere public where you can't divert me from talking – but not too public: around the Cathedral will do, there won't be many people about at this hour.'

They passed through the gate into the green Close, making their way against the tide of visitors thronging the narrow streets in search of teashops and fish bars, pausing for a moment to look at the Cathedral, riding the close mown lawns like a great galleon on an emerald sea. Zoë tilted her head, gazing up at the spire. 'I don't know about familiarity breeding contempt,' she observed, 'but that never ceases to amaze me … that spire; how did they *get* it there? I'd love to climb right to the top but I wouldn't dare. I get vertigo halfway up a stepladder. In fact I feel dizzy just thinking about it…' she gave her sudden throaty laugh. 'I'd better not play Juliet. I'd probably fall off the balcony.'

He smiled and took her hand. 'Perhaps we'll just sit on this bench, then you can admire it from a safe distance.'

'Are you really all right?' She leaned into him as they sat on the sun-warmed bench. 'You sounded awful on the 'phone, all fed-up and growling.'

He put his arm around her. 'Just too much booze and far too many cigarettes; tell me, how was the tour?'

'Pretty good; tiring though because of learning new lines every evening but Marty helped; he's a good mate.' She looked at him slant-eyed. 'But I want to hear about what's been happening to you.'

'Oh, nothing went right after Olivia came back from Devon. We had a terrible few weeks.' He put his head back, closing his eyes. 'The final crunch came when Sylvia Wynn-Davies – remember her? – shot her mouth off about us in Olivia's hearing.'

She sat silent listening to his bald recital of the facts, her acute ear hearing the undertones of bitterness and guilt. She studied the lines about his mouth, the dusting of bright silver showing at his temples, the thinning spot in the blonde curls and wondered if she really did love him, or if it was just the need for someone to need her that made her want to kiss him, and hug him and make him smile.

She was silent when he finished, looking down at the grass beneath her feet, wriggling her bare toes in her sandals. After a moment or two he put his fingers against her chin and turned her face towards his.

'Zoë, I'm going to ask you something, and I want you to think carefully before you give me an answer. Will you do that?'

She was uneasy. 'Yeah, OK. What is it?'

'Do you really want me in your life? Want me more than I have been so far?'

She gave a little jump of fright. 'Jesus wept, what a question to spring on me!' she hesitated, pondering his words. 'What do you mean, "In your life"?' She giggled nervously. 'In a minute you'll go down on one knee and propose.'

He grinned faintly. 'I wouldn't entirely rule that out.'

'Well I think you should.' Her tone was suddenly flat. 'What about your wife? I thought she mattered so much. Make up your mind … do you care about her or don't you, because I'm beginning to get bloody confused.'

'Oh, yes, I care. But she's made it plain that she's leaving me to clear up the mess, one way or another.'

'I told you I didn't want this; that I don't like it.'

Now she was angry and he'd never get a straight answer. He felt despair beginning to well in him as she continued passionately, 'I never wanted to know about her or talk about her. You said she wouldn't go … I thought that we could just have our times, our special times, with nobody getting hurt.'

'Darling, for how long did you think we could do that?'

'For as long as I needed you and you needed me.'

'But I need you all the time.'

'You can't. You still love her.' Her face was set. 'I can hear it every time you say her name.'

'Then why am I sitting here with you?'

He tried to take her hand again, but she pulled away.

'You tell *me*,' she said, and he blanched, hearing in those three words an echo of Olivia's despairing cry over the years: "Why do you do it Giles? You tell me..."

He leaned forward, putting his face in his hands. He said, 'Oh, *Christ*, not you, too!' and she gazed down on his bowed head with sudden shocked understanding.

'You bastard,' she said softly, 'you've done it before, haven't you? That's why you were so sure she wouldn't go; that she'd forgive you ... again.' She gave a short, mirthless bark of laughter. 'And I thought I was the first.'

'No, you're not, but for her you were the final insult.' Wearily he sat up again and faced her. 'There have been other women, right from the beginning. Don't ask me why, because I don't know. But just understand this: there has never been anyone for whom I would have risked so much, no other woman who could have made me turn my back on my wife and son and soon, no doubt, my home. You have got so far under my skin that I'm prepared to do anything in order to be with you, and under any terms you care to make, because I think you may be the only woman to whom I could ever be faithful.' He stopped, spreading his hands and hunching his shoulders; he gave a wry, defeated smile. 'Congratulations, Zoë darling. Here I am: the catcher catched!'

For a few moments she sat very still, then her mouth went down at the corners. 'But you still love Olivia.' It was a statement.

'Yes, and I expect I always will. But there is love, and in love; and in love is what I am with you.'

*   *   *

She slept in his arms, but he lay sleepless, staring into the darkness of the hotel room.

I want a home with you, he thought, not these impersonal rooms with their Bernard Buffy prints on magnolia painted walls, and plastic wipe-clean floors. I want old wood and rugs and flowers. *You want,* his own voice mocked him, *what you had with Olivia – what you are about to walk out on...*

He moved restlessly and Zoë gave a little hiccup of sound and tightened her arm across his chest.

'Yell is going to kill me for this!' had been her last words, as she lay limp and drowsy with spent passion. He had kissed the crown of her head and she had curled into him, and sighed, then fallen asleep.

He closed his eyes but still sleep eluded him. He had taken this enormous, terrifying step into the unknown, with no plans and no ideas for the future. In four weeks she would be gone again; James Yelland had his cast now for Othello; a minor but up-and-coming young lion of the London theatre would be playing the lead, holding Zoë, kissing her, caressing her.

'It's on stage, silly … it doesn't count!' She had laughed at his ill-concealed jealousy at her news, 'I'm just a humble Yelland babe and terribly honoured to play opposite him, so don't be cross.'

The sky was beginning to lighten. He could see the pattern of leaves from the tall lime outside their window moving over the blind. Hell, he was operating at nine. He'd have to go straight to the hospital and snatch an hour's rest first on his office couch … he moved his hand down the curve of her spine his hand caressing her buttocks. She stirred and murmured something into his shoulder. He asked. 'What did you say?' he put his other hand under her head and eased her mouth away from his shoulder, feeling the flutter of her laughter against his skin.

'That I think I love you.'

He kissed her eyes. 'I thought you might if I waited long enough.'

'Bastard,' she said equably. 'Go back to sleep.'

'I haven't *been* asleep!'

'Oh, well, in that case…' She pulled him closer, her hand sliding down between his legs and curling about him. 'You'd better stop talking, hadn't you and –'

'Not on your life.' Deftly removing her hand he sat and swung his feet to the floor. 'I have scalpels to sharpen and stitching to do. Only actors and vagabonds can sleep late.'

She sat hugging her knees, watching him when he returned naked and dripping from the shower, smiling as he towelled himself dry and started to dress. She said, 'I meant it, you know. Whatever love is, I think I have it.'

'Even for an old man like me?'

'Especially for an old man like you.'

He shrugged into his shirt and sat on the edge of the bed facing her, tying his tie. 'You have to promise me that if I'm jealous or too demanding, or if I hold you back from doing all that you need to do, then you will tell me and know that you have the right to go.'

She said, 'Yes, Giles,' and he smiled at her mock-solemn

expression.

'I'm not really being noble. I can say these things now, because I'm dressed and about to leave you, but darling, I've just trodden all over someone else's dreams and I couldn't bear to do the same to you.'

'I won't let you tread on mine.' She looked at him with a sudden, unnerving candour. 'How many other women have you had behind Olivia's back, Giles?'

'My God, what a thing to ask a man who's in a hurry,' he stood up, scooping his car keys and change from the bedside table into his pockets. 'Four she knew about; two, no, three, that she didn't.'

'And before you met her?'

'No use asking about what I might have done during drunken student parties and equally drunken Navy shore leaves; anyway, *they* don't count.'

She lay back with hands behind her head and gazed at the ceiling. 'You louse ... I've a damned good mind to make you meet my mother. She'd pray for you until your socks dropped off!'

He grinned. 'Is that the worst you can think of?'

'Don't be so cocky, you don't *know* my mother.'

'No darling, and if she's as bad as you say I don't want to.' He leaned across the bed, kissing her briefly. 'Go back to sleep. I'll see you tonight.'

*   *   *

He turned the car radio up. Edith Piaf was belting out '*Non, je ne regrette rien*', which suited his mood perfectly this morning. However, considerations other than that of being ecstatically happy with Zoë would soon require his undivided attention.

There must be a meeting soon between Olivia and himself; he hoped there wasn't going to be a tussle over Riversmead. If she wanted to remain there then that would be fine; if not, the sooner it was disposed of the better. In any case he must find a flat nearer the theatre, somewhere quiet and private, where he and Zoë could be alone together.

Yelland, he was sure, would be furious.

Giles was well aware now that Zoë had exceptional talent, that the director was almost fanatically determined that she should become a name in the theatre. To that end he liked her close at hand to coax, bully and rehearse until even he could find no fault. She never complained about the punishing schedule and when Giles tried to show her

126

how Yelland dominated and controlled her life, she looked at him as though he were speaking a language she didn't understand. 'But he does it for *me* … gives me so much time, so much help. I need that; need all I can get. Can't you see? I have to work at it because it has to be perfect. After all he gives me I can't give him less than that.'

But he didn't see, and was as uncomprehending of her as she of him. Although he knew in his heart how fatally easy it would be to repeat the mistakes he had made with Olivia and tried hard not to fall again into the same trap, he needed Zoë so desperately that he was quite unable to see Yelland for what he was – her mentor and teacher; only as a continuing obstacle in the way of the time that they could spend together.

To him Yelland was the Svengali-like figure who controlled Zoë's life and through her, Giles' own. It was a novel situation in which he found himself and his inability to shake off the director's influence was a constant irritant. As the weeks passed he became increasingly frustrated and frighteningly aware that he might not win against someone who held all the right cards.

12

Olivia left Lodscombe on a warm cloudless morning; she was dreading the visit to Riversmead and the meeting with Giles, but soon it would be time for Adam's summer vacation and although she was reluctant to make a decision over the house, the time had come to make up her mind where she and Adam should live. She had been a month now in Devon, but couldn't go on living indefinitely with her parents.

Margot tended still to treat her carefully, as though she were in the early stages of recovering from an illness, when quite often she was raging inside and needed someone uninvolved on whom she could vent her feelings. Her father, although protective of her, still retained what he imagined was a well-concealed fondness for Giles, which made it impossible for Olivia to confide all her own angry emotions of resentment and loss.

She'd begun to spend the greater part of each day, regardless of weather, ranging far along the coast, her newly sharpened eyes seeing the enchantment of sun wind and rain on the changing landscape. Crouched under overhanging rocks or in shallow caves for protection against wet and stormy skies, with seas roaring across the beaches to pound the rocky cliffs, she painted swiftly and with growing confidence. On blue, sun-washed mornings, full of the bright light that hurt the eyes, she filled her canvas with the white crescents of restless gulls swooping and soaring above seas that swelled over and around rocks now sun-kissed and innocent of menace.

When she folded her easel at the end of each day and allowed herself time to think, she had to admit that although Giles' absence meant freedom and peace of mind, not least from worrying about what he might be doing and with whom, she still missed him. Missed most of all his physical presence; the feel of him next to her when she awakened each morning. Once, she dreamed vividly that they were making love, a dream so powerful and intense that when she woke she could feel him still, his weight pressing her into the bed. Devastated, her body aching with desire, she had pulled on her clothes and walked along the beach until the treacherous longings died and her tormented body was again at peace.

But as the days passed she became aware that, although she continued to crave him physically, she was also increasingly content with her new life. She had a future now; freedom to paint, to go where she wished, when she wished, and a peaceful welcoming house to which she could return each day.

In her more honest and introspective moments she had to concede that some measure of her contentment might be to do with a certain sexy, bearded gentleman left behind in Somerset. It was just as well, she thought, that more than an hour's drive separated her from Tom Doyle. In her present state of enforced celibacy it would need very little encouragement from him to let all her years of fidelity to one man fly right out of the window.

*   *   *

Now this morning as she drove towards her meeting with Giles, every mile that passed took her back into the harsher world, where un-palatable facts must be faced and far-reaching decisions made.

Traffic was light and she realised when she was almost halfway that she would be ridiculously early for their lunchtime meeting, and on an impulse left the duel carriageway to follow the leafy lane to Pendene. Not of course, she told herself virtuously, to see Tom Doyle, who may well be making plans to spend the summer half-way across the world with his occasional lover; just that it would be restful to sit in that cool, welcoming house and chat to Bartholomew Kenny.

*   *   *

Barty greeted her without so much as a flicker of surprise, only a smile that sent his face into a thousand welcoming lines of greeting.

'I thought you might come soon. I'll put the kettle on.'

Olivia pushed her hands through her hair and raised her eyebrows. 'Don't tell me a heavenly messenger warned you of my approach!'

He clicked his tongue. 'Tom's laid bare my shameful secret, has he?'

'Umm, you might have told me. Vicars are a bit out of my ken.'

He grunted. 'Some of 'em have been out of *my* ken from time to time,' he admitted. Swinging the kettle onto the range and reaching for a tin he began ladling coffee into a pot. 'When I came back from the war, you can't imagine how parochial and out of touch, smug even, some of my brothers in Christ seemed,' he shrugged, 'but I pottered on alongside them as one does, and made the best of it.'

'Why? Why not do something else?'

He gave a hoot of laughter. 'What else could a fifty plus ex-army

129

padre do for a living? Besides, I didn't say I'd lost faith in God, just that I couldn't see eye to eye with some of his chosen.' He gave her a mildly sarcastic look. 'I can't think you've driven all this way to indulge in theological discussion with *me*.'

'No, I came for the coffee … and I have to meet Giles later; at our house.'

'I see.' He made the coffee then placed the jug and three mugs on the table. 'Tom will be back shortly, in case you were wondering,' he said, then watched the blush rise to her cheeks. He sat down opposite her and folding his arms on the table tactfully changed the subject. 'Now then, tell me all you've been doing these past weeks.'

'Painting, dodging a huge Irishman by the name of Flynn; being utterly selfish in avoiding too much time spent with my parents, who are the very best but not what I need right now.' She kept her eyes lowered, picking absently at a loose thread on her sleeve. 'Worrying about Adam comes to mind as one of my less self-absorbed occupations, and wondering what to do about his, and my long-term future, another.'

'That's a lot of thinking time.'

'I need it. Taking stock of my life to date it seems in retrospect that I've been pretty complacent, if not downright stupid about a lot of things.'… *and still wanting to be fucked by Giles is one of them,* she added silently, *but I'm not telling* you *about that!*

Barty gave another of his characteristic grunts; picking up the coffeepot he began to fill two mugs. That accomplished he slid one of them and the cream jug towards her.

'Would the huge Irishman be Ambrose Flynn, the sculptor?'

'Yes.' She was surprised. 'Now how would you know about him?'

'Oh, he's quite famous, isn't he? And Tom mentioned something about him living your way.' He looked vague. 'I seem to remember he was a bit bothered at one time about Flynn's son and yours.'

She stared at him and he had the grace to blush. 'All right, we do discuss school matters here … Tom's only human, you know.'

'Is he now…' she eyed him over the rim of her cup. *The cagey blighter* she thought, *he didn't let on to me that he was bothered.*

'Well good morning, Mrs Ryder.'

She hadn't heard the door open and turned swiftly, to find the object of her thoughts standing in the doorway, apparently unembarrassed by the fact that he wore only a pair of grey linen shorts embellished with broad arrows and Stolen from H.M. Prison stamped across the front. In one hand he held a towel and a pair of wet bathing trunks, in the other the cat. His tall body was very brown and muscular; deprived of his formal suit he looked younger than at their last meeting. The thick brown hair was longer than she remembered, the dark eyes livelier, his teeth showing in a smile between the clipped moustache and close beard. All he needed, she thought inconsequentially, to pop right up there in a frame on the walls of the National Gallery: *Portrait of a Spanish Grandee,* was a lot of black leather, a Byronic shirt and thigh boots. With an effort she reassembled her flying thoughts. 'We were just talking about you.'

'Really?' he looked over his shoulder as he settled the cat on a cushion. 'I would have foregone my swim had I known *you* had arrived for coffee.'

'I hadn't realised – you must be quite close to the beaches here.'

'Two minutes down the footpath that runs alongside the church-yard. It's a bonus at this time of the year; whenever I have a couple of free periods I can swim, have a coffee with the guv'nor and be back in school in under the two hours.'

He sat down next to her and she felt a quick tingle at his closeness, wondering fleetingly if he was that brown all over. He gave his controlled, close-mouthed smile. 'You must let me show you the beach sometime; it is very popular and gets busy in the summer, but further on around the point there is a little cove, which no one but me ever seems interested in swimming the hundred or so yards to reach.'

Olivia had a sudden very precise vision of swimming to a deserted cove with Tom Doyle and hastily buried her nose in her cup.

'Biscuit?'

Barty was opening a battered tin with what seemed an unnecessary degree of concentration and she came to with a start. 'No. Thank you. I must go now.' She hoped her voice sounded normal. 'It's a long drive and I want some time alone at the house before ... before Giles arrives.'

Doyle stood, slinging the towel about his neck. 'I'll see you to your car.'

She saw Barty's head come up; caught the look he gave his son-in-law, and knew that he was a target for the old man's disapproval. Bland and apparently oblivious of the look, Doyle took her arm as she said goodbye to the old man, then steered her out of the room.

He held open the car door and bending down as she slid into her seat, gave another of those smiles. '*If* you were returning this way tomorrow, and *if* you would care to have lunch with me, I know a very quiet and pleasant place just outside Stargates, where we could talk if you wish; failing that, you could always weep into a large gin and pretend I wasn't there!'

She smiled mistily, feeling perilously close to sudden, illogical tears. 'I should like that very much. Thank you.'

'About twelve-thirty, then; I'll wait at the main road ... just follow the ramshackle old red Singer that will be lurking under the signpost,' he stepped back, 'until then, Mrs Ryder.'

'Until then, Mr Doyle.'

Now for God's sake, Olivia gritted her teeth. *Don't drive your bloody car up a tree just because you are looking as long as possible at that "fine brown frame" now getting smaller and smaller in your rear-view mirror.*

*   *   *

By the time she arrived at Riversmead her mood had changed again. Walking in the quiet summer garden, bending to trail her fingers in the slow moving stream, she felt empty of all but sadness and resignation and not a little guilt. Later, as she moved from room to room of the silent house, that feeling intensified until even her quiet footsteps seemed a reproach.

She had dreaded this coming back to the place where she and Giles had shared so much, laughed and made love; been happy and content. But hadn't most of that been a cruel illusion? Who knows, she thought, maybe I was fooling myself all along. Just how happy had they been, how content? Had even their lovemaking been all she thought? Had all the tender words, the promises made, been worth all the tears and humiliation, the anger and the pain?

She stood in the doorway of their bedroom, facing at last that for the woman she had been it might indeed have been worthwhile, but now she was strong enough to turn her back and put the old life, and her dependence on Giles, behind her. Inevitably there would be regrets and she would perhaps never be completely free from loving him, but the future beckoned with all its promise of new beginnings. Now she felt ready, or almost ready, to make the final break.

It wasn't what life handed you that mattered, she had read somewhere, but how you dealt with it. Well, the good times and the bad were in the past. It was now up to Giles with his Zoë, and herself with...? God knows, she thought, with a rueful grin; shying away from the remembrance of Doyle's smile, probably no one; but all of them – Giles, Zoë, Adam, herself, must somehow make something worthwhile out of what was left.

There was the sound of the front door opening, then the familiar footsteps. He called: 'Olivia?' and for one moment her heart swooped. Then she closed the bedroom door and crossed to lean over the banister rail. 'Hello, Giles,' she said, and turning, began to walk down the stairs as steadily as though this were just another ordinary day.

*   *   *

'You look wonderful.' He handed her a glass of wine; then held the bottle to the light and grinned. 'I see Sandra has been consoling herself again!'

He was like a little boy. Not sure if he was to be chastised or forgiven. On impulse she put the glass down and moved to kiss his cheek. 'She always did; but not for much longer.'

He smiled uncertainly and took her hand. 'If you want to be angry, it's all right.'

'I don't; I've done all that. I've cried and cursed you and wished I'd done something frightful to you – to her, preferably both of you – but today, back in this house, all that finished.'

Still holding her hand he gazed around. 'Yes, I can understand that; it's empty: nothing left but just the memories and these four walls.' His questioning eyes sought hers. 'But it was pretty good from time to time, wasn't it?'

'It was, very good.' She put her head on one side and regarded him soberly. 'Oh, Giles, I hate to admit it, but you really do seem to have changed for the better. That's the first time you've not tried to talk me round.'

'It's the first time I knew it wouldn't be any use!' He slipped his arm in hers. 'Come along. Let's walk in the garden and begin to sort out what's to be done. Then we can go and put Carol out of her misery. Once or twice over the past weeks, I've felt she was about to die of the effort not to ask what was going on!'

*   *   *

It was late evening and they were both tired; glad to sit in the garden of the Bear and Ragged Staff Inn and eat a leisurely meal.

'If you are planning to live in Salisbury I don't know what to do, Olivia was perplexed, her brow creased in a frown. 'Whether to come back to Riversmead, or find somewhere to rent, or buy, in or around Lodscombe; I don't *want* to live here in Hampshire again but Adam must have a proper base and I can't stay at Captains Cottage much longer. They are both sweet, but one should never try to live again

133

with parents once one has flown the nest.'

'Perhaps we should ask Adam what he wants.'

Olivia sighed. 'Yes, perhaps we should. He'll be gone soon enough and he ought to have the choice of where to spend the next few years ... here, or in Devon, regardless of what either you or I want right now.'

Giles put a hand over hers. 'At least your parents understand. I haven't dared to tell father – God knows what will happen when I do. You can bet he'll come over, if only to tell me what a fool I am, as if I didn't know that for myself.'

'I hope he'll still visit at Christmas and see Adam ... and me.' Olivia said. 'I know he can be difficult, but I've never seen why you can't be together for a day at a time without quarrelling.' She gave him a gently satirical smile. 'Come down to Lodscombe with him and I'll sort both of you out!'

'I believe you would. How you have changed.'

'Have I?' She was thoughtful for a moment. 'Yes, I suppose I have. But wait until you see Adam again; I think you'll find he's a bit different too.'

'He 'phoned me last week to ask in a round about way if I'd go down this Saturday. I said yes ... if that's all right with you?' He looked at her questioningly.

'Of course: you don't need to ask, and it might be an opportunity to sound him out about where he wants to live. But be honest with him, won't you? Don't be afraid to let him know how you feel. It's important that he understands.'

He shrugged hopelessly. 'How can he understand? He's still a boy.'

'You'd be surprised,' she gave an enigmatic smile. 'Try him.'

'OK,' he hesitated, 'I've wanted to ask you something all day...'

'Ask away.'

'Have you; I mean, are you...Oh, hell...is there anyone else? You seem so, well, so damned *sure* of yourself...' He stopped and pulled his mouth down. 'Sorry. I'm being nosy.'

'Yes, you are and no, there isn't ... unless you count Ambrose Flynn, who leaps out of the woodwork from time to time and wants to sculpt my head. At least, that's his story. Oh, and of course, there *is* Barty!'

She laughed out loud so that a couple at a nearby table glanced across and smiled at them, as though sharing a secret. She smiled back then lowered her voice. 'You know what we look like?'

'Yes,' he answered promptly, 'like a couple having a clandestine meeting with a view to adultery later.'

'Well, you should know,' she sobered suddenly, giving him a look that was both concerned and inquiring. 'Is it really all right with you?'

'Yes. I don't deserve it nor do I know if it will last,' he grimaced. 'I rather think I'm hoist with my own petard, but I'm doing my best not to mind that the theatre is a powerful, and somewhat daunting, rival for her affections –' He stopped suddenly to stare fixedly at her from beneath lowered brows, 'and just who the hell,' he asked, 'is Barty?'

Olivia smiled. 'Only the vicar,' she said.

*   *   *

They sat on as dusk gathered and the garden gradually emptied of customers. After the landlord had pointedly removed the last of their empty glasses and returned sighing to the bar, they exchanged conspiratorial, tipsy grins.

'Well, what do we do, pissed as we are?' asked Giles. The little silver slivers in his eyes sparkled in the light from the windows as he took her hand, rubbing it against his cheek. 'As neither of us appears fit to drive, I suppose we must stay the night. The question is: what do we play – singles or doubles? Do we go out with a bang or a whimper?'

She watched him dreamily, feeling sexy and thinking of Tom Doyle, naked apart from those shorts. Half closing her eyes she could see the teeth showing in the dark beard, the compelling eyes; the warm brown body close to hers...

But Giles was still holding her hand and they had drunk far more than was good for two people who knew each other so well and were trying to part without hurt. She brought her mind back to the present and focusing carefully on his face said, 'If there isn't a bed-side lamp you get out and turn off the light...'

*   *   *

In an ocean of frilled cretonne and lace she held his thin, sinewy body to her as they made leisurely, familiar, companionable love: moving together in a remembered effortless rhythm before the upward spiral to a gentle climax, the slow, voluptuously lazy descent, the cooling of their bodies and the drift into sleep, her head on his shoulder, his hand on her thigh.

135

She smiled sleepily into the darkness. *Well, we may each have lacked the old* férocité *of the tiger but, drunk or sober,* féroce *or not, it was a lovely way to say goodbye to it all...*

*   *   *

'Hardly a bang!' he observed next morning as they kissed before parting.

She patted his cheek, 'But rather more than a whimper!'

They climbed into their separate cars and drove away in opposite directions.

'And I don't,' she said aloud, putting her foot down and heading for the dual carriageway, 'have one moment's regret or guilt about that, you *louche*, predictable, sexy old bastard.'

13

Olivia drew her car in alongside Doyle's then switched off the engine and waited as he left the little red Singer and came round to open her door.

'Welcome to the Talbot, Mrs Ryder.'

She stepped out, working hard at keeping her leaping pleasure from showing on her face.

He held open the door to the inn, watching as she moved before him into the quiet bar, her dark blue skirt whirling about her legs as she walked; her shoulders endearingly fragile-looking under the thin lawn of her blouse. She was definitely glowing this morning, Tom thought, and wondered was that because of this meeting, or from seeing that idiot of a husband? Had they perhaps said goodbye as he and Jayne always did, with a night of unbridled lust?

Barty had delivered another blunt warning after his last meeting with Olivia. 'I don't know what you think you are playing at; dammit, Tom, the woman is still married, and you said yourself she was out of bounds.'

To which broadside Tom had replied with some asperity that he wasn't, for God's sake, proposing to seduce her, and that if she was the woman he imagined her to be, she would now get on with her life unencumbered by her husband or anyone else, especially a middle-aged schoolmaster.

Taking in her heightened colour but composed expression as she sat opposite him now, apparently giving all her attention to the menu, he was damned if he could tell whether or not he had guessed it right.

She laid down the menu and smiled. 'As it's so warm and there's no chance of a swim today to cool off, I think I'll go for the cold game pie and salad.'

'Splendid. I'll join you,' he looked at her enquiringly. 'Would you like some wine?'

She shook her head, wincing slightly. 'I don't think that would be a good idea!'

'Oh!' He laughed. 'Not even the hair of the dog?'

'Not even that, I can still feel the bite. Just plain tonic will be fine.'

He gave their order at the bar and collecting a beer for himself, sat down again, for once unsure of how to proceed.

She raised her brows. 'It's all right. You can ask questions.'

'In that case how did it go, and where are you heading?'

'It went very well, much better than I expected. In a few weeks this patient will probably be reasonably recovered ... he's a good surgeon!' She made a rueful face. 'As for where I'm heading, I wish I knew. We have agreed, even although it seems a little unfair on him, to let Adam decide if he and I move back into Riversmead when Giles leaves, or if we stay in Devonshire.'

He ran his finger round the rim of his glass. 'That wasn't exactly what I meant when I asked where you were heading.'

'I know it wasn't, but the answer's the same: I honestly don't know. Right now I can't see beyond the moment.'

'In that case, would it be in order for us to meet like this from time to time?'

For a moment she almost panicked. She most certainly didn't want any kind of commitment with this man, attractive as he was, although perhaps in a few months, when she might be rather more sure of herself...

She played for time, propping her chin on one hand, trying to assess what lay behind the teasing, mildly questioning look in those dark eyes. Eventually she asked, 'Are you flirting with me as a prelude to seduction, or is that a genuine proposition?'

He answered her gravely. 'Madam, I am a pillar of moral rectitude and never flirt with married women; come to think of it, you are the only married woman I have ever propositioned – and yes, it is genuine.'

'Then I would like to meet occasionally ... like this,' she shook her head, laughing, 'but you'll take a lot of getting used to. I've spent three years knowing you only at a great distance as the august and rather intimidating Papa Doyle, who keeps my son in order. I'm not terribly sure about the Tom Doyle who wanders around in his shorts and invites me out to lunch.'

'I assure you he is one and the same person.' He watched her with a smile. 'And I am sure you know that I would do nothing to damage the very good relationship I have with Adam. Although I do find you very attractive, and in other circumstances would like to spend a great deal of time with you, I do have a commitment elsewhere; so all I have to offer are a few hours in which to meet and eat and talk. And of course, if you need more ... a shoulder to weep on or a father confessor, there is always the guv'nor. More than once he has fulfilled both of those roles for me, so I can recommend him. But...' here he gave a wry smile, 'he will be alarmingly honest and impartial, always.

So be warned!'

She was silent and thoughtful. The seconds ticked by as she considered his words. Eventually, she gave a little lift of her shoulders and held out her hand. 'I think I can manage on those terms and Barty will do fine for those more intimate discussions.'

He took her hand, 'It's a pact then … for now.'

'Yes; for now.'

He continued to hold her hand, giving her a half-smile. 'Adam has always been something of a favourite with me. Feeling as he must be right now, I'd hate to upset him in any way.'

'I didn't think schoolmasters were supposed to have favourites.'

'They're not.'

She raised an eyebrow. 'Then, why?'

'I noticed when he first came that he has the same birthday as my son.' He looked away suddenly. 'Illogical of course, hopelessly sentimental and unrealistic, but I like to think Jamie might have grown up to be as straight and as just plain nice, as your son. He certainly had as gentle and charming a mother.'

Impulsively, she asked, 'It must hurt so much … to see all those other boys. Why did you choose to do what you do?'

'Oh.' He released her hand. 'Probably *because* of all those other boys; although sometimes I'd quite cheerfully lock them all in a box and throw away the key!'

'Were you always a teacher, or something quite different before the war?'

'Something very different, like my father I was a professional soldier … often a mistake to follow in father's footsteps.' He shrugged. 'It was all right to begin with. I met Rosalind at a university dance; we married ridiculously young while I was still at Sandhurst. After several very good years, enjoying the social life and the travelling, Jamie was born and we settled down, as families do. Then almost immediately after that came the war.' He stared out of the window behind her. 'Afterwards I was in Malaya, then Palestine, then India. I grew sick of it all eventually, chucked it in and went back to University and, well … ended up at Chiltens. I think Barty fiddled it a bit … he used to be the school Chaplain and was on the Board of Governors. I like what I do and I like being near enough to keep an eye on him.'

She grimaced. 'All of those awkward hormone-ridden adolescents; I don't think I could bear it.'

'It has its compensations – and its drawbacks,' he admitted. 'When one teaches English Literature to half-grown young men;

laying before them all the beauty and the sensuality of Shakespeare and Byron and Donne, one has to make allowances for occasional outbreaks of sneaking down over the fields to the beaches with girls, and secreting erotic literature under the mattresses.' She smiled at the sudden twinkle in his eye as he spread his hands. 'I'm supposed to beat them for that, but I have a strong suspicion that some may find that almost as stimulating, so I give them fearsome dressings-down and gate them instead!'

'Adam told me that when you really rip into him he wants to die.'

He laughed outright. 'I suppose it's always nice to know one's efforts bear fruit.'

She gave him a considering look. 'I shouldn't let any of them ever see you in those shorts though, or all hope of keeping them in check would fly right out of the window.'

'I shall keep my shorts for your eyes alone … that is, if you would sometime agree to swim the necessary hundred yards with me to my private beach.'

Enchanted, he watched a dimple appear either side of her mouth before she gazed at him with the same guileless ingenuousness as her son. 'That would be very nice Mr Doyle.'

He grinned and stroked his beard with a thumb and forefinger.

'Call me Tom,' he said.

*   *   *

One evening, a week after the meeting with Olivia, Adam appeared in Doyle's study. 'My dad's coming down on Saturday,' he explained, making a determined effort to appear nonchalant and at ease, 'So if I could have a pass, sir?'

Doyle laid down his pen. Resting his arms on his desk he regarded him intently. 'You'll have a lot to talk about.'

'Ye-es; I'm not sure how long he has, but he won't be here until lunchtime…is it all right if I'm late back?'

'How late?'

'How late can I be?' Adam didn't really know what he'd do with any extra time, but there was no harm in trying.

'Don't push your luck,' Doyle picked up his pen, 'Eight-thirty then, and no later.'

'Thanks, sir.'

He watched him as far as the door. 'Adam.'

'Sir?'

'Even at eight-thirty … or later, if you need to talk over your day,

140

all you have to do is turn that handle you now have in your hand and come in.'

'OK.'

'That's all.' He began writing again, adding, without lifting his head, 'and don't use that vulgar slang to *me*!'

'Sorry, sir,' Adam closed the door quietly, then did a quick shuffle down the corridor. Playing air guitar and shaking his head he warbled: 'He loves me, yeah, yeah, yeah; he loves me, yeah, yeah, yeah, he loves me yeah, yeah, *yeah*!' then as no one was in sight, slid down the banisters then fled to the boot room to kick the wall.

Oh, *God,* Saturday!

What would they talk about? He wished he hadn't asked Dad to come; had even half-hoped if he left it late enough, that Doyle would refuse him permission. Now he'd *have* to see him. It was going to be just too bloody stinking, embarrassing *awful*!

14

At the sight of his son's carefully controlled smile, Giles' heart sank. He pushed open the car door, hoping his own expression was less strained.

'Hop in. I'm sorry I'm a bit late … where shall we eat?'

Again there was the brittle smile, the over-polite speech. 'Macy's, that's if you don't mind driving right across town. They do great puds.'

'Macy's it is.' He drove out of the gates then stopped the car a short distance down the lane. Adam looked at him questioningly.

'You can relax.' Giles turned sideways in his seat to look him full in the face. 'I haven't grown horns and a forked tail!'

Adam swallowed hard. 'I'm sorry … I don't know what to say.'

'Try 'Hello, dad.''

There was a faint tremor of Adam's lower lip. 'Hello, dad, I've missed you.'

'I've missed you too.' Giles squeezed his shoulder briefly, then released him and turned back to re-start the car, 'Now we've got that over you can direct me to Macy's great puds.'

'Sure, into the town and over the bridge…' Adam sat up very straight, holding his eyes wide because they were a bit damp; ashamed at having slipped back, even for a moment, into being a blasted kid. It was going to be an absolute bugger trying to keep everything under control; worse than sex, even…

*   *   *

An hour later Adam pushed his plate away with a satisfied sigh.

'Thanks dad. That was a super meal.'

'It's a long time since you and I have been out together, I'm sorry about that.' Giles moved his own plate to one side. 'I'll try to do better in future. I've been unfair and neglected you these last few months.'

'It's all right. It can't be helped. I know you've been … busy.' There was a slight, sarcastic edge to his voice

Giles noted the tone and the new air of faintly arrogant self-assurance that had become increasingly apparent, once the awkwardness of their first meeting was over. He decided on the direct approach.

142

'Adam, we need to talk, but not here,' he signalled to the waiter for the bill, 'we'll drive around and find somewhere quiet.'

'We could go down to the beach at Pendene.' suggested Adam, 'it's out of bounds really, but that doesn't count if you're with a parent. Drive back towards the school and turn right at the signpost.'

'Why is it out of bounds?'

Adam grinned with some of the old friendly ease.

'Too many places to go for a snog!'

Giles raised an eyebrow.

'Just the place to talk then, so long as we're not likely to fall over any of your peers disporting themselves behind the rocks...'

They left the car at the top of the slipway and walked down onto the long curved beach. It was low tide and the sand was soft under their feet, the only objects in sight a few small boats that lay beside their mooring buoys, waiting for the tide to return and float them again. They sat down under the lee of one of these and Adam loosened his tie, giving Giles another questioning look.

'You go first, dad.'

Giles grinned. 'OK. Suppose we start off with the holidays. Where would you most like to spend them?'

'That depends. I suppose there's no chance of you and mum being together again?'

'That's unlikely.'

'In that case I'd rather spend them in Devon.'

'Actually it isn't only the holidays. In a couple of weeks I'm moving out of Riversmead. Your mother and I felt you should have your say about where you wanted to live permanently, there or in Lodscombe; not just staying with gran and pops there, but in a new house.'

Adam was silent for a few moments. He could feel the slow burn of anger begin and answered without looking at him. 'I don't see the point in returning to Hampshire ... it won't *be* home at Riversmead if you're not there. But I'll have to talk to Mum ... see what she wants.'

He stood up abruptly, slouching back against the keel of the boat and staring out towards the horizon. 'I don't know why you're in such a blasted rush to muck everything up. If you've really split up, then I suppose I'll just have to wait until you can get down in term time to see me, because I won't be passed from one to the other in the holidays, like Bill Marshall is.'

Giles gave a faint, exasperated sigh. 'This isn't easy for any of us. It will take time...'

'Yeah? Well just let me know where I'm supposed to be when I'm not here.' Adam aimed a kick at a large pebble and sent it flying towards the water. 'Why did you do it?' he demanded savagely, 'How could you mess everything up for all of us? How could you stop loving Mum?'

'I haven't; I shall love her as long as I live.'

'That's crap! You don't have to lie to me. I'm not stupid. I saw you with that girl in Salisbury; shit, you could be her grandfather!'

Giles was shocked into silence for a moment, then sighed. 'Hardly that; but I'm sorry. I don't expect you to understand. You have to feel it to know it.'

'I know it all right.' His face was burning and terrible, crude words trembled on his tongue. He thought of Kate. He'd never, ever do such a thing; hurt her as *he'd* hurt mum.

'Right.' Giles was suddenly brisk. 'Let's get this all out in the open, shall we? Olivia tells me I should be honest with you. You won't like what I'm going to say, and you probably won't understand.'

'Try me. I'm really quite intelligent.'

God give me patience... Giles wiped a hand over his face and tried again.

'Adam, your mother and I can't ever just dismiss all that time we had together, and in a way, a very important way, we will always love each other. But for twenty years I've been a lousy, unfaithful husband. In all that time she's known it and either forgiven me, or turned a blind eye. Now she's no longer prepared to do either of those things and I no longer want her to. Believe me it *is* possible to love more than one woman, because that's what's happened to me. I wanted it both ways, but that just won't do and like it or not, what I feel for Zoë now is stronger than the bond between your mother and me … I'm sorry if I've put it crudely but that's the way it is.'

Abruptly Adam turned his back completely, standing as though carved out of granite.

Oh, God, Giles thought. I've blown it. Of all the stupid, bloody things… Impulsively, he touched his shoulder. 'Adam…'

Adam turned, his eyes very clear and cold.

'Well,' he said with exquisite politeness. 'You *are* the one who said it was crude and I couldn't agree with you more. If that's how it's been for twenty years, then Mum's better off without you, isn't she? We both are.'

'Nothing is ever that black and white.' Giles struggled between a desire to either hold him very close or hit him. He knew he was being rather expertly wound-up, but thought in the circumstances it wasn't so very surprising. 'No doubt you think you've every right to say those things, but don't bank on me keeping my temper indefinitely, will you? If I didn't care so very much about both of you, I could have just walked out and saved myself the insults.'

Adam shrugged. 'If we're going to go on with all this, d'you mind if we walk, because right now it's all a bit too much like being up on the carpet before Doyle.'

Giles answered him through gritted teeth. 'If you could stop being such a Bolshie little sod for five minutes, perhaps we can get down to actually *talking*.'

'All right, but hell, dad,' Adam gave him a sideways look compounded of admiration and exasperation, 'you have got one *hell* of a ruddy nerve haven't you?'

*　　　*　　　*

'You will be pleased to know that our son wishes to live in Devon, although he informs me that he needs to speak to you first and see what *you* want.' Giles' voice on the 'phone was weary and faintly disgruntled.

'I thought he might.' Olivia controlled the urge to laugh. Too unkind, she thought; by the sound of it Adam had been a bad boy. 'You sound exhausted.'

'I am.' She could hear from his voice that his mouth would be grim and his eyes a very sharp blue. 'How I kept my hands off him from time to time I'll never know, but we parted friends. More or less.'

'I did try to warn you, and you shouldn't complain; he's just like you.'

'No he bloody well is not! I could have been talking to *you* … all those nicely phrased, breathtakingly polite insults.'

'Don't exaggerate. Anyway, thank you for ringing. I'll give him a call myself tomorrow.'

'Well, well…' Olivia met her parents' mutually inquiring gaze as she put down the 'phone. 'It seems that you and I may find we are not such distant neighbours in the near future, but I shall have to speak very firmly to that son of ours when I ring him tomorrow. I think he's been giving Giles a very hard time!'

*　　　*　　　*

Barty glanced out of the window for the third time then reached for

145

the 'phone.

'Is one of yours missing?' he inquired, when the familiar voice of his son-in-law answered, 'I only ask because there's one wearing your house colours been sat on the big field gate, the one opposite, since he was dropped off from a black Jaguar almost an hour ago.'

'Tall? Skinny? Blonde? Looks like an adolescent Bubbles?'

'That's the one.'

'Hmm … it's almost seven thirty. Ring me again if he hasn't moved in fifteen minutes, will you?'

'I could have a word with him. He may not realise how late it is.'

'He knows. He's just deciding what to do.'

Barty was curious. 'Been rubbing up your crystal ball, have you?'

Doyle chuckled. 'I don't need one. It's Adam Ryder. He's probably had a bad day. He'll work through it. I just don't want to have him sent up to me for turning up after lock-up, that's all.'

At eight twenty-nine there was a knock at his door. Doyle glanced at his watch and put down his book.

'Come in.'

Adam came slowly into the room. 'Just thought I'd report back, sir.'

Doyle assessed the tired face and weary eyes and pointed to the chair opposite his own. 'Sit down. That was a lengthy visit.'

'Not really.' Adam hunched forward on the edge of the chair. 'I stretched it a bit … to have a think.'

'Did you reach any conclusions?'

'Several.' His face darkened. 'But they might not be the right ones…'

'Right for whom?'

'Everyone.'

'It can't be done.' Doyle returned baldly. 'Just concentrate on how you are going to manage what's happened to *you*. The first rule of survival is to get your own head clear and know where you're going, *before* you start playing God to anyone else.'

Adam scowled. 'I wouldn't mind being God for a day; I'd make 'em all think twice!'

Doyle gave him a satirical look.

'You could make *them*, whoever they are, think until kingdom come and still get nowhere yourself. How many times have I told you when you're at the nets not to fluff a really fast ball?'

'Dozens, but I don't see – '

'Yes you do. You know damned well it happens when you let yourself get rattled and lose your head. Now you have to think clearly, keep your temper and not fluff every time somebody rocks you back with a fast ball, because in the next few months there'll be a lot of those coming your way. Use the brain God gave you to work out whether to block it, play it clean or swipe it into the pavilion and lay out friend and foe alike.'

Adam gave him a sly, sideways look. 'That's always supposing that *they* play by the same rules.'

'Don't get smart with me!' Doyle leaned forward. 'Look, in a couple of years from now you'll be setting out on your own, heading for whatever it is that *you* want to do. When you go, just don't leave any mess behind that was of your making.' He paused, adding with brutal candour, 'You are not the only one in this place who has had that particular kick in the teeth. I could name a dozen others who've all survived, in one way or another, so if you're thinking of getting a nice big chip on your shoulder, forget it, or I'll give you hell until it's gone.'

Adam sighed and looked pathetic. 'Speaking of chips, sir ... I haven't had any supper.'

'Then you shouldn't have spent so long sitting on Mr Gara's gate watching his corn grow, should you?'

Adam was baffled. 'How did you know that?'

'I have an all-seeing eye. Go and ask the housekeeper for some bread – you do invariably have a packet of butter on the sill outside your window, do you not?'

'Er, yes.'

'And an illicit toaster in your study cupboard?'

'Ye-es.'

'Then use it, and in future hide it somewhere more original than in a box marked 'Balls,' or I may be forced to confiscate it.' Doyle leaned to retrieve his book. 'Goodnight, and don't forget to 'phone your mother tomorrow.'

Adam closed the door to Doyle's study behind him then leaned back against it for a moment. He swore quietly under his breath. *All-seeing eye, my arse ... and I told Bill that was a daft place to put the toaster. Shit, a bloke can't even fart without Papa knowing about it.*

PART 2

What is love? 'tis not hereafter;
Present mirth hath present laughter;
What's to come is still unsure:
In delay there lies no plenty;
Then come kiss me sweet and twenty,
Youth's a stuff will not endure.

W.S.

15

'How was it?' Giles wrapped his arms around Zoë. She felt light and fragile as a bird as she leaned against him; putting her hands behind his head and kissing his mouth hungrily, before pulling back to give her inimitable grin.

'Tiring, exhilarating, almost a sell-out ... bloody *marvellous*, in fact. But I've missed you like hell ... why didn't you come when we were at the King's? Too busy cutting people up, I suppose. You really are a rat!'

'All men are rats, ducky.' Martin dropped her case on the platform beside her. 'And if you think I'm carrying that any further ... my hands are bruised, positively bruised, with hauling your luggage on and off trains. Giles, do your manly bit and take over.'

'I'll do that all right.' Giles' eyes didn't leave her face; Zoë smiled and pressed herself closer into him.

'Go away Marty, there's a dear.'

'Don't worry, I'm off; here commeth Jimmy, and I can't stand the sight of blood...'

He melted away into the crowd as Yelland came towards them, walking with his light feline step.

'Hello, Giles. I guessed we'd see *you* here.' His voice was smooth and urbane. 'Has she told you how splendid she was?'

'I don't need her to tell me. I saw her here before the tour began,' Giles answered, keeping his arms about her. Zoë shot a mischievous glance at the director then laid her head on Giles' shoulder. 'Peace at last,' she said provocatively.

Yelland's nostrils flared slightly. 'Just see that it stays that way. Line rehearsal nine a.m. Wednesday. Three days rest is quite enough. Giles oblige me by seeing she is in bed before ten-thirty.'

'Oh, most certainly and there won't be any bar-room noises to disturb her now.'

Yelland cocked his head sharply. 'Excuse me?'

'Didn't she tell you?' Giles looked reprovingly at Zoë and clicked his tongue. 'You bad girl!' He turned to Yelland. 'I have a flat in Tylers Row, so you won't now need to worry that she's spending her time with low companions in that sordid bar.'

'How nice.' Yelland's voice was icily polite. He turned to Zoë. 'Nine o'clock Wednesday ... and off the book.'

She put out her tongue at his retreating back. 'Bitch!' she said and hugged Giles' arm. 'Take me to the love-nest, lover...'

*   *   *

She ran through the flat, opening doors and cupboards, touching, exclaiming aloud.

'Wow! So much space ... Giles, you *do* have rich friends.' She burst back into the sitting room, where he stood smiling foolishly at her delight. Throwing her arms around him she pulled him across the room. 'Oh, God, but I've missed you. Come to bed. Oh, please come to this simply wonderful, absolutely *enormous* bed!' She stopped on the threshold of the bedroom and held him tightly again, clutching desperately at his shoulders as though he was saving her from drowning.

He responded swiftly to her fiercely whispered: 'I love you. I do love you', although his hands shook so that he fumbled the buttons of his shirt. Impatient, she pulled it over his head then raised her arms for him to do the same with her dress. Taking his hands she drew him towards the bed.

Then began for them the hunger that could not be denied; when the only reality was their two bodies locked together, each driving the other towards the ultimate carnal pleasure. Their coupling now, after the weeks apart, was short and hard but very sweet. Afterwards, she kissed him with light gossamer kisses, murmuring: 'You are my Benedict, my Oberon, my Orsino...'

'And you are everything I ever hoped for but never thought to find.'

She gave her sudden throaty laugh. 'But not for want of looking!'

'I'm sorry about all the others.' Holding her to him he rolled onto his back, so that her face still flushed from the intensity of their lovemaking, hung above his. 'So will you live with me here or must I "Make me a willow cabin at your gate, and call upon your soul within the house?"'

She kissed his mouth then sat, straddling his hips. 'No chance of that; I'll "Come live with you and be your love..."'

'Jimmy will be furious.'

'I know, but I can deal with him.' She flung her arms wide in a theatrical gesture. 'I can deal with the whole world now!'

'Now and for how long?' He caught her to him, crushing her so that she could hardly breathe, repeating, 'for how long, Zoë. For how long?'

152

She melted into him again, holding his face between her hands her tawny eyes huge and luminous in the delicate triangle of her face.

'How long? What does time matter? We don't set limits, we don't talk about time, there is you and me, and here and now. That is all that matters.'

*   *   *

Olivia and Carol worked methodically, crating china and glass, stacking books, sorting records. It was a daunting task; all the minutiae of twenty years shared living to be sifted through and apportioned…

'I just hope I'll be able to fit all this into the new place,' Olivia paused to wipe a dusty hand across her forehead, 'although I'm only taking the minimum of furniture … I don't know how much of this Giles will want. His place is furnished at the moment but I think he's arranging to have it cleared.'

Carol scowled. 'He's lucky he can call the tune. Mike Robinson's made it easy for him, hasn't he? Renting him his flat whilst he takes a sabbatical in Dubai *and* possibly staying on for a year or so after his time is up; but that's Giles all over, isn't it? He'll always fall on his feet.'

'True. Mike doesn't care what he does with what is in the flat already, so long as he pays for storage.' Olivia held up a vase covered with hideous green and yellow writhing dragons. 'I wonder who gave us this monstrosity.' She put it on one side. 'I think Giles might like that, don't you?'

'He'll be ecstatic!'

Olivia glanced at her watch. 'I'll have to leave this for now, I think. I have an appointment and I must get cleaned up. I'll be back in time for that night-cap Chris promised me … eleven at the latest.'

'Is it a man?' Carol asked as they locked up and began to walk down the lane. 'It must be because you are positively glowing. I expected you to be all depressed and in floods of tears.'

'Rubbish … I've been over that stage for weeks. I haven't time to be depressed. Since Adam began his vacation and we decided on the old Lodge at Pels Point it's been one mad rush.' Olivia adroitly sidestepped the first part of her friend's observations. She knew better than to let her know she was meeting Tom. 'Adam's delighted of course, as he's only a short bike ride from Kate and Liam.'

'How are you getting on with Ambrose Flynn?' Carol was easily diverted. 'Anything happening there?'

'I've agreed to sit for him if that's what you mean … just my head and no lower!' Olivia smiled mischievously. 'He pretends he's a real old *roué*, you know, although I'm beginning to think he's nothing of the sort, just a great big cuddly lion. But I do like him. He makes me laugh.'

'I thought you said he was dangerous.'

'He still might be, given the right circumstances, but he's been a tremendous help. It was thanks to him that the Dartmouth gallery agreed to take six of my pictures and they've already sold four.'

On the drive down to the meeting with Doyle, she pondered on the difference between this evening's companion and Ambrose Flynn. With his big frame and his big laugh, Ambrose in the right mood could be an endearing and attractive man, someone with whom she could feel free and unfettered and able to enjoy a kind of acerbic verbal fencing new to her.

Tom Doyle on the other hand, was a subtle and restrained charmer, in fact, a more emotionally mature and less obviously predatory version of Giles – and equally attractive.

She wondered why he'd suggested dinner in Ringwood tonight. She felt a stab of guilt over these enjoyable but frustrating meetings, overlaid as they were now with an outrageous desire to ask him outright if he wouldn't like to spend a night doing all manner of delightful and shame-making thing to her person.

Twenty years of regular and mainly satisfying sex with Giles had left her ill prepared for sleeping alone. She simply hadn't thought just how difficult it would be to live without a man in her life. She knew she wasn't in love with Tom Doyle, that his attraction for her was physical and lay in his good-humoured, faintly aloof, very obvious masculinity. She also knew that he was attracted to her, but although they had met several times since her last visit to Pendene, so far he'd offered nothing more physical than an occasional touching of hands or a light arm about her shoulders.

He hadn't yet made a single move to kiss her.

She had a sneaking suspicion that Barty might have something to do with his son-in-law's reticence. Either that, or Jayne Foreman was rather more of a force to be reckoned with than she'd at first thought … Olivia wondered just what constituted reasonably frequent sex with Tom's number one occasional lover? Once every six months? Every six weeks? A mad, passionate week-long orgy between war zones?

She sighed and turned off the approach road to begin threading her way through the town traffic to the White Hart.

*   *   *

Giles lay back in his chair feeling at peace with the world. A late sun slanted through the long windows, lighting the large comfortably furnished room and sparking off the decanter on the small table by his side. He thought he might leave the flat just as it was and store his own furniture for now. The muted colours and Art Deco style furnishings suited the lofty, spacious rooms.

In the weeks they had lived together, Zoë had flowered like some exotic plant in this quiet place, and he basked now in her exuberant, unrestrained affection and the pleasure she showed in being with him.

She kept home and theatre apart, learning her lines while he was at the hospital then hurrying back after the last curtain to his waiting arms. She didn't talk shop anymore, nor mention Yelland other than in passing, making it clear, he thought complacently, that he, Giles, was now the most important person in her life.

He was delighted and life appeared perfect. That she could feel anything but equally content and carefree simply never occurred to him.

He stretched luxuriously. Only an hour and a half before the show ended. They'd go out to a late supper tonight, he decided. She'd been unusually quiet and edgy for several days and he thought she was finding the summer run of Candida exhausting; grumbling frequently that a heat-wave was no time for struggling into the unbearably hot and tightly corseted costumes.

The ringing of the doorbell interrupted his thoughts and he left his chair reluctantly, padding down the stairs to the street door in stocking feet.

Yelland stood on the pavement, managing as always to appear suave and at ease. He wore narrow dark slacks and an immaculate white shirt, the cuffs unbuttoned and turned back. Bloody poseur, though Giles, taking in the Byronic stance as his visitor leaned one negligent hand on the wall and sketched a brief greeting with the other.

'Giles, dear boy. So glad you are in. I *do* need to have words with you.'

'I thought you'd be at the theatre.' Giles stood on one side and motioned in his unwelcome caller. 'Straight up the stairs, first left off the hallway.'

'No actor needs a director breathing down his neck once the play goes up.' Yelland climbed the stairs with an easy grace. 'I generally spend my time in the bar and turn the loudspeaker on to eavesdrop, but tonight I thought: "I'll go and see Giles…"'

He stepped into the sitting room looking around and nodding his approval as he sank into a chair. '*Très chic*!'

'Why are you here?' Giles asked bluntly. 'I'm not normally on your list of people you just can't wait to see.'

'Very true.' The slanted eyes in the thin face were suddenly shrewd and hard. 'But I thought I should call and tell you how much I disapprove of what you are doing to my *enfant terrible*, who now appears to be in grave danger of losing her fire and all her wonderful, enchanting, maddening and irreplaceable *awfulness*.'

'She has grown up.' Giles was tight-lipped. 'It was bound to happen sometime.'

The other shook his head slowly.

'Oh, Giles, Giles, you are a philistine whose knowledge of what makes an actress of Zoë's calibre tick is non-existent. She is *not* grown up. She is trying to be the woman she thinks you want her to be.' His lip curled. 'She imagines she has found love with a capital 'L' and maybe she has, although I suspect she has only found the illusion of it in the security you give her. She has never known either before, and it may destroy her when she discovers the difference and disillusion inevitably sets in.'

'I don't agree. You bully her and treat her as a child. I love her and treat her as a woman, and in return she loves and trusts me.' Giles struggled to keep his temper. 'Surely maturity is important to an actress? She can't be an irresponsible child forever.'

'How can I make you understand...' Yelland sighed and ran a hand through his long waving hair. 'Look; in a year or two she may be ready to settle down a little, not much, but a little. Perhaps really love and be able to live comfortably in both worlds. I can't believe you are incapable of seeing how in so many ways she is young for her age, and, despite all that you provide, massively insecure. That youth and that insecurity make her vulnerable, and it is that vulnerability which comes across to an audience and helps make her the artist she is.'

He stood suddenly, taking a few paces across the room and throwing his arms wide. 'My God Giles, I wish I could make you see it. You don't understand the theatre; you tolerate it because you have to, but for her it is her life; her reason for being. She gives everything to it ... night after night. When she is on that stage she weaves a magic that makes the people sitting comfortably in their seats feel as though an enchanted wind is lifting the hairs on the back of their necks. She can make them laugh, then in a second turn around and break their hearts.' He stopped for a moment, staring at Giles with sombre eyes. 'She must keep that special, indefinable something as she matures. One day she will be a truly great actress, but while you stifle her with your kind of love and the trappings of security she will lose it … and that is a crime.'

'I've done nothing to stifle her as an actress; I don't intrude on that part of her life.' Giles felt the first twinge of unease at Yelland's passionate and devastatingly accurate assessment of his beloved. He added almost defiantly, 'It is *she* who keeps that quite separate from our life together.'

'Precisely, and you should be asking yourself, *Why*? Already she is trying to live two lives and not managing terribly well. You may not see it because loving her blinds you to everything else.' He looked with something like compassion at Giles' suddenly averted face. 'But I fear that quite soon you may indeed destroy her as an artist.'

'You are quite wrong. I should never do that.'

'You will. I don't know how, but in a few short months you have tied her to you very successfully. During the past few days she has been faced with the need to make a far-reaching, and for her, bound to you as she now is, a most painful decision.' He paused a few moments, letting a silence hang between them before continuing quietly in a level, measured tone, 'On the thirtieth of October I take the Company on tour to Canada and the United States. We shall be away until early spring. For Zoë it will be enormously important. It could open many doors and secure her future. I have to tell you that she has already intimated to Martin that she may not go.'

'She knows about this?' Giles was caught completely off guard.

'Yes, for the past week.' Relentlessly, Yelland's gaze held his and he asked softly: 'She hasn't told you, has she?'

'No.' Giles stood and walked to the window to stare down onto the trees beneath. 'She's said nothing.'

'Then Giles, that should tell you everything; she is at war with herself, torn between you and all you give her, and her future in the theatre. That future which will always be a battle and an agony and the thing that makes her a creature apart from any other woman you have known, or ever will know. She has genius within her and can *be* that great actress she already gives such promise of becoming. Will you deny her that?'

'Don't put it all on me!' Giles turned on him angrily. 'You may be right, I don't know. I don't pretend to understand what motivates you people. *Carpe diem* appears to be your motto, and to hell with anything else in life; with peace of mind, with comfort and yes, with the despised security.'

Yelland was unruffled by the attack.

'Security is for when we have achieved what we set out to achieve; an actor seldom ever does that. In time perhaps security for Zoë may be a husband, possibly children, certainly a home base, but those things will always come after the theatre, and are all very much in the future. Can you give her what she needs, when she needs it? Can you really wait, perhaps for years, for her to come to you; will you take a back seat for the rest of your life so that she can shine?' He gave a brief, sad smile. 'I think not, unless your love for her is of a strength and depth beyond my understanding.'

'Perhaps it is.'

Giles was shaken by the director's undoubted sincerity. Had he been guilty of treating Zoë as he once had Olivia? He remembered her answer, spoken with such confidence when he'd said he couldn't bear to walk over her dreams: "I won't let you…"

'Give me some time,' he spread his hands helplessly. 'I can't take this all in now. I need to think.' He felt physically ill at the thought of losing her for so many months. He couldn't, he really couldn't face being without her now. What would he do with himself; how could he fill his time away from the hospital?

Now he had burnt his boats. There would be no retreat to a safe familiar Riversmead. No comforting, compliant wife waiting to soothe him, nothing but this temporary home and that theatre around the corner, empty of Zoë as his heart and arms.

What was it Olivia had said that night, aeons, it seemed ago? Something about needing a woman's undivided attention, good sex, home comforts and someone to double as a mother and provide them…?

The memory of her words mocked him. At my age I haven't the moral strength to be able to contemplate even a few weeks, he thought bitterly, let alone months without Zoë here to be all those things for me…

Yelland watched the inward battle apparent on Giles' face, wondering what he would do, this undoubtedly kind and loving, but blindingly selfish man? Would he let Zoë fly free, clear of guilt, or bind her tighter to him?

'I'll go.' Yelland turned suddenly towards the door. 'The ball is in your court, Giles. I've said my piece. Now I leave it up to you.'

Giles looked at the clock as the door closed behind his visitor.

Had it really only taken such a short time to tear his world apart?

He reached out a hand for the telephone and dialled Olivia's number, listening as it rang and rang, eventually pressing the receiver back down on the rest.

Just as well. He shouldn't do that, not even just to hear a friendly voice and seek a little balm for his soul.

He had forfeited that right a long time ago.

16

As Olivia drove into the hotel car park, Doyle stepped from his own car and came across to her with his long, unhurried stride.

'Perfect timing as usual.' He held her door open. 'Did you get all your packing done?'

'Almost, tomorrow morning should see it finished then I'll leave straight away. Carol will see the removal men in and out.'

'You must be tired.' Her pulse quickened as he took her arm. 'I've booked a table … if we go straight in we can drink there rather than at the bar.'

How about a room for the night? She queried silently, as she walked beside him, and almost blushed. All those years of marital fidelity, she thought, and right now I'd be quite happy to behave like Giles at his adulterous worst. Have I really got to the point when I can scarcely wait to be taken to bed by my son's schoolmaster? She sat down and smiled at her companion across the table. *Yes, I bloody well have!*

He returned her smile. 'In case you might wish to rush back to your friends, I thought if we ate early there would be time to talk.'

'They are not expecting me back until late. We could walk down by the river and see if the herons are still there. I know they take the fish and all the anglers hate them, but they are so beautiful and majestic.' She chatted on, making conversation until the waiter had taken their order, poured their wine and departed.

'Why are we meeting here?' she asked curiously. 'Why not wait until I returned tomorrow, when I could break my journey at Pendene? You've done a very long drive just for dinner and a talk. You won't be home before midnight.'

'I won't anyway. I'm staying the night here.'

'Oh.' There *was* something decidedly odd about this meeting. She frowned. 'Is anything wrong?'

'I don't think so,' he put his glass down and leaned his forearms on the table 'although there might be any minute now … there is something I need to tell you.'

She felt a nervous giggle burst like a bubble inside her chest. She asked, 'You've got the sack? Barty's been unfrocked? I know – my house has burned down!' She lowered her eyes, adding a silent: *You're going to Calcutta tomorrow, to fuck Jayne Foreman's brains*

160

out between riots!

For one awful moment she thought she'd actually uttered the last out loud. She looked up and met his amused gaze.

'None of those things – nor, I'm quite sure, the one you just thought off and didn't say!' He took her hand. 'Nothing has actually changed since we made our pact. I am still more or less committed; you are still finding your feet in your suddenly changed world, but tonight, when we have finished this meal, drunk this excellent wine, and leaving aside any visits to observe the herons, I should very much like to take you to bed … if that's something you'd also enjoy, of course.'

'Oh, God!' She jumped then hastily closed her open mouth.

He kept hold of her hand. 'Is that a Yes or a No?'

For a long minute she stared at him, seeing as if for the first time the thin, rather sardonic face, the denial of such a temperament in the unexpectedly lively eyes, the definitely wonderfully sensual mouth within the dark beard, and began to laugh. 'You've taken your time … I thought I was going to have to ask *you*!'

*   *   *

'Very nice!' He lifted her hair and kissed the nape of her neck. 'Who said it's never perfect the first time?'

His long, strong body was stretched along her back, his heart thudding cosily beneath her shoulder blades. She exhaled a slow sigh of deep content.

Now she knew. This was no breathtaking romance, no rapturous erotic blending of body and soul, but a wonderful, grown up giving and taking of pleasure, and a most joyful release. Without any need of words she knew there would be no demands made on either side. No promises sought; no plans to be made or argued over; no decisions to take.

I'm an occasional lover she thought delightedly, and gave a deep contented chuckle. You sexy old devil Tom Doyle. You can put my picture up alongside hers any day of the week!

He felt her laughter and turned her to face him again. 'I must say I can't think what you are sniggering about,' he propped himself on one elbow, his voice mild and conversational, 'I mark that at ninety-nine and three quarters out of a hundred … in red ink!'

She chuckled again. 'What happened to the other quarter?'

'That, Mrs Ryder, is what I'm going to deal with in a very short time indeed.'

'Not until I've called my friends and made my excuses you're not.'

He lay, tracing lazy patterns on her back with a long forefinger as she spoke to Chris, smiling, as the fearful lies issued from her lips.

'What are you going to do about your "sprained ankle" tomorrow morning?' Tom asked as she replaced the receiver. 'Shall I have to rush out and buy a bandage before we leave to make that terrible excuse look authentic?'

'I'm surprised you don't know that a sprained ankle is a female euphemism for having had sex,' she told him. 'I used it for the benefit of the very unworldly Chris, and the pleasure of having the very worldly Carol tying herself in knots trying to guess who sprained mine tonight!'

'Really?' His chest shook in a silent laugh. 'Perhaps you should tell her.'

'Not likely. It would be all over Hampshire in twenty-four hours. Thirty-six and it would have got as far as Chiltens and you'd be out of a job.'

'Possibly, but that's nothing to what the guv'nor would do to me.'

'I saw him warning you off weeks ago. He doesn't approve, does he?'

'No, but not on moral grounds.' Tom smiled. 'Barty's a realist, but he's rather protective of you … and you did need time. I hope I got it right. I've wanted you rather badly, you know. Life can get pretty lonely sometimes'

'Can't it just…' She leaned back against the pillows. 'Yes, you did get the timing right, it was very clever of you.' She stroked the curling dark hair on his chest. 'Tell me about Jayne Foreman. Does Barty approve of what you do with her?'

'How refreshingly straightforward you are,' he grinned and stretched out, crossing his arms behind his head. 'I don't think he actively disapproves. He'd like to see me married again, but doesn't think there's a hope in hell of Jayne and I ever making a go of it. He could be right, although I hope not. I think she may be weakening but when we went to bed in Rome three months ago, she still hadn't quite got the wanderlust out of her soul…' he sat up. 'What are you laughing about?'

'*You,*' she spluttered, 'honestly, I thought Ambrose Flynn was an old *roué,* but I reckon you leave him standing.'

He lay back again, pulling her down onto him, his beard tickling her neck, demanding, 'And what were *you* doing in Hampshire when you went to say goodbye to that Giles of yours?'

'None of your business!'

'Quite right,' he enfolded her purposefully in his long arms. 'So how d'you feel about spraining the other ankle – right now?'

*   *   *

'Ever since the war all the established, ordinary ways of living seem to have been turned upside down.' Margot observed a few days later, watching her grandson standing at the wheel beside Kate as the Morning Star left harbour. 'Before then one hardly ever heard of divorce. People just learned to live with their mistakes, then the children at least were spared having to cope with two separate households.'

Engrossed in tying a difficult fly Clive grunted. 'Not much help to the kids if they have to listen to parents rowing, is it?' He picked up his scissors to carefully trim a feather.

'I wonder if Ambrose Flynn's wife will ever come back – those children could do with some mothering, old as they are.' She shook her head sadly. 'Such a pity; that man needs a wife.'

He snorted again. 'I daresay the curvaceous Miriam keeps him warm at nights.'

'I wish you wouldn't keep on about that. She's a perfectly respectable girl and is getting married in September. He's been asking around the village this past week for someone to take her place.'

Clive sucked the end of a thread. 'He's not such a bad chap; quite likeable when you get to know him. All the same...' he adjusted his magnifying glass, bending again to his task, 'I wish Olivia wasn't spending so much time with him. She's missing Giles and you mark my words, before long she'll need some other man in her life; if it's likely to be Long John Silver's doppelganger up on the hill there, then God help us all!'

Margot turned away, keeping her own counsel. She hadn't missed the change in her daughter since her return from Hampshire, even if Clive had. Someone, or something, had put a sparkle back in her eye, and it most certainly hadn't been Ambrose Flynn.

*   *   *

'You said two hours. It's now two and a half and I've the most ghastly crick in my middle spine!'

'One more minute...' Ambrose worked rapidly, thumbing on clay, smoothing it, turning his head this way and that. He squinted at

163

Olivia. 'Just drop that blouse a bit lower next time, will you. I can't be expected to guess at your shoulders from that prudish bit of clavicle you're showing me.'

'I thought this was supposed to be just my head.'

'It was, but it seemed a pity to stop there. I'd rather do a bust.'

'I bet you would; I thought that was a damned great lump of clay just for one head!' Olivia was waspish. 'I could be painting today instead of sitting here with cramp, whilst you try to get my clothes off. If it rains tomorrow and I can't get along to Bracken cove, I shall do something very unpleasant to you.'

He was unmoved. 'If it rains you can come here again and drop your neckline some more.' He picked up a cloth and began to wipe his hands. 'OK.' He threw the cloth over his work before she had a chance to see. 'You can move now.'

'About time,' she stood, putting her hands to her back and flexing her spine, stopping when she saw him watching appreciatively. 'That's enough of that, Flynn!' She pulled her blouse up to her throat and buttoned it tightly. 'Session's over for today.'

He put a hand on her shoulder.

'Come into the kitchen and I'll feed you tea and biscuits.'

She sat at the table as he roved about the kitchen like a large amiable bear. She'd been wrong she thought, to call him a cuddly lion. Only his head was leonine, the rest of him was vaguely ursine … big and powerful and slightly menacing. But those large paws handled and sculpted clay with a delicate precision that was a joy to watch.

'I'd like to paint you,' she said impulsively and he looked around with a grin.

'Stick to the wild and rugged cliffs and sea – and buildings; they sell more easily.'

'No, I mean it. Could I come sometime when you've finished my head –'

'Bust,' he interrupted.

'Oh, all right then, bust. Seriously … I'd like to. You could get on with your work and I'll just sit in a corner and get on with mine.' She gave him a thin-lipped smile. 'I shan't expect you to pose with *your* shirt slipped winsomely down to your navel!'

He brought two mugs of strong tea to the table, handing her one and pushing the biscuit tin towards her.

'All right. As you're not the sort of female who'll disturb me by nattering nineteen to the dozen, you can paint whatever bit of me takes your fancy, clothed or naked.'

'It's a deal.'

They shook hands solemnly. As she went to draw hers away, he held it captive in his. 'In Ireland,' his long mouth curved into a smile, 'we men spit on our palms first when we make a deal, but when we make a deal with a colleen, we do it like this…' and he leaned forward and briefly kissed her mouth.

She sat quite still for a moment then let out a pent-up, hissing breath. He grinned unrepentantly and raised his eyebrows. 'Well?'

'Perfectly, thank you.' She reclaimed her hand and stood up, observing coolly: 'That's the second time in a fortnight that I've been kissed by a beard.'

His bellow of laughter followed her all the way to his gate.

*   *   *

She walked rapidly away from the studio, thinking she ought to be offended, but although unexpected and unasked for, it had been a very pleasant, inoffensive kiss. Brotherly, almost … She gave a vulgar little snigger. *Who am I kidding?* She jumped down onto the beach and almost collided with an astounded Liam.

'Oh, Lord … I'm sorry; did I wind you?' She caught at his arm as he staggered back against the cliff.

'It's OK,' he quickly recovered his habitual aplomb. Passing a hand over his hair and straightening to his full six foot he said rather distantly: 'I wasn't looking where I was going, either.'

'I thought you were out on the boat with the other two.'

'No, they've gone fishing just around the point.' He fell into step beside her as she started along the beach. 'I had some thinking to do, so I opted out.'

Surprised, Olivia took a sideways glance at him. Although she'd met him several times with Adam, he'd never offered more than a moderately civil greeting and a few conventional words. Now he was tramping alongside her, frowning into the middle distance and looking as though he might be settling into her company for the rest of the afternoon.

There was a long pause. She broke it to say, 'As I've been sitting for your father for the past couple of hours, I thought I could do with some exercise.'

'I know. I was coming in but I saw you there. I didn't like to interrupt.'

He was really quite pleasant Olivia thought, once that cocky God-Almighty expression was off his face.

'Sorry.' He flushed suddenly. 'Am I being rude? I'll clear off if you want to walk on your own.'

'No. I'm only going home and I never mind company. If you've nothing better to do, you're welcome to a cup of tea – or a beer if you prefer.'

'Thanks. A beer would be great.'

They walked on. Chatting intermittently about his boat and the proposed trip to France, he wasn't quite at ease; one minute engagingly boyish, the next assuming the almost comically affected pose of the superior young man. Once he forgot himself sufficiently to start skimming stones across the water then stopped abruptly, ramming his hands into his pockets and walking on with a return of his usual aloof and lordly air.

When they reached the Lodge he was silent at first, glancing around the pleasant, simply furnished, stone-walled kitchen; it was like some he'd seen in Ireland, he thought. Olivia's copper pans were hung on one wall, a vase on the tall pine dresser was filled with garden flowers and the stone flagged floor was partially covered by a woven grass mat. He sat at the square elm wood table, taking all this in while she fetched two glasses and a bottle of ale from the pantry.

'It's OK here. Nice and peaceful.' He watched her pour the beer and push a glass across the table. 'Thanks.'

'I can't quite figure why it's called The Lodge. Tucked away in this little piece of woodland, there is no house anywhere near it might have served.' Olivia sat down, smiling across the table at him. 'If you'd like to stay until Adam gets back you can have tea with us.'

'I ought really to get back.' He fingered the glass. 'Had a row with the old man this morning so I've kept clear all day.' His eyes flickered briefly towards the dresser behind her. 'I left my ciggies behind and I didn't have the cash to buy any…'

She leaned back and taking the pack of Kensitas from the shelf passed them to him. 'I think there's a couple there. I hardly ever smoke now.'

'You don't mind if I do?'

She shrugged. 'It's a bad habit, but you're eighteen, aren't you? I can hardly smack your hand and send you home; if you want to wreck your lungs that's your problem.'

'Thanks.' He lit one quickly with matches he took from his pocket then gave a sudden, disarming grin. Put a beard around *that*, she thought, and you're your father to the life…

She propped her chin on her hand. 'Had you finished all your thinking, or did I interrupt it?' she asked.

'No. It wouldn't have done much good anyway.' He looked

uncomfortable. 'I've finished at Chiltens now you see, and I missed University this year … I didn't want to go anyway. Now dad's on my back to get a job; that's what we had the row about.' He drank some of the beer then sat rubbing a finger on the glass, the frown back in place. 'There's no one to talk to down here. All I get is my father telling me what I should do.'

'You're talking to me.'

'Yeah,' he grinned. 'But then *you're* not going to start telling me what I should do, are you?'

'No, but I might ask you what you want to do.'

'That's easy.' He took a long pull at his beer. 'Design and build boats. Nothing else, just that.'

'Why don't you then?'

He shrugged. 'Boatyards are closing all along this coast. I've been tramping around these past few vacs trying to get taken on somewhere, but no luck. People with loads of money, who can faff about in ruddy great yachts, don't seem to be rushing to buy them with Made in England stamped on their keels!'

She laughed at his sarcasm.

'So where do they buy their ruddy great yachts?'

'Australia – the USA; that's where the money is now,' he was suddenly wistful. 'I know I could do it if I could just get the training; you know, design and build them, and one day maybe even race.'

'Well you'd better start thinking about how to find a boat yard somewhere other than Devon, hadn't you?'

'Oh,' he gave her a bright, confident look. 'Don't worry; I'll manage somehow, even if I have to walk all around England to find one.'

*   *   *

'Come on.' Adam pulled Kate up the last few feet of cliff. 'We'll be home in a couple of minutes. Mum will be out painting and won't be back until late, she never is, so we can have some time in the house alone. I'll walk back with you to Lodscombe later and pick up my bike.'

Kate stood breathless at the top, rubbing at the streaks of red earth on her shirt. 'Hell, Adam. Why can't you walk up the steps like every-one else?'

'It's quicker this way.' He manoeuvred her towards the shelter of some trees. 'How about another kiss?'

She laced her arms about his neck. 'All right. Anyone would think

167

we hadn't been doing this, on and off, all afternoon!'

'Well we shan't get much chance next week, with Liam watching us all the way to France and back … umm! More!' He pulled her closer. With a bit of luck, he thought, he could persuade her onto the big couch with him when they got home. The bunks on the Star were bloody cramped…

'That's all!' She pushed him away and started up the narrow path. 'Come on, what I want right now is some tea and toast.'

Breathless from the climb, laughing and with arms about each other, they walked into the cottage then, at the sight of Liam with his elbows on the kitchen table, sprang apart like startled fauns.

Olivia, turned around from taking cutlery from a drawer, first registering the new arrivals' unmistakable intimacy and sudden confusion, then Liam's knowing grin as he tipped back on his chair demanding, 'What have you done with the boat … and where's all the fish?'

Adam's flush showed dark under his tan, 'She's tied up at Morgan's jetty of course,' he growled, 'and we didn't catch any fish.'

Liam grinned again. Olivia laid the cutlery down carefully before reaching for the plates. She repressed an exasperated sigh; Liam suddenly becoming human and sharing his problems with her she could handle, but sex rearing its ugly head in the shape of his sister and Adam was something else. I should have seen it coming, she thought crossly, Giles would have.

Aloud she said, 'I've persuaded Liam to stay for tea. While we eat you can all talk over plans for the French trip, then I shall be quite sure I know what's going on, shan't I?' and she gave her son a look pregnant with meaning.

Oh, shit, Adam's shoulders drooped. How come, he questioned silently as he began to help Kate lay the table, that mum was onto *him* so quick when dad had managed to get away with it for so long?

*　　　*　　　*

He cycled back slowly from Lodscombe, put his bike in the shed and turned reluctantly indoors. For a few moments Olivia observed him in silence as he stood slumped against the doorframe to the sitting room, and he gazed moodily back at her.

'The trip to France sounds fun,' she said eventually.

'Yes.'

'So long as you are careful … you will be careful, won't you, Adam?'

168

'Yes. You don't have to wrap it up. I know what you mean, but it isn't like you might think.'

She patted the cushion beside her on the couch. 'Come and tell me what you think I might be thinking!' she invited, and at her smile he sat, feeling a certain relief that she wasn't about to fly off the handle straight away.

'Probably that it's serious. It isn't; we only kiss a bit and all that...'

'And all what?'

'Well, *you* know,' embarrassed, he looked at his feet. 'I *am* sixteen now, mum. I'm not stupid and I know what I'm doing. So does Kate.'

'Oh, darling, you don't have to be stupid to get carried away while you're doing 'all that', whether you're sixteen or sixty!'

She wanted desperately to hug him as she had when he was little. Now he was slipping away from her and she didn't want to say, or do, the wrong thing. *Oh, Giles*, she mourned silently, *without you to lend a hand, how am I to deal with this young man and all the problems he'll have to face? I've never been a boy; how can I know what he feels or wants?*

'It really is all right.' He was gazing at her earnestly. 'Kate wouldn't let me, anyway.' He coloured when he realised that implied that he'd already tried. 'Liam's all right, isn't he?' he asked hurriedly. 'I thought you didn't like him at first.'

'I felt he was cocky and too sure of himself. But yes, after talking to him today I think that underneath all that he's probably a nice chap. It's just a pity he and his father don't get on.'

'Kate says it's because they blame each other for their mother going off.' Adam went a slightly deeper shade of pink. He couldn't possibly tell her about Liam finding the naked farmer and his mother on the bed. 'It's all a bit complicated and nobody talks about it; not like us.'

'Are you missing dad?' she asked gently. 'You can do more than speak to him on the 'phone each week you know. You could go up and stay.'

'Yeah. When we get back from France I might – but won't *she* be there? You know ... thing ... Zoë.'

'Probably. How much would you mind?'

'I dunno.' He frowned. 'It'd be a bit weird, wouldn't it?'

'At first, but one can get used to all kinds of things, given time.'

'I suppose so. I'll maybe ask next time I talk to him.' He smiled at her uncertainly. 'I don't miss him all that much: just sometimes. You know, when I want to talk and he isn't here.'

'I know. I feel that way from time to time.'

'I suppose he couldn't come here? Just for a few days, you know. Would you mind that?'

'You could ask. I wouldn't mind but he might feel a bit awkward.'

'OK,' he stood up. 'I think I'll go up and look over my list of stuff I need to take to France,' he paused at the door for a moment, swinging on the latch, 'it's difficult, about girls...' he hesitated, 'dad said they should come with an instruction book!'

Olivia laughed. 'I daresay Kate thinks she could do with one of those, headed: How to say "No" and mean it!'

Fleetingly, she thought of Tom Doyle and his warm brown body covering hers. 'Don't be in too much of a hurry to find all the answers,' she advised. 'Most of them are worth waiting for – so wait!'

17

Giles waited until he had given their order and the waiter had left their table, before asking the hundred and fifty thousand dollar question.

'Zoë, why didn't you tell me the company was doing an overseas tour?'

She took her roll and began breaking it into little pieces.

'Who told you? Jimmy, I suppose,' she swore and he winced.

'Must you use that word?'

She looked at him with narrowed eyes. 'Don't be such a stuffed shirt. I can't be twin-set and pearls all the time.'

In spite of his disapproval, he smiled. 'Somehow I've never seen you as that.'

She continued to stare at him. 'That's how I feel sometimes.'

'But not when you're using that gutter language…'

'I haven't noticed *you* winning medals for restraint. You can leave me in the shade when you start.'

'Perhaps I can, but that's usually only when I'm having a row with someone; even then I seldom go *that* far.'

'OK then, let your hair down and have a row with me here in this nice, middle-class restaurant. Bring a little excitement into your life.' Viciously, she jabbed her fork into the cloth.

'Darling,' Giles leaned across the table to take the fork from her hand. 'Don't wreck the tablecloth, and don't try to pick a quarrel with me because I asked you a question you don't want to answer.'

'You've only brought it up in here because you hope I won't cause a scene. When did Jimmy tell you?' she demanded angrily.

'About ten days ago. So why didn't you tell me yourself? I've been waiting.'

'There was no need,' she avoided his eyes, 'because I'm not going. I told Jimmy so tonight.'

'May one know why?'

'No. One may not.'

For a moment he watched her fingers crumbling the bread. Her head was bent so that he could only guess at what her expression might be. With a sinking feeling in his gut he stood up and reached out a hand to take hers.

'Suddenly, I'm no longer hungry for *haute cuisine* … let's cancel our order and go.'

*   *   *

They bought fish and chips from a late stall in the square and ate them leaning on the parapet of Crane Bridge. Giles watched the round yellow moon reflected in the water, hearing the bell of doom toll within him as he marshalled all his considerable powers of persuasion to put Yelland's arguments as his own.

But she was too quick for him, twisting and turning like an eel, throwing all his reasoning back in his face, eventually rounding on him to demand accusingly, 'Why are you doing this? I don't need you and Yell ganging up on me. I have a right to decide what I do with my life. I'm not bloody dancing to anyone's tune but my own. I'm staying and that's that.'

'Oh, darling, *please* listen to some sense, from me, if not from him.' Giles tried to put his arms about her, but she shrugged away from him and he beat despairing hands on the stonework. 'Zoë, you *must* listen. You are young and gifted. This tour will open new horizons for you and life seldom hands out second chances of that magnitude. If you stay here what will you do? Find some third-rate company and stagnate until Yelland comes to take you back again? You know you would hate that.'

'I doubt that he'd have me; he doesn't forgive easily. But I can manage without him; or I can always follow the other nine-tenths of my profession and rest.'

'And do what? Become a *hausfrau*? Knit socks? Go screaming mad with boredom?' He shook his head. 'How long do you think *we* would last in those circumstances? You'd resent me and in time hate me.'

'Don't talk such bloody drivel,' she swung round on him, sending a cascade of chips into the water. 'I can't do without you now, any more than you can do without me. You made me love you, you bastard and now look where it's got us.'

'Will you just belt up and listen for one minute ... *Christ*,' he smacked an exasperated hand on his forehead, 'this is a bad as trying to beat some sense into Adam's head when he's hell bent on being a bolshie little sod.'

She grinned maliciously. 'Language!'

He grabbed her by both arms. 'You have worked ... slaved, for years to get where you are now – and quite apart from that, what about Yelland? What about loyalty? You can't forever be a spoilt brat: treating people who are relying on you like something that's

172

stuck to your shoe. You've no right to chuck it all up so that you can go on having a nice comfy life with sex on tap and –'

'You *shit*!'

She wrenched away then hit him so hard across the face with her open palm that he reeled back against the bridge; when he straightened again, one hand covering his numbed cheek it was to see her flying along the pavement at a speed that meant he hadn't a chance in hell of catching up with her.

'Bugger, bugger, *bugger*!' He rammed the remnants of their meal into a waste bin and began to walk towards the flat. I must be crazy, he thought furiously. Why on earth should I do Yelland's bloody work for him? He paused as he crossed over the river again. There was a strong eddy under this bridge and the reflected moon waved and leaped in time with his thudding heart.

You're doing it because you love her. If loving means letting go and releasing her from the bonds you have bound about her, however much she may try to keep them, then that's what you have to do – and take the chance that if this is the moment when her career really takes off, she may never come back to you.

He threw a stone at the water, sending the moon shimmering into a thousand ripples of light. 'All right, my love,' he said aloud, 'it seems as if it has to be *au revoir* – I just hope to God I haven't pushed you so hard that it ends up as goodbye.'

*   *   *

She was sitting on the step, her knees drawn up to her chin, and gazed up with mournful eyes as he stopped before her. She caught her lip in her lower teeth and said in a small voice, 'I forgot my key!'

Silently, he opened the door and she climbed the stairs before him. When they reached the top, she went without speaking into the bathroom, and he heard the shower begin to run.

He went into the kitchen and lit the gas under the kettle, the fish and chips lying like lead in his stomach.

*   *   *

Zoë stood unmoving under the shower, letting it pour over her hair, into her ears and eyes and mouth, wishing it was possible to open her head and wash her brain clear.

Now she was back again facing the agony of indecision. She wanted to go, of course she did. Wanted it more than she could

173

remember wanting anything. But Giles ... how would he really be about it when it came to the crunch? He'd talked tonight as though he'd be happy to see her go; hadn't once said he'd miss her or couldn't do without her. Slowly, she began to turn the soap in her hands. Perhaps he was glad of the opportunity to finish their affair. She'd always been afraid that sometime he might get tired of her and go back to his perfect bloody Olivia, and of course, he'd be too kind to come straight out with it, wouldn't he?

She stood back, trying to see herself through his eyes: a short-fused, obsessed, ambition-driven young woman, with no great beauty, no money and a vocabulary that would, as he'd often said, make a hardened old seadog blush. Viewed objectively, it didn't seem a catalogue of pluses that would keep a man like Giles interested for life.

But she had tried so hard to be the sort of woman he wanted; tried until sometimes she thought she'd burst with the unnatural restraints she'd put on her enthusiasms when they were together: for the plays in hand and all the fun and gossip of the theatre. Tears gathered in her eyes. If this was love, then you could stuff it. Nothing was worth all this hurt inside.

'You must talk to Giles ... you owe him that. You can't just make such a decision without.' Jimmy had been coldly distant when she'd told him she wouldn't go on the tour. 'I shall not even begin to tell you how *I* feel. You are a spoilt, ungrateful little girl, and don't deserve the chances you've already been given, let alone to be offered, *gratis*, such an opportunity as this...'

She'd muttered an obscenity that made even him blench. 'You will,' he'd said with icy fury, 'apologise for that *at once!*' and almost in tears she had then bolted out of the dressing room and back to the security of Giles' arms.

Now even he was angry with her...

She wrapped herself in his thick towelling bathrobe and padded damply into the sitting room, just as he came from the kitchen carrying a mug in either hand. 'Tea,' he offered. Without looking at him she settled into an armchair and tucking her feet under her, took the mug with both hands. The overlarge sleeves of his robe fell back and the sudden defenceless pose, the sight of her thin wrists and small hands clutching the cup, sent a wave of pity through him.

She said abruptly, 'If you want to yell at me I shall quite understand.' She stared down into her tea. 'I've never hit anyone before; I've often wanted to, but didn't dare because I thought they might hit me back. I'm sorry.'

'So you should be,' he said severely. 'You nearly busted my

fucking cheekbone!'

'So it doesn't matter if *you* swear?'

'You'd make the Pope blaspheme once a day and twice on Sundays.'

'Yes, well,' she was sulky. 'I'd had enough.'

'Zoë.' He put down his own cup and came to squat before her. 'We can't just leave this. We have to clear up the mess.'

'I know.' Her eyes stung again. 'Look, if it's all over just say so will you. I promise I won't make a scene.'

'What on earth are you talking about?'

'You and me. You're pissed off with me aren't you? You don't have to spell it out. I know a bloody brush-off when I hear one.'

His mouth twitched. 'What happened to the twin-set and pearls?'

'Not really me.' She wiped her nose inelegantly on the sleeve of his robe, giving a pale grin when he winced and handed her his hand-kerchief. 'I only did it to please you. I shouldn't have bothered. I knew I'd never be able to keep it up.'

'Why did you think I'd want you to change? … No. Wait!' He held up his hand as she made to speak. 'I don't need to ask that, do I? Zoë darling, I am so sorry. I've been selfish beyond belief. I could say it's because I love you, but that's a rotten excuse for being so damned smug and pleased with myself, simply because you were making it all so easy for me. All my life I've been a taker. I've tried to be a giver for you, but obviously failed abysmally…'

'I don't care about that. I just don't see why *you* want me to go with Jimmy.'

'Because it's important, because at this moment your future is at stake and because to go is what you want with all your heart and soul, isn't it?'

'You know it is – but I want you as well. I want our life here.'

It was the hopeless cry of a tired child. He took her cup and placing it on the table held her face between his hands. 'I'll keep … remember, you said it: we don't set limits; we don't talk about Time.'

'You really want me to go with the company?'

'With my blessing and with all my heart.'

'Will you…' She gave a hiccup. 'Will you still be here, in this place, when I come back?'

'Yes.'

'And you won't get tired of waiting and find another floozie?'

'Well, I'll maybe have an orgy or two!'

'I love you, Giles; say you love me.'

He smiled, and stood, drawing her up with him. Too full of

emotion to say all that was in his heart, he could only fold her in his arms and hold her close.

Eventually he said huskily, 'Oh, you're all right, Zoë Ormonde,' he kissed her damp head, 'and this old man just loves you to pieces, with or without the twinset and pearls!'

*   *   *

'What are you doing here two hours before curtain up?' Yelland was at his desk conning a script, reading glasses halfway down his long nose. 'I trust it is not to inform me that you can't spare the time to grace this present production with your presence tonight?'

His tone was bitingly sarcastic. Zoë flinched a little, but stuck her chin in the air in the gesture he knew so well.

'I've come to say I'm sorry about last night, and about what I called you. I do want to go on the tour.' She swallowed hard, adding unsteadily, 'that is, if you'll still have me.'

'I'm very touched that you should climb down off your high horse for me.'

'I haven't.' She was disarmingly honest. 'Not for you. I climbed down for Giles.'

'How sweet,' he peered at her over his spectacles. 'I gather you haven't changed all that much if the prospect of leaving this company has failed to curb your impertinent assumption that you may come and go as you please.'

'Are you giving me the push?'

Yelland stared at her stricken face and took pity. 'No. Even if that is something you richly deserve.' He held out the script. 'But you'd better be very sure you are going to stay the course. We shall open with this, and you will need to behave yourself from now on and be very, very good, or I shall not give you the lead.'

Zoë looked down at the clean, fresh wad of quarto sheets. The title leaped out at her from the printed page and suddenly it was Guy Fawkes' night in her head.

He leaned forward, propping his chin on one hand, watching her face. He said, 'Just remember, darling I *don't* want any bloody My Fair Lady; I *don't* want Lerner and Lowe, or Julie Andrews. I want G.B.S. and *you*. Give me every atom of infuriating, out-at-elbows, snotty-nosed brat that you have in you, and you have plenty; bring to life an Eliza that every single person on the other side of that curtain can believe in, and care about, and I may in time forgive even you.'

She looked up from the script. 'You're a bit of an old Higgins

176

yourself, Yell – almost loveable in a way, and I've never really minded that for the past four years you've been such a bastard to me!'

He saw tears in her eyes and felt a most unusual tug at his heart; Giles was right, she was growing up, and he wondered sadly if she would ever again be quite the same stubborn, troublesome, thorn in the flesh that he had battled with for so long. Pushing his glasses up his nose with one finger he held out his hand for the script. 'Forget your lines again and ad lib as blatantly as you did last night, and you'll find I can reach even greater highs. Now go away and leave me in peace.'

'Yes, Yell. Sorry. I had a lot on my mind.'

At his ferocious scowl she backed out then stood for a moment in the silent corridor. From below, sounding hollow and far off, there was a muted burst of laughter and a clang as a stagehand dropped a weight. She breathed deeply, letting all the familiar subtle smells of the building fill her nostrils. Could she ever have lived without it? Would she really have given it all up?

'I don't know,' she whispered, 'I'll never know, because you let me off the hook Giles, and wouldn't put me to the test. I never in a million years would have imagined you could do that for me.'

As she began to walk towards the dressing rooms, to the make-up and the cold cream and the taint of yesterday's cigarette smoke that still permeated the air, she knew for the first time how much she was loved, and how much she loved in return.

18

'If anyone one in that boat has a pair of binoculars, they must be having a rare treat.' Olivia reached for her discarded costume and began to shake it free of sand. Tom pulled on his brief trunks, casting a lazy eye over the motor launch as it idled slowly past the cove. He gave the distant occupants an amiable wave.

'Possibly, but I've no great objections to livening someone else's day, have you?'

She closed her eyes. 'In theory, no. Unless anyone out there happens to have a son at Chiltens and got an eyeful of a naked fellow parent being rogered in the sand by a member of the teaching staff!'

'Oh, well.' He leaned to brush sand from her breast with a light hand. 'Whoever they are they've rather missed the best part.'

'For a schoolmaster you do appear to be distinctly short on a strong moral sense … I can't think why I'm consorting with such a low-lifer.' She turned her back on the boat and shrugged herself into her costume, looking at him thoughtfully over one shoulder. 'Sometimes, when I allow myself to think about us, I'm quite appalled at how easily my persona of old, reliably faithful wife, has degenerated into this. I really can't complain any more about Giles and his goings-on, can I?'

'There is a difference. *You* do not go back and sleep with him afterwards…' He smiled and waggled a thumb at the water. 'Are you ready to swim back? Barty will have the teapot ready.'

She combed her fingers through her hair before tying it back with a piece of ribbon. 'I feel a bit awkward about sitting to have tea with an ex-vicar after this. I always get the feeling that he's reading my mind.'

He laughed. 'Don't worry. He's too busy trying to read mine.'

They swam back slowly, collecting their shorts and shirts from behind the rocks where they had left them, then sat to chat and dry off before dressing and walking back along the cool shadowy lane.

The small cat was seated on the gatepost and jumped onto Tom's shoulder as they passed. He scooped her into his arms, where she lay supine and blissfully purring as he rubbed a gentle finger under her chin.

'Lazy trollop!' He decanted her into an armchair as they stepped into the long sitting room. Raising his voice he called, 'We're back,

178

guv'nor.'

'I know, your moggie told me.' Barty appeared with the tea tray. 'Sheba has some kind of radar device which tells her when Tom's coming,' he explained to Olivia. 'As soon as she goes out to sit at the gate, I put the kettle on.'

'When did this come?' Doyle picked up a telegraph envelope from the mantelpiece and the old man glanced up from pouring the tea.

'Just after you left for the beach,' he looked again at Olivia, holding her gaze as his son-in-law opened the envelope and stood reading, a frown gathering between his brows.

'That's unexpected.' Folding the form again he tucked it back into the envelope. 'Jayne's on her way back from Malaya. She wants to be met at Heathrow on Monday evening.'

For a moment Olivia studied Barty's mild and guileless expression in silence, before asking Tom, 'You mean she's willing to travel all the way down from London in that bone-shaker of yours?'

He grinned. 'She's a tough lady.'

'She'd need to be,' her tone was dry. Again, she had the passing thought that he and Giles had rather a lot in common. Each had that assured, indefinable air of a man who seldom had to work hard at being attractive to women, and that although less the predatory male than her husband, Tom appeared to view fidelity to his Jayne as being a somewhat flexible commodity during her absence. But perhaps that was the way it was with them both...

'I know exactly what you're thinking!' he accused as Barty left the room in search of the biscuit tin, 'but you are quite wrong. I don't make a habit of making love to other women whilst she's away ... only to you.'

'Why me, then?'

'Because you are quite lovely, were very inviting and as lonely and needy as me.' He pulled a face. 'That sounds a trifle bald; but I meant it as a compliment ... you have to admit we were good for each other.'

'And neither of us expected, or wanted, any commitment,' she observed.

He bent swiftly to kiss her cheek. 'That wasn't a primary object, just an added bonus.'

Olivia smiled and patted his cheek. 'Barty is right. You need a wife to keep you in order, and if you really think Jayne Foreman is the one to do it, I can fold my tent as well as the next Arab. You won't even notice I've gone.'

He said softly, 'Oh, but I shall,' and touched her mouth with a gentle finger. 'Don't *you* want someone with whom to grow old?'

'Perhaps. Sometime; not right now, but I like to feel I still have my friends.'

'You have us.' Barty observed as he returned with the biscuits. He looked hard at his son-in-law. 'Hasn't she, Tom?'

'Yes, guv'nor, she has. For as long as she wants.'

Olivia and the old man exchanged glances, his eyes asked a question and she answered it with a faint smile. 'That could be for quite a while,' she said, 'I like to keep my friends.'

*   *   *

Barty listened to the sound of her car receding along the lane, and when Doyle returned he busied himself gathering the tea things onto the tray.

'She's changed a lot.' He commented abruptly, staring at his son-in-law from beneath his brows. 'Standing nice and steady on her own two feet now, isn't she?'

'You could say that.'

'Selling her pictures as well. She must be pretty talented ... soon be completely independent, I shouldn't wonder.'

'You could be right.'

'Still, she must miss that husband of hers.' He straightened up, the loaded tray between his hands and let his gaze rest on Doyle's blandly non-committal face. 'A good thing she's too level-headed to rush headlong into any other disastrous mess.'

'That lady,' returned Doyle with some feeling, 'is as likely to rush into *any* mess, disastrous or otherwise, as you are to mind your own business. What she does is what she wants, and that only after she's given it sufficient thought. She is,' he added with a sudden grin, 'discovering the delights of being a new woman ... and more power to her elbow!'

'Well, I daresay we shan't see so much of her when your own new woman re-appears.' Barty turned to leave the room, giving him an oblique glance. 'One at a time is quite sufficient.'

'Yes, guv'nor, I rather think it is.' Tom laid an affectionate hand on the old man's shoulder. 'Don't worry, when Olivia is ready, and if she feels the need, she'll find the kind of man, and life, that she really wants. As it's unlikely to be with her errant husband, or a pushing fifty schoolmaster, *you* can sleep quiet in your bed, you interfering, manipulative old so-and-so!'

180

*   *   *

Driving back to Lodscombe Olivia reflected that if she'd needed a substitute father, Barty would have filled the position quite admirably. She thought with warm gratitude of the two men she had just left; Tom, comfortable, amusing and sexy, the older man, wise, watchful and protective. Each in his way providing the friendship and support she had most needed over these past weeks.

She sighed, knowing with a sad swoop of her spirits that she would miss Tom and the warm intimacy of their friendship. He had helped her to break away from her dependence, both mental and physical, on Giles; banishing for good the compliant woman who had allowed herself to be duped and manipulated so easily, and freeing her from the nagging sense of guilt she'd carried at walking away from her marriage.

Perhaps the timing of Jayne Foreman's arrival was just right. It would not have been difficult, she acknowledged honestly, to have drifted into something deeper than her easy sexual friendship with Tom, which would undoubtedly have been quite disastrous. One settled housewifely lifestyle with a man was enough. If she really wanted to put back together her fragmented life and career, her priority now must be for personal space and plenty of it.

But still, she would miss him.

She drove on, mentally ticking off the remaining days before Adam returned from France. Reverting to her parental role she realised with dismay that in a little over two weeks he would be back at school, and that before then she'd have to fit in a clothes' buying expedition. She thought rather maliciously that if he visited Giles then *he* could take on that duty. As he'd never before had to undertake such a chore it would at least have the charm of novelty.

About to skirt Dartmouth, she remembered just in time that she had some more canvases to deliver to the Art Gallery, and turned left towards the estuary, feeling the old familiar lifting of her spirits as the sea, blue and sparkling in the afternoon sun, came into sight.

Cruising through the holiday traffic she managed to catch a parking space opposite the gallery. Taking the packed half-dozen new canvases from the boot and tucking them under her arm, she crossed the street. Dodging the meandering cars driven by heat-stunned tourists she ran up the gallery steps, leaping back with a little shriek of surprised alarm as Ambrose Flynn stepped out through the door.

'Just the woman I was looking for!' Deftly, he removed the

181

package from under her arm, and turning her away from the door steered her firmly back down the steps. 'I've spent the past six hours trying to find you. Where do you get to, woman, that's such a secret that not even your redoubtable father knows where you've gone?'

'That's my business – and give me back my pictures – you've just hi-jacked my bread and butter for the next month!'

He gave a bellow of laughter and continued to propel her through the crowd, which parted like a bow wave before his impressive height and muscle. 'Rubbish! Your bread and butter – and jam – are well provided for already. Besides, I have a much better use for these.' He side-stepped into the doorway of the Castle Hotel, pulling her with him, 'Here, toasted muffins and all the tea you can drink. We are going places together, you and I.'

'We are going nowhere together, Flynn.' She tried, but failed to be crushing as he placed her in a chair in the quiet lounge. Seating himself opposite he regarded her with his bright blue gaze.

'How many finished canvases have you right now … apart from these?' He gestured at the package he still carried.

'Perhaps another half-dozen. Why do you ask?'

'Constantine, the owner of the Bloomsbury gallery which exhibits and deals with most of my stuff now, is interested in your pictures and prepared to have a small showing in early November, when some of my pieces will be on exhibition. You could have a modest killing there woman, so just stop giving me a hard time!'

His eyes were dancing with mischief as she stared at him in stunned disbelief. 'Is this your idea of a joke, Flynn?'

'I never joke about the possibility of making good money.'

'Hell's teeth!' She sank back in her chair. 'You really do mean it, don't you? And you must have set it up, you crafty, underhand…'

'Please, no compliments!' He reached across the table, capturing both her hands in his. 'Constantine has only seen a couple of your canvases that I snaffled from the gallery here last week, so you'll need to come to town with me soon and show him more of your work. Then we can start talking how many and which. When I take your bronze up to the foundry next month would be a good opportunity to talk with Andoni – and give you time to produce one, perhaps two more canvasses before the exhibition date.'

He released her hands to lean back and study her with an appreciative eye. 'I like those shorts – and that shirt. A damned sight less prissy than all that Harvey Nicks' bollocks you were wearing the first time I clapped eyes on you! If you're to be seen in my company try not to go back to dressing like a well-heeled suburban housewife. I have my reputation to think of.'

She began to laugh. 'You are the rudest man, but thank you. This means more to me than you'll ever know.'

He swept aside her thanks. 'I'm putting your bronze on show in November. If you weren't such a stroppy wench I'd have been able to make it a nude.' He tilted back on his chair and half-closed his eyes. 'Perhaps I will next time – classical pose, of course – the Copenhagen Mermaid but without the tail; it would be a crime to miss out on those legs of yours!'

'You get full marks for trying, but if I were you I'd find something a little younger. I can't see that a depiction of a forty-plus woman in the buff would exactly cause a stir in the art world.'

He gave a loud hoot of laughter. 'I don't need pert tits and a great arse to create something of beauty,' he said and turned to order their tea from the elderly waitress who had materialised at his side.

'You shocked her,' reproved Olivia, watching the woman's indignant back in retreat. 'She'll probably report you to the management and we'll be thrown out.'

'It wouldn't be the first time for me. I've been thrown out of some of the best bars in County Clare.'

'That I can believe,' she looked at him thoughtfully. 'What made you leave Ireland and come to this country?'

He frowned and examined his fingernails. 'I married an English-woman.'

'Sorry. I didn't mean to pry.'

He said brusquely, 'It was too long ago to bother with. At the time she wouldn't cross the Kentish border to live, let alone the Irish Sea, so I had to make the choice: stay in Connemara or follow my blood. I followed it, and her, to Kent. As it turned out I chose wrongly.' Suddenly his face was heavy, the bold eyes hooded.

'So did I, but it gave me some very good years – and Adam, of course,' Olivia answered sharply. 'You've also had your compen-sations.'

'What compensations?' He asked mockingly. 'Don't pretend you've not been told all about big bad Flynn who hates his kids.'

'I don't listen to gossip; I prefer to make up my own mind, and so far I haven't noticed you beating or starving either of them into submission. Liam's a bit of an adolescent brat and I know you're not exactly his favourite man, but Kate is sweet and Adam tells me she thinks a lot of you.'

He pulled his brows together but didn't look displeased. 'Actually, I quite like her, but Liam...' he shook his head. 'I'm afraid he's a lost cause.'

'Nonsense. That's a terrible thing to say of your own flesh and blood.'

'Is it? You might think the same of your son if he spent half his life trying, by fair means or foul, to get money out of you for booze and pot. He thinks I don't know what he does but he'd have to be up very early to put one over on *me*.'

'He does *what*?' Olivia was horrified. 'Are you telling me that my son has crossed the channel and is now sailing around the Spanish coast on a boat skippered by a delinquent dope-head?'

'Simmer down, woman!' he was amused at her outrage. 'He's hardly an addict. It's only his way of giving two fingers to me … and to every other adult in authority. I should never have let them make the trip if I hadn't a pretty good idea that Kate is onto him. Don't worry; he'll behave himself while she's around.'

'I'll hold you responsible if anything goes wrong,' Olivia promised tartly, then her face pinked at a sudden vision of Adam "kissing and all that" with Kate.

'Now why are you looking like that?' Intrigued, he watched the blush spread. 'You look guilty as hell and worried with it!'

Olivia took a deep breath. 'You do realise that Adam and Kate are, well … *interested* in each other, don't you?'

'If you mean what I think you do, that's a God-awful way of putting it.' He put up a hand to tug at his beard and gave a disbelieving growl of laughter. 'Are you sure … they're only a couple of kids.'

'Those kids are both sixteen,' she returned sarcastically. 'Kate is a lovely young woman, who appears to get very little of the affection she needs at home, and Adam has Giles for a father. I can think of less explosive pairings.'

'And *you* let them go to France together?'

'With your pot-smoking, beer swilling son!'

They glared at each other for a moment before his big frame began to shake with laughter. 'Just imagine the three of them all watching each other! I don't think we need worry this time. Kate won't let Liam out of her sight, he won't take his eyes off your son and your son won't take his eyes off my daughter. All the same I think a spot of straight talking will be in order when they get back.'

'I'm not stupid, you know.' Olivia was annoyed. 'I've already spoken to Adam and warned him to be careful.'

'Oh, aye, and I'll speak to him some more when they get back and frighten the bejesus out of him … and her,' he rumbled. 'I'm the old-fashioned sort of father, who doesn't *ask* any sixteen-year-old lad with his hormones on the boil to be careful around his daughter. I just tell him what I'll do to him if he isn't.'

In spite of herself she began to laugh. 'It's obvious you're no disciple of Dr. Spock.'

'I've never heard of him but I remember what a sex-starved teenager spends all his time thinking about!'

She regarded him with a new respect, but couldn't resist saying pointedly: 'Perhaps sometime you should try some of the straight talking to your own son, instead of arguing and try to starve him out of his unpleasant habits. He might not then need the beer and pot.'

'*Touché*, lady,' his teeth showed very white in the dark beard. 'Perhaps I'll do just that.'

She pushed home the advantage. 'You could also listen to what he really wants to do with his life instead of just nagging him to get a job.'

'I didn't realise an Agony Aunt had taken the lease of the Lodge...' he paused as the waitress re-appeared and waited while their tea was served before continuing. 'I don't know how you come to know more than I do about my own children, but given a few more years I'd say you're set fair to becoming a damned interfering old biddy!'

She helped herself to a muffin and nibbled it delicately, looking at him from beneath arched brows. 'You just keep a civil tongue in your head, Flynn,' she advised calmly, 'or you'll whistle in vain for *me* ever to pose for you in the buff.'

'Oh, I'll whistle all right,' he promised, folding his arms on the table top, 'that I will, and one day my lass, you'll come to me.'

She gave a slow teasing smile. 'Better not hold your breath on that one, Flynn,' she said.

19

Waiting in the airport's arrival hall, Doyle was filled with an un-comfortable mixture of emotions. Despite his efforts to keep his lovemaking with Olivia a step removed from anything deeper than the satisfying of their mutual needs, she had made inroads on his lonely heart. For a warm and deeply sensual man, as time passed the long periods without Jayne had become harder to bear, and he knew he could so easily have let himself become much more than Olivia's "occasional lover."

Just why Jayne was returning at least six weeks earlier than expected he had no idea, but it was damnably bad timing. Only a few days ago he had been making love with Olivia and Jayne had been a long way from his thoughts. The prospect of a sudden return to life with his long time lover was proving more than a little disturbing, and he couldn't rid himself of a nagging feeling of guilt for having taken another woman to bed in her place.

Occasionally, in the past, he had wondered if Jayne ever slept with anyone else during her travels, but neither had ever questioned the other about the time they spent apart. He was still pondering the possibility of a mutual infidelity when he saw her coming towards him across the hall, walking with her confident easy stride, a canvas bag and camera slung over one shoulder.

'Tom!'

Her face lit up in greeting as she saw him. She ran the last few yards to throw herself into his arms, and he hugged her to him, his senses stirred as always at the sight and feel of her. 'I didn't expect you back so soon. How much time do we have?' he asked.

'As much time as you want.' She leaned back to smile up at him as the other passengers from the flight surged around them. 'I've lots to tell you … you'll be bored with me by the time I'm through.'

'Never that,' he kissed her again, holding her face between his hands, tangling his fingers in her short curly hair.

She dropped her bag to the floor and put her arms around his neck, saying huskily: 'I've missed you, Tom Doyle, oh, how I've missed you.'

His heart turned in the old familiar way and suddenly he didn't care how many other men she might or might not have bedded; only knew for certain that she was still the one, the only one who could

186

ever help heal the aching space in his heart for the loss of Rosalind
and his little son.

*   *   *

'Have I left it too late for you and me?' she asked, as they lay in each
other's arms in the hotel bedroom. From the building opposite neon
signs winked on and off, sending red and green lights chasing across
the ceiling, while beyond the windows the muted roar of traffic gave a
passing reminder that the city never slept.

'Too late to do what?'

'Settle down … be your woman, share your bed every night,' she
turned her head into his shoulder. 'Oh Tom, I'm so tired. I've spent so
long proving I could make it in a man's world; could do as well as
anything in trousers. I'm nearly forty now and I've had enough. Sheer
bloody-mindedness on my part of course; I didn't have to prove
anything to you, did I?'

'No. Just to yourself.'

'Well, I've done that … Tom, what do *you* want now?'

He smiled into her eyes, lit by the pulsing lights. 'A wife; a home
… you, only you.'

'And a child – that's if I'm not past it?'

'That too, although I'll be more of a grandfather than a father,' he
was silent a moment then tightened his arms about her. 'What made
you change your mind and come home?'

She was evasive. 'Oh, you know; the passing of time … the old
biological clock ticking away…'

'Nothing more than that?'

'Well, it is almost eight years since I fell in love with a certain
sexy Lieutenant Colonel in Jerusalem, and I've been in love with him
ever since. Isn't that enough?'

He was silent again, before saying quietly: 'I think I should tell
you something…'

'No. Don't.' She put a finger on his lips. 'Just so long as you
don't have regrets if I ever get around to waddling about with several
pounds of baby on board.'

'It doesn't sound as though I'll have time for regrets, or anything
else.' He kissed the crown of her head. 'You'll have to be a mother to
all my other boys as well you know. They've been missing out on the
tea and sympathy dished out by all the other Housemasters' wives.'

'I'm famously sympathetic and make a very good cup of tea.'

'Can you bear the thought of living in my quarters? It's a very

187

roomy flat and well away from all those grubby little things – and there's always Barty to bolt home to if it gets too bad.'

'Do you beat the grubby little things when they are naughty?'

'On occasions; not very often.'

'I don't think I much like the idea of being married to a child-beater.'

'One can get used to anything,' he rebuked, 'and as you are not exactly in the usual run of academic wives, I shall probably find myself confiscating girlie magazines by the ton, and have boys lining up outside my study in droves for retribution. You may have to put cotton wool in your ears to muffle the screams!'

She felt the laughter deep inside his chest and lifted her head to give him a mocking grin. 'You have a sadistic streak, Tom Doyle, but I do love you. Will Barty be pleased, do you think?'

'I should think he'll be over the ruddy moon, darling.'

'How soon can he marry us?'

'As soon as possible; preferably by special licence, otherwise he'll be afraid you'll get away again.'

'I shan't do that. I've burnt all my boats.' She gave a sudden gurgle of laughter. 'I reversed the charges and 'phoned my editor from Kuala Lumpur to tell him I was going to retire and raise babies. He called me something very rude and made it quite clear that nobody at the *News* would have me now at a gift. They like their correspondents footloose and fancy free.'

'And how do you like your schoolmasters?'

She laughed again; straddling him she began to move her hands over his chest. 'In bed and about to give a repeat performance, I hope.'

Much later, on the brink of sleep, she asked: 'Was she very pretty?'

He closed his eyes. 'Uh huh.'

'Young?'

'No.'

She said 'That's all right then…neither was mine! 'Night, Tom.'

'I'm glad to hear that. Goodnight, my love.'

Tomorrow he would 'phone Olivia. He felt an immense debt of gratitude to her; for knowing her and for almost loving her. Grateful too, that they could now remain friends, with no harm done to either of them, or to those they loved.

*   *   *

Watching the Berry Head lighthouse come into sight, Adam was both eager and reluctant to be returning home again. It had been a wonderful, if frustrating, voyage. The only time he and Kate had been alone together on the boat was the time Liam went ashore and got pissed in Saint Lunaire. Kate had been so worried about what the big idiot was up to that they'd wasted hours scouring the countryside for him, when all the time he'd been sleeping it off in a beached rowboat fifty yards along the shore.

If only they'd known … he sighed over the wasted opportunity. They could have necked all afternoon…

But that aside it had been wonderful. The night watch when he had stood alone at the wheel, eyes moving between navigating instruments and sea and stars, had been the most magical and exciting hours imaginable. The sea and everything to do with it, he thought, now that was the way he wanted to live his life.

Forty minutes later they were tying up and he could see Pops, binoculars around his neck waving at them from the cliff-top, and felt a rush of pleasure that his grandfather had been waiting and watching for their return.

*   *   *

From where he stood in his studio Ambrose could see the masthead of the Morning Star rounding the point, flying her distinctive dark blue pennant with a silver star at its centre. Here they were then, back safe and sound.

He frowned a little, remembering his conversation with Olivia.

For so long he'd spent so much time worrying about Liam, and keeping some kind of control over *him*, that he'd hardly noticed how attractive Kate had become, let alone seen that young Ryder was smitten. His frown deepened. He'd soon sort that young man out, but what on earth was he to say to Kate? Did she have any idea of how to deal with hot-handed pubescent youths? He supposed girls talked about those sort of things amongst themselves…she certainly wouldn't have got much help from any of those out-of-this-world nuns at that school of hers. But how could he possibly start on such a subject when there was so little rapport between them? Perhaps he might be able to get around that one if he collared young Ryder first. Get him sorted out, he reasoned, and there should be less need to worry about Kate.

Olivia was right, he though ruefully. His children lacked any kind of love or interest in their needs, and what they couldn't get from him they would look for elsewhere, or turn to even less healthy means to get attention. Now he faced the unpalatable fact that he'd given them little consideration or affection since Paula went. Wrapped in his own fury that she had brought her sordid affair into their home, then as time passed, desperately lonely, he'd been selfishly blind to the needs of his children.

He flinched when he remembered Kate's silent withdrawal and Liam's anguished, helpless anger. No wonder Kate was looking to that boy for affection, and Liam drifting uncertainly into dubious and dangerous waters…

Deep in thought he turned again to clearing a part of the studio for Olivia to work. She'd need space to set up her easel for the threatened portrait. Perhaps if he was very diplomatic she might agree to work here permanently. It would certainly be better than the small room she used at the Lodge.

He stood tugging at his beard. She was seeing someone he was sure, there was no other way to account for all those absences and the glow she had about her. He should have stepped much more carefully right from the beginning: toned down the approach, shown a little more finesse.

He stood with folded arms staring with unseeing eyes at the horizon. How the hell could he have known, all those months ago when he first saw Olivia Ryder crouched over her easel, that she was going to get under his skin like this?

After a while he went into the small room leading off the studio and took the cloth from the clay head. Lightly tracing his fingers over the wide brow, small straight nose and full curved lips, then down over the bare shoulders to the hint of a swelling breast, he sighed. 'Too late,' he said aloud, 'you're too bloody late you old fool.'

Replacing the cloth he returned to his post at the studio window.

*   *   *

Once home again Adam was in no hurry to do any further travelling before he returned to school, his response only lukewarm to Olivia's suggestion that he could spend a day or two with his father to shop for the clothes he'd need for the winter term. He wanted to see his father, of course he did, but he also wanted to spend what remained of his holiday with Kate.

'I'll think about it,' he said grudgingly, when Olivia pressed him. 'I've only just got back … anyone would think you were trying to get rid of me.'

'I'm delighted to have you back, but you did say that you'd like to spend some time with your father.' Olivia was patient. 'I know you hate shopping, but it has to be done and you might as well do it with daddy. You're much more likely to get what you want from him than if you had me breathing down your neck.'

'All right, I'll ring later.'

'What's wrong with now?'

'I can't … I have to go down and help Kate clear the boat. I said I would.' He was already at the door. 'I'll be back in time for supper. Honestly.'

'I'm beginning to know why you used to yell at me that I treated the house as a hotel,' Olivia said to her father when he dropped by later that day, 'all Adam comes home for now is to eat and sleep.'

Clive laughed, helping himself to another slice of cake. 'In a few years you'll be wishing he was back again and taking bed and board for granted.'

She sighed, propping her chin on one hand.

'I know. I wish he wasn't going back to school. I shall be lonely.'

'Really? That isn't the impression your mother has, she seems to think you're happier than you ought to be, and is very frustrated that she hasn't found out why you've been spending so much time away from home.'

'Then she's almost as nosy as you, isn't she?' Olivia answered blandly, 'and I should think you could both find something better to do than worry about where I spend my spare time.'

'I'm not worried, I leave all that to your mother,' Clive licked a finger and began harvesting the crumbs on his plate. 'She may think you've got a man tucked away somewhere, but I know that now you've started painting again you won't be rushing to give it all up to be someone else's little helpmeet.'

She laughed. 'Damn' right, I won't, but I'm not expecting to spend the rest of my days in suspended animation either. However, in future I'll continue to do my best to keep my private life well away from my mama's eagle eye!'

*   *   *

Surveying the end of voyage chaos in the cabin, Adam wondered where Kate was. Liam, he knew, would be off out somewhere, but Kate had said she'd be down on the boat and he wanted time alone with her; to lie on the bunk, stretched along each other from head to tingling toe. They hadn't been like that together since before they went to France, except for those heady few minutes one night on the way out, when Liam had been on watch…

He stood still, gazing towards the door of Kate's tiny cabin, remembering how he had woken in the dark, his body tormented with longing; how he had gone into Kate's small cabin, where she'd let him get under the covers and they'd done much more than just kiss. Of course, they hadn't gone all the way, but she'd touched him, and let him touch her, in all the places they'd never touched before.

His insides went liquid at the memory, and he drew in a sharp breath. He *must* stop thinking about sex all the time. It had been bad enough before the French trip, now it was becoming impossible. If they did anything like that again when they were alone and with no Liam on the other side of the bulkhead, he knew neither of them would be able to stop.

Resolutely he began stuffing all the oddments of paper, bits of leftover food and other detritus in varying degrees of decomposition and unpleasantness into a paper sack, and thought about his proposed visit to his father.

Ever since his exam results had arrived he'd known he'd have to face up to him sooner or later. Mum had been tactful and hadn't said much about the cock-up he'd made of his science papers, but he knew Giles was unlikely to be so lenient. He was not the most patient of fathers and Adam was especially wary of him since that awful scene in the car last Easter.

Sudden footsteps on the deck above made his heart gave the familiar thump; Kate was here at last. He scrambled to the cabin doors, exclaiming loudly: 'About time, gorgeous … and I hope you're alone!'

'I'm that all right!' Bending almost double Ambrose Flynn eased himself down the steps into the cabin with Adam in startled retreat before him, 'although it's a long time since anyone called me gorgeous.' He stared from beneath drawn brows. 'I take it you were expecting my daughter?'

'Er, yes. I was, actually.' Adam had backed as far as he could and was now pressed up against Kate's cabin door.

'Well, she'll not be along tonight. I found a little job for her to do so that we could have a cosy chat … man to man.'

Adam couldn't imagine anything he'd like less than a cosy chat with this intimidating giant of a man, who was quite clearly on the warparth. An awful sick feeling invaded his stomach and he had to fight a sudden need for the lavatory. It wasn't as if they'd actually *done* anything, not really, he told himself in an effort to bolster his courage.

Making a supreme effort he levered himself from off the cabin wall. Looking Ambrose straight in the eyes with an expression Doyle would have recognised, and interpreted, at once, he said with ingenuous innocence, 'That would be very nice, sir. Would you like a cup of coffee?'

'Not particularly.' Ambrose was amused and impressed by this unexpected show of well-mannered deviousness from one so young, and decided to honour him with a full frontal attack.

'I've come to ask you a straight question and I need a straight answer.' He placed both hands on the table and leaned forward menacingly. 'Are you having sex with my daughter? And I do mean S-E-X in *all* its glory!'

Adam jumped, all his *sang froid* deserting him, 'Shit, no, sir!'

'That's good. Let's keep it that way, shall we?' Ambrose gave his tooth-gleaming pirate smile, 'because should you decide to do anything so rash as to actually get your leg over, I give you fair warning that I shall take great pleasure in personally flaying the skin off your arse and feeding it to the fishes.'

Adam was stung into sudden terrified indignation. His voice rose. 'You ought to know that Kate wouldn't let anyone go too far.'

'That sounds to me as though you've tried!'

'Yes … no, well, not really, that is…' He was scarlet with shamed embarrassment. 'What I mean is we haven't, you know, *done* anything … not really.' At the look on his visitor's face he faltered and stopped.

'No? Well just cool it, will you. In a couple of years – when of course you will know *all* about being responsible adults – what the pair of you choose to do with each other then is your own business. Until such time it's still very much mine.' Suddenly, he pointed a threatening finger. 'And I shall be seriously annoyed if you *ever* do anything to upset or cause that splendid mother of yours any grief, simply because you can't keep your dick in your pants when you're around my daughter. Understand?'

'Yes, sir.'

'Have I your word on that?'

'Yes, sir.'

'Good.' Ambrose sat and spread his arms on the table. 'Now, while we continue our little chat, and before I help you to finish clearing this tip, how about that coffee?'

*　　　*　　　*

After Ambrose had left Adam sat alone in the darkening cabin, mulling over the past hour, silently acknowledging that he had been well and truly hamstrung, but marvelling that Kate's father had been such a decent chap to talk to once he'd finished giving him hell. Eventually, feeling ashamed and foolish, he put his hand under the mattress on his bunk, feeling for the unopened little blue packet that had caused him so much embarrassment to buy from the chemist in St-Malo. Opening up the rubbish sack he pushed it down far beneath all the litter then tied the neck of the bag tightly with twine. He'd ask pops to burn the sack on his bonfire along with the garden rubbish and that would be that. He would, as Kate's father advised, cool it; but not too much. A chap couldn't be expected to turn into a saint overnight and he didn't want Kate to think he'd gone off her.

* * *

'You are terribly late.' Olivia glanced up from her book. 'I've had my supper, but there's cold meat and salad in the pantry.'

'Sorry, mum … it's all right I'm not very hungry. We cooked some chips.'

She eyed him speculatively. 'Is something wrong?'

'No.' His eyes were a soft limpid blue. 'I've been thinking … I ought to give dad a ring in the morning. If it's all right with him I could go on Wednesday and come back Sunday, couldn't I? I think Kate's going to be pretty busy and we won't be taking the boat out much, so I'll still have some time here with you before term starts.'

She studied him for a few moments in silence. He wasn't looking flushed and moody as he often was after he'd been alone with Kate. 'Did you two get the boat cleaned up?'

'Kate couldn't come. Her father helped me.'

'That was kind of him.'

'Yes. I'm tired, mum. I think I'll go straight up.'

Concerned, Olivia eyed him more closely. 'Are you *sure* there's nothing wrong?'

'Yeah, of course I am.' He drifted over to the staircase then paused a moment with his hand on the rail. 'You know, mum, I think Kate's old man fancies you!' he said, then exploded into laughter and fled up the stairs, leaving a completely nonplussed and uncomprehending Olivia staring after him.

* * *

194

The following morning she left for her day in the studio, wondering uneasily exactly what had passed between Ambrose and her son the previous evening. When she'd tried to question Adam at breakfast he'd stonewalled her in the most irritating fashion. Before she could settle to work she would have to ask Ambrose, even if she was unlikely to get any more sense out of him than she had from Adam.

Ambrose was already working when she arrived in the studio and she went straight into the attack.

'Have you been talking to Adam?' She set out a large sketch block on her easel and began sharpening a pencil.

'Good morning to you, too, darlin' – and what makes you think I might have?'

She looked at him over the top of the easel.

'Because he came back last night in rather an odd mood and mentioned you'd been down on the boat with him.'

'We did have a chat…'

He was standing with one hand half covering his face, apparently engrossed in studying the sketches spread on the table before him.

'And?' she prompted after a few seconds silence.

'And what?'

She said patiently, 'What did you chat about?'

'My daughter of course: he assured me I have nothing to worry about, because he isn't *actually* having sex with her,' he regarded Olivia with an air of mild surprise. 'Why are you looking at me like that, and with your mouth open?'

Olivia was baffled. 'Why on earth should he say such a thing?'

'Probably because I asked him,' he moved the sketches about with an absent forefinger, 'and as he would appear to be quite embarrassingly honest I believed him.' Bending to scoop a ball of prepared clay from the bin he settled it on his plinth with a thump. 'I suppose that as spotty adolescents go, he's not at all a bad specimen.'

Olivia tested the point of her pencil against her thumb and looked thoughtfully at the back of his head. 'Careful Flynn!' she murmured, *sotto voce*, 'your soft under-belly is showing!'

*   *   *

'Your dad's all right.' Adam volunteered as Kate joined him on the jetty, 'he helped me clean up the boat last night.'

'Did he? I'm sorry I didn't come down. He asked me to finish clearing the part of the studio your mother is going to work in. I thought you'd have left cleaning up aboard until this morning.'

'Um,' he leaned over to dislodge a crab from a pile with his fingernail and watched it plop down into the water. 'We had quite a talk; I thought he might have told you.'

'No. What did you talk about?'

'Oh, this and that … all sorts of things: I was a bit fed up because mum wanted me to go and stay with dad before term starts and I didn't really want to go.' He dislodged another crab. 'You know I made a real muck up on some of my exams?'

She giggled. 'You mean getting C minuses for biology and chemistry? Does it matter?'

'It does if your old man expects you to read Medicine.'

'Oops!' She pulled a face. 'Well, you certainly cocked that one up, didn't you?'

'Yeah. I was getting a bit panicky because I know he's going to be livid.' He grimaced. 'Somehow, when your dad finished … well, finished telling me something and we'd started to get a bit matey, I sort of told him about it. He said that if *he* ever had to give anyone bad news, he gave it to them straight, even if it meant he had to get the hell out of it bloody fast afterwards!'

She laughed, her eyes sparkling. 'Sometimes he can surprise you and be really nice. Even Liam say's he's getting quite human. Dad actually smiled at *him* this morning.' She leaned her arms on the wall next to his and added, 'He's still in shock.'

'Who is?'

She looked around as Liam joined them, hitching himself to sit beside her on the wall.

'You are, after dad was so agreeable at breakfast.'

'Yeah. Ruddy weird it was *and* he caught me as I was coming out just now and gave me a quid.' Liam gave a snort of laughter. 'We'd better go up to the shop and spend it before he changes his mind and asks for it back.'

He led the way up the hill to the village store, still trying to puzzle the reason for his father's unusual good-humour. So far as he could see nothing had happened to bring about the change; Ambrose was as usual wrapped up in his work, and there was still the problem that *he* hadn't yet managed to find a job, so there was bound to be another row sooner or later … Liam began to walk more slowly, allowing the others to go on ahead. The only thing that *had* changed, he thought suddenly, was that Adam's mother seemed to be around quite a lot now.

He scratched his head. That couldn't be it. The old man was off women, had been for ages, even if he couldn't help giving the eye occasionally to a pretty one, although he'd soon clam up if they tried to get too close. He could even be like a bear with a sore head with Miriam, who could be pretty flirtatious when the mood took her.

For a few moments he allowed his mind to dwell on Miriam's considerable charms. At one time he'd thought he was in with a chance there, until that wanker Alex Finch turned up with his sports car and guitar and his bloody Beatle haircut.

He sighed. You needed plenty of filthy lucre if you wanted to keep a girl. He'd just *got* to earn some money soon; beside the expense of taking out a girl he was clean out of grass again.

20

'We'll have to rush around and get your things on Saturday.' Giles scowled at Adam. 'If you'd given me more warning you were coming I could have arranged things better – I can't just cancel a half-dozen operations at such short notice.'

'You'd have to if you'd been run over by a bus.' Zoë pointed out reasonably.

'That would be the result of my own carelessness, or an act of God; an entirely different matter from neglecting my patients in order to outfit this useless waste of space.'

Adam mumbled, 'You and Mum seem to think I need my hand held. I don't, I can get what I need for myself.'

'That's right.' Zoë winked. 'Just give him the money Giles and let him get on with it.'

'You have to be joking – I wouldn't trust him on the loose in London with so much as a shilling of my money.'

Zo offered carelessly, '*I'll* go with him if you like and make sure he doesn't buy anything too sensible.'

Giles looked grim. 'I don't actually feel like giving him anything but a damned good hiding after those bloody awful exam results.'

Adam's face fell. Zoë glanced at him then shot Giles a challenging look; he shrugged and gave a wry smile in return. 'Very well, I suppose I've already given him a hard enough time. When will you go?'

She smiled back at him, miming a kiss then turned her tawny eyes on Adam. 'I've nothing to do tomorrow until curtain up,' she offered. 'We could get an early train to Waterloo in the morning and have ourselves a great time down the Kings Road.'

Adam was transfixed and faintly alarmed at the thought of spending a whole day in the company of this extraordinary female. He didn't know what to make of her. Quite prepared to hate her on sight and show his immense disapproval of her presence in his father's life, he'd been completely outmanoeuvred by her at their first meeting, when she hadn't attempted to either apologise or hide their relationship. *It's happened,* her manner said clearly, *it's one of those things, so don't fight it,* and he'd found himself won over before he'd had a chance to even start giving her the cold shoulder.

Now he was grateful that she was there to deflect some of his father's anger. He looked hesitantly at Giles.

'Could we, dad? It would be great. Bill Marshal would be absolutely *green*!'

'All right, all right,' Giles held up a warning hand, 'but school clothes first; the rubbish later…' He turned on Zoë. 'And don't you *dare* encourage him to get a ridiculous haircut, a tattoo, an earring or any of those bloody awful pansy shirts, or I won't be held responsible for what I do to him … and you!'

'No darling; trust me. Now, I've got to get moving for the matinee,' she linked her arm in Adam's. 'If you'd like to come with me now you can sit at the back in the director's seat, then afterwards we could do a quick tour backstage. It's quite fun, and Colin might let you play with his lighting desk if he's in a good mood.'

'Great!'

Adam was already on his feet and Giles gave another wry smile at the resilience of youth. The previous evening his son had taken the full force of his anger over the poor exam results, remaining sullen and miserable until Zoë's return from the theatre, when her exuberant spirits had effectively dispelled the air of gloom hanging over the flat. Before his son's visit Giles had been on edge, dreading Adam's reaction to his lover, but all awkwardness had vanished with her arrival; she had played her part to perfection and Adam had regained both his spirits and his dignity. Now, as Giles watched her making a comrade of his son, he wondered just where real life ended for her and the acting took over…

He doubted if even she knew the answer to that one.

*   *   *

'Did anyone ever tell you that you are a genius?' he asked, as they waved Adam's train out of sight on the Sunday morning.

'I've been called a lot of things, but never that.'

'Well, you've worked some kind of magic on my son and I call that genius.' He put his arm about her shoulders as they left the platform. 'The last time we were together he gave me a very sticky time. Now, after a rather difficult start, for which you no doubt blame me for playing the heavy father and threatening to beat him, he treats me like a nice old man whom he doesn't mind humouring, and whose opinion on unimportant matters he's prepared to tolerate. He even let me take him to the lab without complaining.'

'He is easy to like … but then I love his father so that gives me a head start.' Zoë gave him a teasing glance. 'He doesn't have your temperament, though, does he?'

'No, that is entirely his mother's.' Giles shrugged. 'He's placid and easy-going until something really rouses him, then he can turn in a second. But he's over it quickly and throws you completely by being either humbly apologetic, or obliquely funny. That's pure Olivia and not a bit like me.'

'I think I might like Olivia, d'you suppose we might meet one day?'

He answered shortly, 'Possibly; in the fullness of time.'

She said, 'I don't mind talking about her now; particularly since I've met Adam.'

'We'll all have a lot of talking to do to each other soon. I've arranged to see Noel Travis, my solicitor, next week. Riversmead has been sold at last and there are a lot of loose ends to tie up ... then there is the matter of the divorce.'

She looked reflective and paced along in silence for a while before she asked, 'Why all the hurry?'

'It's unfair to everyone to let it drag on.'

'Giles.' She stopped and faced him. 'I'm not going to marry you, you know ... not yet, anyway. Perhaps never.'

'A contradiction in terms, if ever I heard one!' His smile was strained. 'I'm not pressuring you now, but I can't promise not to ask you at some time in the future ... and Olivia may want to be free. I owe it to her not to try and hang on.'

'Sorry. I didn't mean to blight your plans.' She smiled reassuringly. 'It's just that I think *we're* doing fine as we are, don't you?'

'Whatever you say, my darling.'

But I want to be sure of you, he thought. I may see Yelland's point of view; I may even have schooled myself in the knowledge that you will keep on leaving me, but I want to know you'll always come back. Marriage, even for you, my love, would be a powerful bond.

He smiled and squeezed her shoulder. 'Let's go home and open a bottle of wine to celebrate being just two of us again.'

'Well, we know where that will lead, don't we?'

He looked down at her, all his love in his eyes. 'I must be crazy to think of tying myself for life to a woman who can read my mind so well.'

Zoë laughed up at him; putting an arm about his waist she corrected, 'Not crazy, lover; just brilliant!'

*   *   *

200

Olivia took up her brush and laid the first stroke on her canvas with a steady and confident hand. She had poured over her sketches for a long time before this moment, studying in detail her impressions of that leonine head.

She didn't intend a portrait as such, preferring to show him immersed in his work, with the cluttered untidy studio providing the background to a rather shadowy figure. Content to use her skill to catch the essence of the man absorbed in his creation rather than make a study of his face, she realised now, when she had finally come to capture him on canvas, that beneath the mixed façade of flirtation and provocative rudeness lurked an unmistakable charismatic charm, something, she thought, that might prove fairly lethal at very close quarters…and working alongside him in this studio *was* rather close quarters.

As she watched he swayed back on his heels to assess his work, then leaned forward to touch the clay with powerful but delicate fingers and she paused for a moment, her brush in mid air, caught in a sudden rush of perception.

I was wrong about you, Flynn, but I think I've found you now…you are neither lion nor bear, nor an old roué. You are a massively talented, extremely attractive, definitely sexy man, with what Carol might call pizzazz, and I like you, I really do; but I think that liking you is about as far as I'm going to let myself go…

*   *   *

'As I can see how you hate being a gentleman of leisure, I thought you could make better use of your time by learning to do something useful.'

Ambrose dropped his keys, closely followed by a small red folder, next to Liam's empty breakfast plate. 'Going on the premise that if you can drive a Land Rover you can drive anything, I've arranged for your first lesson at nine-thirty this morning. The instructor's name is Godsend, so let's hope he lives up to it!'

Having delivered himself of which bombshell, Ambrose left the room, closing the door very firmly behind him.

Liam and Kate stared at each other.

'What the hell has got into him?' Liam rolled his eyes, trying to keep his astonished delight from showing. He picked up the provisional licence and opened it. 'It's true … he isn't having me on, my name is right here in black and white!'

Kate, transfixed with her spoon halfway to her mouth, stared blankly back at him. 'Search me … you must have done something right. Can I come and be your back seat driver?'

'No you bloody can't. Just because your boy friend's away until tomorrow doesn't mean I want you sticking to me like glue.'

'Louse,' she answered equably and continued with her breakfast. 'If we're not sailing I shall go and see Adam's mother, she said I could any time. I'm not going to hang around here listening to you gloat.'

He grinned. 'If she was younger, or I was older, I could fancy her.'

'You fancy anything in a skirt that isn't actually hideous.' Kate was scathing. 'Why don't you get yourself a decent girl instead of hanging around the village hall with your tongue lolling out at all the local tarts?'

'Thank *you*! Decent girls expect to be wined and dined and sit in the best seats in the cinema, while the local tarts, as you so rudely call them, settle for fish and chips and Slapton beach.' He stood up, pocketing the keys. 'However, if I have a set of wheels, anything is possible.'

She stuck her tongue out at him.

'Dream on, he'll not let you have it for *your* version of back seat driving.'

*　　　*　　　*

With a certain degree of enjoyable malice, she watched as, with a cacophonous grinding of gears, the Land Rover bunny-hopped up the hill. *Poor old Mr Godsend*, she thought, turning to begin the walk along the cliff path to Pel's point, *rather him than me*!

Kate was pleased at the opportunity to visit the Lodge alone. At first she'd been cautious about Olivia's overtures of friendship. She found chatting easily with Adam's cool, elegant and she suspected, very clever mother, daunting, and had kept her distance, but when on closer acquaintance she had discovered Olivia to be completely unaffected and friendly, her reserve had crumbled. Now she grasped eagerly at any chance to visit the cottage, sometimes resenting even Adam's presence there.

She thought it was probably because Olivia had changed and was no longer quite so elegant, and therefore so much more approachable. Her smart clothes had been discarded in favour of cotton skirts, or shorts and casual shirts. Her hair was longer, and when she was painting tied back carelessly with a scarf, or any odd piece of ribbon or tape that came to hand. Now it was easy to chat, even to let her guard down a little and talk about her father and Liam.

It's because she is calm and comfortable and really interested in what you say, and she doesn't ask awkward questions; not even about the amount of time Adam and I spend together, Kate mused thoughtfully, as she made her way through the woodland surrounding the cottage, and she always looks pleased to see you, even if she's working.

She longed to talk, really talk to Olivia, like you could to a best friend or a sister … or mother. Kate shied nervously away from that last thought. From what she remembered of her mother, she didn't think there would have been many intimate mother and daughter confidences exchanged *there*.

At the edge of the pheasant strip she stopped for a few moments and stood looking down the grassy slope towards the Lodge garden, where she could see Olivia bending over some plants. She wondered if she could ask her about boys: how to manage things. Sometimes, when she was alone with Adam, even though he hadn't asked her again to do the things they had on the boat when they were sailing to France, she was almost frightened by her own feelings. Afraid that one day she might not be able to help wanting him to go too far. That would spoil it all but what was she supposed to do when the feelings started?

Once or twice lately she had seen her father watching her, a softer expression in his eyes than she'd ever seen before, and had almost blurted out some of her troubled thoughts. But it had been so long…she couldn't remember what it had been like to really talk, and just the thought of even hinting to him about some of the things that she and Adam had done together made her go hot all over.

Olivia straightened from staking and tying an overlarge clump of delphiniums, and for the moment Kate put aside her worries; waving and calling a greeting she bounded on long coltish legs down the slope.

'You must be psychic.' Olivia held the gate open for her. 'I was going to ring your house with some good news when I'd finished in the garden; I've found an absolutely lovely woman who lives half way between Pels Point and Lodscombe, and is willing to help at your place every day and see to the meals. She's also going to give a hand clearing up here a couple of afternoons a week.' Olivia gave a cheerful grin. 'Painting and housework just don't mix with me, I'm afraid. Pushing things into cupboards as a way of keeping the place tidy is all right, but I'm rapidly running out of cupboards.'

Kate gave a gurgle of laughter. 'Dad never puts anything away, even in cupboards, but I'm really pleased to know I shan't get stuck with the cooking every weekend when Miriam leaves. I'll have enough to do working for my A levels.'

'Sit down, I'll get some coffee.' Olivia moved the simmering kettle further onto the hotplate and spooned powdered coffee into mugs. 'What are you planning to do?'

'Law, I hope … it's about time there were more women in that. Not that I particularly want to end up as anything too hair-raising, like a Q.C, or a judge … a nice country town solicitor's office of my own would do me.'

Olivia smiled. 'My father was a barrister. I remember going to watch him when he was in court in Exeter and hoping everyone would know I was his daughter. I thought he was terribly handsome and distinguished, all got up in his wig and gown, and I was absolutely devastated when he lost a case, because I just knew he must be right and the other chap wrong! He would take me into the Rayleigh when the court rose and feed me tea and buns to console me.'

'Perhaps I'll aim a little higher … I rather fancy the wig and gown, although I should hate losing.' Kate folded her arms on the table, fixing her blue gaze on Olivia's face. 'Adam said his dad wants him to do medicine, but he isn't sure he wants to do that, is he?'

'Isn't he?' Olivia masked her surprise. Well, well … Tom had said it could be a mistake to follow in father's footsteps; perhaps Adam might be feeling that way … hence the ghastly exam results. 'He hasn't said anything to me, but he'll have to make up his mind what he's going to do before gets down to *his* A levels.'

Kate began to stir sugar into her coffee. 'He ought to go into the Navy. Liam says he's got a mathematical brain and is brilliant at navigating. He reckons he's a born sailor, but not a yachtsman. He says it's the sea Adam's crazy about, not the sailing.' She shrugged, and grinned. 'I can't see the difference, but Liam can.'

Olivia sat cradling her cup in both hands, wondering if the information being offered was coming first or second hand. She thought Adam was sufficiently like Giles to play his cards close to his chest, and he might be just too uncertain about his father's reaction to have said anything, even to Kate.

'Has Adam discussed this with you, or mentioned the Navy?'

'No. I don't know if he's thought about it. I just know he's not keen on being a doctor.' She looked suddenly hunted. 'Oh, crumbs! You won't let on that I've said anything, will you? Men are so touchy, aren't they? You never know when you're treading on their corns.'

Olivia smiled and asked dryly, 'You've already discovered that, have you?' I wish I had, at sixteen.'

Kate looked down into her cup. She felt her stomach begin to quiver and took a deep breath. 'I'm discovering quite a lot of things about men at sixteen … whether I want to or not.'

Olivia thought she knew a good opening when she saw one. Meeting Kate's suddenly uncertain expression she answered reassuringly, 'I imagine you are. I seem to remember that quite a few took me by surprise at your age, and I don't suppose things have changed very much, have they?'

*　　　*　　　*

Ambrose heard the front door being closed very quietly and left the studio to discover that Liam had already disappeared into his room. He rapped on the door and walked in without waiting for an invitation.

'How did it go?'

Liam jumped to his feet. Hell, the old man never *ever* came into his room. 'OK. I suppose.' He strove to be his usual surly self, which wasn't easy with the pleasure and excitement of the past hour still churning inside. 'It went all right.'

'Good, because you're on a crash course for a week, starting on Monday.' His father surveyed him impassively. 'Naturally, I want something in return for my generosity.'

Liam curled his lip. 'Like what?'

'Like you handing me any wacky baccy you may have secreted about your person, or this room, and a promise not to buy any more with my money.' Ambrose scowled at his son's startled expression. 'You do know what a promise is, don't you?'

Liam sat back down on the edge of his bed, gnawing at his lower lip in silence. 'Yeah, but I haven't got anything left,' he said grudgingly at length. 'I couldn't afford the French stuff and you can't exactly buy it at the village shop.'

'What did you do with the money I gave you the other day?'

'Spent it on crisps and stuff for us to eat on the boat, 'n I got some fags.'

'So it wasn't a complete reformation.' His father pointed a sudden threatening finger. 'Now look here, all this bloodyminded, infantile snot-nosed behaviour has got to stop. You may not like me and sure, there are plenty of times when I don't like you overmuch, but I'm not going to sit back and watch you making a bloody fool of yourself –

205

an' me.' He paused to yank a chair from against the wall. Plonking it down in front of his stony-faced son he straddled it, and laying his arms along the back said succinctly, 'You are not leaving this room until we've thrashed out where it is you think you are going with all your pot smoking and booze; so take that feckin' sulky look off your face an' start behaving like a man, or I may just break a lifetime habit and really lose me temper.'

Liam smirked. 'Your brogue's showing, Daddy-O!' then at his father's expression moved hastily back across his bed and slouched against the wall. 'All right, all right; don't blame me for not bursting into song because you've suddenly noticed I exist.'

'Well now, you're going to notice that *I* exist as something other than a source for keeping you supplied with your various adolescent versions of a baby's dummy.' Ambrose bared his teeth in a sudden ferocious smile. 'You never know … in time you might even get to like me as a father.'

'You reckon?' Almost there was an answering smile. Ambrose gave a roar of laughter and slapped his knees.

'Yeah, man, I reckon!'

'You're too old to swing,' Liam drew his brows together in a scowl at having exposed a chink in his armour. 'Why the sudden change anyway? You haven't bothered about me for years.'

'Not quite true, I've bothered about you all right. I just haven't let you know.' Ambrose stood up quickly and turned away. 'Kate's not back so I'll start lunch and you can tell me all about your life's ambitions while we eat … and I still want that promise.'

He left the room abruptly. Liam sat staring for a minute or two at the chair he'd vacated then shrugged and followed him. Lounging down the stairs his hands in his pockets he stopped at the open kitchen door. 'Want a hand?' he asked grudgingly.

'You could toast some bread.' Ambrose reached for a tin of beans and Liam groaned aloud.

'Not more of those ruddy things, da, when Miriam's gone I reckon you and me will be farting for England!'

'What then? I'm not up to her version of *cordon bleu.*'

There was a silence. From under lowered brows Ambrose watched the struggle taking place on his son's face. Eventually Liam passed a tongue over his lips and suggest gruffly: 'So let's go to the pub.'

'Might as well.' Ambrose didn't risk meeting his eyes, but added an equally gruff, 'better make it quick though. Unlike you I can't spend all my waking hours sitting on my arse. I'm working to a deadline, you know.'

When aren't you? Thought Liam cynically as they walked up the cobbled street, then gave himself a metaphorical kick. *Don't be such a rotten sod! At least the old man's trying; I just wish I could figure out why!*'

*   *   *

'I like the casual clothes you've bought, but I'm surprised Giles let you get away with one or two of them ... this, for instance.' Olivia held up a double-breasted brass-buttoned Naval overcoat that must practically brush his ankles. Remembering Kate's confidences she repressed a smile. A spot of wishful thinking, perhaps?

'He didn't.' The tips of her son's ears glowed. 'Er ... *she* did ... Zoë; we went shopping down the Kings Road and Carnaby Street. Everyone's wearing things like that in London now. Great, isn't it?'

'Fab,' she agreed dryly, 'all you need now is the cap and a row of medals to go with it. So you got on all right together?'

'Yeah. She's OK; not really pretty or anything, except her eyes, but just funny and sparkly...' He coloured and looked away. 'I didn't want to like her, but somehow, well, you can't help it really.'

'It's all right.' Olivia smiled. 'You're allowed to like her. It would be pretty unpleasant for dad if you didn't.' She slipped the coat over her shoulders and pirouetted slowly. 'What d'you think, does it suit me?'

'Yes, but it's for me, mum,' he grinned, 'wish I could wear it for school. Papa would absolutely foam at the mouth.'

'And with good reason.' She delved deeper into his case then straightened slowly, holding at arm's length a green shirt with a long pointed collar and purple flowers rioting across the front. '*Adam –* really!'

He blushed. 'Don't tell dad. Zoë hid it at the bottom of my school things, she said...' he stifled a giggle, 'that she was thinking of getting him one for his birthday!'

Olivia's mouth curved into a smile. 'Then she has more courage than I have.'

He giggled again. 'Or me.'

21

'Kate said she had lunch with you on Friday.' Ambrose spoke with his back to Olivia, who continued painting in silence. He turned around and glowered. 'She came back looking about thirty-five and called me Pop!'

'I hope you were flattered.' She paused, and regarded him narrow-eyed. 'You've no idea how funny you look when you try to cover your embarrassment by growling and showing your claws.'

He studiously ignored the jibe. 'What did you talk about?'

'Women's things. What subjects did you discuss with my son the other week?' she countered.

'Men's things!' His mouth twitched. 'Do we call a halt to play or keep the ball in the air a little longer?'

'We-ell, I wouldn't mind batting the subject of Liam and his driving lessons back and forth for a while, not to mention the visit the pair of you made to the pub.'

'I knew when I saw your father there that news would travel fast.' He sat back on his stool and grinned. 'OK, so it's a gas. Laugh all you like; it was you started it all by lecturing me about my kids.'

'Naturally, it would be my fault. It almost always was…'

She caught herself up, closing her mouth firmly and he sat and watched as the colour crept up her cheeks. Moved by her embarrassment at the sudden unguarded moment he asked softly: 'It goes on hurting, doesn't it?'

'Yes, it does.'

'Well, that gives us something in common, quite apart from a clutch of awkward adolescents to push and shove in what we hope is the right direction.'

'You hope.' She gave a faint grin. 'I'm not entirely sure that *I'm* going in the right direction.'

For a long moment she found herself held by his vivid gaze. Her colour deepened; she gave a nervous little laugh and turned again to her canvas. 'You're getting to be very astute in your old age, Flynn. Perhaps we should both get on with our work.'

'I can't.' Suddenly brusque, he strode to the door. 'You've broken my blasted concentration. I might as well put the kettle on.'

He stood against the range, leaning both hands on the rail.

She's got to you, you bloody fool, and all you can do is run; and with good reason. She doesn't need some emotionally crippled old fart in her life; she doesn't want *anyone, except perhaps whichever beard it was she kissed first ... and how do I know what she does or doesn't want?* He gave a grim smile. *I know because I've been there and back more than once these past five years...*

'How long does that kettle have to boil before we get coffee?' Olivia spoke behind him and he gave her a sphinx-like glance over one shoulder.

'Tea. I forgot to order the coffee. Miriam usually shops but she's had other things on her mind: like screwing the boyfriend rigid every night.'

He reached for the canister and took the teapot she handed him. He cleared his throat. 'I suppose I was rude in the studio – and just now? I haven't quite got used to having a wo – to having anyone around when I work. I'm sorry.'

'No need.' She sat at the table watching him. 'I started it. I didn't know you were touchy about your age.'

'I'm not.'

She grinned. 'Out with it then, Flynn: how old are you?'

'Fifty-six,' he was truculent, 'how old are you?'

'Let's say you have almost a ten year head start on me.'

'So mind your elders and betters, my girl.'

'All right, mister. You're not so old you are allowed to get tetchy.' She stood to fetch the milk jug to the table and set out two mugs. 'I'm only taking a short break. I aim to finish today.'

His heart plummeted. 'So soon?'

'I'm a fast worker.' She smiled. 'I bet you've had a peek or two under the cloth when I'm not here.'

'I've done no such thing, woman. Have *you* tried sneaking into the back room to see your bust before it's cast?' He sat opposite her and began to pour the tea.

'Certainly not. But I'll unveil for you tomorrow...' She broke off at his involuntary sly smile and flushed again. 'Correction: I'll unveil your *portrait* for you tomorrow!'

In her confusion she dropped a lump of sugar into the cup he handed her and stirred absentmindedly. He watched in silence for a moment, before observing mildly: 'You don't take sugar.'

'I do today!' she snapped. He took out a handkerchief and waved it above his head and she laughed. 'All right. Sorry. Truce then. At least until tomorrow when I'll be out from under your feet.'

'You don't have to get out.' He was hunched over the table, head lowered so that she couldn't read his face. 'I never use the whole studio and you don't really have decent facilities for painting at the Lodge.'

'That's a very kind offer but you are used to working alone; having someone around all the time must disturb you.'

'Perhaps I can do with a little of that.' He leaned his elbows on the table and watched her face. 'Besides, apart from our little sparring matches, which if we are honest we both enjoy, you are a very peaceful person to have around.'

She hesitated, sipping at her tea, making a face at the sweetness. 'I suppose it might work. After all, when I'm through with your portrait, and weather permitting, I'm mostly out and about, aren't I?'

'It's a bargain, then?'

He smiled, leaning across the table and holding out his hand. Remembering how he had taken her by surprise the last time he'd moved to seal an agreement with her she said briskly, 'Just you spit on it first, Flynn, and keep your distance!'

He gave his rumbling laugh. 'You too.' She put out her hand and he smacked his big palm down on hers. 'Done.'

*   *   *

Halting on their way to the back door, Adam, Kate and Liam stood transfixed, staring in at the kitchen window. '*Jesus*!' Liam spoke in hushed and awed tones. 'Either my old man's making your ma an indecent proposal, mate, or he's just sold her a bloody horse!'

Ambrose turned swiftly at the concerted explosion of mirth from beyond the window and made a threatening fist at the three faces. 'Clear off, you grinning idiots, damn you. We're having an artistic conference!'

Shrieking loudly the three fled to the harbour, where they flung themselves down on the Morning Star's deck, rolling around in paroxysms of laughter.

'Did you *see* them?' wept Kate, wiping her eyes on her shirt. 'Talk about Scarlet and Rhett!'

'Or Fred and Ginger!' choked Adam.

'More like Bluto and Olive Oyl!' Liam howled and set them all off again.

Adam held a hand to his aching side. 'What were they really doing?'

'Making a pact.' Liam raised his head from the deck. 'That's what the horse-dealers do at the fairs in Ireland. I remember from when pa used to take me over on holiday. Why? What did you think they were

210

doing?'

Adam went faintly pink. 'I don't know any Irish horse dealers, do I? For all I know they might have been limbering up for a fight!'

'Not those two.' Kate gave a knowing, sly look at her brother. 'You are a thickie Liam. You can't see what's under your nose, can you?' She grinned at Adam. 'Don't look so innocent, *you* know, don't you?'

'Know what?' Liam knit his brow. 'What's the mystery?'

Kate gave a loud snort of laughter. 'Dad fancies Adam's mother but she doesn't know it yet, stupid.'

Liam gaped. 'Omigawd!' He tilted back on his chair. '*That's* why he's become halfway human! Brilliant ... but she's much too good for *him*!'

'Don't get carried away. I don't think she's even given it a thought,' Adam said. 'I definitely don't want Kate as a sister and I don't need a father, I already have one of those ... and I don't know what *you're* so pleased about, she'd bloody soon sort *you* out if you stepped out of line.'

'Oh, *please*!' Liam was fervent, clasping his hands together and rolling his eyes, 'your mother is quite something and I'd just love to be sorted out by her! But dad's almost bound to cock it up, dismal old git that he is, so you've nothing to worry about, you ungenerous, greedy sod.'

*   *   *

'Load of yobbos!' Ambrose jumped up to watch the three career down the hill. He turned back to Olivia, his eyes glittering. She met his furious gaze and for a few moments tried valiantly to stifle her own mirth before breaking down completely. For a moment he stood glaring at her bowed head and heaving shoulders then sat down again, muttering an unintelligible string of oaths beneath his breath.

'I beg your pardon?' Olivia raised her head and dabbed at her streaming eyes with a handy corner of the tablecloth. '*What* did you say?'

'Never you mind. It is the Gaelic, and you don't want to know.'

He continued to glare, lips pressed tightly together. 'Sorry!' Olivia clasped a hand over her mouth, her eyes made enormous with the effort not to laugh, and slowly the line of Ambrose's mouth began to break. An audible rumble started deep inside his chest, erupting finally into a roar of laughter.

She rummaged in her pocket for her handkerchief and wiped her eyes again. 'This is all terribly juvenile, Flynn.'

'I don't think I've ever seen a woman that merry before,' his eyes snapped with laughter. 'Are you sure you'll be able to continue painting after all that?'

'The muse is strong upon me…' she stifled another snort. 'For two pins I'd change your expression to match the one you had just now – I thought you were going to throw a fit.'

'I damn' near did.'

A companionable silence fell between them and they sat smiling at each other across the table.

Like emeralds, Ambrose mused, *her eyes are like emerald pools, deep enough to drown in.* Slowly his own eyes travelled down her neck to the vee of her shirt; the top buttons were undone and he could see the beginning of the hollow between her breasts. He wrenched his eyes and thoughts away. *My God, had he really suggested they continue to work under the same roof? I'm mad,* he thought, *stark, staring mad. This woman has never given even the slightest hint that she sees me as anything other than a rude old lecher whom she's determined to keep at arm's length. Added to that I still have a wife and she still has a husband. Even if she were willing, I wouldn't just want a quick roll in the hay. I'd want much, much more than that.*

Olivia noted his expression and the direction of his eyes and flushed, stifling her involuntary response to his look. *No more occasional lovers*, she admonished silently.

She was past wanting one of those, thanks to Tom, who had given her all she needed, when she needed it. When she was ready to start again, without walking into absolute disaster, it was highly unlikely to be with anyone as volatile and unpredictable as Ambrose Flynn.

He eyed her sardonically for a moment, then pushed a hand through his hair and pursed his lips. 'Back to work, I think, don't you?'

She finished her tea and stood, gathering her composure about her like an invisible shield. 'Without a doubt, Mr Flynn,' she said, and led the way back to the studio.

*   *   *

'After this morning's little exhibition,' she told Adam severely, 'what you need is a jolly good slap around your leg.'

'Sorry, mum, was Liam's dad as furious as he looked?'

'I think that would be rather an understatement. All three of you behaved disgracefully. I should think the entire village heard you caterwauling your way down the hill.'

'It was pretty funny, mum … both of you spitting and whacking your hands around like that…' Adam suppressed a giggle then widened his eyes at her expression. 'Sorry again!'

'Don't dig yourself any deeper. Just keep quiet and lay the table.' She turned aside to hide a smile. 'I suppose you thought that if you stayed away long enough it would all have blown over? Well it hasn't. I've a good mind to make you go over tonight and apologise to Ambrose.'

'Oh *mum,*' he began to lay the cutlery with the injured air of a wrongly accused felon, then asked with sudden formality 'You know something mother?'

'What?'

'You can be really rotten sometimes; you're not like you used to be. You've changed.'

'Is that so?' she answered dryly, 'well so have you, and judging by this morning's little incident I reckon it's about time I pulled you up … by the ears, if necessary.'

*   *   *

When Adam arrived at the boat the next morning Kate and Liam were already busy cleaning and polishing on the upper deck. Kate greeted him with a hideous grimace. 'Dad tore us both off an enormous strip when we got back last night.'

Liam gave a dismissive snort. 'All piss and vinegar! Underneath you could see he was laughing at us.' He grinned. 'He's definitely mellowing, so I reckon you two were right … it must be *lurve.*'

Adam fell silent; taking up a tin of Brasso and a rag he went aft to start polishing the rails. He worked slowly and thoughtfully, remembering that when Ambrose had cornered him on the boat that time, he'd been tickled to hear the ferocious Flynn's deep voice soften every time he'd spoken about mum. Then it had all seemed a bit of a joke and he'd thought it funny enough to make that idiotic remark when he got home.

But she *was* spending a lot of time with the big man and she *had* changed.

He stared thoughtfully up at the pink house on the hill, remembering how he had always been able to get around her to shield him from his father when a storm was brewing. Now she sometimes had a look in her eye that quite clearly said if he stepped too far over the line with *her,* then he'd better watch out.

He loved his mother, of course he did, and he'd always tried to do as she asked. But his father had been the final authority to be obeyed; the one who laid down the law and punished him if necessary. Now, she'd suddenly assumed that role in his life. It was all very confusing and a bit humiliating.

And just suppose she did like that bearded Irish giant; liked him a lot. What would she do? Would it be like dad and Zoë? Would she want to *live* with him? The way she was now, he thought glumly, she'd do it if she wanted to, even if it gave gran and pops and everyone else in Lodscombe a fit, which it probably would. He didn't want anybody coming along to mess up his life again and spoil everything. He was only just getting used to being without dad. Perhaps if he really showed her how much he hated the idea she'd give up spending so much time with Kate's father. There were plenty of ways he could do that.

He gazed out over the water, remembering what Doyle had said to him that time he'd wanted to run away: "Don't leave any mess behind that's of your making." Belatedly, he faced up to the fact that even now his mother might be lonely enough to need company other than his own; that when he'd left school she would be alone all the time and that couldn't be right, could it?

He sighed. It seemed he'd better start watching his step with the big man, and not make any more trouble for his mother or himself.

22

Zoë stretched like a cat against the pillows. 'Just think: three whole weeks with no theatre and no rehearsals … just you and me with all that much time to do with as we wish!'

Giles grinned back at her as he stood before the bedroom mirror, buttoning down his collar. 'Not quite, darling. I can't get away until Friday.'

'Could we spend this weekend in London?'

Giles wrinkled his nose. 'Why London? It stinks.'

'I need some clothes; warm ones for Canada. Jimmy says it'll be freezing by the time we arrive. As we're now into September the West End stores will have all their winter stuff in. I promise I'll do all my shopping in one fell swoop.'

'All right … where would you like to go for our holiday? How about Basingstoke? Or, I know, maybe Walthamstow or Croydon?'

She gave a splutter of laughter. 'Somewhere warm, please, just to set me up for the frozen wastes of Canada, and New England at Christmas.'

He was suddenly sober, his smile fading. 'I wish we could have been together then.'

'So do I,' she caught her lower lip between her teeth, 'Giles, are you quite sure?'

'Yes.' He summoned a smile. 'I can wait. There will be other Christmases.'

'What will you do? Please don't spend it alone.'

'I may go to Paris … save my father coming over here and creating mayhem.'

'What does he do in Paris?'

'Nothing much since he retired, apart from wining and dining and playing cards with his old cronies. He was in the Diplomatic Corps and has lived in France since the war; most of his friends are in Paris anyway. He and Olivia get on like a house on fire. She's always visited him quite regularly and they talk on the 'phone, but even she's funked telling him we've parted.'

'Will you tell him about us?'

'I think I shall have to. He'll give me absolute hell because he's very fond of Olivia. He won't like missing out on his Christmas visit either, and of course he'll want to see his grandson. I suppose I could take Adam to Paris with me if he wanted to come. It would take the pressure off Olivia.'

'But he wants you to go to Devon for Christmas. He told me when we were out together.' She was watching him closely.

'That might be difficult.' Giles turned from the mirror. 'And you would hate it if I did.'

'Not really. Not any more.' She grimaced. 'I shouldn't be so sure of you, should I?'

'No, but I rather like it.' He crossed the room and taking her face between his hands bent to kiss her mouth. 'You are all I shall ever want, or need, and I shall wait for you with as much patience as I can summon … which may not be much, but at least I'll try.'

She traced his features with a finger, then kissed him lightly and pushed him from her. 'Go away, or I shall never get out of this bed.'

'Come and have lunch with me. The Crown at Ranleigh.'

'Is that a good idea, so close to the hospital?'

He shrugged. 'They have to know some time, and frankly I don't much care any more. Sometimes I'd just like to shut up shop at the hospital and go.'

'Don't be silly. You'd be miserable as sin.'

'I don't mean give up surgery.' He smiled. 'But I've been in a nice comfortable rut at Ranleigh for a very long time now and I'd like a change.'

'To where?'

'Don't know. I haven't thought about it that deeply yet. I might take a sabbatical and do bugger all for a year!' he kissed her again, 'I must go. See you at lunchtime.'

She wrapped the counterpane around her and went to the window to watch him cross the road to his car. As though he sensed her eyes upon him he turned, saw her watching, then smiled and waved before ducking into the driving seat.

Giving a return wave as he drove away she went back to sit on the edge of the bed to imagine being married to him and starting every day of her life this way. After a few minutes she lay back across the bed to contemplate the ceiling with narrowed eyes. 'I couldn't do it,' she said aloud. 'I'll never ever make a proper wife. Jimmy's right. Theatre first, home life a poor second, and that only for a few weeks at a time, then off I go again…' she sighed heavily. 'Darling Giles, I do love you, even if Jimmy doesn't believe it, but will you really go on loving me when you know that other part of me will always win?'

For a moment she cocked her head as though listening, then said conversationally: 'You know, God, if darling mummy is right and you really are up there in the wide blue yonder, stop combing your long white beard and lend a helping hand now and again; give me a shove in the right direction, because I'm buggered if I know which way to jump to keep everyone happy – and that includes *me*!'

*   *   *

Adam sat in the back of the Land-Rover, wedged between the wooden case that carried Ambrose's sculpture of his mother, and Olivia's crated canvases. He was horribly conscious that he would be in for a certain amount of leg-pulling when seen rolling up at Chiltens in this battered vehicle; his chauffeur the undeniably flamboyant Flynn.

True, Ambrose had trimmed his beard for the occasion and tamed his hair and wore shoes and socks in place of the usual sandals, but his green corduroy suit was worn and comfortable, his shirt boldly checked and innocent of any tie. In place of that item was a knotted blue silk scarf. Still, Adam had to admit that he was rather fun to be with. As the miles rolled by he spun outrageous yarns; from time to time burst into song in a mellifluous baritone, and was altogether in roaring high spirits.

Seated beside Flynn, Olivia laughed, occasionally joining in the singing while turning frequently to smile reassuringly at Adam, as though to let him know that she understood his feelings and was there to see everything was all right.

At first when she'd told him he had to share their journey to London as far as the school, he'd baulked at the idea. Why couldn't she take him back alone as she always had in the past, he'd demanded, adding sulkily that he would take the train; that he wasn't going to be seen arriving back escorted by any scruffy great Irishman with clay in his hair. Although he had apologised later he still felt embarrassed at how childishly selfish he must have sounded and made great efforts now to be sociable. The business of taking a back seat, both in the figurative and literal sense, in order that his mother could enjoy Ambrose Flynn's company was, he acknowledged moodily, proving bloody difficult.

Olivia watched him in the rear view mirror and read some of his thoughts, sensing too that he was hiding other well-buried worries that he was not yet willing to share with her. If Kate was right, those were most likely to be about his future choice of career, but she couldn't force him to talk if he didn't want to, and so far he had confided nothing, remaining tight-lipped and uncommunicative about Giles' reception of his exam results and what, if anything, he was

217

going to do about them.

She supposed she would just have to watch and wait until he was ready.

*   *   *

The first people they saw as they drew up before the school steps were Tom Doyle and his new wife. Thank God, Olivia thought as Ambrose helped her down from the Land-Rover, that Tom had been so prompt in 'phoning with his news; it had given her the time to make occasional casual reference to his married state commonplace. At least Adam wouldn't gape or commit any frightful faux pas, and she could meet the somewhat farcical situation with composure.

'Mrs Ryder, Adam,' Doyle shot a startled glance at Ambrose then recovering swiftly took Olivia's hand, keeping his eyes and mouth firmly under control, 'and Mr Flynn … I didn't expect to see you here today.'

'I didn't expect to be here, but curiosity drove me.' Ambrose gave Jayne an appreciative once over, and smiling broadly took both of her hands in his. 'Congratulations. About time this place had some new blood … and very attractive new blood it is!'

Olivia muttered a caustic 'Blarney!' under her breath then greeted the new Mrs Doyle with a smile: 'I admire your courage. Wild horses wouldn't get me to stay here surrounded by your husband's charges, fond though I am of my own.' Beside her she was aware that Adam was gawping admiringly at Jayne, eagerly taking the hand she offered and giving his wide ingenuous smile.

'Hel-*lo*, Mrs Doyle!' he breathed, so like Giles that for a moment Olivia teetered between a desire to laugh and the itch to smack him.

Doyle eyed him sternly. 'That's quite enough from you. Try to remember that you are now a senior member of this zoo.'

'Yes, sir,' Adam turned to Ambrose. 'Cheers, thanks for the cabaret; 'bye, mum.' He gave Olivia a nonchalant wave before running up the steps to disappear through the open doors.

Doyle gave her an inquiring glance. 'Everything all right there?'

Olivia gave a lift of her shoulders. 'So-so.'

'Shall I dig?'

'Please.'

'In any special area?'

'Father's footsteps … I think.'

The two onlookers silently registered this exchange between people who were only too obviously intimate enough to use that

218

particular kind of verbal shorthand.

Oh, ho, thought Jayne, so she's the one!

Ah, ha, deduced Ambrose, so that's the beard she kissed before mine!

Blissfully unaware that they had given themselves away, Mr Doyle and Mrs Ryder resumed their polite exchange of small talk, until another set of parents arrived, when they shook hands again and parted without a backward glance.

*   *   *

'No more music?' Olivia gave Ambrose a sideways look, 'five miles at least with never a word, and not a single aria.'

He concentrated on the road ahead. This was not, he decided, the moment to start asking questions, however much he might want to confirm that Doyle had been the reason for her frequent disappearances in the fairly recent past. Although as the damned man was now well and truly married, he supposed that gave some ray of hope for the future. Anyway, if he did ask she'd more than likely tell him to mind his own business…

He gave a non-committal grunt. 'I've just about exhausted my not inconsiderable repertoire on the musical side and was wondering if you still wanted to travel down to Hampshire by train tonight? Wouldn't you rather stay in town? There are plenty of comfortable hotels, you know.'

'Thanks, but I really ought to stay the night with Chris and Carol. We've been neighbours and friends for years. Besides, I do rather miss letting my hair down to another woman.'

'Ah. Wouldn't I just like to be a fly on the wall when you do.'

She laughed and settled back into her seat. 'Don't let your imagination run riot, Flynn. Just get us to London in one piece and I promise I'll relay any really juicy bits on the way back tomorrow.'

'I may hold you to that. If I pick you up from this Carol's place when I've finished at the foundry, say about midday, will that be about right?'

'Fine. But be warned. She's a huge fan of yours so it won't just be hello and goodbye. You'll not get away until you've had a good and probably highly indigestible vegetarian lunch!'

He groaned. 'God save me from gushing women, especially vegetarians.'

'I should think that's a small price to pay to have me out of your hair for the evening.'

'But you won't go tonight until we've had dinner, will you?' he asked quickly. 'We have to celebrate.'

'You know *you* have nothing to worry about.' She made a wry face. 'Your pal Constantine may change his mind when he sees what I have to offer.' She hunched her shoulders. 'Quite honestly, I'm scared stiff; in fact I wish I was safely home in Lodscombe painting pictures for the local gallery to sell. I don't think I'm ready to fly quite so high just yet.'

He took one hand off the wheel to lay it briefly over hers.

'Don't worry, you'll fly all right: and higher than you think. I know these things. I'm in the business, remember?'

'I still wish you hadn't persuaded me to bring your portrait. I don't particularly want that to go on view. It's the first portrait I've done in an age and I really only painted it for myself.'

He shrugged. 'Don't be selfish. It's a beautiful piece of work and deserves to be coveted by someone with taste … and a lot of money! After all, you can see my ugly mug in the original any day of the week. Surely to God you don't want your version of it to hang on your sitting room wall?'

She smiled mockingly. 'Don't flatter yourself. I was going to hang it by a piece of string over the damp patch in the scullery.'

He whistled through his teeth. 'That's my girl!' he said.

*　　　*　　　*

Ambrose finished his conversation with Constantine and joined Olivia where she stood at the gallery window, gazing out at the passing traffic. 'Feeling better now?' he asked, placing an arm about her shoulders.

She smiled. 'I'm walking on air. It's a long time since I was paid quite so many compliments.'

'You deserve them.' He kept his arm about her and joined her in watching the busy street. Suddenly, he gave his growling laugh. 'Nice pair of legs over there!'

Following the direction of his gaze Olivia felt her knees buckle.

On the pavement opposite the gallery, Giles and Zoë Ormonde walked hand in hand, her long legs matching his stride. Olivia saw Giles bend towards her upturned face as she spoke, then tilt back his head to laugh like a boy, and the girl hugged his arm and laughed with him.

'It's all right. I have you.' Olivia realised Ambrose was clasping her shoulders with both hands and guiding her to a chair. 'I thought

220

you said you were feeling better? I didn't realise you were *that* nervous.'

'It has nothing to do with nerves!' Olivia fought her way through the enveloping fog of emotion, furious at the involuntary shaft of pure uncontrolled jealousy that had raced through her. 'I thought I'd passed being knocked off course by Giles, but the bastard's still at it!'

'You've lost me.' Still holding her shoulders, Ambrose sat back on his heels, peering up into her face. 'You're not hallucinating by any chance, are you?'

'No,' she began to laugh unsteadily. 'That girl … the one with the legs … that was Giles she was hanging on to. Now you've seen what he left me for.'

He looked gravely into her eyes. 'I don't see he got such a big deal,' he answered, 'the legs are great, but she's absolutely no arse at all.'

'No good to pose for your tail-less mermaid then?' Olivia's voice shook with laughter but her eyes were bright with tears.

'Useless,' he returned firmly. 'No tits to speak of, either!'

Olivia's mouth crumpled. She dug her nails into his arm, whispering urgently: 'Flynn, just get me out of here for a few minutes, will you? I think I'm going to have hysterics.'

Andoni Constantine watched through the window as his celebrated client whisked through the swing doors to stand on the crowded pavement, bellowing with laughter and holding in his arms the gallery's most recently acquired *artiste,* who was weeping tears of mirth, or pain, or both onto his checked shirt and looking as radiant as a weeping woman could look.

Andoni shrugged; the English, such an extraordinary people.

23

Olivia wound down her window, letting the rush of air cool her head. 'Carol will dine out on your visit for months. I had no idea you could be so gallant.'

'My good deed for the year,' Ambrose grinned. 'I quite like a spot of hero-worship, now and again.'

'And you ate all that vegetable curry without turning a hair.'

'*Noblesse Oblige* ... and it was an excellent curry.' He turned his head momentarily to glance at her face, noting the pallor beneath her tan and the shadows around her eyes. 'At the risk of getting a snappy back answer, I'd say you look as though you could do with a good night's sleep.'

'Um, I slept badly.' She leaned her head back and closed her eyes. 'I had one of those dreams; you know – or perhaps you don't – the sort when you find yourself in the past and can't quite believe it when you wake and find you are back in the present...'

'And remorse is crawling over you like so many invading ants,' he supplied as her voice trailed away.

She kept her eyes closed. 'There speaks a man who's been there; I couldn't have put it better myself.' A faint flush crept under her skin. 'Yesterday he looked so happy and just for that moment I hated him so much.'

'He's not worth sleepless nights.'

She opened her eyes and stared straight at the road ahead. 'How would you know?'

He shot her a quizzical look. 'I know an undesirable character when I see one; I've been one myself for years!'

Her mouth twitched. 'I suspect that's a quote.'

'You suspect right.'

She was silent again for a moment then sighed and said forlornly, 'I once told him he was an awful husband and he was terribly hurt. He said that was nonsense; he was a perfectly good husband but just hadn't managed to be a faithful one. It's that sort of breathtaking double-talk that makes a woman start thinking she's the one being unreasonable.' She skewed round in her seat to ask him, 'Were you a perfectly good husband?'

'Not particularly, but at least I was a faithful one.'

She studied his frowning profile and gave another sigh. 'Sorry.

I'm feeling a bit of a cow today. I enjoyed spending the time with Chris and Carol, but perhaps it wasn't a very good idea to go back there and see Riversmead again. Especially after the shock of spotting Giles and his piece ... and it was the weirdest evening.'

'In what way?'

'Oh, I don't know. It's hard to explain.' She closed her eyes again. 'Just watching Carol: all the fuss over getting the meal. The damask cloth and matching napkins, candles and after dinner mints, and I thought: 'what an absolute load of bollocks!'

She turned to stare at the deepening crow's feet around his eyes. 'You can laugh, but I used to do all that. It seemed important at the time. Now I can see I never ever did it for me. All that time-wasting and effort was for Giles, because that was how he liked to live. I can't get over how unbelievably idiotic I was to give up everything important to me, in order to minister to his every whim and keep him in the style to which his stupid cow of a mother had accustomed him.'

'You'll be telling me next that youth has passed you by and all you can see on the horizon is an old age full of resentment and regret.' He was blunt and forthright. 'Put a sock in it, woman! Life is for living. You should go down on your knees and give thanks for getting the chance to have another stab at it. After all you did once tell me that you'd had some very good years.'

The barb went home and she was stung into sarcasm. 'All I need is to be stuck in a travelling confessional with a philosophising bloody Irishman who is, needless to say, hardly in a position to play God.'

He didn't answer and she stared moodily out of the window, watching in silence the passing scenery. She shouldn't have snapped at him like that, she thought, it was all the fault of that bastard Giles for kicking her feet from under her by prancing around with his bloody girl friend.

An hour passed almost in silence. She couldn't shake off her feelings of resentment and niggling jealousy. To hell with you, Giles, she thought rancorously, I don't really want you in my life anymore, and certainly not second hand, so why does just the sight of you stir me up and make me so bloody miserable?

Suddenly she noticed they were nearing Pendene and was overcome by an almost desperate need to see Barty again; to sit with him in the cool familiar room and talk of anything but Giles. Momentarily she hesitated before asking tentatively: 'Flynn, d'you mind if we call in on a friend of mine? It won't take long and I'd like to see him. You don't have to meet him if you don't want to, but I think you'd like him.'

'If it will sweeten your temper, I'm prepared to make a diversion to Timbuktu!' he growled, and wondered if she knew just how wistful and lost she sounded. Or how much he would have liked to take her in his arms as he had yesterday, when they'd stood together on a London street and she had wept on his shoulder.

*   *   *

He stopped the Land-Rover before the cottage. 'D'you want to go in first?' he asked. 'See if anyone's at home. It looks pretty deserted.'

'I expect he's down the garden, he usually is.' Olivia climbed out. 'I'll go and see.'

Following the path around the cottage, she paused for a moment to savour the heady scent of the old-fashioned rambler rose climbing the side wall. The gravel path was meticulously raked and the borders of late summer flowers bloomed in an orderly manner. In the face of such pristine splendour she was suddenly conscious that her linen slacks and silk shirt were creased with travelling, and her hair, which had started the day in a neat coil on top of her head, was now escaping in waving tendrils about her face.

Barty, looking up at the sound of her footsteps, saw only the tanned skin, the casual clothes worn with careless elegance; the sunglasses pushed up onto the dark hair, and thought that he had never seen her looking lovelier. Putting down his basket of apples he held out both hands.

'I knew today was going to be special,' he smiled and bent to kiss her cheek. 'I even have a bottle of homemade wine in the cooler.'

'A large one, I hope.' Olivia laughed, tucking her arm in his as they turned towards the house. 'I'm on my way back from London via Hampshire. We took Adam to school yesterday...'

'*We*?' he queried.

'Don't pounce like that, Barty!' She smiled. 'I have brought a friend.'

He stopped and turned her to face him. 'Have you seen Tom and Jayne?'

'Yes. They seemed very happy; very content'

'Any regrets?'

'None,' she hesitated. Looking up into his eyes she asked, 'Have you forgiven us?'

'Of course,' the old man gave a down-turned smile. 'I wasn't angry with you, but with Tom. Although Jayne was leading him something of a dance, I knew that they loved each other and felt they

224

belonged together. I thought he had no right to keep meeting you.'

'Barty, was it your doing that made her suddenly decide to give it all up and come back to Tom?' Olivia asked, 'Did you warn her about what was happening?'

'I hoped you weren't going to ask that. Yes, I cabled her.' He gave a glance at her questioning face and hunched his shoulders. 'I suppose I shouldn't have, but I didn't want you to be hurt … and he wasn't the man for you, was he?'

'He might have been.' She sighed and gave a little shake of the head, 'but it wasn't for love that we went to bed; it was because we were both lonely. And I needed him, Barty. I was missing Giles – physically, emotionally and in every other way. Tom made me laugh and see life could still be fun and he made me feel like a woman again. I suppose you think it was wrong to become lovers without love?'

'Possibly, but I'm not so sure.' He took her arm once more in his and began walking again along the gravel path. 'Perhaps I shouldn't have meddled. I don't know. I'm just an old busy-body who thinks he knows what's best for everyone.'

'Like God, you mean?'

He lowered his brows, looking down into her mischievously innocent eyes for a moment, before giving his slow smile. 'Yes, my dear, *almost* like God, the difference being that He *does* know what He's doing!'

Ambrose had left the Land-Rover in the lane and was leaning on the closed gate as they appeared around the corner of the cottage. Straightening, he stared for a moment then gave a huge grin and sketched a genial salute.

'Hello, Padre, you left the khaki God-squad then, did you?'

'Hello, Wingco, I see you've had *your* wings clipped!'

Olivia gazed from one to the other. 'You two know each other?'

'You could say that.' Ambrose came through the gate and clasped the old man's hand warmly. 'You look one hell of a lot better than the last time I saw you. Older, but healthier.'

'I've heard all about Olivia's neighbour, Flynn the sculptor. I thought we may meet again one day.' Barty, his face wreathed in smiles and still grasping Ambrose's hand, turned to Olivia. 'I first met this lunatic when my convoy was blown up sixty miles beyond Bengazi. He'd spent three days flying at about fifty feet above the desert, in a Mosquito that had holes all over the fuselage and appeared to be held together with string, refusing to give up until he found we few survivors who were making our way back to camp.'

'That was before I realised they were headed by a Proddy vicar who shouldn't have been with an armed convoy in the first place, let alone lead a trek across a desert teeming with Panzers,' Ambrose interrupted rudely, 'if I had I might have stayed in the mess.'

But Barty wasn't to be silenced. 'If you ever want to really embarrass him, ask if you can see the medal he got!'

Olivia grinned at her discomfited and thunderously self-conscious companion. 'A medal – just fancy, better lead us to that bottle of wine now though, Barty, he's looking as though he may drive off any minute now and leave me stranded.'

With some ceremony Barty uncorked the wine, poured and handed each a generous measure, then settling into his chair raised his own glass. 'Here's to times past and a better future,' he looked at Ambrose and gave a sly grin, 'you've no idea how much I know about you; I hear you have a very pretty daughter and an awkward, anarchic son.' Ignoring Olivia's involuntary blush and Ambrose's continuing black looks he sipped at his drink then smacked his lips appreciatively. 'From all that I've heard I imagine *he* probably takes after his father!'

*   *   *

'If I'd known it would turn out to be a boozy old boys' reunion, I'd have taken the train home.' Olivia wrestled with the Land Rover's recalcitrant gears as they joined the traffic outside Dartmouth. 'It's a good job one of us had the sense to stay sober.'

There was no reply. She glanced sideways and saw that Ambrose had fallen asleep, his arms folded and his chin tucked comfortably into his chest. She tried to picture him younger; smooth shaven and uniformed. He would have been quite something, she thought. He still was, come to that...

The sudden remembrance of seeing Giles and Zoë Ormond cut across her pleasant musings. Again she shrank from the memory of her involuntary anger and jealousy, and wondered how she would have managed those few frightening moments without the immediate and unquestioning support that this man had given her. In contrast to Giles' familiar, confident embraces and Tom Doyle's less accustomed and dominant ones, it had been a novelty to be encircled by Ambrose's competent arms and feel the reassuring laughter shaking his big frame.

To be held closely against that broad chest had been rather more than just pleasant and comforting. Once she had recovered from her near hysterical outburst, she'd been both startled and gratified to find herself feeling cheerfully and agreeably sexy. Stopping at a red light she stole another glance at his face.

His eyes were open and he was watching her with his bright unblinking gaze. 'Hello,' he smiled, 'and who might be troubling you now, me darlin'?'

'You are!' she replied tersely. The lights changed and she crashed the gears.

He smiled again. 'Oh, good,' he said, and settled back contentedly into his previous somnolent state.

*   *   *

Doyle put his head around the kitchen door where Jayne was preparing supper.

'Darling, I have Adam Ryder due in ten minutes. He might be glad of a cup of tea before I'm finished.'

'I hope you're not going to batter him,' she looked up from chopping onions, 'because I'm clean out of cotton wool.'

He laughed. 'In about half an hour then … and some cake…'

*   *   *

Adam sat on the edge of his chair, watching Doyle cast an eye over his O-level papers. Looking up after a prolonged pause, the master asked casually, 'Are you happy with these grades?'

'They're all right, I suppose. About what I expected.' Adam was cautious. Doyle's expression as he'd read the exam results and form reports had been closed and inscrutable. 'My mother didn't say much but my father wasn't exactly overjoyed.'

'I'm not surprised. You'll have to work harder at those science subjects if you hope to get into medical school. That is what you're supposed to be aiming for, isn't it?'

Adam stared out of the window into the early evening mist. He was finding this session hard going at the end of a long day. Trapped by the soft cushions and fat brocade arms of the easy chair he felt at a disadvantage. He'd expected to be in Doyle's study discussing the essay on Shelley he'd sweated over to hand in yesterday, not invited into his sitting room to delve into the thorny matter of his choice of a future career. He decided it might be safer if he was a little vague. 'I'll try harder this year, sir.'

'You have a very bad habit, Ryder of dodging the issue;

227

something I've had to tell you about several times before.' Doyle dropped the papers on the floor and leaned back, folding his arms. 'I don't know exactly what you've done to upset him, but Mr Parrar tells me you are wasting his time in his class as you have no natural aptitude for biology; in fact, you are a disaster. Quite a stumbling block for a prospective medical student, one might think.'

Adam was embarrassed. 'He has it in for me because I was sick on my dead frog, that's all, sir.'

'Good Lord,' Doyle was startled. 'Were you really?'

Adam was defensive. 'I didn't expect it to stink like that when I cut it open.'

'A small matter, one might feel, compared with butchering a full-sized human cadaver reeking of formaldehyde.' Doyle couldn't help showing his amusement and Adam flushed.

'I expect I'd get used to it.'

'Are you quite sure you want to?' Doyle persisted. 'After all, why struggle to get a few embarrassing Cs doing something that makes you sick, when you've more than a fair chance of getting straight As in Maths and English and a very creditable B plus in everything else?'

'I don't think I could tell my father I'm not really interested in being a doctor. It's sort of always been expected I'd do medicine, you see.'

'Not good enough … this is *your* future we're discussing. Whatever you do, whether medicine or road sweeping, you should do it not because it might please someone else, but because it pleases you.' Doyle smiled suddenly. 'I really don't think either your father, or any prospective patients would approve of you wielding a half-hearted scalpel, do you?'

Adam gave a reluctant grin. 'I suppose not.'

'So, are you going to tell me what you do want, or am I as usual going to have to drag the truth out of you?'

'It's difficult.' Adam avoided his eyes. 'Everyone's going to think it's just something I've dreamed up in the holidays and say it won't last … like someone wanting to be a cross-channel swimmer after managing one width of the baths.'

Doyle sighed. 'Just stick to the point.'

'Well, I've spent most of these holidays sailing: really sailing, not just tacking around the coast with a picnic basket, and I can't think of anything better than spending my life at sea.' Adam frowned with the effort of putting his thoughts into words. 'It isn't just being out on the water and having a cracking good time; it's plotting and navigating that's the best part; especially at night when you're alone with just the sea and stars, and you know it's all up to you. I know it sounds stupid, and it's hard to explain...'

'Just sailing around in a yacht isn't exactly a practical career prospect, is it?'

'Oh, I wasn't thinking about *yachts,*' Adam was dismissive. 'They're OK, but only for fun. No, I want to do it properly: go into the Navy and serve on a frigate or a warship ... or even an aircraft carrier.' He narrowed his eyes, gazing into the middle distance, oblivious for the moment of anything beyond the dream.

'Then don't you think it rather dishonest to go along with something you've already decided isn't for you?'

The question jolted Adam out of his visionary thoughts. He looked crestfallen. 'I suppose it is.'

Poor little blighter thought Doyle, as if he hasn't got enough on his plate. 'If you really feel that's what you want, then you'll just have to find the courage to follow it through, won't you?' he said gently. 'You could at least have come to me and discussed it before now. It would have saved you a lot of worry and been much better in the long run.'

'I thought you'd try to make me change my mind,' Adam admitted honestly. 'My father will, and he'll be absolutely furious. If I tell him now that I want to chuck medical school for the Navy, he'll give me a really hard time – be sarcastic and say something like, if I took a ferry across the channel in a storm I'd soon feel differently about spending a life at sea.'

'You'll just have to find out the hard way by telling him, won't you?' Doyle's tone was dry. 'If you can face up to *me* when you're in trouble and live to tell the tale, you can surely manage to face up to your own father when he's at a safe distance on the other end of a telephone!'

'I suppose so.'

Doyle asked suddenly, 'What do you think your mother will have to say about such a change of plan at this late stage?'

'I think she'll be fine about it.' Adam's expression lightened and he grinned. 'I expect she'll be glad not to have to do my washing and ironing any more.'

Doyle smothered a smile and jerked his head towards the door. 'Well, what are you waiting for? Go and find out!'

*   *   *

Armed with a handful of sixpences, Adam dialled his first number with trembling fingers. When Giles answered he took a deep breath, 'Dad? I need to tell you something…

*   *   *

'Don't be such a bloody fool!' Giles was incredulous. 'You can't just suddenly up and change course like that. I won't have it … nor will I countenance any son of mine wearing bell bottoms and working for peanuts.'

'But I want to do it properly … go to Dartmouth.' Adam's voice trembled, but he stood his ground. 'Anyone would think I was rushing off to join-up as a deck hand. I need to get all my A levels first.'

'And what is suddenly wrong with medical school?'

'Well, nothing. I'm just not cut out for it. Dead things make me puke…'

'The purpose of being a doctor,' Giles interrupted with heavy sarcasm, 'is to keep your patients alive. You're not supposed to kill them off then throw up on them!'

'You know what I mean.' Adam found he was holding the 'phone so tightly that his fingers had gone white. Which is worse, he thought feverishly, fighting this out now with dad or going back to tell Doyle I've flunked it? He relaxed his grip and took another deep breath. 'I'm sorry if it makes you angry, dad, but I've made up my mind.'

'I can't believe this.' Giles almost howled, and Adam could imagine him clutching his brow. 'Now just you listen to me because I know what I'm talking about. Being in the Navy has nothing in common with sailing a bloody yacht to France and back. You have no idea of what you'd be letting yourself in for. I served aboard for four flaming years and though as a medic I didn't have the worst of it, it was still hell … and Dartmouth is nothing like school; it's exams and square bashing and a discipline that should have gone out with Nelson and didn't … and if you survive all that and think the worst is over, just wait until you've tried being at sea in a storm and are chucking up the entire content of your stomach in the heads … you'll soon change your mind then, believe me!'

There was a muffled explosion at the other end of the line and Giles held the receiver away from his ear for a moment before replacing it to ask suspiciously, 'Adam, are you by any chance laughing at me?'

'Of course not,' Adam stifled his mirth. 'Sorry … what were you saying?'

Ten minutes and a great deal of acrimonious discussion later, he

230

rang his second number.

'Are you quite sure?' Olivia asked as he finished speaking. 'It's a big step, isn't it?'

'Yes, I'm sure, mum.'

'Have you rung your father?'

'Yes.'

'And?'

'He wasn't pleased but I think he said it was OK in the end.' Adam skated swiftly over the full content of Giles' explosive reaction. 'I know he thinks I won't stick it out, but I will.'

'All right, darling, if that's what you want,' Olivia gave a small, relieved sigh. 'Just as long as you realise it's going to be a lot tougher than university and medical school … and don't think you're going to start sending your washing and mending home, will you? I just might have let you do that if you were at university, but sailors do that sort of thing for themselves.'

When she had put the phone down she stood looking at it with a puzzled frown, then stared blankly at her reflection in the kitchen mirror. 'Now what did I say that was *that* funny?' she asked aloud.

*   *   *

'Tea and cake?' inquired Jayne, as Adam returned.

'Please, Mrs Doyle.' He looked with studied attention at the laden tray she set down before raising innocent eyes to Doyle's face. 'After all this, do I get supper as well, sir?'

'Tell me the results of your 'phone calls *now*, or you'll be out of that door minus cake *and* supper.'

When Adam finished relaying an edited version of his conversation with each parent, Jayne laughed and Doyle gave his sardonic smile. 'I suppose,' he said, 'that you think you're very clever to have been almost one hundred per cent accurate in predicting their reactions.'

Adam finished his cake and licked a finger thoughtfully. 'Well, sir, they do say it's a wise child that knows its own father … and mother too, I suppose,' he said and grinned unrepentantly at Doyle's repressively lowered eyebrows.

*   *   *

As the door closed behind their visitor, Jayne began to gather up the cups and plates. 'If the rest of your boys are half as nice and have half the charm of that one, then you're a lucky man, Tom,' she observed.

He gave a derisive snort. 'Adam Ryder is not 'nice', he is a pain in the neck and has caused me more trouble than the rest of them put together. The thought of having him right under my nose for another year makes my blood run cold.' He reached for his pipe. 'But I grant you the charm. Another couple of years and he'll be absolutely lethal.'

She paused to give him an enigmatic smile. 'If I was sixteen I'd find him pretty lethal right now, and it isn't difficult to see where he gets *that* from, is it?'

Tom blew down the stem of his pipe. 'It runs in the family, I believe.'

'From what I saw the other day it positively gallops!'

He reached out a long arm and pulled her down onto his knees. 'Could it be, Mrs Doyle, that you have been attacked by the green-eyed monster?'

She laughed and ruffled his hair. 'You *said* that she was old!'

'No,' he corrected, 'I said that she wasn't young.' He narrowed his eyes. 'How did you know?'

'My journalistic instincts for a good story; one day I'll tell you how you both gave the game away.' She kissed him, slowly and thoroughly.

He looked at her mouth in silence for a few seconds then kissed her back. 'One day,' he promised, 'I'll hear your confession about *your* old man. Right now I can think of better things to do.'

'You can? Such as?'

He bent to whisper in her ear and she gazed thoughtfully into the distance.

'Interesting,' she said, 'and tempting. However, there is just one thing…'

'What's that?'

She gave him an innocent wide-eyed smile. 'After all that, do I get supper as well, sir?'

24

Ambrose appeared in the open doorway of the Gatehouse, holding an envelope aloft. 'The visit we made to Barty seems to have borne fruit; he's been in touch with his vicar pal in Kent, who's spoken to his son with the boatyard in Suffolk. He builds racing Catamarans and if Liam gets himself up there ASAP he'll have a job at last.' He grinned at Olivia, who was seated at the kitchen table, 'I thought you'd like to have the news with your breakfast.'

'I've already had it, thank you, the breakfast, that is,' she pulled a face. 'I must say I'm surprised Barty remembered anything you talked about last week, considering you sank a couple of bottles of that vicious brew between you, but I'm glad for Liam's sake that he did.' She pushed a hand through her hair. 'I've also got some news. Adam 'phoned last night to say he wants to join the Navy.'

'Was that a surprise?'

'Not really. Kate told me weeks ago that's what Liam said he should do. Going by what Adam *didn't* say, I'd hazard a guess that Giles threw a horrendous wobbly at the news. However, he seems to have calmed down eventually and agreed.'

Ambrose perched on the edge of the table next to her and shook his head. 'I could have told him it's useless to expect your children to share your own passions. I'd have quite liked at least one of mine to show some sign of artistic talent, but I doubt if either of them could produce anything recognisable as Art, even with a Painting by Numbers kit.'

'Perhaps one massive dollop of artistic temperament is enough for any family.'

'You are too kind ... but probably right.'

'Will you take Liam to Essex?'

'No. He wants to go on his own, by train. He doesn't yet like me enough to be trapped in a car with me for hours with no hope of escape. I suspect it will be a long time before he'll allow himself to unbend that far.'

'But things are better between you, aren't they?' Olivia was quick to sense the hurt beneath the dry remark. 'He talks about you in quite a different way now.'

'We have a lot of ground to make up.' He smoothed the letter with his hand. 'I thought I might get him some kind of vehicle when

233

he's passed his test. You never know. He may want to come home occasionally.'

'Perhaps he will, if he thinks you'd be pleased to see him,' she suggested gently.

Ambrose leaned back, folding his arms and frowning. 'It's not that easy.' He stared at her in silence for a few moments then said abruptly, 'I didn't want either of them, you know, but Paula had hardly combed the confetti out of her hair before she was pregnant, and fourteen months after Liam there was another one!'

'Of course it was nothing to do with you, was it?' He sounded so disgruntled that Olivia couldn't help the sarcastic retort.

'With Paula, it was all or nothing. Trying to practise birth control with a woman who acts as though she's got a hot line to the Vatican is no joke. She very quickly discovered she was no more maternal than I was paternal; after Kate's birth she spent all her time watching the calendar to make sure it didn't happen again. It was the last straw when she decided to watch it with someone else, then upped and left me with the pair of them.' He frowned, pulling at his beard. 'Liam thinks it was his fault that she went. As I never bothered to tell him it wasn't, I can't blame him for keeping me more or less at arm's length.' He paused for a moment before adding, 'You don't know how I envy you. I would like just once to have him look at me the way your son sometimes looks at you.'

Under his unwavering gaze Olivia felt her colour rise. 'Perhaps I'm a better Agony Aunt than you thought.' She felt her pulse quickening and cast around fruitlessly for some suitably light and deflecting comment, suddenly very much aware of how close they were to each other. His hand rested on the table beside her arm and she could feel the warmth of him through the thin cotton of her shirt.

At length he broke the silence to say quietly, 'I'm beginning to suspect that you're better at a great many more things than I'd realised,' and leaning down he kissed her mouth.

'Oh, hell,' she jumped up and found herself caught in the circle of his arms. 'If I'd known you were going to do that, Flynn, I wouldn't have let you over the doorstep this morning.'

'Shhh,' he held her cosily against his chest. 'I'm not going to ravish you, woman … I just want to see if you feel as good as you did last week.'

She slid her arms beneath his crumpled linen jacket and said without thinking, 'You didn't kiss me then.'

'Nor did I,' he bent his head again, 'but I can soon remedy that.'

This time it was the real thing. His lips on hers were firm and

warm and he explored her mouth with the thoroughness of a connoiss-
eur. With a small sigh she responded, tightening her arms about him
and letting her body curve into his. When after what seemed a very
long time he lifted his mouth from hers, and still keeping her wrapped
in his arms asked conversationally, 'As beards go – how was it for
you?'

Olivia caught a steadying breath through her tingling lips and
surveyed him gravely. 'Difficult to judge, I'm afraid. I've had only a
limited experience of beards, *per se.*'

'Two are enough for any girl,' he answered succinctly, then stood
her away from him and put his hands on her shoulders. 'I think we
should go for a walk, Mrs Ryder, or I may forget I'm almost a
gentleman.'

Grateful that he was giving her space and time to recover from the
turbulence his kisses had aroused, and still a little breathless she
answered, 'I'll come for a walk with you only if you'll stop calling me
Mrs Ryder.'

He took her hand. 'The tide is out, Olivia, so we'll walk the strand
to the studio, where I shall feed you coffee and cake, whilst you tell
me your life story.'

'Give me one good reason why I should do that.'

He grinned, his pirate grin. 'I told you mine, didn't I? Only a
snippet, I know, but there isn't much else … at least, nothing I'm
prepared to tell you about just yet!'

*   *   *

Her hand fitted comfortably into his as they walked along a beach
newly washed and smoothed by the morning tide. When they rounded
the point she shivered slightly in the freshening wind; filled suddenly
with an amazing feeling of content he tucked her hand into his jacket
pocket, keeping it there curled into his palm.

This time she hadn't stopped him kissing her; her body had been
pliant and eager and the temptation to make love to her strong. But it
had been a fragile moment, and an inner sense dictated she was not
yet ready to make a commitment; that for the present he should step
back and let her go. He looked at her face, the skin glowing pink
under her tan, hair loose and blown about by the wind, and tightened
his hold on her hand.

I don't need to rush this, I can wait. The thought surprised him.
He wanted her; God, how he wanted her, but she needed time and
space and so did he. They had each paid the price of loving too much,

235

too soon. This time they must both get it right, because this was something just too important to spoil or let slip away.

After a while she looked up, smiling. 'Remember when you said you'd whistle, and that some day I'd come to you?'

'That I do. What about it?'

'I wonder if you would mind *not* whistling for a little longer.'

'Is that all?'

'For now. Am I asking too much?'

'No. It'll do.'

A fine rain began to fall but they walked on at the same leisurely pace. There was no hurry now, no hurry at all.

<h1 style="text-align:center">25</h1>

Zoë's letters to Giles came regularly, never less than two a week, full of her travels and the success of the tour; the generosity of their hosts.

"You just won't believe," she wrote, "the kind of parties they give. Oh, how I wish you could be with us here in Toronto. We eat steaks so big they hang over the side of the plate and we dance and party until dawn. It is the most fantastic place. The buildings are so enormously tall that I feel like an ant about to be squashed at any moment. If I walk more than twenty yards I get lost and James is tearing his hair because I have to keep taking cabs. Darling Giles, I miss you so much. We shall have ten days Christmas vacation in New Hampshire, but what will I do with all that time to re-charge my batteries if you are not there to charge them with me? All other things apart I am tired. TIRED! I don't see how I can be as I go to my bed (alone) each night, and only get up in time for lunch. When I have worked out the time zones in Boston, I shall 'phone you on Christmas Day and to hell with the expense…"

It wasn't hard to picture her in such a setting, she was one of those rare people who could fit easily into any company, any situation, as much at home in a ballroom as a bar. Giles smiled. No wonder she was tired; working in the theatre every day and partying half the night. He looked out of his window over a grey, wet November morning and felt the constant dull ache in his heart surge into painful life. Another month to Christmas, then three more before she would be home again.

He left the remains of his breakfast and wandered restlessly around the flat, coffee cup in hand. When the newspaper thumped onto the mat he went down to fetch it then settled into an armchair, skimming through the pages, his mind half on Zoë; half on the printed pages. Suddenly, a name leaped from the Arts page. 'The Constantine Gallery, Bond Street: An Exhibition of Bronzes by Ambrose Flynn. Ceramics by Antoine Fauvre, Paintings by Olivia Ryder.'

'Good grief!' He stared in stunned disbelief. Adam had said she'd been selling paintings to a gallery in Dartmouth … but *Constantines*?

He reached for the 'phone.

*   *   *

'Hello Giles! The Exhibition? Yes that's right. On Saturday.'

Olivia, he thought, with some irritation, sounded as though he was merely asking after her health. 'You might have told me.'

'What did you expect … a gilt edged invitation?' Her voice held an undertone of amusement. 'Sorry, I should have said something, but I've been so busy it's all rather crept up on me, and art isn't really your thing, is it? Anyway, it's on for a fortnight so there's no rush.'

He hesitated. 'I'd like to come for the opening if that's all right.'

'Sure. If you don't see me, it means no one is buying my stuff and I'll be hiding in the office. At least, with Flynn and Antoine exhibiting, you won't be the only one to turn up.'

'I'll be there, but I can't make it until the afternoon. I've a hypochondriac p.p who thinks he'll die if I don't see him on Saturday morning.'

She gave a gurgle of laughter. 'We'll look out for you.'

He replaced the receiver, face creased in a puzzled frown. What did she mean, 'We?' Just who were 'We'?

*   *   *

After a dry-mouthed, thirty panic-stricken minutes hiding in Andoni's plush office, Olivia had conquered the worst of her nerves. Now fortified with a stiff brandy she ventured out into the Gallery.

'Oh!' With mingled pleasure and pain she saw the red Sold sticker by her portrait of Ambrose.

Until now she hadn't admitted, even to herself, how much she wanted to keep it. She had wanted to have it labelled "not for sale" but Ambrose had teased her out of it. Now some stranger would be free to make what they might of the cluttered studio, with dust motes rising on a shaft of the morning sun, lighting the absorbed face and craftsman's hands of Ambrose at work.

'I like it … No, more than that, I love it,' he'd said, when he first saw his portrait. 'I've always seen myself as looking like a cross between Captain Kidd and God!'

'This is good, yes? Your first sale for Andoni … and the bronze, that too has found favour with a buyer.' The gallery owner watched Olivia with amused, knowing eyes. 'That is one of Ambrose's best pieces. It has…' he waved his hands expressively. '*Éclat* … Passion, it is beautiful.'

'Yes.' She looked at the bust, finally cast and finished, feeling the colour creeping up her face. When she had first seen the finished work she had been stunned into silence. The image Ambrose had created

238

was disturbing: the half-closed eyes in the cool face; the underlying sensuality of the full mouth, the long neck and delicate shoulders, the beginning of a curved breast. To the viewer it hinted tantalisingly at unseen depths; the secret, yet to be discovered woman within. It was quite simply erotic.

'What do you think of my Aphrodite?' he'd asked her, to which she had replied truthfully that it made her feel as though she stood naked in a room full of strangers, and he had laughed and said, 'Precisely!'

'Is it sold?' she asked now, feeling the sudden prick of tears behind her eyes.

'But, yes … almost immediately; it is a masterpiece.'

The hours passed. A few more red stickers appeared by her work. She had little time to talk with Ambrose; he was constantly in demand but sent continual encouraging glances or smiles to her where she was busy in her own right, buttonholed by earnest enthusiasts and keen-eyed critics alike.

She was beginning to wilt when he appeared suddenly at her side. 'Quickly,' he whispered, 'let's take a breather before everyone stampedes for the champagne and sandwiches in the little gallery,' and hustled her unceremoniously through a side door.

In the sudden cool peace of the quiet room, the long central table laden with food and bottles of champagne, she gave him an over bright smile. 'Congratulations, you sold my bust!'

He saw the question behind her eyes and kept his voice carefully light. 'Congratulations, you sold my picture!'

Before she could reply Constantine appeared, flinging open the door and sweeping a group of critics and favoured clients before him. Champagne corks popped, toasts were drunk and they were once again swamped in talk and laughter.

*   *   *

It was a little after two o'clock when Giles reached the gallery. Pushing open the swing doors he stepped into a room filled with a bewildering conglomeration of people, ranging from the well-barbered, Saville Row suited men and expensively dressed women, to casually clothed artists and critics of both genders. Immediately facing the doorway was the central plinth with the bronze of Olivia in pride of place.

God Almighty!

Glancing furtively around him, Giles advanced upon it, feeling

239

everyone in the room must know that the half-veiled eyes, the languorous slope of the shoulders, the full, slightly parted lips were almost exactly as Olivia looked when she made love.

He was still trying to collect his scattered thoughts when, across a sea of heads, he saw the dark, grey-flecked mane of Ambrose Flynn towering above everyone else in the room. Even at a distance, Giles could see the sculptor's smiling eyes were fixed firmly on a woman, whose back he could just glimpse through the crowd surrounding them. As he moved closer the woman turned and he saw it was Olivia.

Giles couldn't believe his eyes. Where was the neatly styled waving hair? The tailored suit and blouse she would normally wear to such an occasion? Who was this stranger with hair piled with artful carelessness on top of her head; who wore grey corduroy slacks, with a tweed jacket over a red, high-necked sweater, and still managed to look a million dollars ... 'God Almighty!' he repeated under his breath and at that moment she turned and saw him. He slammed a smile on his face and went to meet her.

Olivia watched him cross the room; the tilt of his head, the curve of his mouth, his gaze intent upon her face as he threaded his way towards her, made her heart skip a beat. Oh, Lord ... and she'd imagined she was over him completely.

'Hello Olivia.' He took her hands in his and kissed her on both cheeks.

'Giles ... you should have come an hour ago.' Amazing, she thought, my voice sounds perfectly normal. 'You've missed all the smoked salmon and champagne.'

'I didn't realise it was you at first,' he said truthfully, 'you are ... different.'

'Look,' she smiled and took his arm, 'I panicked about nothing ... see those sold stickers? I'm still pinching myself.'

He studied her paintings in silence. They were splendid. Powerful and arresting, utterly truthful to the menace as well as the beauty, of the sea and coast she knew so well and loved so fiercely. This is what I spent twenty years preventing her from achieving, he thought. How did she stifle all that talent and turn herself into something so totally alien to all this as a suburban housewife?

With pain he remembered the young, carefree, unconventional and outrageously funny Olivia he had first met; the Olivia who had loved him so much that she had sacrificed everything in order to become all that he wanted her to be. Now, in this confident, talented woman he could see the person she should always have been, could always have been, but for him. His eyes lingered on the portrait of

Ambrose, aware, that like the bronze, it had a subtle intimacy, as though artist and subject shared a secret.

Olivia was speaking again, claiming his attention. 'Giles, this is Ambrose Flynn...'

'Yes.' He summoned a smile as the sculptor held out a hand in greeting. 'I saw your photograph in the window.'

Olivia looked down at the clasped hands. One long and slender, above it the sharp white cuff with the gold links, the immaculate dark grey Crombie sleeve. The other big and powerful, a brown and blue check unbuttoned cuff showing from beneath well-worn brown corduroy. Nothing, she thought, could have drawn the line more sharply between the two men.

'Mother and dad will be coming tomorrow.' She was quick to fill the threatened awkward pause. 'Dad refused to come today; he said he'd rather wait until the worst of the arty crowd had cleared off.'

Giles laughed and relaxed. 'Now that sounds exactly like Clive. I wonder he ever let you near a paintbrush.'

She smiled and took his arm again. 'I was his daughter and I could do no wrong. Now come along, you must see everything. We can safely leave Ambrose to his fan club for a while. He quite likes a spot of hero-worship, don't you, Flynn?'

'That depends on the worshiper.'

Giles noted the easy camaraderie and the exchanged smiles and felt an unreasonable stab of jealousy. It's because of that damned bronze, he told himself. How, unless they were lovers could the man have seen that expression on Olivia's face? He shied away from the unwelcome thought, then allowed a wry inward smile at having the nerve to mind. What did it matter, anyway? He had Zoë, at least, part of the time. Olivia was happy; why should he grudge her the pleasure of another man's company?

But all the same...

He forced a grin and pressed her arm. 'All right; educate the philistine if you must, but only if you'll let me take you to dinner tonight ... I'd like to talk about Adam and the Christmas holidays.'

He spent an hour at the gallery. As the door closed behind him Ambrose was immediately at her side. 'All right?' he asked, and she leaned back against him, turning her head with a smile.

'I'm fine. I can handle anything today. I've said I'll have dinner with him tonight; he's leaving tomorrow and it's a good opportunity to sort out a few outstanding matters – mostly to do with Adam.'

For a moment his look was searching, then he gave a half-smile. 'Why should I mind? Where is he staying? Not the Balmoral, I hope.'

'What ... Giles stay in Kensington?' She gave a splutter of laughter. 'He's at the Regent Palace. Anything five hundred yards away from Knightsbridge or the West End would be unthinkable!'

'That's all right then.' Ambrose gave his rumbling laugh. 'I trust you made it clear that we have separate rooms. I don't want to wake up to find a scalpel at my throat.'

'Now why should he do that?'

'Because for a moment back there he was jealous as hell.'

'Was he?' She considered for a moment. 'Well, there has to be a first sometime I suppose,' she gave him an impish smile. 'But I doubt he'll make a habit of it.'

'To make sure my jugular remains intact you could tell him he doesn't have a reason.' Briefly, he touched his lips to the crown of her head before adding an almost inaudible, 'Yet!'

*　　　*　　　*

Giles asked, 'Would you mind if I asked Adam to spend the New Year in Paris, with pa and me?'

He'd waited all the way through dinner and their amiable discussions over finance; the not so amiable discussion about Adam's future; his own idea of taking a sabbatical and the minutiae of problems associated with such things, before coming to the point. Olivia was amused. It was a novelty to have him quite so deferential. In times past he would have told her his intentions then patiently but firmly dismissed any objections she might make.

'I don't mind and I should think he'd jump at the chance. Did he tell you he'd quite like you to spend Christmas at Lodscombe?'

He took a gulp at his brandy. 'he did, but I'm not terribly enthusiastic. You'll be spending a part of it at least with your parents and I don't think I'm quite up to that yet.'

'Well, yes. I can see Christmas dinner might be a problem,' she acceded reasonably, 'but you'll have to face them sometime. Adam needs to keep contact with you as much as possible, but he can be pretty stubborn over the prospect of being posted between us like a parcel.'

Giles looked hunted. 'I'll think about it.' In an automatic return to the old intimacy he put a coaxing hand over hers. 'Livvy, darling, don't push me too hard. I'm finding this evening difficult enough as it is.'

She considered the hand lying on hers. I'm all right, she thought. Not quite out of the wood, but nearly there. It's a nice enough hand

242

and it's warm and comfortable and almost sincere, but I really don't need it to be doing anything to me other than this.

She smiled and gave his fingers a squeeze. 'Why don't you break the ice with my parents tomorrow … wait until they've been to the gallery, then meet them somewhere for tea?'

'Would that be a good idea?' He thought for a moment. 'Perhaps you're right. I'll give it a try.' He grinned, the old confident Giles returning with a rush. 'Will you tell … no,' he caught himself up, 'will you *ask* them to meet me? Say three-thirty at Harrods. Then after tea Margot can be in the right place, and with just the right amount of time left to spend money while Clive and I sit and talk in peace.'

That's my boy, thought Olivia; organising everything to fit in with what *you* want. She gave his hand a brisk pat. 'You nearly had me fooled,' she said, 'for a time I thought the leopard really had changed its spots!'

*　　　*　　　*

When she returned that evening Ambrose was waiting for her in the hotel bar, two glasses and an uncorked bottle of red wine before him on a small table. As she sank into a chair he leaned to pick up the bottle.

'I thought you might not return and that I should have to drink this alone.'

She looked at him with gentle irony. 'Where else might I have gone?'

He busied himself pouring the wine. 'To the Regent Palace, perhaps?'

She accepted the glass he offered and gave a small shake of the head. 'No,' she stared down into her wine. 'I had to find out if I could spend an evening alone with him without still wanting to go to bed,' she admitted.

'And could you?'

'Yes … Oh, yes!'

He let out a long breath. 'Thank God for that.'

'You knew, didn't you?'

'Uh-huh.'

'Then thank you for not saying … or showing it.' She was silent for a few moments, turning the glass in her fingers. 'I fell for Giles the first time I laid eyes on him,' she said, 'he was, well, just about the most beautiful thing I'd ever seen and sexy as hell. Now, I can despise his morals, even hate him from time to time, but still get pleasure at the sight of him walking towards me. Why?'

He said, 'Because it takes time to detach oneself from being the other half of love.'

'I suppose so.' She looked at him soberly. 'Oh, Flynn, it hurts to fall out of love.'

'Tell me something I don't know.'

'How long did it take you to stop hurting?'

'Quite a while; repairing my damaged pride took even longer.' He smiled, 'but it's been knitting very rapidly over the past few weeks.'

She looked at his strong assured face. The wide-set eyes gazed steadily back, and with sudden heady delight she knew that once again she was standing on the very edge of love.

26

When Olivia collected Adam for his last exeat weekend before Christmas she found him in bubbling high spirits.

He flung himself into the car, with scarcely more than a 'Hi, mum!' before launching into an enthusiastic outpouring of his future plans.

'I've found out all about Dartmouth ... I can go September after next if my As are OK and they'll have me. D'you realise it'll take almost four years – four *years* – before I actually get to be a ship's officer? But you go to sea for three months after the first year ... I hope it'll be the Med; wizard wearing whites and getting brown knees...'

Olivia listened patiently until he ran out of steam. 'Did your father speak to you about going to Paris for the New Year?' she asked at the first pause.

'Yes, and he told me he's coming down for a couple of days at Christmas. Fab, isn't it? When we go to Paris grandpa's taking me to the Moulin Rouge...'

'Oh, is he?'

'Yes. And there's going to be huge New Year party at some Hotel. Mum, I've *got* to have a dinner jacket, a white one – and a cummerbund. Every one is wearing them for parties over there, grandpa said...'

Olivia gritted her teeth in a genteel sort of way and put the car into gear.

'Adam, dear, in all the excitement, you won't forget to tell grandpa I send my love, will you?'

'Couldn't you come with us?'

'Another time. I have a feeling that after this Christmas I may be glad of a little time alone to recover, without Nico here.'

'Liam wrote to me. He said his dad's bought him a car and that he'll probably be home for Christmas too. He reckons the boatyard is great. Him and a friend, a girl I think, are sailing to the Channel Islands for the New Year...' Adam broke off; suddenly gruff and trying to appear nonchalant he said, 'I don't suppose Kate could come to Paris? It'll be boring for her at Lodscombe on her own.'

'Well.' Olivia tried not to laugh. 'You'll need to ask four people about *that* ... Giles, Ambrose, Grandpa and Kate!'

245

'Yes, well,' he grinned, embarrassed, 'you'll help, won't you, mum? You know: sort of sound out her father before I ask. He's a bit … well, a bit fierce sometimes.'

'I imagine he is,' she answered dryly, and wondered again just what *had* constituted Ambrose's "little chat" all those months ago, and if he had carried out his threat to "frighten the bejesus" out of her son. As Kate had brought no more personal worries for discussion, perhaps the good old-fashioned heavy father approach had borne fruit.

She took her attention from the road for a moment to glance at her son's profile and sighed inwardly. Yes, he had grown up, the bloom and curved lines of childhood gone. Beside her now was a tall loose-limbed young man, very like Giles in looks, but with a certain gentleness about his mouth and eyes that spoke more of the romantic dreamer and less of the self-confident, manipulative charmer.

You'll do, she thought, but I hope no one ever breaks *your* young heart…

*   *   *

'I have something to show you.' Ambrose said, coming up behind Olivia as she stood at the window, watching Adam and Kate start towards the bus stop and an evening at the cinema in Dawlish. He took her arm and led her towards his small, comfortably untidy office behind the studio. 'I need your advice on where I should put this…' He pushed open the door then stepped back a pace as she stopped on the threshold.

'You didn't sell it – oh, Flynn!' She turned with shining eyes. 'What a terrible liar … how *could* you?'

He ran a hand over his hair. 'I didn't tell you I'd sold it,' he protested, 'you told me.' His eyes sparkled with sudden devilment. 'I thought I might put it in the living-room window.'

'Over my dead body; I won't have every local youth ogling at *that*.'

'Then it will have to be my bedroom.'

'With a cloth over it, I should hope … you certainly let your imagination have full reign, didn't you? No wonder Giles was so put out; he as good as said it was indecent.'

'What a low mind your husband has.' He put his arms about her. 'The bedroom it is, then.'

'If you must.' She turned in his arms and kissed him. 'Thank you for not selling me.'

He stood motionless, holding her very close. She could feel the steady beat of his heart against her own. After a while she raised her head to stare accusingly at his mouth. As the faint sound issuing from between his teeth became steadily louder and more melodious, she put a hand either side of his bearded face, bringing it down to hers.

'I know perfectly well, Flynn, what you are doing. I could hear that whistle if I was standing in the Lodge a mile and a half from this room…'

*   *   *

They lay quietly at first; smiling into each other's eyes, delighting in their intimacy as the slow delicate touch of mouth and hands deepened desire.

'Why have we waited so long?' Olivia asked, 'and why have *I* found it so hard to trust my own feelings?' Ambrose kissed her eyes swiftly then spoke with his mouth against hers.

'Perhaps we both were too scared to trust again,' he murmured, 'but let go now, Olivia my love, and trust me as I trust you.'

The hands that shaped clay with such delicate precision touched her with tenderness, his long, clever fingers on in and around her, his mouth following where his fingers led. She stroked her hands down his back, pulling him closer, and they moved together with a fluid seamless sensuality, like dancers in a slow waltz. 'Oh,' he dipped his head to her breast, '*this* is going to take a little time!'

Much later, bodies slicked with sweat and limbs still wrapped about each other, they lay quiet and spent. After a while he raised himself, and cupping her face in his hands brushed his lips across her mouth, murmuring, 'Well, me darlin', whoever would have thought we could manage anything as perfect as that?'

As his bemused blue eyes gazed down into hers, all the doubts and misgivings of the past months were finally swept away. We are partners, she thought; all that matters or will ever matter is that we share this love, and this trust. This is the elusive something I thought I should never find. It is the light in the window. It is coming home at last.

And Ambrose watched the changing shadows of her face and knew that each had found the other half of a new love.

*   *   *

'Don't go to sleep,' he whispered, easing his arm from beneath her head. 'Our offspring will be thundering home very soon'

247

She lay limp and still, keeping her eyes closed, 'I know, but I'm trying to forget.'

'Stop playing possum for a minute and look at me, Olivia.'

She opened her eyes. 'Umm … Yes?'

'We have a problem … at least I have.'

She sighed. 'I knew there'd be a catch in it somewhere.'

'I suppose that depends on your point of view. You see I don't know what you and Giles may have decided, but Paula is never going to agree to a divorce. She'd rather live in sin for the rest of her life than divorce me and have to leave the Church.' He hesitated then confessed, 'In all honesty I couldn't force her. Actually she didn't leave me, you know. She might never have done. I threw her out.'

Olivia's shoulders shook slightly. 'That was very rough of you, Flynn, but in a way she's right: perhaps one should only be married once. I don't think I could make all those solemn vows again.'

'In that case,' he raised himself on one elbow, 'will you consider being unmarried to me until death does us part?'

She smiled. 'As you put that so nicely, then yes, I will.'

He smoothed her hair with a gentle hand. 'If I can't be your husband then I will be your lover and your friend; I will be a shield and a sword over you…'

She traced his lips with her finger. 'And I will be your port in any storm.'

In the darkened room his teeth showed, white as a gull's wing. 'Well then, we can't say fairer than that, now can we, me darlin'?'

*　　　*　　　*

'Mum, have you been out here this evening?' Adam stood at the open door to the scullery, a concerned look on his face.

'No. Why? What's the matter?'

'It's this patch on the wall. Something's happened to it.'

'Oh, Lord, and I thought it was getting smaller!' Picking up a cloth to dry her hands, Olivia crossed the room and he stood aside hastily to let her pass.

Suspended on a tattered piece of string from a rusty, six-inch nail, her portrait of Ambrose hung crookedly over the diminishing damp patch on the scullery wall. For a full half-minute she stood staring at it, before turning accusing eyes on her son, who backed away quickly and held up both hands in defence.

'He told me to do it! He said it was an early Christmas present!'

'Oh yes? And what did you get in return?'

Adam grinned. 'He said Kate could come to Paris if it's all right with grandpa and dad … Mum,' he stared at her face in sudden consternation. 'Mum, you're not crying, are you?'

'No. I've got some dust in my eye,' she laughed shakily. 'Now take that damned thing down will you, and hang it properly in the sitting room.'

Taking the cord Ambrose had given him from his pocket and fastening it to the hooks in the picture frame, he asked, 'You do like him, don't you, Mum?'

'Yes.'

'Good, because he likes you a lot, Kate says.' Briefly, he lifted his eyes from his task. 'I don't so much mind going away now when I know you've got someone else here as well as gran and pops … and he's really an awfully decent sort of bloke, isn't he?'

'Awfully decent,' she agreed.

Adam bent his head as sudden colour flooded his face. 'Mum, do you more than like him? Are you … do you … you know … with him?'

'Yes to all those questions.' Olivia stood very still, aware that her heartbeat was keeping time with the loud tick of the old wall clock. 'Do you mind?'

For a moment he hesitated, then 'No,' he said quietly. 'No, I don't mind at all.'

Briefly she touched his shoulder and he looked up and smiled. Picking up the hammer and picture hook she said briskly. 'Now, if you think you've made that all ship-shape and Bristol fashion, we shall give it pride of place over the mantelpiece.'

'I can't think why he wanted me to hang it on that bit of string in the scullery in the first place,' Adam's face wore a puzzled frown as he followed her in to the sitting room with the picture.

She looked back at him over her shoulder and smiled.

'I imagine it's all a part of him being an awfully decent sort of a bloke and not leaving you out of things,' she said.

*   *   *

'Thank you, everyone, that's all for now.'

James Yelland watched his cast trail away after the word rehearsal for that evening's performance. God, but he was tired. So was everyone. It was a relentless treadmill. Three plays at each new venue: Monday and Tuesday *Twelfth Night*, Wednesday and Thursday *Venus Observed*, Friday and Saturday *Pygmalion* and alternate Sundays spent travelling overnight to the next theatre, the next lodgings.

It was a punishing schedule, particularly for the older members, although even the youngsters, Ellie and Martin, Ferdie and Zoë, all of whom were usually so determined to dance and party half the night, were beginning to wilt. Particularly Zoë, whose demanding roles seemed to be sapping even her hitherto seemingly inexhaustible energy at a worrying rate.

He watched the gang of them now as they came towards him in a chattering bunch, noting the bruised violet shadows beneath Zoë's eyes; the tight black trousers and black polo necked sweater she wore serving only to emphasise the angular lines of her body. He frowned, putting out a hand to stop her as she was passing.

'Zoë. Just a minute.'

She wrinkled her brow. 'What is it? Did I get it wrong?'

'No, of course not … when do you ever,' he smiled. 'But you look twice as knackered as anyone else, even Granville, and he's damn' near seventy. You really must rest more. Remember, that film chap is coming to see you this Friday. Besides, I promised Giles I'd return you undamaged, and now just look at you…'

'I do rest, so stop nagging Jimmy. I'll be all right after the Christmas break, we all will.' She giggled suddenly. 'Did you know Granville reckons he's going to spend the whole time skiing?'

'He bloody well isn't; if the old fool breaks a leg, whom will I have to play Pickering and Malvolio?'

'You, I suppose,' she linked her arm in his as they began to follow the others from the hall. 'Honestly though, it's tougher than I expected. Americans are wonderful audiences, but so enthusiastic off stage they exhaust me. I just want to go somewhere quiet and peaceful for the break. I don't want to party or ski or do anything the slightest bit energetic. I think I might just sleep for the whole ten days!'

She left him at the tall brownstone house where they were staying, with the excuse that she had shopping to do, but in reality to escape his sharp-eyed observations. Stumbling sleepily from her bed at noon, late for the line rehearsal, she hadn't had the time to make-up as usual, to smooth concealing pan-stick under her eyes and work colour into her cheeks.

Roll on March, she thought grumpily, and a nice drizzly, blustery Salisbury day; the grass around the edges of the cathedral thick with daffodils, their petals becoming translucent in the rain, and the early almond blossom lying like greying pink confetti on the pavements…

Barnsville was no shining city of building-block towers, open parks and wide streets, but a rather depressing town with mainly old plank or brownstone houses at one end, at the other shops, a brash new supermarket and modern single storey dwellings like coloured boxes.

It was freezing; the packed snow piled high along the sidewalks a dirty white, while in the roadways steam rose from the central heating vents to hang like ectoplasm in the still, cold air. She wandered downtown in search of a drugstore, listening with fascinated concentration to the accents around her, trying them out in her head. She'd like to do an American play some time, she thought, Miller, O'Neill or Tennessee Williams: Something dark and tragic. *The Glass Menagerie,* perhaps.

But she *was* tired. Last night, waiting in the wings for her cue, for several panicky seconds she'd lost concentration; only the sight and feel of her recent change into ballgown and tiara clueing her into which scene she was about to enter.

She shivered. If only Giles were here. A sudden desperate need for him caused a warm, treacherous stirring of desire and she increased her pace, thinking that she'd have energy enough if he were to appear on this dismal street. Then they would race, hand in hand, back to her room with the elaborately swagged drapes and the flowered wallpaper, and make wonderful, noisily exciting love on the mock Shaker bed, sleep a little, then begin all over again…

STOP! The crossing sign flashed. Patiently she waited at the snow-encrusted curb until it commanded WALK, when she was carried across the road in a surge of wool-coated, fur-capped humanity, all apparently hell bent on getting somewhere faster than the next man.

She pulled her own coat collar up over her unprotected ears. In eight days from now she would hear his voice. *Ring me on Christmas morning when you have managed to crawl out of bed,* he had written. *I shall be staying with Clive and Margot until the twenty-seventh, after that I'll take Adam and Kate over on the ferry and drive down to Paris. I shall never make it through the empty hours unless I can hear your voice and tell you all that is in my heart…*

Zoë hunched deeper into her coat thinking: you in Devonshire and me in New Hampshire … and the whole bloody Atlantic between us!

She made for the neon lights and warmth of a diner and settling herself onto a high stool at the pink plastic and chrome bar, smiled at the platinum blonde, dark-rooted waitress who leaned negligently against the counter, her jaws moving rhythmically on a wad of gum.

'Whaddal it be, hon?' The woman shifted the gum from one side of her mouth to the other. 'We got ham, egg an' fries or hash browns, waffles an' syrup, beans an'…'

'Just coffee and one of those chocolate cakes, please.' Politely she interrupted the recital of what had all the hallmarks of a long litany. 'I'm really not very hungry.'

The woman leaned on the counter, settling for a chat. 'You British?'

Zoë grinned mischievously. 'How can you tell?'

'It's that Limey accent … it cracks me up every time!' She gave a whinny of laughter and lifted the round glass jug of coffee from the machine behind her. 'Cawfee an' cookie comin' up.' She pushed a full cup across the pink plastic counter then slid the cake onto a plate and handed it over, together with a paper napkin decorated with a fat grinning male face and a legend proclaiming that this was Joe's Diner. She watched as Zoë gulped at the coffee then offered: 'You look like you'd do better with the ham n' eggs, hon; been sick have you?'

'Sick?' Zoë was startled. Christ, did she look that bad without half a pound of Max Factor on her face? She summoned a smile. 'No, just tired.'

'You wanna take care of yourself, kid.' The waitress peered into Zoë's cup. 'You wanna top-up? It's free.'

'No thanks. This is fine.' She sank her teeth into the cake, watching herself in the mirror behind the counter. Who wouldn't look like a walking corpse in this cold?

A huge man in motorcycle leathers, his long hair tied back in a ponytail, lounged in to sprawl across the bar and the waitress, swaying on patent leather stilettos strolled towards him, parking her gum en route by the coffee urn before asking, 'Hi Frankie, whaddal it be today then?'

The sound of his low suggestive voice and the waitresses' answering shriek of laughter put Zoe's teeth on edge. Screw you, she thought rancorously, you go right ahead and enjoy yourselves. I am, as you Yanks say, bushed, used up, clapped out, up the Swannee without a paddle … and I think I've just about had this particular town up to my frigging back teeth!

She brooded quietly. Martin and the rest of the boys and girls could have their fun and games over Christmas; get drunk, fuck and be fucked in turn by the entire population of New England if they wished. She would stay at the Holiday Lodge in Vermont with Yell and Piers Conway and comfortable middle-aged Becka Francis; sit by a log fire and watch in comfort, while all the big macho guys and hulking sporty wenches broke their arms and legs on the ski slopes.

Shit. She gazed at her reflection with hollow eyes. *I'm becoming one of the "Why don't you all grow up and behave like responsible adults," brigade... She gave a stifled giggle and pulled a face. Well, whaddaya know, hon, I seem to have joined the dismal old bugger shower at last ... Mummy would be pleased!*

27

Margot jabbed a sprig of holly into the Christmas pudding. 'Is it going all right? Are they still talking?' she asked in hushed tones.

'Of course they are; you don't expect them to start tearing each other apart as soon as we leave the room do you?' Clive Trevellyan was amused. 'They're both civilised people. I know Giles is a bit jumpy, but that's only because he's waiting on his 'phone call.' He splashed the heated brandy lavishly over the pudding. 'Get that lot down them and with the rest of the booze they already have on board they'll be sweet as a pair of turtle doves!'

Margot stopped in the act of striking a match. 'If I were Olivia I should just hate him talking to that girl…'

'Well, you're not Olivia and I have a feeling that she's now got precious little reason and even less desire to complain about anything *he* might choose to do – and for God's sake light that pudding before all that expensive spirit evaporates!'

'What on earth are you talking about?'

He uncorked the brandy again and, pouring another measure into the warm pan still sitting on the range, he said patiently, 'Try listening to what your grandson *is* and your daughter *isn't* saying and you'll soon find out.'

'Don't be ridiculous.' Margot struck another match. 'Just open the door, you mischief making old fool, and let me get this to the table.'

*　　　*　　　*

Giles sat in Clive's sagging leather armchair in the study, cradling the 'phone close to his ear, listening to Zoë's voice coming clear across the miles.

'Is that you, Giles? Oh, hell, now you are there I don't know what to say!'

Hearing her rich husky laughter, then the sudden falter and catch in her voice, his heart seemed to turn in his breast. 'Keep talking,' he urged, 'I want to hear your voice. Tell me where you are, what you are doing…'

'I'm in a beautiful log cabin with a blazing fire and snow piled around the windows and a huge Christmas tree … outside in the snow, would you believe, and all covered with lights … and I love you, I

254

love you. What are you doing?'

'Sitting with my feet on an extremely smelly and inefficient oil heater; outside this window are a mere few inches of snow, the Christmas tree is very definitely indoors, the lights have blown twice, I'm full of Christmas dinner ... and Zoë darling, I do miss you so.'

'I hoped you might. We've only just had breakfast, so it will be hours before we get around to *our* turkey and plum pudding.'

'What are you doing today?'

'Being lazy. Yell and Becka have gone to Mass, so I expect I shall play backgammon with Piers, which is tedious as he always beats me. I have entirely the wrong kind of mind for board games.'

'Keep away from him. One old man is quite enough for you to be going on with!'

'But Giles,' she giggled, suddenly sparking into life, 'he's my Higgins and my Orsino and most fabulously sexy and beautiful. He isn't old and I love him to distraction, at least I do on stage.' She lowered her voice. 'Actually, off stage, he's a bit of a stuffed shirt and if I have to look at another picture of the wife and kiddies I shall definitely throw up...'

Giles sat back, smiling and nodding as though she could see him, cramming as much as possible into the few minutes they had. 'Give me your number ... I'll call you from Paris on New Year's Eve.' Writing down the figures he did a quick calculation in his head. 'I'll ring at nine in the evening, Paris time. I won't make it later in case I can't get to a telephone, so make sure you're in your swanky log cabin at the right time.'

She laughed. 'I suppose I can do that...'

'You'd better,' he threatened, 'or else I shall come and find you...'

He heard her last gurgle of laughter and 'Oh, yes please, Giles!' before the pips sounded and the line went dead.

For a few minutes he sat with closed eyes, his throat tight and painful with suppressed emotion, then sighed and rubbed both eyes with the heels of his palms.

When he returned to the sitting room a few minutes later, Adam was helping Margot to serve coffee while Clive snoozed peacefully in his armchair. Olivia glanced up as he entered, stretching out a hand to him along the back of the settee where she was sitting. 'Everything all right?'

He smiled and squeezed her fingers. 'Everything's fine.' He held onto her for a moment then took a deep breath, and letting go of her hand asked briskly, 'Now, after coffee, who's for a walk over the headland before it gets dark?'

'No!' said Margot and Adam together and Olivia made a face.

'Take dad, he needs to reduce that paunch.' She leaned forward and shook her father's knee. 'Wake up, dad; walkies with Giles, who'll cheer you up by telling you what happens to old men who don't take enough exercise.'

Clive opened one eye and settled more comfortably into his chair. 'I *know* what happens, and on the whole I think I prefer a heart attack to hypothermia … wake me at suppertime.'

Olivia lifted her shoulders in a defeated gesture. 'OK, Giles, I'll come with you, if no-one else will, but only if Mother puts a little something extra in the coffee to keep out the cold.'

*   *   *

Ambrose leaned both hands on the windowsill, watching Liam pelt Kate and the somewhat Amazonian Alex with snowballs, before being driven back towards the house by a ferocious counter attack. As the back door slammed behind him the two girls whooped in triumph and returned to their interrupted task of building a snowman.

'Like a pair of ruddy silly kids!' Liam stood in the doorway, tousling snow from his hair. 'Alex has gone mad … she's never seen snow before.'

'I don't suppose she has,' Ambrose returned dryly. 'South Western Australia isn't exactly noted for its harsh winters.'

Liam crossed to the fire and squatted down, holding out his hands to the warmth. 'You didn't mind me bringing her, did you? She only came over in July on a student exchange, so doesn't know anyone much, apart from the people at Norwich Uni.'

'I don't mind, but didn't her uncle and aunt feel a bit put out?'

Liam grinned. 'No. I reckon they were relieved. Maggie has every relative for miles around to Christmas dinner, and all Arthur'll want is to get away from everyone and wander undisturbed about the boatyard to see if he can spot anything Mick and I have done wrong.'

'Job still going all right, is it?' Ambrose was carefully casual.

'Yeah. Great.' Liam looked up, but didn't move as Ambrose came to sit by the fire. 'Alex's dad runs a charter business … hires out crewed yachts to rich businessmen for cruising: New Zealand, Hawaii, the Cook Islands – all that sort of thing. He's thinking of going in for Catamaran racing in a year or two though; perhaps do the really big stuff eventually. You know … the Fastnet and the America's cup.'

Ambrose watched him through half-closed eyes. 'Expensive business,' he commented.

'That doesn't matter.' Liam shrugged. 'He's loaded. He wants his brother, that's Arthur, to start designing a super racing Cat right away and Arthur says I can do some of the dogsbodying on it.'

'Sounds as though you won't have much time to spend your hard-earned pay.'

'I'm saving most of it...' Liam sat back, hugging his knees. He averted his head but not before Ambrose had seen the tell-tale colouring-up. 'Thought I might go back with Alex when she's finished her year,' he said casually, 'y'know, just for a look.'

'Excellent. Go while you can. I'll give you a hand with the fare.'

'You don't have to,' Liam struggled for a moment, then rolled his shoulders, as if loosening some invisible constraint, 'but, yeah,' he smiled suddenly, 'that'd be great. Thanks, da.'

Ambrose felt as though he was tiptoeing through a minefield. This was the longest, and certainly the most intimate conversation, they had ever had and he was acutely conscious that either of them might at any moment shatter it with an incautious word. 'I like Alex,' he said after a short silence, 'how long have you known her?'

'She was staying there when I arrived.' Liam relaxed, leaning back on his hands. 'I go up to Norwich to see her most weekends. You know, for a meal and the cinema and – er, things.'

Ambrose put a hand to his mouth to cover his smile. 'I'd like you to know,' he ventured, 'that while you're here you don't *have* to spend your nights, or at least a part of them, sleeping on this uncomfortable couch.'

An expression of mixed embarrassment and horror chased across Liam's face as Ambrose continued, 'It's just that the stairs creak and you wake me when you're creeping up and down them in the small hours.' He scratched at his beard, giving his son an amiable smile. 'Like me, you're not exactly built for creeping. Better to stay up there, I think, and let me get my beauty sleep.'

Liam averted his eyes, mumbling, 'Well, if it's OK with you.'

'Oh, leave me out of it.' Ambrose heaved himself out of his chair and made for the door. 'I have my own set of strategies to work out. Your lot didn't just invent sex, you know, some of us have been at it for quite a time...' he stopped in the doorway to deliver his parting shot. 'Just remember, looking after your lady is a bloody sight more important than making hasty and perhaps careless visits, while trying to pull the wool over *this* old man's eyes!'

Liam looked at the closed door for a minute, then turned again to stare into the fire. He gave a down-turned smile. 'Thanks,' he said softly, 'thanks a lot, you artful old sod.'

*   *   *

'I'd better meet this Kate before we all go off together.' Giles spoke abruptly as they were walking along the cliff path. It was colder than he'd realised and he wished he'd stayed indoors by the fire. Too much food and drink was playing hell with his gut. 'I must say Adam seems very keen on the whole family, including Flynn the elder; he's hardly shut up about them all since I arrived.'

He was feeling miserable and spoiling for a squabble, Olivia surmised correctly and decided wisely not to be drawn. She said, 'You'll like Kate. She's sensible and intelligent ... and very pretty. They have a boy/girl thing going but they both know the rules and they won't step over the mark. Ambrose has sorted Adam and I've sorted Kate, so you and your father can sleep sound at night.'

'Good, God, is there anything Ambrose Flynn *hasn't* managed to do for my family?'

She heard him struggling to be reasonable before he lost his temper; she gave him a warning look. 'Don't push it, Giles. One has to deal with matters as they arise. If you aren't around, someone has to lay it on the line. Adam was beginning to exhibit all the symptoms of developing into an adolescent jack rabbit, and it wasn't within my powers to know what he was wanting and feeling. It took a man to appreciate and deal with that.'

'You're right. Sorry,' he controlled himself with an effort. 'I know I have to make a lot of adjustments. He's growing up by leaps and bounds, and I don't really know where I'm at with *you* anymore.' He stopped suddenly, pulling her around to face him. 'I've changed too, you know, and have also got into the habit of laying it on the line ... you may take a swing at me if you don't like this, but it is Flynn, isn't it? You are in love with him?'

'Yes. It is, and I am.'

His lip curled slightly. 'It's reciprocal, I hope?' He couldn't control the sarcasm.

'Yes, it bloody well is, you snide bastard!'

They stood for a few moments glaring at each other, before the farcical aspect of the situation overcame them both and they collapsed into sudden helpless laughter. 'Honestly,' Olivia wiped her eyes with her woolly gloves, 'after all you've done, you have the nerve to bring me out in the freezing cold and start harassing me about *my* love life

… I don't know why I don't just push you over the cliff.'

'Because I still love you and you love me … after a fashion.' He caught her hand and started along the path again. 'Be my friend Olivia. By all means smack me back into place when I get up your nose, but don't cut me out of your life completely.'

'I couldn't if I tried, but please, Giles, just promise not to bully Adam any more about wanting to go his own way – and let him see you trust him to look after Kate without having you breathe down his neck all the time.'

'Cross my heart and hope to die…'

'You'll meet her tomorrow so be your usual charming self and don't embarrass either of them.'

'Yes, ma'am.'

'Adam needs you to approve of him.'

'Yes, ma'am.'

'Giles,' she said, 'just shut up, will you!'

'Yes ma'am.' He winked, she giggled and winked back. He said, 'Race you to the lighthouse?'

She released his hand and began to run along the narrow path through a sudden flurry of snow. With a shout of laughter he started after her, and they ran together as they had done on a Christmas Day twenty years before, when a young Olivia had first brought home a young Giles for a cautious parental approval.

For the last time, he thought as they ran; we're doing this for the very last time. Hopefully they might always be friends, and go their separate ways without regret, and without pain. He would be a better husband the second time around, if Zoë gave him the chance, and try to treat his son as the man he was so rapidly becoming.

And always love Olivia at a distance.

When it came to the final reckoning he thought, letting go gracefully was perhaps what love was all about.

28

Ambrose heaved Kate's suitcase into the boot of Giles' car then turned to put an arm about her shoulders.

'Got everything? Passport, money, handkerchief, spare hair grips?'

'Everything.' She leaned into the warmth of his arm. It was still a new sensation and she wanted to prolong it, feeling almost weepy at the moment of parting.

Sensing this he put both arms about her, hugging her to his chest before releasing her with a growled: 'All right, then. Behave yourself now!'

'Yes, dada,' Kate went on tiptoe to kiss his cheek. With a quick smile at Olivia she scrambled into the car, then leaned to wind down the window. 'I'll send a postcard … not a rude French one. Something tasteful,' she grinned as Giles started the engine, 'and I'll wave to you from the top of the Eiffel Tower.'

Adam pulled her back onto the seat. 'If we ever get there. 'Bye mum, 'bye sir…' He wound the window up and grabbed Kate's hand as the car began to roll forward. 'Eight glorious days in Gay Paree,' he was gleeful. 'Hurry up dad; we don't want to miss the ferry.'

Giles glanced in the rear view mirror, saw the clasped hands and the way they sat as though glued to each other from shoulder to knee, and shuddered. He hoped Olivia was right. She'd seemed pretty positive everything was under control, but all the same he'd see these two had rooms as far apart as possible. Groaning softly and wrenching his mind away from the memory of what he'd been doing at sixteen, he put the car into gear. Despite his earlier philosophical thoughts about parenthood, after all these months of carefree living it was no joke to suddenly have to revert to being a father again.

*   *   *

The sound of the car engine died away. 'Eight days…' Ambrose was thoughtful. 'What shall we do for eight whole days … and nights? With Liam and his girl in Guernsey and those two in Paris, we could be terribly lonely!'

Olivia said gravely, 'We could see each other now and again, I suppose.'

260

He considered this with equal gravity before suggesting, 'How about tonight?'

'Sounds good.'

'Your place or mine?' he asked.

'Oh, mine. It's rather more off the beaten track than yours.'

'And what shall we do to pass the time?' he enquired. 'You might as well know that I don't play Strip Poker, Scrabble or Monopoly.'

'We'll think of something, but right now I think we should go inside. There are more curtains twitching along this street than one normally sees in a month of Sundays.'

'Let's give them something to twitch about then,' he pulled her to him and wrapping his arms around her, kissed her very long and hard, full on the mouth.

At Captains Cottage, Margot watched Giles' car out of sight, then glanced towards Ambrose's house. 'Do you see *that*?' she turned astounded eyes on her husband. 'What on earth does that man think he's doing?' she demanded.

'Kissing our daughter … and pretty thoroughly at that,' Clive tapped the stem of his empty pipe on his teeth. 'She does seem to be enjoying it!'

'I can see that,' Margot snapped.

He grinned. 'Considering that for these past few weeks it's been practically lit up in neon lights over her head, it's taken you long enough to twig!'

She said tartly, 'You weren't so observant months ago when she was quite obviously sloping off with someone else.'

'No, but then she wasn't in love with *him*, whoever he was.'

'My husband, the expert…' she took his arm. 'Oh, well, at her age she has the right to do as she wishes I suppose, with or without our approval. But I must say it will be awkward having to run the gauntlet every time I go to the stores. That nosy old Bridie will be having a field day when she opens up tomorrow.'

'It won't be any more embarrassing for me than when we slipped away for that week-end in Bude, remember? I'd just signed into the hotel as Mr and Mrs Horatio Golightly and you said, "Will you keep the key, Clive or shall I?" right out loud in front of the manager. I wonder we didn't get thrown out.'

She smiled reminiscently. 'The bed springs twanged, didn't they? We ended up on the floor.'

'We did.' He dropped a kiss on her head. 'So after your gaffe at the reception desk all those years ago, what have we to fear now from Bridie Cadacombe and the rest of the village gossips?'

*   *   *

'Do you think we've actually heard the last of *I'm Dreaming of a White Christmas*?' queried Zoë, playing with the dial of the radio, 'it would be "quaite naice" as my mother would say, to have a small gap at least between that and Auld Lang Syne.'

'I trust you did you daughterly duty and sent your mama a Christmas card.' Yelland stretched his long legs to the fire. 'Or is such a natural happening quite beyond your devastatingly honest little ken?'

'Quite beyond. She hasn't acknowledged my existence since I joined your "Immoral Concert Party" as she so charmingly put it. A Christmas card from me would probably bring on a heart attack.' Zoë left the radio and sank into, rather than sat on, the long sofa before the fire. Resting her head back against the cushions she said, 'I should have gone to Mass with you and informed her by telegraph. The thought of my being in the clutches of an emissary from the Pope would have finished her off completely.' She looked at him solemnly. 'She's Low Church, you know. Very, very low … in fact practically subterranean. Doesn't approve of all that scraping and bowing and lighting candles … did you light one for me, James darling?'

'I did.' He observed her through half-closed eyes. 'We're very waspish today, dear.'

'Yes, well, I bet you were never forced to sit in a freezing tomb every Sunday, listening to some old fart preach hell fire and damnation at you.'

'Very true. I wore a pretty lace surplice and choked the faithful with incense.' He asked suddenly, 'Just how much do you weigh now?'

She screwed her eyes tight closed. 'A real gentleman wouldn't dream of asking a lady such a question…'

'Don't be tiresome,' he admonished severely. 'Giles would be very cross indeed if he could see you now…' He looked at her accusingly. 'Becka tells me you had a whacking great nose bleed last night.'

'Interfering old cow; it's all her fault. I've caught her ruddy cold and its playing hell with my sinuses.'

Relapsing into silence Zoë lay down full length on the couch. Watching her companion from the corner of her eye she could see his gaze sharpen and realised with despair that she couldn't hide this awful thing any longer. She turned her head, her eyes huge, something

262

like fear in their tawny depths. 'Oh, Yell,' she gulped, 'I'm sorry, but I do feel most awfully ill and I think it's rather more than a cold.' She tried to smile. 'I must have what Marty calls a galloping lurgy … how awful if I've still got it when we open again.'

Yelland left his chair to kneel by the couch and take her hand. It felt cold; he put the back of his own hand against her forehead. 'Just how long, my sweet,' he asked gently, 'have you been feeling "most awfully ill?" and how many nosebleeds have you had on the quiet? Better come clean now; Becca *has* been talking.'

'Just a few, and only for a little while.'

'And what else? The truth please.'

Her eyes filled with tears. 'I bleed a bit when I clean my teeth and my bones ache, they really do, deep down inside. Please don't be angry with me, Yell. I thought I would feel better after this break, but I don't. And I'm so *tired…*'

'I'm getting a doctor out to you right now.' He stood up and made for the door. 'You move before I get back and I swear I'll tan your blasted hide!'

'Drama Queen!' she flung after him with a sudden resurgence of spirit, then sank back again, the tears spilling over.

'How the bloody hell should I know what's wrong with her?' Less than a minute later Yelland's voice rang loud from the hallway. 'That's what you're supposed to tell me, so get out here will you – ASAP!'

There was silence for a moment, then she heard his voice again, clipped and icily calm. 'Now you just listen to me, you cretinous, supercilious unprofessional *twat*; I don't give a monkey's fart whether or not it is New Years' Eve, nor do I weep because you will have to put the chains on your tyres. Making house calls in the snow may be a novel experience for you, but I have a collapsed girl here looking like the wrath of God and burning with fever. Any inconvenience this causes you is of monumental unimportance to *me…*' She heard him gather his breath for a broadside. 'You have,' he spat explosively, 'exactly twenty fucking minutes to get your fat arse over here before I come and get you.'

She coughed on a weak laugh as he came back into the room and sat beside her. 'That told him,' she said, and kissed his hand. 'Thank you, James, for fighting my corner with such panache. Giles couldn't have done it better.'

'I'll get you to bed … come along, don't lie there like a dead fish,' he ordered, 'put your arms around my neck…' he scooped her into his arms, masking his shock at her fragility, grumbling, 'and hang on. I'm not as young as I used to be.'

With gentle detachment he helped her to undress, found warm pyjamas and a towelling robe, wrapping her like a mummy before settling her in the bed and pulling the covers over her.

'You'll miss dinner if you're not careful,' she said mournfully.

Her eyes glittered feverishly, the violet shadows beneath them like bruises on her pale skin. He stood looking down on her for a moment, before turning away with a crisp, 'Never mind about missing dinner. I'll go down and watch for that pompous prick. See if you can sleep a little.'

When he had gone she lay staring at the ceiling. 'Well blow me, I just hope the pompous prick has something in his little black bag to put me right before Giles calls.' She closed her eyes and curled onto her side. 'Only a few hours to go; I *must* be back on my feet by then...'

*   *   *

'Should we let them go on their own?' Giles peered at Kate and Adam as they piled into the taxi with a crowd of other young people. Adam, in white sharkskin jacket, red cummerbund and black dress trousers looked alarmingly adult and sexy, and Kate, wearing the blue velvet mini dress his father had insisted on buying her, far too pretty and toothsome to be let loose without a minder.

'This is Paris, not some Hampshire village,' Nikolas Ryder had brushed aside Giles' protests as a delighted Kate had stood in the boutique that morning, watching the dress being swathed in tissue paper and laid carefully in its gold and black stripped box. 'To be out of fashion at a New Year's dance at Antoine's is, for any young woman, quite unthinkable!' Now he said sharply, 'Stop hopping about like a cat on hot bricks, Giles,' and stepping back into the house, shut the door firmly. 'Adam has more sense at sixteen than you had at twenty.'

'Thanks, pa, but you might not be so *blasé* if you'd seen the size of that girl's father.' Giles was ironic but gave him the beginnings of a smile. 'Now what have you got planned for the rest of the evening?'

Nikolas glanced at his watch. 'I suppose we must wait for you to make your telephone call before we stroll down to join the grown-ups at Marco's.' He bent to take a cigarette from a silver box to ask with pointed sarcasm, 'As a matter of interest, how is the lovely Olivia?'

'Beautiful as ever and flowing through life with a newly acquired somewhat acerbic assurance, and an equally newly acquired man with

264

his own brand of particularly maddening self-possession!' Giles was equally sarcastic. 'As they are both artists of considerable talents they will probably have an amazingly happy life together, punctuated by fairly explosive disagreements, which I'm sure will scarcely ripple the waters of their content.'

'Good,' Nikolas tapped the cigarette on his thumb nail then flicked his lighter, watching him through a haze of fragrant Turkish tobacco smoke. 'She always did deserve better than you.'

'Don't waste your breath trying to needle me, father. I'm not such an easy target now. I've changed as well.'

'I had noticed.' Nikolas sat down hitching his trousers meticulously over his knees. 'Tell me about your Zoë.'

'That's a rash invitation; once started I tend to run with that particular subject,' Giles hunched his shoulders. 'The potted version is that she is disgracefully, heart-breakingly young. She has the most beautiful eyes, the most terrible hair-cut outside the Roland Petit Ballet, and a voice that makes this man's spine tingle and his thoughts turn to just one thing … at least it does when she isn't swearing like a navvy,' he looked his father in the eyes and grinned, 'not at all your sort, pa.'

'Might have been, once upon a time,' Nikolas shot his cuff, looking again at his watch. 'Better make your call from the bedroom, then I shan't be tempted to eavesdrop.'

Giles contemplated him in silence for a few moments, before observing, 'I've been waiting for you to try and cut me down to size in your usual inimitable way … I hope you're not saving it all up for later when you have an audience.'

'Put your mind at rest, Giles. I've always thought you an untrustworthy cad where women were concerned, which is hardly surprising in view of your track record, but I believe that this time you are sincere. So long as Olivia and Adam are not suffering unduly I'm happy to offer my congratulations. Providing, of course, that you manage to stay faithful to *this* one. But then that remains to be seen, doesn't it?'

'Thank you, for that vote of confidence.' Giles' tone was dry and good-humoured. 'You always were a master of the back-handed compliment.'

He went out, closing the door carefully behind him. 'Cheeky old sod!' he exclaimed under his breath, and turned to climb the spiral staircase to his bedroom. Once there he heeled off his shoes and lay on the counterpane, seeing Zoë in his mind's eye, pulling him towards her with a husky, "Let's make love *now*."

He checked his watch then picked up the 'phone and began to dial.

29

Olivia dozed on the couch, her head in Ambrose's lap, thinking hazily that these last few days must be the best, and certainly the most peaceful, that she had ever spent. She had learned so much more about her man in this short space of time: that he invariably growled and grumbled in the early mornings between bed and breakfast, like a volcano on the verge of eruption, that he never read newspapers or magazines, but poetry during the day, and crime novels for relaxation at night. That he could, as now, spend long periods close to her in amiable silence without his thoughts necessarily turning to bed, although when they did the result was always both spontaneous and combustible.

The 'phone rang suddenly, she groaned and swore. 'Tell whoever it is to bugger off.'

Ambrose clicked his teeth. 'Naughty!' He put down his book. 'It must be your parents; Clive said they wouldn't last out until midnight – I expect he wants to wish us an early New Year.' He reached out his hand and unhooked the receiver. 'Good evening, this is the Amelia Bracegirdle Home for Fallen Women...*Who*?' he sat up, suddenly tense. 'What? Say that again, will you...'

Olivia watched his face uneasily and saw the sudden sharpening of his eyes as he held the receiver tight against his ear, deliberately muffling the caller's voice.

'Who is it?' she asked as he handed her the telephone.

'Don't panic. It's nothing to do with Adam or Kate. Giles wants to speak to you.'

She listened, her face taking on a greenish pallor, while the hand holding the telephone shook. Ambrose placed his own hand on her shoulder and felt the tremors running through her. He could hear Giles' voice, quick and light, Olivia answering, 'Yes. Yes, of course ... I understand ... Is Nico up to it, or shall I come? Ring me when you know...' She said, 'Darling, it may not be that bad ... take care...'

She put the phone back on its rest and sat staring at Ambrose with bleak eyes.

'He's leaving for the States tomorrow on the first flight he can get. Zoë's been taken to a hospital in Boston and James Yelland's asked him to get there as quickly as possible.'

He asked compassionately, 'Do you always go that colour when you hear bad news?'

'Probably.' She tried to smile, her eyes glistening. 'Oh, Flynn, I wish I didn't know him so well,' her voice rose. 'He's trying to be so brisk and professional, but I can hear the panic … he won't say the words but he *knows* what's wrong and he's so frightened…'

'Hush,' he pulled her to him, holding her gently, 'easy now, my love.'

The hands that could rouse her to the heights of passion now moved slowly over her neck and shoulders, and under their calming warmth she slowly relaxed. 'How do you always know what I need?'

'I'm the seventh son of a seventh son…' He put his lips against her forehead. 'You're not quite over him yet, are you?'

'Yes and no. I still catch what he is feeling. Stupid, but in some strange way I still feel responsible if he's worried or unhappy. I always did.' She looked up for the reassurance of his smile. 'You are good to me.'

'Nonsense!' he growled, with assumed ferocity. 'Don't you go maudlin on me woman. If you've got over your incipient hysteria you'd better tell me what's happening about our children … do we need to fetch them home?'

She sat up in the curve of his arm, pushing her fingers through her hair. 'No. Nico … that's Nikolas, Giles' father, says he will keep them there for the full holiday if that's what they'd like, then bring them back in Giles' car. He's seventy six but still fighting fit, and Giles says to let him do it, if you agree.'

'Sounds fine.' He raised his eyebrows. 'Nico? That's a young name for an old man.'

'When Adam was small he always called him Grandpa Nico, because he couldn't say Nikolas. He dropped it as he grew up but it stuck … it became a sort of joke and Giles calls him Old Nico behind his back.'

She smiled then and he said, 'That's better, you're almost back to your natural colour. That shade of pea green doesn't suit you.'

'It never did.' Olivia leaned her head back on his shoulder. 'Are you really the seventh son of a seventh son?'

'No. Only the third out of three boys and two girls.'

'Where are they all? You never speak of them.' She wanted to keep him talking; anything to keep from thinking about the agony in Giles' voice.

'There are only two of us left now.' Swiftly he picked up on her need. 'There *was* Michael and Kieron and me, then Siobhan and

Maeve. Michael was killed in Normandy shortly after D-Day, and Kieron died in a Jap POW camp. Maeve caught polio and died ten years ago. Siobhan and I were the lucky ones. I'll take you visiting one day; she's married to a dentist and lives in Yorkshire.'

'What about your parents?'

'Both died relatively young … too hard to go on when you have to keep mourning your children.'

'That is so sad. What made you and your brothers join up? You didn't have to, and I thought your lot in the South were pretty ambivalent about our war.'

She felt mean in pressing him about his past; it was obviously painful, but now he'd started she was unwilling to let the subject drop.

'Oh, didn't you know,' he was cuttingly sarcastic, 'all Irishmen love a fight.'

'Rubbish. I refuse to accept that as a reason.'

'Well, let's just say that as a family we don't like bullies.' He was laconic now. 'My father fought them the first time and Michael, Kieron and me just followed on the second time around.' Picking up his book again he began to leaf through it. 'There's a very good poem somewhere here that says it all.' He found the place and began to read in his deep, rich voice.

> *'First they came for the Jews*
> *And I did not speak out –*
> *Because I was not a Jew.*
> *Then they came for the communists*
> *And I did not speak out –*
> *Because I was not a communist.*
> *Then they came for the trade unionists*
> *And I did not speak out –*
> *Because I was not a trade unionist.*
> *Then they came for me –*
> *And there was no one left*
> *To speak out for me.'*

She shivered and he put his arm about her shoulders. 'It's sad to think that our offspring and their pals don't really want to know.' He was pensive, pulling at his beard with his free hand. 'Even the nicest, least bolshie ones have a kind of arrogance … have you noticed? A certainty that what they want they will get, Bomb or no Bomb – and they haven't a clue what it was like for us, or what it was all about, nor, I suspect, do they care.'

She asked. 'Were we ever like that?'

He shook his head. 'No. We didn't have that time or those choices. Someone said, 'Go there, do this', and we went there and did it, which is why our generation will always be different from those who come after.' He gave her shoulder a squeeze. 'What did you do in the war, granny?'

'Me? I was Second Officer Heyward I/C WRNS Pay, somewhere in Scotland…' She twisted her head to look up at him. 'I bet you didn't know that at one time there was a Russian Air Squadron stationed across the border?'

'You're joking.'

'I'm not; they were incredible. Just sex on legs really. It was rather like the Midwich Cuckoos. All of a sudden the place was full of blonde, blue-eyed Slav babies. The village maidens were jumped so fast that half of them imagined they were having a virgin birth!'

He closed his eyes, his mouth twitching at the corners. 'You paint a touching picture of a village life filled with olde worlde charm.'

'It had its moments.' She was ruminative, twisting a thick lock of his hair in her fingers. 'Giles and I had just started sleeping together when I was posted to Scotland, and almost immediately he joined a convoy escort ship in the Mediterranean. I knew he was spending his leaves in the sin ports of North Africa and was pretty miffed that none of the sexy Russians came onto our base and offered to relieve my frustration. Our section officer said it was the uniform that put them off. "Why fight your way through Wren issue black lisle hose and navy passion-killers when easier alternatives are to hand?" was how she put it.'

Ambrose said, 'I bet you'd have turned *me* on; I remember having any amount of fantasies about those nifty black stockings!'

She thought, this evening is made for confidences. I wonder if we would be talking like this if Giles had never made that call to America. Aloud she asked, 'Do you mind very much about Giles?'

'No. Do you mind about Paula?'

'Of course not, but she is no longer a part of your life as he still is of mine.' For a moment she was thoughtful, then suddenly smiled. 'But her Ambrose is not my Ambrose, any more than Giles' Olivia is yours. We are different people to each other.'

He laid his hand against her cheek and turned her face towards his. 'I do love you so.'

She rubbed her head against his hand. 'I don't think I want to see the New Year in with a glass in my hand, do you?'

'No.' He kissed the crown of her head. 'Come to bed.'

*   *   *

The frost-rimmed windows sparkled under a cold hard moon; somewhere a rocket whooshed through the air to explode in a burst of coloured stars. Ambrose murmured 'Happy New Year!'

She was silent, holding him close.

He said, 'There is a place I would like to take you when spring comes again,' his voice was dreamy and his arms warm around her. 'A short way from Galway, short in Irish miles that is, stands a long low house under a blue hill. There you can lean on the stable door and watch the Atlantic rollers pour clear across from America and fling themselves over the rocks. At evening you can walk the shore and climb Pardoe's Head where, if you are lucky and keep very still, the seals will come to sing for you.'

'Too perfect. There must be a catch…'

'There is.' His laughter rumbled. 'It's called Mica. Five foot nothing of seldom-sober deviousness. He has one tooth, a cockle eye, a tongue that could cut steel – and an absolute God-given conviction that he is the owner, and I the caretaker, of Kilora!'

'I'm not surprised. You can hardly be a frequent visitor.'

He was silent for a moment then said quietly, 'It is not a place to be alone.'

He kissed her throat then bent his head to put his lips against her breast. Looking down she could see the dark shape of his head and shoulders against the paleness of her skin, and was pierced with a sudden sharp protective love that was close to pain. He was shedding the last defensive layers, opening his thoughts and feelings to her, as she had to him. All the barriers are coming down, she thought, and felt a deep and tender content.

Cradling his head in her arms she lay smiling into the darkness as he sighed once before beginning the drift into deep untroubled sleep.

*   *   *

All Adam could feel was a hot, all consuming anger. He sat stiffly on an upright chair his hands clasped tightly together and looked at Giles with burning eyes. 'If you're going so quickly she must be very ill.'

'I think she is.' Giles watched him through the cloudy beginnings of a headache.

'You *know*, don't you? Why don't you tell me? You don't have to wrap it up, I told you before … I'm not a kid.' His voice was hard

271

with accusation.

Giles gave in. Said the words he didn't want to give tongue to; not even in his own thoughts. 'I think she probably has a particularly rapid form of Leukaemia.'

Adam blanched. 'She's going to die, isn't she?'

'Yes.'

'Soon?'

'Yes.' Giles turned his head away.

Kate put out her hand. 'Adam, don't. Can't you see its bad enough without you hammering at it?'

He rounded on her furiously, demanding, 'What am I supposed to do; pretend it doesn't matter; that I don't care? That it will all go away in the morning?'

Nikolas put in gently. 'Adam, it is the morning, and nothing is going away, not for anyone, and certainly not for your father.'

'I'm sorry, but it doesn't seem to make any sense. I can only think how much fun we had, how much she laughed...' tears gathered in his eyes. 'I'm just so bloody angry that I want to find someone to blame and hit them.'

'That makes two of us.' Wearily, Giles raised his head. 'I'm certainly not going to say it will all look better after a few hours' sleep; it won't. But sitting around and trying to find a reason for the totally unreasonable is not only futile, it is stupid and childish. Go to bed, Adam. I'll talk to you again before I leave. Goodnight Kate. I'm so sorry your evening has ended like this...'

Adam flushed at the dismissal. Tight mouthed, he followed Kate from the room.

'You were hard on him,' Nikolas accused as the door closed behind them. 'This is his first brush with real tragedy and you cut him down.'

'I know.' Giles' voice was bleak. 'But he's told me more than once to treat him like a man. OK, so I'll treat him like one and he may thank me for that when he gets the next big kick in the teeth that life will undoubtedly hand him. If he can't take it, I'm quite prepared to go back to treating him as a child.' He added bitterly, 'No *man* can afford to go around being that vulnerable.'

His father was silent. After a few moment Giles sketched an apology with both hands. 'You're right. *I* can't afford to be that vulnerable, but I am. I just hope Adam never ever has to feel as I do now,' his voice broke, and he put his head in his hands, moving it slowly from side to side, 'and I don't think I can bear it, father. I really don't think I can...'

*   *   *

Adam wrenched angrily at his tie then paused, arrested in the act of unbuttoning his shirt. He could hear the murmur of his grandfather's voice then the chink of glass. But there was another sound he couldn't identify. He strained his ears. It was clearer now, but still it took him several minutes to realise that what he could hear was the sound of his father, weeping.

He went to the bedroom basin and splashed cold water over his face and hair, then raised his dripping head to stare at himself in the mirror.

'You stupid, selfish pig.'

He watched his own tears begin to trickle down his wet face, and snatching up a towel scrubbed them away. Then he left the room and walked quietly down the long landing to Kate.

She was already in bed. The bedside light was still on and he could see her eyes were wet and red-rimmed as his own. She said, 'Go away,' but he shook his head and crossed to sit on the bed beside her.

'I'm sorry. I was rotten to you. Can I stay?'

'Of course not. You know we said we wouldn't...' she was in tears. 'Go *away*,' she said again.

'I don't want to do anything ... for once I don't feel like it,' he tried to smile. 'I won't even take my clothes off ... just let me have the counterpane. Let me stay, and be with you...' he put his head down onto the pillow next to hers, 'please, Kate. I don't want to be alone tonight...'

*   *   *

Much later Nikolas left an exhausted Giles asleep on the couch and slowly climbed the stairs. He paused at Adam's door then turned the handle quietly. For a long minute he stared at the empty unruffled bed, then closed the door and walked the length of the corridor.

Silently he opened the door of the end bedroom.

In the light from the bedside lamp he saw that Kate slept, lying on her side, one hand tucked beneath her cheek. Beside her, still in his party finery sprawled Adam, one arm across her body, his long limbs tangled into the quilt and eyelids twitching restlessly. Nikolas took a spare blanket from the box at the foot of the bed and spread it over his grandson. He stood gazing down at the two tear-stained young faces for a moment before stooping to turn out the light.

Moving with an old man's gait, he left the room as silently as he had entered and walked back down the staircase to keep watch over his sleeping son.

30

'Acute Myeloblastic Leukaemia … she is already in the final stage.'

Giles bowed his head at the confirmation of his worst fears. The tubby, grey-haired Dr Lou Coburn, Head of Medicine at the Holy Cross Hospital in Boston averted his eyes.

Beside Giles, James Yelland moved restlessly. 'What does that mean?' he asked, 'what can you do for her?'

The doctor spread his hands helplessly and Giles answered for him. 'It means she is dying and that there *is* nothing to be done.' He looked up at the doctor. 'How much does she know?'

He shrugged. 'She hasn't asked and no one has told her. We waited for you. But she is a very astute young lady, and I'd take a pretty certain bet that she at least suspects.'

'So would I.' Giles glanced at Yelland's ashen face then back at the doctor. He asked, 'Could you leave us for a while? We need to talk and I must have some time to clear my head before I see her.'

'I simply can't take this in.' Yelland turned bewildered eyes on Giles as the door closed. 'She said she was tired … we all were, and I nagged her for not resting enough. But *this*!' he shook his head in disbelief. 'A week ago she was chucking snowballs at me … was it my fault? Did I work her too hard?'

'No. You can put your mind at rest on that point. No one's to blame … except perhaps, the boffins who split the atom.' Giles leaned his head on his hand. 'This is the Twentieth Century scourge, Yelland; we have sown the wind, now we are reaping the whirlwind. If you must blame someone or something, blame it on what we did to Hiroshima and Nagasaki. Blame the criminally insane tests in Arizona and the Pacific. Blame the stupid bastards who've gone on testing bigger and better bombs ever since and filling our atmosphere with poison, but don't blame yourself.'

'You're a doctor … can't you make them do *something* to help her?'

For a moment Giles lost his precarious self-control. 'I'm a surgeon, not God Almighty; if Christ Himself came down from the cross, He couldn't help,' he spat out the blasphemy then pulled himself up short at the appalled expression on Yelland's face. 'I'm sorry, but it's hard to be in my line of work and still be so fucking helpless.'

James took a handkerchief from his pocket and wiped his palms. 'What will happen? How will she...' his voice faltered.

'You said she has a cold. If that hasn't already developed into pneumonia, it almost certainly will as she now has no immunity to infection. She will die within a few days.' Giles tried his best to soften the brutality of what he was saying. He had seen death so many times, in all its guises; he could face even this one with a certain detached weighing of the possibilities. He put out a hand to rest it on the other man's shoulder and added gently. 'That really would be best ... for her.'

'Otherwise?' Yelland's face was white.

'She will die from some other massive and certainly more painful infection of spleen, or liver, or kidneys. Or will simply bleed to death.'

The silence in the room was so complete that Giles could hear his watch ticking. He thought, if I don't get out of this room immediately, neither of us is going to be able to make it for hours...

'I'll go to see her now. Give me fifteen minutes,' he said, and summoned a smile. 'That's about all I shall manage on my own...'

*   *   *

Any hope he may have had that the end was not very close died at his first sight of her as she lay on her back in the white hospital bed, her fragile form outlined beneath the covers. She was deathly pale, the telltale bruises showing livid on her bare arms, but she smiled when she saw him, and raised her head. She said, 'Better get me out of here, Giles, these beds are only made for one.'

He bent to kiss her forehead, but she pulled him down and kissed his mouth.

'I shan't break in half ... yet,' she waved a weak hand at the nurse, who stood discretely by the window, 'don't be afraid of shocking Anna. She doesn't shock easily.'

The nurse smiled at her. 'If you promise to behave, I'll leave you for ten minutes.' She turned to Giles. 'I'll be just down the hall if she gives you trouble.'

As the nurse left the room Zoë said, 'Her name is Anna Capaldi, isn't she wonderful?' she raised beseeching arms. 'Hold me, Giles. No one will disturb us. Anna will see to that.'

He lay down beside her and took her in his arms. 'I can't turn my back can I, without you get up to something?'

'That's what Jimmy says. Poor James! He looks so alone. He's sent the Company on without him, did you know?'

'Yes.'

She lay quiet in his arms. 'Giles, have you ever lied to me?'

'No. In that you are unique.'

She stared into his eyes. 'Can I ask you the question?'

He stroked her hair. 'I'd rather you didn't, but I can see you must.'

'You don't have to answer. I'll know if you don't.' She didn't flinch. 'I'm not going to get better, am I?'

Her breathing was fast and shallow. He cradled her head. 'Don't talk, my love, just be still and close to me.'

'How long?'

'Not long at all.'

'*Oh, shit*!' she said, then curled into him in the old familiar way, and he held her fast, letting her hot tears seep through his shirt to spread as a burning stain over his heart.

By the time Anna Capaldi returned, Zoë had fallen into a restless sleep. Giles slid his arms from around her and sat up. He listened to her breathing, watching the rapid rise and fall of her breast for a few moments before turning sombre eyes on the nurse. 'I think it might be an idea to ask Dr Coburn to get some oxygen in here.'

'I already have; its coming soon.' Her face was full of concern. 'Are you all right? You must need to rest.'

'Oh, there'll be time enough for that later.' He looked at her more closely. 'Have you been with her since she arrived?'

'Yes, I'm her day nurse. I'm here until the night nurse takes over at eight.'

'Well, I hope *she* won't mind sharing with a man, because I'll be staying!'

'That's all right.' She smiled. 'She's used to that, we all are ... Mr Yelland hasn't left her side for more than a few minutes until today, when he went to meet you.'

Giles moistened his dry lips and gave a crooked grin. 'Then it might get a little crowded in here later...'

*　　　*　　　*

Through the sixty long hours that followed, Giles and Yelland, old enemies now drawn together in shared sorrow, kept vigil seated on either side of her bed; in turn they dozed and woke and dozed again; ate mechanically the food brought to them; dozed and woke and watched as the oxygen cylinders emptied and were replaced, and her

277

breathing became more laboured, the periods when she was conscious less frequent.

On the second morning, when Yelland had left the room briefly to visit the hospital chapel, she awakened looking luminous and rested and almost well.

'Remember when you took me to Biarritz before the tour?' she whispered huskily. 'I told Jimmy how you wouldn't let me go to the Casino and gamble, and he called you a tight-fisted bastard! Let's go again this year.'

He played the game with her. 'And watch you lose all my money? I think not.'

'We could still sunbathe at Eden Rock.'

'I'll buy you a new bikini.'

'Did you know a film man came to see us?'

'Uh huh. James told me you made a hit with John P. Goldfarb the Third.'

'He wants to make me a movie queen…' her voice began to fade. 'I said I'd have to ask my chap about that…' Giles kissed her hand and for a brief moment saw the ghost of her old smile. 'When I'm a rich bitch, Giles darling, you can gamble in the casino with my money.'

'I shall wait with baited breath…'

That night, he struggled from an exhausted sleep to hear her husky whisper, 'Oh, Jimmy … I'd fight if I wasn't so bloody tired. Look after Giles for me, won't you? Sorry about Cleopatra and not making it to the National for you, but now, "the odds is gone and there is nothing left remarkable beneath the visiting moon…"'

As the beautiful voice faded away Yelland leaned his head on the hand he held clasped in his own; when he spoke his voice was soft in the semi-darkness of the room. 'I didn't need to wait for you to do your stuff with the serpent, my darling girl. For me, you have *always* been, "a lass unparalleled."'

On the other side of the bed, Giles stayed silent and motionless, unwilling to move and break the spell between these two, now joined by an invisible cord of intimacy that was almost tangible; understanding for the first time, the pride and depth of love James Yelland had for his young protégé. She was nearing the end; Giles could feel it in every fibre of his being; he looked at the other man's bent head with a compassion that for the moment transcended his own sadness and grief.

How she was all things to all people, he reflected: to himself the beloved lover, to James the light that never would be dimmed. To

Marty she was a pal, a mate, to Adam a needed, generous friend.

We only live on in the people who know and love us, he thought, *and all of those whose lives she has touched will remember Zoë. Remember her talent and the way she could shock and tease and love. She is that "bright particular star", the one who will never grow old; but stay on in the memory of us all as the ever young, the ever loved.*

At that moment Yelland looked up, reading his eyes, silently acknowledging the message they held: that very soon there would indeed be for them both, "nothing left remarkable beneath the visiting moon."

*   *   *

Nikolas broke the news to Adam and Kate when they appeared for lunch. Giles had 'phoned an hour before, sounding drained and exhausted in defeat.

'Can you get them home in a day or two, father? There's still so much to do here. There is the funeral on Monday and I shan't leave for some time after that... They'll both need time in their own homes before school starts again. Will you get in touch with Olivia and tell her what's happened, and let her know when you'll be arriving?'

Now Nikolas told them quietly and gently that it was all over; there would be no more waiting for the news that no one wanted to hear.

Kate sat white and silent. Adam left the table and went out onto the terrace, to stand for a time hunched against the railing, staring out over the roof-tops to where the grey dome of Notre Dame merged into a leaden, snow-filled sky.

Eventually he turned away and re-entered the room. 'I don't like to think that dad is alone,' he said abruptly, 'someone should be with him.'

'Someone is ... James Yelland from the theatre company. He's been with him all the time.' Nikolas trod carefully. He wouldn't put it past this grandson of his, now suddenly controlled and adult in his grief, to demand that he should immediately fly to his father's side. 'Giles wants you to return home now. You both need your own people, and they need you.'

'You'll stay with us in Devon, won't you, grandpa, just for a while? After all, *you* might need us.'

'If your mother will put up with me,' Nikolas smiled and Adam gave a shaky laugh.

'You can have my bed. I'll sleep in the spare room, it's smaller

279

but warmer!' He turned to Kate, pushing down the awful hollow feeling, hoping he could keep a hold on it until he could be alone. It wasn't fair to make other people as miserable as him. He gave her a faint, strained smile and asked, 'Come for a walk down to the river? You never know what might turn up.'

'You mean, wait for the *Star* to come sailing up the Seine?' Following his lead she returned his smile. 'Rotten weather for sailing though.'

'Sissy,' his voice shook, 'you can't always sail in sunny waters...'

For an hour they walked, muffled against the cold, before he left her in Notre Dame and walked down to the river to lean on the parapet and weep alone, but by the time Kate joined him again he had washed his face at a fountain and only his swollen eyes gave him away.

She said simply, 'I lit a candle for you as well,' and he smiled and took her hand and they walked back silently to his grandfather's house.

*   *   *

'That bloody woman!' Yelland was almost comical in his rage. 'That disgusting, unnatural, sanctimonious old *bitch*; any cat's a better mother than she's ever been!' He stared at Giles, eyes snapping with fury. 'I 'phone all the way from bloody America to her snug little bungalow in Frinton-on-Sea; I break the news that her only daughter is dead and offer to fly her out for the funeral and she says, 'What daughter? I don't have a daughter,' and puts the 'phone down on me ... May she rot in hell.'

Giles smiled fleetingly. 'I have an awful feeling that if she *did* turn up Zoë would find some frightful way of making her displeasure apparent!'

'You're right, of course. I wouldn't put it past madam to chuck down a damn' great thunderbolt if she had one handy!' Yelland sat drumming his fingers on the arm of his chair. 'I shall have to rejoin the company next week,' he said abruptly. 'Come with us for a week or two, Giles ... not your scene, I know, but you shouldn't be alone. Not yet.'

'Thank you, but I will find a corner here to lick my wounds before going back home. Although for what reason I'm going back at all, I can't at the moment imagine.'

'What will you do?'

'God knows; I was planning on taking a sabbatical soon.' Giles narrowed his eyes, staring out of the hotel window, where sudden

280

brilliant sunshine was melting the top layer of snow on the rooftops below. He had been, he remembered, taking that year out to spend more time with Zoë. 'I might even come back to the States,' he said, 'there's some very exciting research work in heart and lung surgery going on here in which I'm keen to be involved. I might pursue that line … put out some feelers before I go home.'

'You'll be a long way from your family if you decide to work over here.'

Giles answered quietly, 'But closer to Zoë.' He shrugged. 'The world gets smaller every day. I shall see that I don't drift apart from my son, but I'm on my own now, and I think I could manage my life better here.'

*   *   *

He saw the freesias in the florist's window. Hothouse flowers that would soon wilt and die in the snow, but he bought them, and made his last trip out to the little cemetery by the church on the far side of Boston common.

Squatting on his heels he scooped the fresh snow from the mound and laid the flowers. He said, 'Time to go home. I'll keep an eye out for Jimmy and Marty for you … but I shall be back before very long. Just try to keep out of trouble…'

Say hello to our flat for me. Her voice was close in his ear as he walked away, *have an orgy or two if you like … I won't mind. Not much, anyway*!'

*   *   *

'Saying thank you is not nearly enough.'

Anna Capaldi took the hand he offered. 'We shall miss you and James, Dr Ryder.'

'My name is Giles.'

She smiled warmly. 'Then we shall miss you, Giles.'

'I shall be back, I hope at the end of this year. Not here, but over at the Hartington Institute. That is if everything goes well with visas and work permits and all those other tiresome bits and pieces that keep the bureaucrats busy.'

'To have fresh work to look forward to will be some help I'm sure. It helped me.'

He raised inquiring brows. 'You needed that?'

'We'd been married ten years when my husband was killed in

281

Korea.' She was matter of fact, 'he was an Army Medic. Nurse training seemed a good way to keep the faith. I never regretted turning my back on the old life and starting all over again.'

Giles buttoned his coat and pulled on his gloves. 'I'll let you know if it works for me…'

<h1 style="text-align:center">31</h1>

When they stepped from the car, Kate went into Olivia's open arms. Adam pulled a face then summoned a wry smile. 'I don't really mind sharing, but when you've quite finished with my mother, I'll have her back!'

Ambrose put an arm about his shoulders. 'Stop harassing the women folk.'

Adam's eyes crinkled. 'I thought that's what men were for.'

'Amongst other things,' he growled. Releasing Adam, Ambrose held out his hand to Kate. 'Come here, Katerine. I've missed you.'

For a moment she clung to him as she had when they'd said goodbye, and he kept his arm about her as he held out his hand to Nikolas. 'Welcome to the madhouse. Clive is indoors toasting crumpets, Margot's lining up the tea cups and there is sufficient whisky left to keep both you and me happy for the rest of the evening!'

'Thank God for that.' Nikolas rubbed his hands. 'I can think of any number of things I'd rather do than cross the English Channel in winter,' he clasped Ambrose's hand and kissed Olivia's cheek.

As Adam hugged her, Olivia whispered, 'Everything all right?'

He gave her a steady smile. 'It is now.'

*   *   *

Later, when everyone else had left and Adam reluctantly given in to exhaustion and gone to bed, Nikolas sat before the dying fire and gave Olivia a rueful smile. 'I'm sorry if I'm disrupting your peaceful holiday.'

'There will be other days, and I want you to stay; it would please me and help Adam.'

He gave her a sideways glance. 'You picked a very different fish from the pond this time, my dear; are you happy with him?'

She threw back her head and laughed. 'Rather a big fish, but I'm very happy.' She sobered suddenly and was quiet. 'Poor Giles,' her eyes were sad. 'I can't imagine how he is feeling now, or how he'll cope.'

'I think he's hoping for a few days here when he returns.'

'He can come ... and stay, as long as he needs. I told him that

283

when we spoke on the 'phone last night.'

He gave her a warning look. 'Be careful, Olivia. He may just be running to where he thinks he can find an answer to his loss.'

'I have to help him, Nico. I can't turn my back.'

'I know, but you have an infinite capacity for caring, sometimes at the expense of your own needs. And there are others to consider.'

'Flynn and I are grown-up people,' she answered him gently. 'We can make space for Giles.'

'Perhaps, but Adam and Kate have to fit in there somewhere.'

'It won't be easy,' she acknowledged, 'for Adam in particular, but he'll soon be back at school where he has a very understanding house-master ... also Barty, a wise old friend who may offer a bolt hole and a listening ear from time to time,' she gave him a candid look, 'and they both have Flynn and me. All of us are used now to talking things over.'

'I'm a nosy old man, I know, but have you two been living together?'

'Isn't it obvious?'

'Then how are you and your Flynn going to manage your lives if Giles is here for any length of time?'

'With some difficulty, but there is always the studio ... sacrosanct to artists only; I daresay we shall survive.'

'I'm sure you will,' his tone was dry and amused. 'Although even when Giles is gone, I imagine having those two youngsters still popping back at regular intervals will cause you a few headaches. You can hardly openly share a house in this village until they are off hand. To say the least, it would make things awkward for them.'

She smiled. 'We shall tell them the truth but keep to our own houses and save them any embarrassment while they are home. After all, in another year or so Adam should be at Dartmouth and Kate at University. When that happens, we shall give up trying to be discreet and rock Lodscombe to its foundations by going to live in sin in Ireland.'

'Ireland?' He was startled. 'Why on earth do you want to go and bury yourselves in Ireland?'

'We want,' she said, smiling at his concern, 'to walk our own shore in the evening and have the seals come to sing for us...'

*   *   *

The flat was cold and unwelcoming. Giles walked around turning on the central heating and lighting the gas fires, then stood, still huddled

284

into his overcoat. Staring out onto the wet slush that was snow in an English city he frowned and said aloud, 'I don't think this is such a good idea,' then cocked his head, waiting.

'*Give it time. Spring will come again...*'

He pulled off his thick, woollen, Boston-winter scarf. 'Bugger spring. What about now?'

'*Language, Giles*!' he heard the echo of her laughter.

Picking up his plastic bag of groceries he went into the kitchen and rattled plates to break the silence.

*   *   *

In the early hours of the morning he awoke with a heart-stopping thump, and reaching out into the darkness, swept his hand over the empty pillow.

For an hour he lay, sweating and wide-awake. Now, back here in the bed they had shared, came the full anguish of knowing that he would never again hold her in his arms; that a part of him had died with her. He felt cold and empty, and totally alone; before him a high, dark wall that he didn't want to climb.

He remembered that there were Sommeil tablets in the bathroom cabinet and swinging his legs out of bed, fumbled with the switch on the bedside lamp. He *had* to sleep, if only to stop the thoughts whirring around in his head. He walked unsteadily into the bathroom and taking out the bottle, stood staring at it for several seconds before unscrewing the cap and tipping the contents into his palm, registering then that the bottle was large and almost full; in fact there were enough of the little pink tablets to put a fair-sized insomniac pony to sleep.

He took a long, clinical, professional look at his face in the mirror.

The eyes staring back at him were dull and sunken, the skin dry, with deep vertical frown lines between his eyes. He thought: I need a haircut, a shave, and a reason for living. He fingered the tablets in his palm; this was what those without compassion and understanding called the coward's way out. Why not take it?

Again he studied his face in the mirror and answered himself: *Because it would make all the love, all the life we had null and void, as though it had never been. It would leave Nikolas without a son and Adam without a father.*

And it would leave Olivia without ... what? He grimaced painfully at his reflection. 'Without a pain in the neck!' he said.

Tipping his hand he sent the tablets down the lavatory and pressed

285

the handle; returning to the bedroom he pulled aside the curtains and taking a blanket from the bed, wrapped it around his shoulders then settled into the cushioned wicker chair by the window to wait for morning.

As dawn broke he was in the car, speeding towards the one sane, familiar thing left in his life.

Back to Olivia.

Just for a little while, he thought, as the car ate up the miles. I know I can rely on her. She won't have changed that much and I won't bother her for long. I just need to walk and talk with her and know that she still cares. Then perhaps I can return to Ranleigh and the hospital until it's time to go back to Boston. And maybe by then the wall will have fallen and I can start all over again without anyone to hold me up, or point me in the way that I should go.

32

In the cottage on the cliff there were good days and there were bad for Giles. At first the bad predominated, but gradually they evened out so that he woke some mornings with a lifting of the spirits and the hope that today would be the day he turned the corner. Even when the feeling didn't last beyond noon, it gave him some hope for the future.

And Olivia found an old, practised patience: leaving him alone when he withdrew into himself; giving freely of her time and attention when he needed to talk. Sometimes they walked in silence in the cold winter weather, sometimes sat before the fire while he talked of Zoë, and tried, tentatively, to make plans for a future without her.

But she heeded Nico's warning.

Because there were times when she felt him beginning to exert the old pressures, the old manipulative charm, and twenty years of shared living had given her a finely developed antenna for the direction of his thoughts and his unconscious body language. So she struggled to keep the delicate balance between, never allowing the compassion and warmth she felt for him, and his close dependence on her, to spill over into physical intimacy.

Escaping to work in the peace and tranquillity of the studio was an antidote to the tension and sometimes despair of those weeks. An intoxication and re-birth of self to lie in Ambrose's arms and have him make love with a new, demanding fierceness that was both exciting and disturbing. By tacit agreement they avoided discussing how long it might be before they could be alone again: to recapture the tranquil warmth of those few days, when nothing of the outside world had intruded on their delight in each other. But as time passed, tension and dissention crept insidiously into their time together.

They began to clash verbally over slight and unimportant matters; trifles that in the past would have caused nothing more than a temporary irritation, but now frequently erupted into abrasive and hurtful exchanges, leaving Olivia exasperated and unsure and Ambrose retreating into sullen silence.

But one evening when Giles was dining with Clive and Margot it was brought brutally home to her how much Giles' presence at the cottage was costing Ambrose: that beneath his apparent acceptance of the situation, there was a volcano of anger and frustration ready to erupt.

287

After a day of discord between them, with each barricaded behind a wall of taciturn resentment, he watched, eyes clouded and dark with anger as she cleaned her brushes with unusual concentration and thoroughness, her back pointedly turned from him.

'How much longer is your bloody ex going to be in *your* house?' he demanded with sudden venom.

'Until he's ready to go,' she answered evenly. 'I'm not pushing him out.'

His mouth twisted in contempt. 'I don't doubt he's banking on that. Pretty good at hiding behind your skirts, isn't he?'

Olivia took her shoulder bag from the table. 'I'm tired and I'm going home.'

He said crudely, 'No chance of a quick fuck, then?'

'The way I'm feeling right now? No chance at all...' as she made to pass him he caught her arm, jerking her into a rough embrace. Angry, she made to pull away. 'Leave it, Flynn. It's been a lousy day, don't make it any worse.'

His big hands gripped her tightly above the elbows. 'Too busy rushing back to welcome your precious Giles home to get into my bed are you? How d'you think that makes me feel?'

'Jealous as hell by the look of you ... now let me go, damn you.'

Forcing her lips apart he ravaged her mouth. Silently she fought him while the blood pounded in her ears and her body fought its own battle between fury and lust. Ambrose, even in this foul and savage mood, could still set all her nerve ends jangling and swamp her with desire. Finally he took his mouth from hers, glaring down with hard blue eyes. 'Whose bed is it to be then – Giles' or mine?'

Infuriated she twisted spiteful fingers in his hair. 'No contest, you bastard; there never has been. But I don't like caveman Flynn; so let me go and don't try it again.'

For a moment his hands tightened, fingers digging into her flesh and making her flinch. Then his shoulders slumped; he raised one hand and touched her bruised mouth. 'You stop scalping me,' he offered, his voice thick with emotion, 'and I'll stop short of rape!' He released her and as she unclenched her fingers from his hair, rested his forehead against hers. 'I'm sorry. I can't help it; all the time he's here I'm afraid.'

'Of what?'

'That somehow he'll persuade you he can't live without you.'

Shaken she put her arms about him. 'That's what it's all about isn't it ... all this squabbling and fighting? We are both afraid of the same thing: *I'm* on edge most of the time, expecting him to make a move – and make it he will, sooner or later: but darling, if we just trust each other it won't matter if he does.' She hugged him close. 'I'm sorry for Giles, and yes, I'm still fond of him and want to help him, but there is no competition; so no more strong arm tactics: promise?'

'Promise.' He rocked her gently. 'I love you so very much.'

She smiled, leaning back in his arms. 'Well, are you going to show me how much, or must I beg for it?'

He gave his old growling laugh. 'Come along – no cave man tactics, I promise.'

'Oh, I don't know…' teasingly she tugged at his beard. 'I've rather changed my mind. So long as you stop short of dragging me to bed by the hair I reckon a spot of Neanderthal sex wouldn't exactly come amiss…'

'Monkey sex,' he said, 'is even better.'

*   *   *

After that evening there was an easing of pressure, with both of them less troubled and disturbed by the cuckoo in the nest, able again to tease, argue and disagree without hurt, Ambrose once more frequently bursting into his big, rumbling laugh and making love to her again with tender lips and hands.

*   *   *

Almost a month after his arrival, Giles awoke one morning with his head suddenly clear and the realisation that this particular morning was different. As he shaved, watching his eyes in the mirror, he thought, I'm not cured, or healed, or even particularly glad to be alive, but I can *feel* again, and that has to be good…

He went downstairs and into the kitchen as Olivia came in from the garden with her hands full of snowdrops. 'Just look!' she exclaimed, holding them up to him. 'The first sign of spring.'

He smiled, and his eyes were brighter than she'd seen them since that day he'd come, cold and grey and desperate, to bang upon her door and beg, "Help me Livy: help me or I shall go under…"

'They come early here, and even earlier in Cornwall; do you remember the flower meadows at Porthcurno, where we took our leave one February during the war?'

'Yes, when you spent a whole afternoon staring at the legs of the girls picking daffodils,' she answered dryly, then smiled again and

289

bent her head to the flowers.

It was then that the nascent desire that had begun to stir in him again sprang to sudden, almost overwhelming life; the remembered feel and look of her when they made love, vivid and clear.

'Livy…' He took a step towards her and put out his hand, daring to make the move he had so often been on the very verge of making these past weeks. She raised her head to give a half-sad, half-warning look that stopped him in mid stride. For several moments they stood motionless, until Giles broke the spell. Giving a rueful hunch of one shoulder, he turned to stare out of the window at the white fluffs of clouds riding a hard blue sky.

Not quite spring yet. Not for him anyway.

If only … but it couldn't be. Of course it couldn't. Olivia had her new life; for her there could never be any return to those past days of mixed pleasure and pain. He spoke with his back to her. 'It's time I went, Livy. Now, before I start slipping back into the past. It would be so easy, you see.'

'Yes.' She put the flowers down and began to fill the kettle.

'I'll leave today … I thought I'd stay with Chris and Carol for a day or two before I return to work.' He turned to face her, elaborately casual. 'I've appreciated the hospital granting me the few weeks leave but I need to get back into harness. And I must open up the flat. It will need airing after all this time. It felt dampish when I got back from the States.'

'Will you be all right?'

'I have to be. I'll get back to the hospital and work until I leave for Boston at the end of the year. And I want to spend some time with Jimmy Yelland when he gets back. Make sure he's all right.'

She said, 'You know you can always come if you need a break. Bring Jimmy with you, if you like.'

'I think I've been around long enough.' He gave a faint smile. 'You need your life back, and Ambrose needs his woman.'

She said gently, 'He's got her and I have him. Now and forever.'

Giles leaned forward and kissed her lightly on the cheek. 'Unfortunately, I never really doubted that!'

*   *   *

Ambrose and Olivia settled back into the routine of work and shared living with little now to disturb them. They continued to fight occasionally, make up rapidly and grow a little closer each day. The weeks passed with only the minor disruption of Kate's easy presence at weekends and an occasional flying visit from Liam. Even Adam's appearance at Easter caused little more than a ripple.

He had put on a late spurt of growth, shooting suddenly past Giles' six feet and developing an impressive breadth of shoulder. Deep-voiced and filled now with a calm, controlled energy, he ate prodigious amounts of food and from time to time, vied subtlety, but determinedly with Ambrose for Olivia's attention.

No natural expert in the intricacies of family life and relationships, Ambrose watched with admiration Olivia's handling of both her son and his daughter and found Adam's increasing willingness to defer to him on occasions, or to lay before him the odd thorny problem to resolve, gave him a pleasure he found impossible to put into words. Even Liam's visits, filled as they were with his plans to return that autumn with Alex to Australia, were amiable and passed pleasantly without any major confrontations.

But the immediate and simultaneous arrival of Kate, Adam, and the long summer vacations aroused mixed feelings of pleasure and dread in Ambrose's heart, as he viewed the probable effects on them both of weather warm enough to inspire long walks, and even more protracted expeditions aboard the Morning Star.

Without Liam's inhibiting presence, such a close companionship between a girl who was fast becoming a lovely young woman, and a very assured and attractive young man, was a combination that may well make for headaches all around.

*   *   *

'I'm going down to the boat, mum ... and sir!' Adam grinned at Ambrose, who growled and threw a piece of clay.

'Just take her for a sail and leave us in peace for a while, will you. We're both busy, and the thought of having you hanging around for the next six weeks is enough to send me into an early grave.'

'It doesn't do a lot for me either,' Adam gave Olivia a mischievous glance, 'Mum, will you tell Kate where I am when she gets here?'

'I should think she'll probably guess,' she answered dryly, 'but yes, when she's had a chance to change and catch her breath, I'll send her down.'

Ambrose gave him a particularly piercing look. 'If you're sailing together, see you do just that and nothing else!'

'Like what?' Adam dodged, brushing at his sleeve as another piece of clay came flying, 'hell, Ambrose, give over; this is a new

291

shirt!'

'Get out then.'

'I go; I go. Tell Kate to *hurry*....'

'And behave yourselves, blast it.' Ambrose bellowed after him. He grinned wolfishly at Olivia. 'Sorry.'

She gave him a loving, exasperated look and returned to her easel. Slowly the echoes of Adam's presence died and the room settled to the normal sounds of brush on canvas and the slap, slap of wet clay.

Ambrose worked with concentration, whistling faintly through his teeth, conscious as always of Olivia at the far end of the studio, a constant source of pleasure and delight. In retrospect, the fears that had consumed him a few months ago seemed merely foolish, but still, he was glad to be back as the only man in her life. Sometimes, he had seen Giles look at her in a way that had made his heart freeze. Once or twice, he thought, it had been an uncomfortably close shave, but now he could see and touch and love her without feeling that dark shadow hovering at his back...

*   *   *

'Gosh! I could hear you singing when I got off the bus.' Kate slid down the cabin steps and into Adam's arms. 'Somebody leave you a fortune?'

'No, it was just the thought of having a simply tremendous snog with you!'

They collapsed laughing onto the bunk and he kissed her vigorously until she pulled away, warning: 'Take it easy, I've only just been let out of the nunnery and there's seven weeks to go before the cloisters claim me once again.'

'All the more reason...' he slipped his hand under her blouse, 'I've been banged up for three months with a hundred and twenty hairy blokes, which might be fun for you, should you ever be in that situation, but it's been bloody frustrating for me.'

She surrendered to his caresses for some minutes, then, 'Better get sailing,' she warned, gently but firmly prizing his arms from around her, 'if we stay here much longer we'll have dad appear on deck ready to defend my honour.'

'Oh, *God,*' Adam rolled over and sat up, cross and dishevelled. 'It's like dying of thirst and having someone hold a bottle of water just out of reach! Hell's teeth, Kate, this time next year we'll both have left school, so why should we wait? What's so magical about being eighteen that means we can do then what we can't do now?'

292

She was patient. 'Because *you* promised dad and we both agreed to wait.'

'Oh, all right,' scowling, he combed his fingers through his hair, 'but *they* didn't wait did they?'

'That's different – if you're practically in your dotage I daresay you need to get cracking as soon as possible.'

He groaned. 'Jesus, Kate, I spend ninety-eight per cent of my waking hours, and probably most of my sleeping ones, thinking about sex … another year and I'll be a nervous wreck.'

'I'm amazed you find the time,' she said primly. 'I'm working far too hard to have time for thinking about that sort of thing.'

He grinned. 'It's different for you.'

'Chauvinist pig!' She began to fasten her blouse. 'Actually, I think about it a lot but *honestly* … imagine getting preggers like Sylvie Harrison up at the pub and having to get married before you'd had any real life outside of this place.' She shuddered. 'Sweet sixteen and looking like Mamma Cass!'

'Don't,' he paled. The thought of Kate's slim body swelling into such grossness was revolting. Probably Sylvie Harrison's bloke had thought he was being careful; but nothing was foolproof and he and Kate were hardly in a position to rush off and get married if it happened to them…

He jumped down from the bunk. 'Come on. We'll get the sails up and catch the best of the day. We can skinny-dip in Pels cove.'

'Are you kidding … it'll be freezing there.'

'As it's probably the only chance I'll get to see you in the buff, I'll risk the cold.' Adam chuckled. 'And if I must stay a virgin, I might as well be a clean one.'

*　　　*　　　*

Ambrose watched their return from his vantage point by the studio window; Adam's arm close around Kate's shoulders as they walked up the hill. She was laughing, her head tilted upwards, reminding Ambrose of the day in London, when he'd seen Giles and Zoë together. He frowned and tugged at his beard.

'Those two…' he glanced round as Olivia came into the room; he beckoned her to join him at the window, 'they're going to be too much alone together now Liam's away.'

She tucked her arm in his. 'Better face facts, Flynn, we can't expect them to stay pure and chaste indefinitely.'

'The silly buggers think they know all about it now and expect to jump into bed before they're out of rompers, but they're still only a couple of kids.' He scowled. 'You don't think they've already…?' he left the question hanging in the air.

'No, I don't, although if it was up to Adam, they probably would have by now,' she answered him dryly. 'Fortunately your daughter has more common sense than my son, so you don't need to worry; she knows how to manage him.'

He scowled again. 'All I can say is, roll on next year. Once they're out of my sight and responsible for themselves, they can do as they wish and take the consequences … it'll be no use then to come running to me if they make a muck of their lives.'

'Ach, but you're a hard man, Flynn,' she mocked him and put her arms about his neck. 'Give them a bit of space to enjoy the holiday. We have nice, normal kids. Kate works hard at school and is a delight to have around and Tom has nothing but praise for Adam these past months. He's handled Zoë's death and Giles' stay here without being knocked too far off course. We've a lot for which to be thankful.'

'So we have, but that doesn't alter the fact that I'll be damned glad when September comes again and they're both safely back in school.'

Olivia shook her head reprovingly and he laughed, tightening his arms about her as he bent his head to hers. 'T'is all your fault, woman, for you set them both a shocking example!'

'See that?' Adam paused and jerked his head towards the studio window. He made a rude noise through pursed lips. 'Snogging again … you'd think at that age they'd be past it, wouldn't you?'

33

Clive cast a glance up at the darkening sky and sniffed dubiously at the faint dampness in the air.

'It's been a great summer but I reckon we've had the best of it.'

'Um,' Olivia stood with her hands in the pockets of her skirt. She gazed down to where the Morning Star lay deserted at her moorings. 'Next summer will be our last for actually living here. We'll be back fairly regularly, though.'

'I'm glad to hear it.' Margot wrinkled her nose. 'I don't fancy having to do that sea voyage very often, and I most certainly wouldn't fly.'

Clive grinned. 'A parochial woman, your mother.'

Margot sighed. 'We'll miss you, but at least we'll see something of Adam and Kate, particularly Adam as he'll be close by.'

'Perhaps,' Clive looked amused. 'I have a suspicion he might find other things to do than visit a couple of old fogies.'

Olivia linked her arm in his. 'He *likes* old fogies, look how well he gets on with Barty. Tom says Adam walks down to see him two or three times every week.'

'Oh, anyone would get on with Barty…'

That was true, thought Olivia, as she walked back to the Lodge, although he firmly refused to go visiting and leave his garden untended, the old man appeared to get great pleasure and satisfaction from holding open house to all of them. Even Giles had been drawn into the circle of Barty's friends. An odd friendship for two such disparate men, but one that she knew Giles valued.

'You look very pensive, are you missing our brood?' asked Ambrose, as she entered the cottage. 'Here, a nice cold G & T,' he kissed her. 'I've missed *you.*'

'I've only been gone an hour.' She smiled and took the glass. 'But yes, I am missing them. And now there's only Christmas and the Easter holidays when they will really be with us. After that they'll want to spend all the time they have together before they go their separate ways … what was it you said you called it in Ireland?'

'The time between school and getting to grips with the world?' He smiled. "Running the Country."'

'A lovely and very poetic way of putting it, but it makes me feel a little sad … and old.'

'Never mind,' he said comfortably, 'when they're gone we two can be Darby and Joan and sit in our rocking chairs either side of the hearth and reminisce!'

'I didn't say I felt *that* old.' She smiled at him over the rim of her glass. He grinned and sat back, stretching his feet to the range.

'I'm glad they've had a good summer. You were right, you know. Kate does know how to handle him. For a while I thought he was just too overwhelmingly sexy for her to resist.' He grinned. 'All that self-control … she must take after me!'

'Of course,' Olivia sat on the arm of his chair and ruffled his hair, 'you are exceptional. After all, you were able to concentrate wholly on your work whilst a scraggy old woman posed for you!'

He tilted his head back and smiled wickedly. 'I'm hoping that the same ravishingly stunning mature woman will pose for me again soon … without that prissy shirt.'

Her eyes sparkled, 'This time, Flynn you may get lucky,' she teased, 'just so long as you continue to keep your mind on your work.'

He slipped an arm about her waist. 'I think you should prepare for it to be a very "hands on" sort of experience … after all, I have to get your proportions absolutely right.'

*   *   *

He took her to Ireland the following April; flying from Bristol to Dublin and spending two leisurely days driving their hired car, an elegant, but somewhat elderly and asthmatic Zephyr Zodiac, through all the vagaries of an Irish spring; running the gamut of weather that ranged through brilliant sunshine, thick white mists, streaming rain and the softest of breeze-blown drizzle.

It was years since he had done this journey by car and he was moved by Olivia's delight; seeing through her eyes the beauty of the changing colours and forms of his homeland, as they passed through a varying countryside of brown peat and lush green grasslands, on their way to the rocky coast and blue hills of Galway.

When they stayed the first night in the bar of a small town on the banks of the Shannon, Olivia was enchanted with her first taste of Gaelic hospitality, Ambrose watching in amazement as she devoured an enormous amount of fresh-caught salmon and white fluffy potatoes running with yellow butter. 'Keep eating like that,' he warned, 'and we'll soon be too poor to afford petrol for the car.'

'I'm just making the most of my opportunities,' she assured him, 'we shan't be doing this very often, shall we?'

'No, in future we fly as close to home as possible. I just wanted you to see what Ireland was like, coast to coast.' He leaned back with folded arms as she pushed away her empty plate with a satisfied sigh. 'It beats me how you can eat so much and stay the same size.'

She smiled. 'I wouldn't if I did this every day.'

'Tomorrow we shall be home and Mica will likely try to serve you stewed kelp and tatties. His cooking is guaranteed to keep anyone thin, mostly because it's too disgusting to eat,' his eyes teased and she laughed, reaching across the table to take his hand.

'Don't lie to me, Liam told me you live like a king when Mica cooks.'

'Did he now?' he smiled, and stood, pulling her to her feet. 'Come along. We'll walk this meal off with a nice stroll through the evening drizzle then come back and be sociable in the bar over our pints of Guinness.'

She tucked her arm in his as they walked by the river. 'I wonder what Adam will make of all this?'

'If there are fish in the rivers, and my daughter to come home to, he'll be happy.' He gave a rumble of laughter. 'Like me, he's a simple man!'

*   *   *

His house was all Olivia could have hoped for. Several times over the past year she'd wondered if her easy acceptance of a future in this country had been if not foolhardy, at least somewhat rash. But she had trusted him so completely that it was no surprise to see the beauty of the place, the whitewashed stone house nestling beneath a blue hill, with the ocean rolling in over rocks no more than a hundred yards from the door.

As she stepped from the car, he touched her shoulder lightly. 'Does it feel like coming home?'

'It feels ... perfect,' she answered truthfully.

'You haven't met Mica yet,' he laughed, and putting an arm about her opened the wicket gate and led her towards the door. As if on cue the top half swung wide and a small, wizened face appeared in the opening.

'Ach. It's time ye returned, Flynn ... where's your belly gone, man? An' that poor lass ... I can see her bones!' The apparition flung open the lower half of the door, a huge, one-toothed grin splitting its face. 'Come in now, for I've a rabbit stew on that will stick to your

297

ribs and put some meat on the pair of you!'

'Seaweed and tatties, my foot,' Olivia poked a finger into Ambrose's taut stomach as they sat at the table and the old man reverently set the plates of fragrant stew before them. 'I can't wait to see that belly come back!'

Mica was like a gnarled old sprite, alternating between caustic exchanges with Ambrose, and dancing comical exaggerated attendance on Olivia, but he was sensitive enough to disappear once the meal was over, leaving Ambrose to take her through the house.

It was a warm and welcoming place; the interior with unexpected angles to the walls and uneven boards on the floors. At the front of the cottage one long living room faced the sea; to the rear was a galley kitchen, the windows framing a view of the distant blue hills. An additional wing built to one side formed an L-shape, housing a lofty studio and store rooms, and at the end, Mica's own quarters.

When they returned to the comfortable living room, Olivia leaned on the sill of the open window, breathing in the clear air and gazing over the stretch of wide green grassland to where the sea washed the rocks. 'How strange to think of living here, with Giles opposite us across that water.'

Ambrose put his arms around her and rested his chin on her head to ask with mock seriousness, 'Do you not know woman, that it's a very dangerous matter to mention your ex-husband when your lover is about to take you to bed?'

'Not at all,' she answered, 'It merely adds a little spice to life and reminds me again how very lucky I am.'

As they began to climb the stairs to their bedroom he paused for a moment to look down at her and say, 'I hope you've realised that Mica will make himself your slave and probably drive you crazy.'

She smiled and tugged at his beard. 'Nice,' she said, 'I've always wanted a slave.'

He put his arms about her, holding her close.

'Ach, woman, don't you know that you already have one of those?'

*   *   *

Adam shouldered the rods and began to follow Barty along the riverbank. 'I wish you'd come down to Lodscombe this year, Barty. It'll be our last summer in Devon. I want to take you out in the Star to fish around the wrecks.'

'I'm a little too old and creaky for that, my son,' Barty's eyes twinkled, 'and I wouldn't like to leave my garden for the greenfly and wasps to take over.'

Adam thought: I shall miss him, and the fishing and all the cups of tea and the talk. Right from the beginning, when Doyle had first brought him down to the cottage, they'd hit it off. They didn't talk much but shared their time companionably, working in the garden or fishing, sometimes walking to the beach and collecting seaweed for the compost heap. He gave an unconscious sigh. There seemed an awful lot that he'd be saying goodbye to in six months' time.

'You're gloomy for a man who's just had a great afternoon's sport.' Barty commented.

'I was just wishing everything would stand still for a bit, that's all.'

'Ah, but it won't, so make the best of what you have while you have it.' The old man's face wrinkled with laughter. 'There are two periods in your life when you spend an awful lot of time saying goodbye to places and people. One is when you're growing up and leaving them behind, the other's when *they're* growing up and leaving *you* behind. In-between, it's nothing like so bad.'

Adam laughed. 'I'll try to remember that in September when I'm doing the leaving.'

In September his father would be back for a while; long enough for Adam to get to know him again before he went to Dartmouth. Sometimes he felt guilty over how little he missed him, how hard it was to remember what they talked about and did before Zoë. And he'd been glad that he was already back at school the first time that Giles came to the Lodge after her death, because he wouldn't have known what to say or do. Awful, really, not wanting to be with him. The last time he'd seen his father at home had been months ago, just before Giles went back to America. Then Adam had still felt a little awkward and uneasy to see both his parents sharing the same house again.

Once, he might have seen it as a chance for them all to get back together, to be a family, but it was too late for that. His mother was really happy now and it was good to have Ambrose as a part of his life. Perhaps in time even Dad would find someone else, and then he wouldn't have to keep feeling guilty, thinking of him always walking alone, with no Zoë to tease him and make him laugh…

'A penny for them,' Barty pushed open the garden gate; he gave him an enquiring look and Adam summoned a smile.

'I don't much like this growing up and growing away, Barty. I can't help wondering what's waiting out there for *me*.'

'A good long life with those you love, I hope.'

'I wish that could be the same for dad. I've thought a lot about him lately; how lonely he must be. I wish I'd found it easier to talk to him when he was here.'

'Talk will come in time.' The old man was comforting. 'It comes with age – the older you get, the more you talk. Look at me!'

'Oh, you're a one-off, Barty.' Adam grinned. 'I've a long way to go before I catch up with *you*.'

34

For Giles, the months spent in Salisbury before leaving England had been painful, with its inevitable reminders of Zoë. Each time he entered the flat, or walked by the river or turned a corner, he was conscious of the relentless pain of loss, whereas here in Boston, her presence was warm and close and very real. But over eighteen months after her death he was still adrift; only his work and the easy friendly atmosphere of the Institute providing him with any satisfaction or pleasure. He had no heart to try and make another relationship; no woman attracted him except for Olivia, and that had only been a blip in his misery, an impossible dream born of his need and her compassion. But still he was lonely and longed for love.

So it was with mixed feelings that he returned to England to see his son, to spend time in Lodescombe with him before he took his first major step away from home.

He went first to Salisbury to see James Yelland, to drink and reminisce, something that caused both of them an equal measure of pleasure and pain. On his first night back, a little drunk and in confidential mood Giles had said, 'I suppose I have to face that now I shall most likely spend the rest of my life alone. But I have money, a good year of research behind me, and soon I'll be back as a full time, active surgeon in a first class hospital. I shouldn't complain, but I do!'

Lying back in his chair, with his chin resting on his chest, Yelland had gazed owlishly over his own glass, replying in his clipped actor's voice. 'My dear man, *I* have been left with egg on my face more times than you can possibly imagine, and every time I've said the same as you; but,' he raised his glass, 'over the years I have cultivated that most useful and sanity-saving philosophy of the great Micawber: that something will always turn up,' he hiccupped slightly, 'and it always has!'

'Maybe, but there aren't many Zoë's around in this world, and I don't think I'd want one, even if there were.'

Yelland leaned forward, focusing with some difficulty on his companion's face. 'What you need, Giles,' he said earnestly, 'is a nice, comfortable woman, a lot nearer your own age, or, failing that, a nice young man!'

Giles grinned. 'If that's all I have to look forward to, James, I think I'll go it alone and leave the nice young men to you…'

*　　　*　　　*

Giles took his eyes off the road for a moment to glance at Adam. The boy makes me feel my age, he thought glumly; next birthday I'll be fifty-six and still a sex-starved bachelor. He smiled grimly to himself.

Where had all the flowers gone, indeed?

He spared another fleeting look at his son, suddenly feeling quite ridiculously proud; at least he'd got *something* right; Adam had greeted his return with a warmth and obvious pleasure that lifted Giles' heart, the memory of their last strained goodbyes of a year ago erased by Adam's spontaneous and cheerful 'Hi, dad!'

As they passed the signpost for Pendene, Giles said, 'When I've dropped you to make your visit, I'll go down to see Barty; d'you want me to pick you up later?'

Adam shook his head. 'No, I'll walk down over the field path when I'm through. I'd like to see him again before I leave.'

He didn't say that he'd be glad of the walk from school to Barty's cottage to snatch some time to be alone. Tomorrow he would start his new life, and that, combined with being alone in his father's company for the first time in almost a year, was making both stomach and voice uncertain from time to time. He was surprised and disconcerted at how emotional he had felt at being with him again and didn't want to make a fool of himself.

He wondered how Kate was getting on. Ambrose hadn't been his usual gruff and uncommunicative morning self when Adam had left home that day, but had sat looking determinedly cheerful, as though nothing momentous was about to happen; as though taking his daughter off to university was an everyday event. But Adam had seen the way Olivia squeezed his shoulder as she passed, and the looks they exchanged, as though silently acknowledging the uncertainty they were feeling about losing both of their children at once.

Cambridge, Adam thought, was a hell of a long way from Devon. Still, he and Kate could talk to each other on the 'phone, then there'd be the holidays in Ireland next year. And you never knew ... Ambrose had hinted that he might get him a car as he had Liam. He let his mind dwell on the heady possibility of driving to spend the odd weekend with Kate, well away from prying eyes; he wondered if she would be the same, or if time away from him, with other friends, would have changed her...

'Wake up!'

He came out of his reverie to find Giles flashing him a quizzical

302

look, and gave a self-conscious grin. 'Just thinking; it's a good job gran and pops are staying put. It'll seem odd; me still in Devon, Kate miles away in Cambridge, you back in Boston again, Mum and Ambrose in Ireland.'

He glanced at Giles' profile and was moved to say, 'I'm sorry about medical school, dad, but it wouldn't have worked for me. Really it wouldn't.'

Giles gave a resigned shrug. 'I know that now, you chump.' He swung the car into the school gates. 'Here you are … go and make your good-byes. Don't forget, we have to be back in London at a reasonable time for you to get a good night's sleep. You have to be at Paddington early to join all the other poor sods…'

Adam said loftily, 'You mean the chaps of the Murray Six entry!'

Giles gave a snort of laughter, 'I'll think of you all being marched from the station when you arrive back in Devon. It won't be anything like going off to school each term.'

Adam grinned. 'Can't be that much different; anyway, if they really want to, anyone can get used to anything.' He opened the car door. 'See you later, dad.'

He walked quickly up the steps, through the tall doors and along the familiar corridors that he had left over three months before. Half the house was on exeat; the few fellows he met who remembered him said a vague 'How goes it, Ryder,' and passed on.

He was no longer a part of their lives.

He rapped on the well-remembered door and Jayne answered his knock.

'I'm glad you came to say goodbye. Tom will be pleased.' She smiled and took his hand. 'You *are* allowed to kiss me now!'

He returned her look with grave deliberation. 'Oh, ra-*ther*!' he said and leaned to salute her French style, with a kiss on either cheek, before following her through the study and into the sitting room. A splutter of laughter escaped him at the sight of Doyle, seated in an armchair, nursing his baby daughter. 'Good morning, sir, I didn't realise you'd be so busy!'

Doyle greeted him with his usual ease and gestured at the bundle in his arms. 'I'd offer you a hold but she might do something unfortunate over those nice clean trousers.'

'I don't mind.' Adam was suddenly shy, taking the baby he held her awkwardly in the crook of his arm. He touched the dark hair with a cautious finger. 'She looks awfully new … and look, she smiled. Gosh, I didn't think they did things like that so soon – smile and that.'

Doyle gave him a pitying look. 'They do any number of other

things as well that are nothing like as civilized!'

'Oh, I don't know...' Adam stopped himself in time from voicing the notion that he'd quite like one of them himself one day, but Doyle seemed to pluck the thought out of the air. He grinned wickedly. 'You do that too soon, Mr Ryder,' he said, 'and there you will have made a very expensive mistake!'

An hour later he stood at the window to watch Adam stride away down the drive then looked down at Jayne as she came to put her arm through his. 'You miss him, don't you?' she asked.

'Yes. He was always rather special. He filled a gap in my life.' Tom smiled and squeezed her arm against his. 'But all the same, I hope our daughter doesn't bring home anything like him in twenty years' time, or I may begin to get seriously worried!'

* * *

At Paddington, Giles parked just outside the station and they both climbed out of the car and stood facing each other, falling into one of those awkward pauses that so often come at important meetings and farewells. Giles broke it, smiling he held out his hand. 'Good luck. I'm giving up my rooms at the Institute in a week or two, so write to me care of the Holy Cross Hospital until I get settled into an apartment. '

Adam gripped his hand tightly. 'Goodbye, dad. See you at Easter. You can show me all the sights of New York!'

'Ten days will be less than perfect but better than nothing.' Giles gave a wry smile. 'I'll be over in the summer to Ireland for a couple of weeks, so get the rods ready. If Ambrose is to be believed, the fishing is out of this world and the salmon just give themselves up.' He clapped Adam on the shoulder. 'Now clear off and join your motley crew; I have to ring Lodscombe and hear how Kate got on yesterday.'

He leaned against the car and watched his son walk away from him. When Adam was no longer in sight he shrugged and got back into the car. 'Pity,' he said aloud, 'he would have had one hell of a bedside manner!'

* * *

Giles placed his canvas grip in the car and closed the boot, then turned to put his hands on Olivia's shoulders. 'Thanks for giving me these few days here and thanks for letting me take Adam to London and see him on his way. It meant a lot to me.'

304

Olivia kissed his cheek. 'If you call in to see Chris and Carol before you leave again, give them my love. As soon as Adam gets a free weekend I've said we'll pick him up and spend it with them. He's dying to fish Bracken Pond again.'

'I must take him around the unit when he comes over at Easter and show him all the bits in bottles' Giles said, 'you never know, after a spell of naval discipline he may change his mind about going to sea.'

She said 'You have no hope at all. He'll love the life. The only drawback for him now is that he'll see much less of Kate.'

'And a good job too.' Ambrose growled. 'We've spent the past two years keeping our fingers crossed and praying hard!'

Giles grinned and put out his hand. 'Goodbye Ambrose. Thanks for holding the fort so well. Good luck, both of you, for the exhibition. I wish I could be in London to see it.'

'I'll send you a photograph of my mermaid when she's cast.' Ambrose gave his pirate smile and wrung his hand. 'Until next year…'

He put an arm around Olivia as they watched the car out of sight. She sighed. 'I still hate to see him so alone. I'm sure it will be good for him to get back into hospital life again after so long, but I don't know how he can bear to return to that particular one after all that happened there.'

'Oh, I think it shows that he's at least on the way to recovery.'

'I hope so.' She put her hand in his as they began to walk down the cliff path towards the shore. 'I shouldn't like to think he might slip back into the mess he was in when he first came down to Pels Point.'

'Well, he had you to pull him out of that, and he's managed to cope on his own in Boston this past year.' Ambrose stopped and turned her to face him. 'Time to stop worrying about him, Olivia, he's a big boy now.'

'So he is.' She put her arms around him. 'I don't think I ever thanked you properly for not going completely over the top when I spent those weeks picking up the pieces.'

He gave her an oblique look. 'You gave me a few nasty moments and I wasn't exactly Mr Reasonable, was I? Sometimes I still can't believe you didn't go back to him then.'

She was genuinely astonished. 'Why on earth should you even begin to think that?'

Ambrose hunched his shoulders, looking out across the water. 'Well, he's prettier than me for a start,' he said, and gave a half shamefaced grin. 'Perhaps out of pity or a kind of guilt, or love, or whatever; it *might* have happened. I thought so anyway. You seemed to be so close to him … and you were still his wife then.'

'Only technically; don't be so ridiculous Flynn. I was looking after him, not *sleeping* with him. Honestly, the things that go on in your head. I didn't think you were the jealous kind.'

'Neither did I, until it dawned on me that your Giles may have taken a tremendous knock, but was still a rather dangerously attractive bugger to have around any woman.'

'He always will be; he can't help it.' Olivia took his hand in hers again. 'Come along, I want to walk along the shore with my favourite man.'

He grinned, 'I'm thinkin' it's powerful good to be just the two of us together again at last!'

She smiled. 'Save the brogue until we get there, Flynn.'

He lifted her hand, turned it and kissed her palm, 'Ach, but I love you, woman…' he swept the breeze blown hair from her face and swinging her into his arms held her, swaying gently, his cheek against hers. Olivia leaned on him until the feel of his skin against hers and the strong steady beat of his heart began to work the familiar magic. She smiled and lifted her face to his. She said, 'Let's walk later.' Linking hands again they began to walk back along the pathway from the shore and up towards the house on the point.

POSTSCRIPTS

*'When you really want love,
you will find it waiting for you'*
                              Oscar Wilde

Giles

He pulled the Packard into a space before the hospital and wrestled briefly with the hood mechanism. There were so many buttons that he hadn't yet figured out which did what. He missed the leather seats, the polished wooden dash, and the smell of petrol in the Jag.

He sat for a few minutes looking at the green and white building. For over a year he'd passed it regularly, but been inside only once. That had been three months ago, when he was being shown over the new cardiac surgery unit that was to be his place of work from now on.

For one panicky moment he thought: This is a terrible mistake, I shouldn't be here; I should be back in the UK, up to my eyes in chest cavities and patting nurses' bottoms; or meeting Jimmy again after the theatre and sinking a bottle of the hard stuff between us...

Time to stop looking back, Giles. Zoë's faintly mocking voice was in his ears.

Ah – all very well to say that, my love. Doing it is the problem.

Oh, balls to that!

He smiled, Language, Zoë...

The palms of his hands were moist; absentmindedly he rubbed them on his knees. It was hot for the end of September, but a cool breeze came through the open window and he could smell the ocean. He leaned back and closed his eyes for a moment, thinking of Olivia and Ambrose as he would always see them now in his mind's eye, hand in hand, walking along the shoreline on the other side of the Atlantic...

'Why, hello; welcome back, Dr. Ryder.'

He opened his eyes. Anna Capaldi stood beside the car, smiling with genuine warmth. He stepped out and took the hand she offered. 'Giles,' he reminded her, 'we agreed to drop the formalities a couple of years ago.'

'Oh, sure, I hadn't forgotten.' She walked beside him towards the hospital steps. 'I guess everything will seem strange to you, working here after the peace and quiet of the Institute. It can be crazy sometimes, but we're OK when you get to know us.'

They began to climb the steps. He gave her a sideways look. She wasn't young and she wasn't a conventional beauty; her nose was too blunt and her mouth a little too wide, but her eyes were lovely and her voice pleasant and low. He glanced down at her left hand; still only the same plain gold band. He remembered Yelland's tipsy advice the night they had hit the scotch together and his own glib response … ah well, he thought; horses for courses…

An old remembered blip kicked in gently under his ribs.

Go on, Giles. Ask her. It's time to start living again…

With a sudden surge of confidence he held open the glass door and smiled down into her eyes. They were like Olivia's, he thought, deep and warm and calm. He said, 'I don't suppose you would have time to show a stranger to this side of town the best romantic spot to wine and dine a lady tonight?'

There was no coquettish hesitation, just a look of frank appraisal before her mouth again broke into her wide smile. 'If Italian's your idea of a good meal,' she offered, 'my mother makes a great Ragu Bolognese, my father orders his vino by the crate from Uncle Toni's vineyard in Verona, and my brother Ferdy plays a mean violin.'

'And who sings "O Solo Mio?"'

She pushed open the door and looked back at him over her shoulder.

'I do,' she said.

Olivia

She finished unpacking the last box and sat back on her heels, delighting in the sight of her own furniture and belongings blending with those of Ambrose'. After all the upheaval of the move it was both pleasure and relief to find their separate goods and chattels in harmony.

Getting to her feet she walked through the house to stand for a few moments in the doorway of the big lofty studio, looking at her easel and stacked canvases and Ambrose's big bin of clay, remembering how they'd sometimes clashed and argued at Lodscombe. She supposed they always would. Two opposing temperaments sharing the same workspace were bound to erupt occasionally. Here at least, she thought, they had plenty of room to fight!

Climbing the crooked, well-worn wooden staircase to the bedrooms under the eaves, she let her thoughts go forward to the future, to when Adam, accompanied by Kate, would sail the Morning Star to Ireland, where the boat would lie at anchor in the small sheltered harbour of the nearby village of Castermere. Olivia smiled a little wryly to herself, doubting that she and Ambrose would see overmuch of either of their children during the period of Adam's leaves from Dartmouth. They were now a very grown-up and self-contained pair, still needing little company apart from that of each other.

Pushing wide the long window of the low-ceilinged, whitewashed room that was her own and Ambroses' own retreat from the world, she rested her arms on the sill and leaned out to gaze along the ribbon of road that wound along the coast, seeking to catch a glimpse of the Land-Rover returning from Galway; amazed that after even just an hour or two apart, her heart could still leap with pleasure to know her man was on his way back home.

She heard the sound of the engine before he was in sight and made her way downstairs and out of the stable door, only to find that Mica had beaten her to the gate. 'Himself's on the way,' his one good eye snapped gleefully. 'It'll be a while yet before your ears are quicker than mine.'

She smiled. 'I wouldn't dare reach the gate before you, Mica ... you might go off in a huff, and then where would we be?'

He leaped for the running-board as Ambrose drew to a halt before the house, and hanging onto the door demanded, 'Did ye get the flour, man … an' the eggs? I'll boil them hens o' mine for broth if they don't lay again soon, an' meself wanting to make a batter the night!'

Ambrose growled, 'In the back,' then jumped down onto the road and pulled Olivia into his arms, 'It's your face I want to see first, not that old devil's,' he said, kissing her then turning to scowl at the old man. 'We're off along the shore Mica, so you needn't bother about getting your ear to the door to hear what I'm saying!'

Leaving Mica grumbling beneath his breath and burrowing like a ferret for his eggs, Ambrose took her hand as they began walking along the water's edge. 'You know, if we'd a 'phone here he'd be at the crack of the door every time the bell rang.'

'You shouldn't tease him so,' she admonished, and he grinned unrepentantly.

'He loves it, and there's nothing he enjoys more than thwarting me at every opportunity … he always has!' Tightening his hold on her hand he gave a sigh of contentment. 'You can't think how happy I am to be here at last with you, Mica and all…

'Did you get your call through to Andoni?'

'Uh, huh. We take all our work over at the end of next month, ready for the showing. He sent a kiss, the cheeky devil.'

She smiled up at him. 'I was beginning to think you might not be back in time tonight. This is our first really peaceful, really alone evening and I didn't want to go without you.'

He grinned, 'Oh, ye of little faith.'

'Yes, well. I know you when you get talking, Flynn.'

They walked on into the closing day, their feet leaving tracks in the firm, wet sand, and when they reached the big flat rock known as Pardoe's Head, climbed it to look out over the grey Atlantic.

He stood with his arms around her and his head against hers, watching as the curious black and grey heads appeared one by one, bobbing in the swell of the tide, lifting whiskered snouts to the heavens and honking plaintively at their audience of two.

'Not up to the Salisbury Cathedral choir, are they?' Olivia chuckled. 'They remind me of Adam, who can't sing a note.'

'Those two,' Ambrose mused, 'do you think this teenage love, or rather, lust thing, is likely to endure.'

'You want my honest, considered opinion?'

'I do.'

Olivia sighed. 'It's possible, but unlikely; Kate is quite a feminist, and has her sights firmly set on her career. When he leaves Dartmouth

Adam could be at sea for months at a time, and he may have inherited sufficient of Giles' less attractive genes to make it difficult for him to be both absent and faithful.'

'Sounds as though there may be breakers ahead,' Ambrose whistled through his teeth. He asked glumly, 'When do you suppose parents can stop worrying about their offspring?'

'Probably never, but I guess that's something we shall have to find out.'

He gave a gusty sigh, 'On a kind of wait-and-see agenda?'

'Yes,' Olivia laughed, 'something like that.'

*   *   *

The sun crept down behind the horizon, stars appeared in the darkening sky; one by one the sleek heads vanished again beneath the water, leaving only a widening ripple on the calm surface to show their passage back to the open sea.

Ambrose kissed the back of her neck and turned Olivia in his arms. 'Time to go home,' he said.

Matthew's Daughter

Matthew's Daughter is the second book in a Cornish Trilogy and follows Caroline Penrose, as she returns from her wartime service in the WAAF to her father's flower farm in Cornwall. But once home she finds a number of obstacles and family conspiracies impeding her path to peace…

ISBN 978-0-9555778-2-6

The Changing Day

The Changing Day the final book in a Cornish Trilogy, begins in 1940, when a meeting between WREN Joanna Dunne and Navy Lieutenant Mark Eden is the start of a love affair that at first seems unlikely to stand the test of time. She is 22, single and an Oxford graduate; he is 36, married and in civilian life a country vet. She is attracted but not looking for romance, he is attracted but not looking for commitment and, as Joanna soon discovers, he is the black sheep of his family and has a very murky past.

ISBN 978-0-9555778-3-3

Available from Sagittarius Publications
62 Jacklyns Lane, Alresford, Hampshire SO24 9LH

A Very Private Arrangement

When in the spring of 1934, fourteen year old orphan Anna Farrell is transported from a life of drab, penny-pinching, genteel poverty with her cousin Ruth, to the elegant, affluent Bloomsbury household of distant cousin Patrick Farrell, and his manservant, Charlie Caulter, she is at first blissfully unaware of the well hidden secret kept by the two men, until a meeting with the quasi-charming Madame Gallimard and her sons becomes the catalyst that threatens to tear her world apart.

Against the backcloth of WW2 and a diversity of places and people, with her beloved Patrick and Charlie to smooth her path through the inevitable pitfalls of first, second and last love, Anna matures from naïve young girl to confident young woman, well able to cope with the men in her life – and some of the women in theirs.

ISBN 978-0-9555778-4-0

Return to Falcon Field

Ryan Petersen, a professor of European Literature at a New England University, accepts a year's exchange lectureship in London. But in coming to England the cynical, detached Ryan has a hidden agenda: to find the woman with whom he had a passionate wartime love affair over twenty years before.

He returns to the now derelict airbase of Falcon Field and the nearby Hampshire village of Hawksley, to begin a journey into the past; one that proves both painful and inspiring as he re-discovers the man he once was, and perhaps could be again.

ISBN 978-0-9555778-5-7

Available from Sagittarius Publications
62 Jacklyns Lane, Alresford, Hampshire SO24 9LH